SYDNEY WILDER

Confessions of a Virgin on a Dating App

Cover Illustration by Mary Dublin
Instagram: @bookcoversbydublin
authorsdublinkendsley.com

Edited by Hailey Thompson
Instagram: @haileythompson_author
cafeamarewriting.com

Paperback ISBN: 979-8-218-47980-0

To the women across the globe,
suffering from endometriosis,
or any reproductive disease.

To those yet to be diagnosed,
for those who have had their symptoms
brushed off or ignored,
this one is for you.

And of course, for my fellow nerds.
May you enjoy all my silly tabletop references.

Trigger Warnings

Attempted sexual assault, religious trauma, stalking, drug scars/mentions of past drug use, mentions of alcoholism, divorce, sexual shame/stigma, STDs, miscarriage, medical injections/needles, mentions of self-harm

Table of Contents

Prologue

"IT WON'T FIT."

Those three words were the first indicator that something was wrong.

Very wrong.

I winced as he struggled above me, his enamored joy twisting into frustration as his face turned red. Tyler was nearly twice my size – a foot taller than me and wrapped in lean muscle from years of athletics and weightlifting. I, on the other hand, was barely five foot two and on the verge of being unattractively thin. A minute ago, I had been fretting about exposing my A-cup breasts and wondering if his pelvis would crush my tiny, protruding hip bones.

Now I had much bigger problems.

I winced as he tried again, attempting to relax my legs as they quivered uncontrollably. This hadn't been my idea, but after much persuading, I had agreed to let my longtime boyfriend take my virginity. After all, we were *that* couple, together since freshmen orientation at our tiny Christian college campus. Always at each other's sides, unwaveringly loyal to each other, and sickeningly in love.

I cheered in the stands at his football games, and he gave standing ovations at my choir recitals. We were a perfect match, and Tyler told me he intended to propose as soon as we graduated.

"So, since we're going to get married anyway," he had insisted. "I want to do this now."

I initially balked at the suggestion, feeling nauseous with betrayal. I was concerned that my loving boyfriend was one of *those* guys my parents had warned me about. *All they want is sex,* they'd told me. *And they'll say just about anything to get it.*

But over the past few weeks, as he continued to bring it up, I gradually warmed up to the idea. *We've been together for almost four years. He loves me. And he's right – if we're going to get married anyway, what does it matter?*

Although my knowledge of the biology behind intercourse was limited, I'd always seen it as a warm, romantic act – the strongest declaration of love in the whole world. My campus's education on the subject was minimal, focused more on drilling abstinence into students' heads than divulging any useful information on how it all worked.

For that, I had to turn to the internet. And the resulting web searches nearly flipped my stomach inside out.

But Tyler had insisted that everything would be alright.

"I'll make it romantic," he told me. "I'll put rose petals on the bed, get some nice candles. I'll even sneak in a bottle of wine."

His last promise made me even more uncomfortable, as alcohol was strictly forbidden on campus. But as the day came closer and my stomach-turning internet searches intensified, I decided that slight intoxication wasn't a bad idea.

But I'd never had wine before, and it turned out I was a lightweight. One glass had my head swimming in a hazy fog, and the rose petals strewn across Tyler's dorm room bed did little to calm my nerves. Even the candle was nauseating; an overly sickly-sweet fall scent that lingered in the back of my throat.

I'd expected it to be unpleasant. My internet searches told me that it might sting, or there might be some blood.

What I didn't expect was for my vagina to deny entry altogether.

"Maybe we should try another position?" Tyler suggested.

My thighs clenched. I was already nauseous, uncomfortable, and quivering with anxiety. If we were going to do this, I wanted to at least be lying down.

But I loved Tyler, and I wanted him to be happy. So I reluctantly agreed to try more positions. Most of which I wasn't comfortable with, and all of which resulted in the same issue. I knew virgins were supposed to be tight, but this seemed extreme. It was as if there was a wall at the entrance to my vagina, blocking off all access.

I jolted. Tyler was getting more forceful, taking out his sexual frustration on my shaking body. He tried again, pushing harder this time.

And I screamed.

It burned like I'd never felt before. It was as if my vagina were being torn in half.

"Avery!" Tyler hissed, clamping his hand over my mouth. "You've got to be quiet! They're going to hear you!"

By *they*, he meant the dorm RAs. My neck craned toward the half-empty wine bottle on Tyler's nightstand. Like alcohol, sex was forbidden on campus. Which meant we had to be discreet.

"This isn't working," I whispered, clenching my throat as I fought back tears.

Relief washed over my naked body as Tyler's grip loosened. He sighed and shook his head, flopping down on the too-small twin bed beside me.

"It's okay, Avie," Tyler whispered in a soothing voice, rubbing my bare shoulder. "I know the first time is tough for girls. Let's call it a night, and we'll try again some other time."

"Okay."

No amount of throat-clenching helped. The tears cascaded in smooth curves down my cheeks, leaving tiny stains on Tyler's pillow.

"Hey, hey." He turned toward me, engulfing me in his tanned, muscular arms. Soothing shivers ran down my spine, like I'd just stepped into a warm beam of sunlight.

All my anxiety, fear, and pain melted away under the heat of his touch. Even if sex was an awkward, painful, confusing mess, I couldn't deny how good his unclothed body felt pressed up next to mine. I curled into his embrace, our arms and legs locking together.

It will be alright. I reassured myself as my eyelids fluttered closed. *After all, we love each other. This is just another challenge for us to overcome.*

With my nerves settled and my breaths deep and slow, I almost forgot that I wasn't supposed to be there. I wasn't supposed to be in the men's dormitory at a Christian college lying naked in bed with a man I wasn't married to.

But at that moment, everything felt right. At least, right enough for me to relish our alone time for the next few hours.

Sex or no sex.

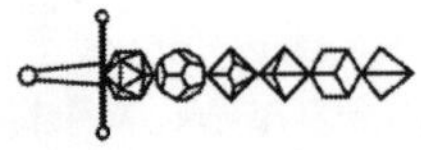

WE TRIED AGAIN.

And a third time.

And a fourth.

With every attempt, Tyler had new suggestions. Enough lube to drown my entire pelvic region. Lidocaine cream that set my insides on fire and didn't numb a thing. Every position imaginable, including some that seemed to defy the laws of gravity.

They all ended the same way. With Tyler becoming increasingly irritated, and me still being a virgin.

We decided to try one more time. It was three weeks until college graduation, and my roommate had made a trip home for the weekend, which meant that Tyler and I had my dorm room all to ourselves.

But with that arrangement came problems. Tyler's bed was at ground level – mine was a loft with barely two feet of clearance to the ceiling. My dorm room was also much smaller, as the women's dorms were older with awkward layouts.

But it would have to work. Tyler agreed to come over at 9 p.m. By then, the sweltering Florida sun would be well below the skyline, making it easier to sneak into the women's dorms with a contraband box of condoms.

He'd offered to bring wine again, but I decided against it. I disliked the feeling of being drunk, and it hadn't blocked out the pain the last four times.

Tyler was optimistic, but I was full of dread. He arrived shortly after the nighttime darkness settled in, slipping silently into my dorm room like a fugitive. From his backpack, he pulled out a large box of condoms and two bottles of lubricant.

"I brought extra supplies," he chuckled, but it did little to ease my nerves. He sensed my fear and pulled me in for a tight hug.

I smiled, his familiar soothing warmth washing over me as I breathed in the scent of his Old Spice. That warmth caused a faint bit of hope to flicker in my chest.

It's okay.

Everything will be okay.

You can do this.

It started as it always did – us unceremoniously stripping our clothes with plenty of kissing and cuddles. That part I loved. I could kiss Tyler all night, running my hands over the muscles that lined his back and shoulders. It brought out all the warm, lusty feelings that I knew were supposed to be there.

But then it was time, and every muscle in my body clenched. I had come to expect the pain now, and my body reacted accordingly. It was like a reflex.

We fumbled for a while, trying the same few positions that we always did. Tyler taught me some breathing exercises, and we focused on relaxing my thigh muscles, which were as rigid as steel.

"You've got to calm down," he insisted. "Tensing your body will only make it worse."

"Easier said than done," I grumbled.

Tyler tried again. As usual, the wall was up, blocking his access. He readjusted, pushed, and readjusted some more, but it made no difference.

And if he pushed too hard, which sometimes happened, I'd be left screaming in pain with my insides on fire.

"Gah!!" I shrieked, my thighs squeezing his hips like they'd crush them. Tyler grimaced, but this time, he continued pressing into me.

"AH!! Tyler, stop!"

He still didn't. His face was tight and red with frustration as he pushed deeper.

"You're hurting me!!"

I went to shove him off me, but he was twice my size and wouldn't budge. I struggled and screamed under him, my whole body on fire with panic.

I didn't care who heard me.

I didn't care if he got upset.

I needed this to stop.

Finally, I managed to pull one leg up to my hip, and a swift kick to Tyler's genitals sent him tumbling to the floor.

My chest was shaking so badly that I could barely breathe. My mouth hung open, inhaling like I was starved of oxygen as Tyler writhed in pain on the floor.

He turned to face me; his frustration replaced with rage.

"What the fuck, Avery!?"

My blood chilled in my veins.

Tyler never cursed.

"Hello?"

The knocking sound was like a nail being pounded into my ears. I saw Tyler's face fall in horror.

"Avery," the voice outside the floor continued. "This is Madison, the RA down the hall. I heard a scream. Is everything okay in there?"

I didn't answer. Neither did Tyler. It was as if the whole world was melting into a puddle around me.

There was another knock, then the metallic chime of keys.

"Avery, I'm coming in."

My stomach fell to the floor.

We'd been caught.

Chapter 1

Five years later

CRAP.

I'm going to be late.

Not that it mattered much. I didn't even know the guy, at least not in person. All I had to go off were a few profile pictures and the texts we'd exchanged the night before. But he seemed nice enough, and I figured he wouldn't judge if I were a few minutes late.

After all, I told myself, *Downtown Orlando is a nightmare during rush hour. He may end up being late himself.*

I rested my elbows on the steering wheel, grateful that I now worked from home and rarely had to deal with this awful traffic. Not only was the city full of highways that wound overtop each other in erratic rollercoaster patterns, but the drivers were often less than polite. The main road leading to the coffee shop was jammed with bumper-to-bumper traffic, with horn beeps and sudden stops a frequent occurrence as the crowd of cars inched forward.

Finally, after going two miles in twenty minutes, I made it to the parking lot. Despite the traffic, Orange Blossom Coffee was a wonderful first date spot – a cozy, inviting space with rustic décor and tons of live plants. I preferred coffee over dinner for first meetups – it was cheaper and less of an investment, leaving either party free to bow out with no hard feelings. But Orange Blossom was also downtown, which meant that I was subjected to the absolute worst of the city's rush-hour traffic.

But this was the place he picked, I sighed. *And I didn't object.*

As I turned off the ignition and stepped out of my well-worn Camry, I wondered what he'd look like in person. From my experience, men were pretty good about having updated photos on their profile. But people were always different in real life.

Plus, I chuckled, *his profile says he's six feet tall. Let's see if that's really the case.*

As I entered the shop and eyed the slender man standing next to the pastry display case, I knew it had to be him. The shop was crowded, full of patrons chatting and sipping at the maze of tables, but he had one distinct feature in his profile photos – a head of vibrant, curly red hair.

He noticed me too, and greeted me with a cordial hug and asked what I'd like for coffee. After I spouted off my usual to the barista – a hazelnut iced coffee with oat milk – I took a moment to study his features while we waited for our order. He was shorter than his dating profile stated, likely five foot nine, and his teeth were more yellow and crooked than I'd expected. But being such a short woman, I'd never cared about height, and my coffee addiction didn't leave me with gleaming white teeth either.

A few minutes later, we plucked our respective drinks off the counter and settled into one of the few remaining empty tables. We each took a long first sip, and I noticed while I'd gotten an iced drink with a straw, his was in an opaque cup that wafted with steam as he set it on the table.

"What did you get?" I asked, realizing that in my contemplative haze, I hadn't paid attention to his order.

"Hot chocolate."

"Ah," I remarked, taken aback by the flat tone of his voice. "Good choice. I suppose it's kind of late for caffeine, but I've always had a coffee addiction."

I chuckled, attempting to lighten the mood. He sat stiff as a board, his face devoid of emotion, and the normally cheery atmosphere of the coffee shop suddenly felt heavy and awkward.

"I don't drink coffee."

I coughed as I took a second sip through my plastic straw. Once again, his tone was flat and dull, and it sent a prickly feeling down my spine.

Then why did you pick a coffee shop for a first date?

I sighed and set my drink on the table, watching as condensation droplets formed on the clear plastic cup. *Ok, deep breaths. Maybe he's just nervous. We just need to get the conversation going.*

"So, uh, Anthony," I gulped, momentarily forgetting his name. "You said you're an engineer?"

"Yup."

"What kind?"

"Mechanical."

I froze, dread engulfing my brain and making my scalp ache.

How am I supposed to reply? I know nothing about mechanical engineering. Can't he give me an answer longer than a single word?

He couldn't. We managed to draw out the mostly one-sided conversation for another hour, with me asking sentence after sentence of questions and his replies being tense and blunt. His face was still devoid of emotion, but he downed his non-coffee drink in record time and started fidgeting with his fingers in his lap. I swore I even saw a bead of sweat slide down his forehead.

I took a deep breath. *Relax, dude. We're just getting to know each other. It's not a job interview.*

It was a shame, because we had many things in common. His answers, although awkwardly short, revealed a lot about him. He liked video games, especially shooters, because of how much he played them as a teenager. He was a fellow *Creatures & Crypts* enthusiast, which was always a huge plus for me to find in a potential boyfriend. He also enjoyed reading, especially fantasy novels, and his favorite place to be on a sunny Florida afternoon was the beach.

On paper, he checked all the boxes: a decently cute guy who was financially stable and shared my love of geeky things. It should've been perfect.

But it wasn't. While his fidgeting fingers told me he was anxious, his dull expression told me he was bored. I couldn't figure out which one it truly was, but I couldn't continue dating this guy if we could barely hold a conversation.

My gaze flicked up to the old-fashioned, copper-rimmed clock hanging from the wall. We had been there for an hour and a half, and it had felt like an eternity. But it was only ten minutes until eight, meaning that if I left now, I'd still have time for some gaming before bed.

"Well, Anthony, I enjoyed meeting with you," I said. I went to stand up, and his tense expression didn't change. "But it's getting late – I should head home."

"Alright. I'll text you later."

I exhaled. I was hoping his reaction to seeing me leave would give me more clues.

Was he relieved? Disappointed? Does he wish I would stay longer?

We exchanged another brief, awkward hug. But as I walked out to my car, I felt relief wash over me as soon as I settled into the muggy seat. Now that the sun was setting, the steering wheel wasn't scalding hot, and I could guide my car out of the parking lot without getting first-degree burns on my palms.

Since the traffic had cleared out, it was only a fifteen-minute drive back to my apartment on the edge of downtown. It was a modest abode – a single-story, two-bedroom townhouse with bright yellow paint and a brown shingle roof that needed replacing. Rows of patchy bushes separated the interconnected townhomes, and I'd stuck a massive potted monstera plant next to our front door to give it some liveliness. It kept the front porch from looking too bare and sterile—from revealing that it was home to two broke twentysomething women who had other priorities than decorating.

I stepped onto the front porch, my eyes scanning the dirt that lined the cracks in the concrete like blood vessels. *Maybe I should get a pressure washer,* I sighed as I fiddled with the front door lock. *Make it look like this place isn't the women's equivalent of a bachelor pad.*

I smiled as Cassidy's cheery folk music echoed down the narrow main hallway. I could tell by the sounds and smells coming from the kitchen that she was making dinner.

"Good evening, girlie!" she shouted once I was near the kitchen.

Her auburn hair, which was even curlier than mine, was piled high atop her head, and her black-rimmed glasses framed a small, round face. In one hand was a dirty spatula, which she used as a microphone as she twirled around the kitchen, belting out the lyrics to her favorite songs.

Having a roommate wasn't ideal, but Cassidy was my best friend, one of the first people I'd met when I moved to Orlando five years earlier. We loved each other to death, but living together often made us fight like sisters. It both strengthened and frayed our relationship at the same time.

"Sooooo?" Cassidy cooed in a singsong voice as she plopped her elbows on the counter. "How'd it go?"

I didn't reply, but the slight grimace on my face gave her enough of an answer.

She chuckled. "That bad, huh?"

"Well, no." I plopped down at the dinette, picking at the paint chipping off the back of the antiquated chair. "That's the thing. It was *just* okay. We have a lot in common, but he's really quiet. I couldn't tell if that was just his personality, or if he was nervous."

"So do you think you'll go on another date with him?"

I shrugged my shoulders. The old Avery would've said yes. I would've given it another chance. But six months and half a dozen men into my online dating adventure, my optimism was starting to wear thin.

"Honestly... no. Because I shouldn't feel wishy-washy about it. If it had been a good date, I would have butterflies in my stomach, giddy at the possibilities. Whether or not I'd go on a second date with him wouldn't even be a question."

"Agreed," Cassidy remarked as she stuck her spatula into the pan of fried rice she was making. "Have you eaten dinner yet?"

I shook my head. "Did you make enough for two?"

Cassidy grinned as she scooped the fried rice into two bowls. "You know I always do."

We ate our meal at the dinette in silence. I knew Cassidy was tired, as her job as a vet tech kept her away from home and on her feet all day. And I was too busy swimming in my own tangled thoughts to make conversation.

The past five years had consisted of me putting the pieces of my life together after my expulsion from college.

I had been caught red-handed by my RA, naked in bed with the man who was supposed to be my whole future.

But everything changed after I left campus. Tyler's parents were wealthy alumni, and they made a hefty donation to save his son from the same fate. He was suspended for two weeks, but unlike me, he still graduated. He still walked across that podium and accepted his diploma while the woman he had promised to marry was nothing more than an empty chair.

He ghosted me after that. I never heard from him again, and after a few weeks, I stopped sending him desperate text messages. Getting kicked out of college wasn't the real problem – I could always apply elsewhere to finish my degree. And I knew that wasn't the reason why Tyler left me.

The real reason, the one that had haunted my love life for the past five years, was my inability to have sex. It seemed cruelly ironic – that my pure, innocent self, one raised by two devoutly religious parents who wanted me to follow in their footsteps, would be incapable of rebelling. Purity was no longer a shield, a symbol of my morality to wear with pride.

It was a punishment.

"Wow, you were hungry," Cassidy noted, staring at my empty bowl while hers was still two-thirds full.

I frowned. I tended to scarf down food when I was angry. I was no longer alarmingly thin like I was in college, but I would always have a wiry figure with very little body fat, even in places where I wanted it to be. *Fast metabolism*, my parents had told me. Which made sense, because they were both sticks themselves.

I waited for Cassidy to finish eating her dinner, and then we both scrubbed dishes and wiped down countertops until the kitchen was sparkling clean. Our home was plain, with mismatched, hand-me-down furniture and cheap plastic kitchenware, but we never let it get too dirty.

Cassidy sensed my foul mood and asked if I wanted to watch a movie, but I declined and slunk off to my room. I didn't feel like socializing that night, even with my best friend. And Cassidy was always understanding of other's emotions, so she didn't mind if I became a recluse for the rest of the night.

I settled at my desk and watched my PC monitor blare to life. My room was simple: a twin bed shoved in the corner to allow for more floorspace, an old 32-inch TV with a Kindle Fire stick shoved in its side, and my favorite spot in the whole room – my L-shaped computer desk. At one end was my work laptop, which was hooked up to two monitors that had been supplied by my employer. At the other end was my elaborate gaming PC, whose parts glowed in a variety of rainbow colors within its sleek white case.

I absentmindedly flipped through my gaming library, running into the common scenario of having hundreds of games but no idea which one to play. I eventually settled on a generic-looking platformer I had bought on sale a few weeks earlier. It was optimized for controller play, which meant I could lean back in my plush gaming chair and relax without having to be hunched over my keyboard.

I wrapped a fist around my long, curly brown hair, sweeping it up in a messy bun to keep it out of my face. I scrunched my face up at my reflection in the computer monitor, observing how my freckles twitched as my nose wrinkled. I was a bit odd-looking, having inherited my pale skin and plethora of freckles from my Scotch-Irish father, and my curly dark hair and petite figure from my Greek mother. I was no model, but most people considered me pretty, and I'd never had any trouble getting dates based on my appearance.

Maybe if I put on some makeup to cover my acne scars... or painted my fingernails...

Ugh, Avery, stop. Quit worrying about guys. Empty your mind and game.

That worked for a little while. I wasn't usually a big fan of platformers, but this one had a cheery, vibrant art style, one that reminded me of a Disney movie. I was almost finished with the tutorial, my thoughts finally settled and at ease, when my phone rang and caused me to jolt out of my seat.

I flipped my phone over. MARIA & JAMES MURPHY.

No. Nonono.

I plopped the phone face down on my desk. I couldn't deal with my parents right now. They knew little of my life in Orlando since I kept my distance and only visited them once or twice a year for the holidays. And even that felt like too much. It sucked me back into my former life, one of two-hour church sessions and cliquey youth groups and suffocating under the weight of my parents' lofty expectations. The fact that I was almost twenty-seven and still unmarried was a heinous crime in their eyes. It was a major reason why I fled the Florida panhandle and settled much further south.

I clenched my teeth until the phone went to voicemail, praying they wouldn't leave another two-minute-long message begging for me to visit.

My phone buzzed again a few minutes later, and I audibly groaned. *Looks like my prayers aren't going to be answered tonight.*

But once I got the courage to pick my phone back up, I realized the notification wasn't from my parents.

It was from my dating app.

The rational part of my brain told me to hurl the phone onto my bed and ignore it. For most of my twenties, I had been on a journey to find myself – to gain independence and figure out who I was outside of my controlling parents' grasp. But last year, seeing the number *26* on a birthday cake hit me like a sack of bricks. I was an adult now. One who was officially closer to thirty than twenty.

After several years away from my family, I determined that I actually *did* want to get married. I wanted a handsome, sexy, sweet husband who I would wake up in bed with every morning. Who I'd cook all my meals with and who I'd kiss goodnight before I fell asleep. We'd play games until 2 a.m. on the weekends, compete in *Creatures & Crypts* events together, and spend hours debating our favorite TV shows and movies. I wanted a husband who I'd share my life with, build a home with, grow old with.

A long time ago, a different version of me thought that was Tyler. But it had been five years since we broke up, and I was more than ready to move on.

But I couldn't.

Because there was always my big secret.

The reason why he left me in the first place.

I was yet to make it past the third date with any of the men I'd met, which meant I was yet to spill the ugly reality of my sexual history. For years, I had feared being a disappointment, being rejected for something I had no control over. But what scared me even more was ending up with a man who would violate me the same way Tyler did. One who wanted to solve my problem with force.

But I also had hope. Hope that the right guy would love me enough to look past my sexual problems. That he would be patient and understanding. That he would help me overcome this horrible obstacle without judgment.

I took a deep breath and unlocked my phone screen.

Sure enough, I had a new message in my app.

> *Hey, I saw in your profile that you play Creatures & Crypts. That's so cool! Who is your favorite class to play?*

I chuckled. My fingers hovered over my phone screen, ready to type out a response.

Maybe this guy would be it.

Chapter 2

I WALKED INTO CRITICAL GAMES THE FOLlowing evening with my gaze locked on my phone.

The same warnings echoed in the back of my head like they always did. *Don't get attached too early. You haven't even met the guy. Remember how Anthony turned out.*

Yet I couldn't help but feel giddy. It all started the night before, when I fired off a quick response to his question before checking his profile.

He was one that I'd hoped would match with me. His profile picture was stunning – a clean-shaven, handsome face framed with golden blonde hair and a dorky yet glorious smile. His main photo was a headshot that showed off his broad shoulders and white-toothed grin. The second photo was him at one of the Disney parks, licking an ice cream cone and making bunny ears over someone that I assumed was his brother. And from that photo, I could tell that he was *tall* – his profile stated he was six foot three.

But his third photo was the one that really got my heart racing. It was him lying on the shoreline at the beach. He was shirtless, which showed off his tanned, chiseled physique. But his muscles weren't the only thing that caught my eye – I also noticed an intricate Gyarados tattoo snaking its way across his chest.

Fit, handsome, and geeky.

I was sold.

We'd stayed up until midnight texting each other. It was all superficial – we listed our favorite video games, movies, and TV shows, feeling each other out for compatibility.

His name was Tristan. He was a big Nintendo fan, since those were the only consoles his parents would allow him to own until he was a teen. His all-time favorites were Pokémon and Zelda, and he claimed to have played every game in both series. In addition to video games, he spent most of his college years as an MMA fighter until too many backaches forced him to quit. *But he's clearly still stayed in shape,* I noticed, scrolling back to the picture of him on the beach.

When I asked about *Creatures & Crypts TCG*, he said he'd played a few times but would love to get more into it. He'd just never had anyone to go to a game shop with.

Maybe that could be me, I blushed, not daring to actually type those thoughts.

Maybe we could...

Ow!

I stumbled backward, realizing that I'd been completely lost in thought and not looking where I was going. I'd bumped into a man with shaggy jet-black hair and a similarly colored sweatshirt who was carrying several boxes full of inventory.

He turned around and smirked at me, and I frowned.

It was just Devin, the owner of Critical Games.

And I knew he was about to start teasing me.

"Hey, watch where you're going, Avie," he chuckled as he set the boxes on the counter next to the cash register. He rolled up the sleeves of his sweatshirt, revealing a silver chain-link bracelet and the intricate dragon tattoo that trailed up his entire arm.

I scowled. "Stop calling me that."

He had started calling me Avie a few months ago, after discovering it was my parents' pet name for me when I was a kid. I knew he meant no harm, but that nickname still stung five years later.

Because the only person who ever called me that, besides my parents, was Tyler.

"Why not? Nicknames are fun," Devin shrugged, prying open the boxes and placing stacks of packaged *Creatures & Crypts TCG* cards on the counter. "You can call me Dev if you want."

"That's not equivalent. Avie is too childish. That would be like me calling you Devy."

"You can call me that too."

I huffed. "You're a pain, you know that?"

"Same as always."

When I first moved to Florida and met Devin, I found him insufferable. He was everything my parents had taught me to avoid – a pierced, heavily tattooed goth guy a decade older than me who was known for pressing people's buttons. He teased me for years, but I eventually realized I was being too uptight and started playing along. Now he was more like an older brother – endearing and annoying at the same time.

But the worst part was that, upon catching a glimpse of my phone screen a few weeks ago, he had learned of my online dating adventures. And like any obnoxious older brother, he was eager to insert his opinion on the matter.

"Who're you talking to this week?" he asked, leaning forward to see my phone screen. My shoulders stiffened—his face was annoyingly close to mine. He always seemed to have total disregard for my personal space.

"It's—ugh, here, I'll show you. Just don't be creepy."

I flipped the screen to Tristan's profile and handed Devin my phone. He pursed his lips as he scrolled through the photos, eventually giving me a subtle nod.

"Not bad. Nice tattoo."

I chuckled, "What do you have now, like, twenty?"

"Sixteen," Devin grinned, pulling down the collar of his sweatshirt. A comet with a d20 for its nucleus sat in the center of his chest, just below his neck. I recognized it as part of Critical Games' logo. "Got this one last week. Anyway, you signing up for *Creatures TCG* tonight?"

"Yup."

Devin ushered me over to the register, where he charged me the $5 fee and stamped a point on my rewards card. And while he did so, my brain drifted elsewhere. Something about seeing Devin's bare chest made me feel... *weird.* He was very pale, which fit his goth aesthetic, but he looked like he had some muscle under those baggy clothes. He was clearly fit, but since he lived in sweatshirts even in the hottest months, it was hard to tell.

As I went to sit down, my phone buzzed again. I studied the growing crowd – the shop was divided into two rooms, one for retail and one for gaming. In the gaming room, about twenty patrons were clustered around the six long tables, chatting and trading cards. I was the only woman there, which happened often. Cassidy had to work late that night, which meant I would be on my own.

My pocket buzzed again as I slouched in my chair. I pulled out my phone, eager to read Tristan's latest message.

You go to a game shop every Friday night? That's so cool! Where is it?

"Hey Avery!"

My typing fingers were interrupted by a sudden shout. I looked up and immediately grinned. It was Aaron, one of my closest friends at the shop. He hadn't been able to make it in a few weeks, so I was surprised to see him. I was also surprised that he'd dyed his hair a new color—bright lime green.

"Hey!" I waved back as Aaron slid into the seat next to me. "Is Cass coming tonight?"

I shook my head, "She has to work late."

"Ah."

Aaron's frown caused a knowing smirk to light up my face. He hadn't been subtle about his crush on my best friend. But Cassidy was oblivious, and Aaron was too big of a chicken to ask her out, which meant that I had the joy of watching him fawn all over her every time all three of us were at the shop.

"Anyway, what decks did you bring?"

Aaron began pulling out his own deck boxes just as Devin shouted that they would be starting in a few minutes. I pulled out my phone again, my eyes lingering on Tristan's last message as I typed a response.

It's near downtown. It's called Critical Games. Anyway, we're about to play the Creatures & Crypts TCG, so you probably won't hear from me for a few hours.

I smiled as I hit send. This was good for me. I needed to spend the night enjoying a card game with my friends and not fretting over my dating life.

And just as Devin began announcing pairings, my phone buzzed one more time.

Sounds fun. Have a great night!

"ALRIGHT, EVERYONE, WE'RE GOING TO START TCG Night," Devin sauntered over to the gaming tables and gestured for the crowd to pay attention. "I'm assuming you're all here for the *Creatures & Crypts TCG*?"

There was a collective nod.

"Excellent. Now, I know we sometimes have some newbies in the crowd. Does everyone know how to *play C&C*?"

"*C&C*? I thought this was *Magic: The Gathering*!" a sudden voice sprung from the crowd, eliciting a few giggles.

"Shut up Chris," Devin scowled playfully. "Alright, go find your assigned pod and get started."

Thankfully, Aaron and I were together for the first game. The *Creatures & Crypts TCG* was a four-player trading card game, played with 100-card decks centered around a single "captain" card. It had been my favorite trading card game for years, ever since I first walked into Critical Games when I moved to Orlando.

Devin was the one who taught me how to play. And he was the one who helped me pick out my first *C&C* deck.

Ugh, I grimaced. *Why are you even thinking about him right now?*

Another vision of his chest tattoo flashed in my mind, and I clenched my hand of cards tighter.

I forced myself to shift my thoughts back to Tristan, endlessly wondering what he would be like in person. If he'd look like his profile photo. What his voice would sound like. If he would be able to carry on a conversation.

I knew I was jumping the gun. I shouldn't have felt butterflies before I'd even met the guy. But I couldn't help it. Especially since I knew that if the first date went well, I'd be head over heels for him. I was already halfway there.

I frowned when I realized that he hadn't actually asked me out yet.

"Uh, Avery?" Aaron nudged my shoulder with his. "Your turn."

"Oh, thanks."

Goddamnit. Focus.

I'd been so distracted that I hadn't realized that I was winning. My opponent directly in front of me had a strong start, but that also meant the rest of the group quickly ganged up and knocked him out of the game. Aaron and my other opponent both had decent board states, and while I hadn't attacked anyone yet, my *lifestealer* deck had been gaining me an alarming amount of life. I sat at 62, while my opponents, having taken a lot of damage knocking out the other player, were at 29 and 18.

I gulped. I was winning, but that meant I was also now the main target.

A few more rounds passed. I took some big hits, knocking me down to 43 life by my next turn. I cringed, realizing that I could've prepared for this situation better if I hadn't been so lost in my own thoughts.

Sadly, I couldn't recover. Both men teamed up to knock me out in two more turns, and they faced off head-to-head to determine the victor. I was pleased that it was Aaron, and I gave him a congratulatory fist bump as he went up to the counter to claim his prize cards.

"I'll get you next round," I teased as I brushed past the counter and headed for the restroom.

Chapter 2

"You wish!"

I closed the single-stall bathroom door behind me and settled on the toilet. And just as I did so, a wave of fatigue washed over my body, causing me to lean back against the plumbing.

Ugh, why do I suddenly feel so dizzy?

And... sore?

I tore off my jeans and underwear at lightning speed. It was just a few red spots, but it was enough for my insides to twist.

I knew what was coming. The pain was mild now, but it wouldn't be later.

I took a few deep breaths as another searing pulse trickled through my body. I had maybe thirty minutes to get home and crawl in bed before the worst of it came.

Disappointment flooded through my veins. I'd have to drop out of TCG Night and head home.

I flushed the toilet, washed my hands, and exited the stall with a hand over my lower abdomen, trying not to appear as sick as I felt.

Aaron and the others were preoccupied; hunched around a table and flipping through their card binders. Devin was the only one on the retail side of the store, punching away at the computer keyboard. From the restroom entrance, I could see the back of his head, sandwiched by a pair of ears pierced with silver studs.

"Hey Avie," he grinned as I approached the counter. "How can I help you?"

"I'm dropping," I croaked as another wave of pain slammed into my abdomen.

"Ah ok. You sure? It's only been one round."

I nodded, pressing my fingers deeper into my stomach.

Devin's smirk faded away, replaced by genuine concern. "You okay?"

"Yeah, I'm fine," I grumbled as I stepped away from the counter. *I'm certainly not telling him about my period problems.*

"Well, alright then. Have a good night."

I pressed my shoulder into the front door and shoved it open. A bell chimed above my head as a muggy, warm summer breeze whooshed past me. It was a short walk to my car, but I was already stumbling by the time I made it to the driver's seat.

I started up the ignition and caught a glimpse of myself in my rearview mirror. My abdomen throbbed again, and I saw my reflection squeeze her eyes shut in pain.

This is going to be a long night.

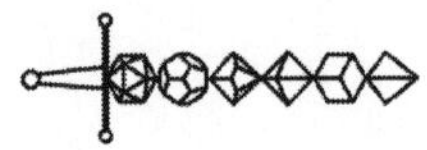

GOD, MY HEAD HURTS.

My eyes fluttered open the following morning, and the first thing I noticed was that I was sore, lightheaded, and still exhausted even after ten hours of sleep.

I placed a hand on my aching forehead as I lay sprawled out in a star shape on my bed. My back and limbs were covered in dried sweat, and my bedsheets were unusually humid and sticky. The morning after bad period cramps felt much like I imagined a hangover would.

But at least the pain was gone. I was no longer crippled by it, alternating between sitting on the toilet with my head buried in my knees and curling up in a fetal position on the bed. I was no stranger to pain—I'd broken my collarbone at age six, torn my knee open at age fourteen, and caught severe COVID at age twenty-four. But in my almost twenty-seven years of life, nothing else had ever compared to the pain of my period cramps.

Chapter 2

My uterus still felt achy and tender as I sat upright in bed, trying to shake the dizziness from my cloudy head. But the worst part about my periods wasn't the pain. That I could deal with, even if it meant sobbing in bed for hours until exhaustion pulled me into a fitful sleep. With my various ailments over the years, someone had always been there to help me. My parents rubbed my head and reassured me as I had my collarbone x-rayed and my knee stitched up as a child. Even Cassidy took care of me when I had COVID, slipping food, water, and medicine through my door so she didn't catch my illness.

Other ailments got sympathy. But as a woman, I had learned that no one gives a damn about your period cramps. You're expected to suck it up, not complain, and act like nothing is wrong.

No matter how much it hurts.

At least it's over.

I slunk out of my bed like a snail and stumbled into my attached bathroom. Once I caught a glimpse of my puffy, sallow face in the mirror, I wrinkled my freckled nose in disgust and splashed cold water on my face. It was Saturday, which meant I didn't have to worry about the fact that I'd slept until 11 a.m. I had no plans, so it was my day to do whatever I wanted.

No plans...

Wait...

Shit.

I dove out of the bathroom, scrambling for my nightstand. My phone was still there, although I hadn't plugged it in to charge in my period-pain-filled stupor. But it was hanging on at 5% battery life, and I unlocked my phone to discover that I had three notifications.

One of them was spam, but the second one was from Aaron, asking why I'd left the night before. I groaned, making a mental note that I'd need to come up with an excuse for that later. *Maybe I'll tell him I had food poisoning.*

But the final notification, the one that had my immediate interest, was from Tristan.

I popped open my dating app, eager to read his message.

Hey! How'd TCG night go?

The timestamp read 11:26 pm, long after I'd gotten home from Critical Games. Whether I was in the throes of my disorienting pain episode at that time or already asleep, I had no idea. But I'd still ignored his message the entire night.

I scrambled to write a response, but after a few seconds, I pulled my fingers away from my phone screen and took a deep breath. *Why are you panicking? You don't know this guy. It's no big deal.*

Besides, being late to respond makes you look less clingy.

Good morning! Yeah, I got home really late last night. It was fun! No wins, but that happens a lot. I played a lifestealer deck most of the night.

I hit send with a satisfied smile. It was a sweet, cheery, friendly response. One that a confident, mature, interesting twenty-six-year-old would send. Not one that was still in her pajamas at 11:15 am and in desperate need of a shower.

Just as I undressed, ready to settle under the soothing stream that poured out from the shower nozzle, my phone buzzed with another notification.

That's cool! By the way, since it's Saturday… are you free tonight?

Chapter 2

I stared blankly at those words for several minutes, the shower still fizzling behind me. It was the question I'd been waiting for, but somehow it sent panic bubbling up my stomach and into my esophagus.

Yes. I am.

Would you like to get a drink at Mulligan's tonight?

My heart thumped in my chest, but Tristan's words also tightened the knot in my throat. Mulligan's was an Irish pub in Oviedo, near the university. I knew it was a popular first date spot, but I wasn't a fan of alcohol. Plus, I was a lightweight, and one beer was usually enough to make my head spin.

I sighed. *But their food is pretty good. And I do really want to meet him.*

We exchanged a few more back-and-forth messages, settling on meeting at 6 p.m. that night. He offered to pick me up, but as eager as I was to meet him, he was still a stranger, and I wasn't ready for him to know where I lived. So we agreed to meet each other there.

Thanks, Avery. Can't wait!

He can't wait. The butterflies started rustling again.

I smiled and put my phone down, high on excitement. But as I came back to reality, I realized that it was now 11:45 a.m., and my shower had been running behind me for half an hour. The whole bathroom, and most of my bedroom, were cloaked in a humid fog.

I chuckled at my stupidity and jumped in the shower, scrubbing myself off in record time. As I emerged, the previous night's painful grime now washed off me, I ran a towel through my long curly hair and patted my face dry.

Of course, I'd have to tell him my secret eventually. It would be a make-or-break moment in our budding relationship, and I had no idea if he'd be willing to work things through with me or bail as soon as I told him. But I had to take this chance. Deep down, I prayed that for the right guy, my sexual dysfunction wouldn't matter. That it would be a problem we could solve together.

Maybe Tristan would be that guy.

Chapter 3

THE BUTTERFLIES REMAINED, FLAPPING AND jostling around in my stomach, in the hours leading up to the date. Not long after I showered, Cassidy knocked on my door and asked if I wanted to go grocery shopping. It was our roommate tradition—wandering down the aisles, wheeling the cart along, stocking up both on food and gossip. So, I happily agreed.

Cassidy weaseled the news out of me while we were in my Camry, and asked me a million questions about my newfound love interest while we shopped. I answered most of them cheerfully, but when Cass started asking more personal questions, I could feel my cheeks start to burn.

"And remember," Cassidy grinned as I scanned the coffee aisle, eager to find a dark roast that wasn't too bitter. "If you two ever need some alone time... just let me know. I'll slip out of the townhouse for a few hours."

"Cass!" I whisper-yelled under my breath, practically throwing the bag of Orange Blossom French Roast into our cart. I could feel that my face was on fire.

"What?" she asked innocently. "It'll come up eventually. You always gave me privacy when my ex was over."

I pushed the cart forward, refusing to make eye contact with Cassidy as my stomach clenched. "It's too early for that. I haven't even met the guy."

"He's hot, though."

"He's hot in his photos. There's a difference."

"And what if he's hot in real life too? What if you decide to—?"

"*Cass*," I replied flatly, through gritted teeth. "I'm not talking about this in the middle of a grocery store. Let's have this conversation *after* I've had a few dates with the guy."

"Whatever you say," she replied, a devious grin on her face.

Once we returned home, we put the groceries away, made a quick lunch of peanut butter and banana sandwiches, and retreated to our separate rooms.

Mine felt like it was closing in on me as I sat on the bed, phone in hand. It was 3 p.m., meaning I had two and a half hours to kill before I left for my date with Tristan.

Normally, any free time would be spent playing video games, but after about thirty minutes of *Stardew Valley,* I became too restless to sit in my cushy gaming chair. I racked my brain for any more errands that I needed to run; anything to get me out of the house and keep my mind from fretting over my upcoming date.

I eventually decided on the nearby pet store, but I entered the place feeling like an idiot. I had no pets, and therefore no need for any food, treats, or other supplies. But I was a huge animal lover, and while finances were often tight at our townhouse, I'd always dreamed of having a companion.

But as cute as the rescue puppies and kittens in the displays at the front of the shop were, they weren't the animals that interested me. Instead, I wandered to the back of the store, able to smell them long before I could see them.

I knew people often turned their noses up at ferrets, but I had been enchanted by the wiggly little cat snakes since I was a teenager. There were two in the enclosure—an albino male and a dark sable female—and they immediately perked up and hopped towards me as I approached. I lowered my hand into the enclosure, and the pair clamored up my arm, their tiny claws leaving little white lines on my wrist as they begged to be held.

I scooped up the female, holding her close to my chest and breathing in her scent. Ferrets certainly were musky, but their smell had never bothered me.

I hung out with the ferrets for a half-hour and spent another half-hour wandering around admiring the fish tanks. Since it was a Saturday, the store was packed, and the staff didn't seem to mind a lonely young woman lingering around and interacting with their animals.

But as soon as my phone showed 4:30 pm, I scampered out of the pet store and made my way home.

Forty-five minutes later, after another quick shower to ensure I'd gotten all the ferret scent off my body, I stood hopelessly in front of the bathroom mirror, flat iron in hand. I had debated straightening my hair, but not long after I'd plugged the iron in, I decided against it. I usually wore my hair in its natural, curly state, so I figured it would be best to let Tristan meet me that way.

Prior to struggling with my hair, I'd spent twenty minutes laying multiple outfits on my tiny twin bed, torn on what to wear. *Nothing too formal, but not too casual either. Should I dress cute? Sexy? How sexy is too sexy?*

I eventually decided on an emerald-green dress with stretchy fabric that hugged my chest and waist before cascading into a flowy skirt. I paired it with strappy brown sandals and a little sterling silver dragon necklace that Cassidy gave me years ago.

Finally, at 5:30 pm, I was ready to leave.

Tristan lived in Oviedo, close to the university where he worked as a financial aid assistant. I lived near downtown Orlando, about thirty minutes away, but I didn't mind driving to his area to meet.

Oviedo was a unique place, once the "rural" part of Orlando now overtaken by student housing and college bars. There were still unique bits of its history left though, and I drove past a few farms with squabbling chickens and grazing horses on my way there.

I paused for a few minutes after pulling into the parking lot at Mulligan's, enjoying a few brief moments of silence with my ignition turned off. There was a low rumble of voices in the distance – the pub was already packed, but it looked like most of the outdoor seating was still open. It was an unusually cool night for a Florida summer, with the temperature and humidity dropping enough to make the evening air bearable for outdoor activities. I enjoyed the way it soaked into my skin as I exited the car and stepped toward the pub.

At first, I thought I'd made it there before him. Which I always hated, because it meant I had to stand around fidgeting with my thumbs while my heart pounded with anticipation. But upon entering the crowded pub, I heard an unfamiliar voice shout my name.

"Avery?"

It was more of a question than a greeting. But as the crowd parted and I caught a glimpse of the blonde-haired boy standing next to the bar, my heart did a happy flip in my chest.

Even in the dim light of the pub, I could tell he was gorgeous. He was tall and tan, with remarkably blue eyes and waves of golden blonde hair. He wore a loose, collared button-down shirt and a pair of jeans—not too casual, not too formal.

He must've also been pleased by my appearance, because he immediately broke into a grin. His teeth were impossibly straight and white.

We exchanged a quick, friendly side hug before settling at the bar. We made awkward small talk for a few minutes, until we realized it was far too loud to hear each other and Tristan suggested we head outside.

"Sounds great," I agreed.

I slid off my barstool and walked toward the patio when I felt a brief brush of fingers against my spine. A warm, happy jolt of electricity ran up my stomach.

I loved when guys did that, ushering me along with a gentle hand on my back. And unlike my date with Anthony, I felt the sparks immediately.

As we took a seat at a metal table outside, I hoped that the conversation would match up to the physical attraction.

And thankfully, it did. After the first few awkward minutes, our conversation began to flow. It started with superficial topics—hobbies, pop culture references, favorite things. He asked me what I liked for video games, and I answered that I bounced around, but my favorites were farming sims and MMOs.

That made Tristan's face light up, because it turned out he was a big World of Warcraft player. That resulted in a twenty-minute conversation comparing different races, classes, and builds, although it was obvious that my knowledge of the game paled in comparison to his.

About an hour into the date, we began discussing our personal lives. I told him I was from a small town in the Florida panhandle, that I had two younger brothers, and that my birthday was July 18.

Tristan was twenty-nine years old. He was born in California, but his parents decided to switch coasts when he was five. He had a younger sister and a younger brother, both of which were teenagers who still lived at home.

Tristan also had a pet, an adorable, vaguely-hound-looking mutt that he happily showed me photos of on his phone. His birthday was November 24, which he said he enjoyed because it was always on or near Thanksgiving.

Unfortunately, this brought up more family talk, which left me in a bind. I didn't like to discuss my parents or my brothers, who I saw little of and had spent the past five years trying to flee from. But being there with Tristan set a tiny spark of hope in my heart. I couldn't tell if he was religious, but he seemed like a sweet, stable guy who my parents would approve of. Maybe trips home would be easier with a boyfriend to serve as a buffer.

But eventually, the conversation swung back around to hobbies, and Tristan eagerly asked me about Critical Games. I explained to him how the *Creatures & Crypts TCG* worked, and what sort of decks I liked to play. He seemed eager to learn, and he asked if I could take him with me sometime.

I said of course, and I could feel the heat rising to my cheeks. But I broke out in giggles when I realized he was blushing, too.

"Do you play the regular *Creatures & Crypts*?" he asked. "The roleplaying game?"

"I used to all the time," I replied. Critical Games hosted a bunch of sessions on Sunday afternoons. "But then work got too crazy. Still, it's something I want to play more of."

"That's great!" Tristan grinned. "I have a friend group that plays on Wednesday nights. We alternate houses, but we always have plenty of snacks and beer. You should join us sometime."

"Sure!"

I realized I may have said that too enthusiastically. More blushes on both sides.

The conversation continued. Nervousness melted away into comfort, and the hours ticked away until I realized it was nearly 10 p.m.

I chuckled. Four hours had passed in the blink of an eye.

That was a wonderful sign.

But Tristan had to leave since he had a family commitment early the next morning. The thought of saying goodbye sent shudders of anticipation down my spine. Not just because I was sad to see him go, but because I didn't know if he'd try to get physical.

I wasn't opposed to a kiss on the first date, but I hadn't met a guy that I liked enough to do it. But I could feel my attraction to Tristan pulsing through my whole body, setting off sparks in my nervous system and making my heart hammer in my ears. I decided I'd let him take the lead, but if he did try to kiss me, I certainly wouldn't object.

And sure enough, in the parking lot as he led me to my car, he did. I was nothing more than a simple peck on the lips, securing our attraction to one another without taking things too far. But it still made me feel like I'd just downed a bottle of wine.

Our grins spread wide across our faces as we said goodbye, and I hopped into my car feeling light as a cloud.

Before I'd even made it home, Tristan texted me about a second date.

And considering it had been my best online date by far, I immediately said yes.

Chapter 4

IT ALL CAME CRASHING DOWN THE NEXT morning, when reality finally slapped the butterflies away.

No matter how well things went with Tristan, I would eventually have to tell him.

I tossed the sheets off my legs and pulled down my underwear, cursing my vagina for being such an uncooperative pain in the ass. I realized that I was getting a bit too hairy down there. It normally wasn't an issue since no guy had seen my genitalia in five years, but last night's successful date left me feeling the urge to shave.

I didn't have an electric razor, so a manual one would have to do. Twenty minutes later, it was patchy and uneven, but significantly less bushy than before.

Now feeling more confident, I rifled through my underwear drawer until I came across my illicit secret: a small bullet vibrator. It wasn't even an inch wide, and only a few inches long, but it was the only one I could muster up the courage to buy.

Chapter 4

I still remembered that day, walking into *Sweet Romance* trembling like I was headed to my own execution. Because that was exactly what my parents would to do me if they ever found out I was buying a *sex toy*.

It had taken a lot of self-reassuring to get that far, telling myself that this was strictly a medical device and not something that would get me sent to the gates of hell. I hadn't been with a man in years, and I needed to start *somewhere*.

But a year later, I'd made little progress. I could stick it in maybe half an inch before the burning started up and I ripped the little device out in pain. Even the vibrating feature didn't help, although it did feel nice on my vulva.

But today, I was determined. I would push through the pain and get this stupid vibrator in my vagina, no matter what it took.

As I laid in bed with my legs awkwardly spread open, the familiar burning sensation caused me to hold back a scream. But I fought against the pain, even with my thighs clenched like iron and sweat pooling on my temples.

Eventually, my leg muscles gave out from being so tense, and I stopped. Even with the most determination I'd had in years, the vibrator hadn't even made it in an inch.

I took a few deep, heaving breaths, ready to try again. But as soon as I slid the device back in, a knock as my door sent my limbs into a frightened spasm.

"Hey Avery, you in there?"

It was Cassidy. I scrambled toward my dresser, hurriedly shoving mounds of underwear on top of the incriminating sex toy before slamming the drawer shut.

"Uh… I'm not dressed."

I cringed, squeezing my eyes shut. I was both embarrassed and in pain, my vagina burning from my futile masturbation attempt.

"Well, I'm headed to Critical Games for *Creatures & Crypts* in about an hour. Want to come?"

My first thought was no, as I hadn't been able to make it to *C&C* in weeks due to my work schedule. I was super behind and would have no idea what was going on or what the backstory was for the campaign. Plus, I was naked, unshowered, and not up for socializing. But I didn't have any other plans for the day, and I knew if I ended up sitting around the townhouse all day, I'd regret it.

Plus, I thought to myself, *it'll be good practice for playing with Tristan's group.*

I sighed, realizing I was once again jumping the gun.

"Yeah, just let me shower and get ready," I shouted at Cassidy through the door.

I started up the shower, flopping on my bed with my phone as I waited for the water to heat up. I went to check my messages and realized I had two of them.

The first one was from... *Devin Lancaster?*

I momentarily forgot that I had given Devin my number a year ago, back when I was still going to *Creatures & Crypts* regularly. *But why on Earth would he be texting me right now?*

Part curious and part nauseous, I opened the message.

> *Hey Avie. Isn't this C&C deck yours? I found it under one of the tables this morning while I was cleaning.*

Shit.

I scrambled for my gaming bag – a retro-controller-themed backpack that I kept all my *C&C* decks in. The *lifestealer* deck wasn't there. I then noticed that Devin's message had an attachment. It was a photo, and I immediately recognized the sun-and-moon-themed deck box.

I must've left it behind on Friday night when I wasn't feeling well.

Yeah, it is. I'll come get it later today.

You know C&C is today, right? You should play.

Yup, I am. Cass asked me to come.

Sweet. Sam is out today, so I'll be substituting as your Crypt Master.

I groaned and plopped my phone on the bed. If I was going to go to a *C&C* session, I really wanted it to be with my regular group. I liked Sam; he was an easygoing, balanced Crypt Master who ran equal parts roleplaying and combat. Devin usually ran the children's group, which meant he had a very… *different* playstyle. He made all his characters talk in funny accents, threw weird puzzles into every dungeon, and spent far too much time plotting out elaborate roleplay sessions at his fictional town's pub.

I debated staying home and spending my afternoon playing video games. But I'd already told Cassidy that I'd go, and Devin was currently holding my *lifestealer* deck hostage. Plus, I had to admit, Devin was a good CM. He was great at making the kids laugh, and his table was always the loudest and most enthusiastic one in the shop.

That was when I decided to check my second message. And while Devin's text had surprised me, this one made my blood run cold.

Hi Avery. How's it going? I haven't heard from you since Thursday. Did you want to meet up again soon?

It was from Anthony. I hadn't contacted him since our lackluster date a few days ago.

I gulped. I didn't want to ghost him – I had been on the receiving end of that cruel practice and knew how awful it felt. I just needed to let him down gently.

Hi Anthony. Thanks for reaching out! I had a nice time, but I don't think we're compatible relationship-wise. I wish you the best of luck though!

I re-read my message twice before hitting send, carefully plotting my words like a work email to a client. Friendly and professional, but firm.

The little "typing" bubble appeared immediately next to my message and stayed there a suspiciously long time. I exited out of my messages and browsed social media for a while, cringing when I saw a *very* long message pop up in my notifications.

Are you sure? I'm sorry, I know I was kind of awkward. To be honest, I don't date much and I was really nervous. But I felt we had a lot in common, and I'd really love to get to know you better. Would you like to get dinner with me at—

I threw my phone on my bed, clasping my fists to my skull and trying not to scream.

I knew that online dating was hard, especially on guys. I got nervous on dates too. But I wasn't interested in him, and nothing irritated me more than men who couldn't take no for an answer. Because as tough as online dating could be, it only worked when there was mutual attraction. I never understood pushiness; why waste emotions on someone that wasn't interested?

I decided to retract my former promise to not ghost the guy, as his begging didn't deserve the dignity of a reply. Despite my earlier reservations about *Creatures & Crypts*, I was now relieved that I had somewhere to be for the afternoon. This guy's message had sent chills down my spine, and I didn't really want to be alone.

I walked away and stepped into the shower, leaving Anthony's whiny message untouched on my bed.

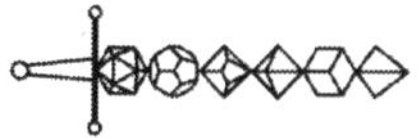

CRITICAL GAMES WAS SURPRISINGLY EMPTY FOR a Sunday afternoon.

Cassidy and I arrived fifteen minutes before the start time, surprised to find most of the tables unoccupied. The only people in the store were Aaron, two preteen boys I didn't recognize, and of course, Devin, who was standing behind the counter.

Aaron immediately rushed over to us, excitedly babbling on about how much fun this was going to be. And, as was usual when Cass and I were together, I was invisible. Aaron's focus was strictly on my adorable curly-haired best friend. I did my best to hide my smug, knowing smile as the pair approached one of the gaming tables and sat down, still lost in conversation.

Devin didn't even try to hide his. He looked like the Cheshire Cat as I spun around and approached the front counter.

"You think he's ever going to grow a pair and ask her out?"

"*Devin*," I hissed, throwing a pretend swat his way. He laughed, his snake-bite piercings gleaming a deep onyx black color under the fluorescent lights.

"Anyway, where's my C&C deck?"

"What, you mean *this* deck?" Devin fetched my sun-and-moon deck box off a high shelf behind the counter, clasping it in his upright fingers like a prized jewel.

"Yes. Give it to me."

"You playing at my table today?"

I huffed. "*Yes*. Now gimme."

Devin made an elaborate show of presenting the deck box to me, that stupid cocky grin still plastered on his pale face. I proceeded to unceremoniously snatch it out of his hands and scurry off toward the gaming table.

Weirdo.

But once I was settled in my seat, I couldn't help but glimpse back at him out of the corner of my eye. His black sweatshirt, one containing a band logo I didn't recognize, slid up his torso as he placed *C&C TCG* booster boxes onto the top shelf behind the counter. It exposed about an inch of his lower stomach, revealing the bottom of another of his tattoos. One that I had never seen before.

My face seared red as I quickly turned away.

"So where is everyone?" I asked, pulling Cassidy and Aaron away from their starry-eyed conversation.

"There's another *C&C TCG* event going on downtown," Aaron explained, running a hand through his lime-green hair. "At the convention center. I bet it's attracted all the game shop nerds like a magnet."

I sighed. As much as I wanted to go to one of those events, they were incredibly expensive, nearly rivaling Disney ticket prices. Cassidy and I weren't quite ramen-noodle-level poor, but the rising cost of living in Orlando had taken a big bite out of our paychecks for the past year.

Chapter 4

"Indeed, the event is going on all weekend," Devin's voice crept up behind us as he sat down at the head of the table.

"Speaking of which, why doesn't Critical Games attend?" Cassidy asked.

Devin shrugged. "I don't have the staff to man both the shop and the event. And if I went myself, I'd lose too much money closing the shop for the weekend."

Ah, that makes sense. I had always wondered what it was like to maintain a game shop. Devin had one or two employees that managed the shop on Mondays and Tuesdays when he was off, but other than that he was the sole staff member at Critical Games. I wondered how long it had been since he had a weekend to himself.

"Alright, ladies and gentlemen." Devin gestured around the table as he adjusted his Crypt Master screen. Normally, multiple tables were playing on Sunday afternoon, but today there was only one. There were five of us players—me, Aaron, Cassidy, and the two boys, who introduced themselves as Liam and Cole.

"Okay, does everyone have their characters? Remember, at this point, you should be level eight."

Eight!? It really had been a while since I played.

I reached into my backpack and pulled out a folder with my character sheet. I stared at my handwritten notes from several months ago and sighed. My character, an Infernal sorcerer named Sorcha, was a measly level three.

I sighed. Which was louder than I had anticipated, because everyone's heads swiveled towards me.

"Sorry, don't mind me," I muttered, embarrassed. "I'll level up while you guys start."

"That's okay," Devin replied. "I'll start everyone off with some roleplay at the pub."

"Thanks."

I gripped a borrowed pencil in my hand, my eyes flipping back and forth between my character sheet and my *Player's Guide* as I updated my stats and spells. But while I worked, my ears kept tabs on Devin's roleplaying session, especially the two boys. They were preteens, both about twelve years old, and each had the same wiry builds with mops of sandy brown hair. I wondered if they were twins.

Devin ran a roleplaying session at the *Drunken Donkey*, the in-game tavern that Aaron had stupidly named while he was intoxicated. But the name made Liam and Cole giggle, and they burst into full-on hyena laughing once Devin started roleplaying at the barkeep in a ridiculous Scottish accent.

I couldn't help but laugh myself. He sounded like a drunken Shrek.

Within ten minutes, I was all leveled up and ready to enter the bar scene. My Infernal, a demon-like character with horns and a tail, was all charm and sass. I couldn't wait for her to mess with Devin's dopey, dwarven barkeep.

"Well 'ello 'ere, 'lil lassie," Devin turned the accent up to eleven, and my face was turning bright red from trying not to laugh. I usually hated how his antics prevented my character from keeping her composure, but today I needed the humor.

Between Devin's accent and my stupidly red face, the whole table was cracking up. We were all so preoccupied that we barely noticed the doorbell chime as someone stepped into the shop.

But as soon as I saw the visitor, all the laughter drained from my face.

Is that... Anthony?

Chapter 5

WHAT THE FUCK IS HE DOING HERE?

He strolled through the front door, hands shoved in his pockets as he whistled quietly. At first, I told myself to calm down. Maybe it was just a coincidence that he was there. After all, he did play *Creatures & Crypts*.

But then his eyes locked with mine, and the look on his face made sweat start beading up on my temples.

I remembered telling him about Critical Games over text, before our failed date.

This was no coincidence.

"Hello there." Devin stood up, greeting Anthony like he would any customer. "May I help you?"

Anthony was quiet, his eyes still locked on mine as he shuffled around the store. I gripped the edge of the table until the blood drained from my knuckles.

"Just looking around," Anthony replied nonchalantly, and I forced back a scowl. *Liar.*

"Alright. Well, my name is Devin. Let me know if you need anything."

Our game of *C&C* continued; except this time, I barely paid attention. Even Devin's comical accent couldn't save me from my panic. He attempted to continue his barkeep's conversation with my character, but I struggled to squeak out one-word answers. Behind the table, Anthony was pacing up and down the shelves, browsing the merchandise while shooting long glances in my direction.

Thankfully, no one seemed to notice my thinly veiled terror. Devin went around the table, allowing each player to perform any desired tasks at the bar. Aaron's character, being a bard, wanted to serenade everyone in the room, while Cassidy's rogue character swindled patrons out of their coin with her magical gambling dice.

I laughed along, pretending that my throat wasn't full of marbles and that I couldn't feel Anthony's gaze boring holes into the back of my head.

It's okay. Calm down. Don't panic. Everything is oka—

"Mind if I join your game?"

Yes. I hunched my shoulders as I realized Anthony was standing directly behind me. He was so close that I swore I could feel his breath on my back.

Yes, yes, yes. I very much do mind.

"We're sorta in the middle of a game right now," Devin replied, scratching his head. "But we run tables every Sunday afternoon if you want to stop by next week."

My spasming muscles loosened as relief trickled through my veins. For once, I was incredibly grateful for Devin's presence.

"Well, can I just watch?"

No. No, nonono—

"Uh," Devin paused for a moment. Even he seemed uncomfortable. "Sure, I guess. Grab an empty chair."

Chapter 5

Anthony sat next to me, his chair just inches from my own. I pressed a palm to my cheek, refusing to glance in his direction.

God fucking damnit. Go away, you creepy, stubborn, low-life basta—

"Sorcha?"

I looked up, my cheeks still burning from Anthony's unwanted presence.

"You speak Demonic, correct?" Devin continued.

I nodded.

"Well, the only quest on the job board today is written in Demonic, and you're the only character at this table who knows that language."

"Ah, okay," I sat up straight, feeling sweat on my palm as I pulled it away from my face. "Well, I guess I should read it."

"Excellent," Devin pressed his hands together. "Follow me to the back, and I'll tell you what the note says."

I nodded, grateful to be able to step away from the table. This was a common occurrence at *C&C* sessions; if only one character could understand a written language, they'd be pulled aside and told the message in secret. It was then up to them if they wanted to divulge the information to the rest of the party.

Normally, the CM would lead the player to the far end of the gaming room, a few feet away from the tables. I was confused and a bit concerned when Devin led me all the way past the retail area and into the back storage area next to the restrooms.

"Uh, okay." I glanced around awkwardly. The storage room was incredibly cluttered, but also perfectly organized, with labels on every pile of boxes. In the corner was a minifridge and a table with two chairs, the makeshift staff breakroom. "So, what does the message say?"

"Forget the message," Devin replied coolly, and I gave him a funny look. He pointed out the door, back toward the gaming tables. "Is that guy bothering you?"

I had been grateful for Devin before, but now I felt indebted to him. There was no message in Demonic. He made it up so he could pull me away from the table and ensure I was okay.

It gave me the sudden urge to hug him, but I quickly brushed the feeling away.

"Yes," I admitted in an exasperated tone. "I met him on my dating app. We met up, but I wasn't interested in a second date. And... he didn't take it well."

"Oh boy." Devin ran a hand through his choppy, dyed black hair. He looked frustrated and... *angry*? "I'll be right back."

"Devin, wai—"

He was already gone. I was frozen in place, hands balled into worried fists as I fretted over the awkward situation I'd caused. *Maybe this is just a coincidence. Even if Anthony is being creepy, I don't have the right to make him leav—*

A sudden shout made me jolt. Someone was yelling, and it wasn't Devin.

I bolted out of the storage room to see Anthony, red-faced and pissed, yelling obscenities at Devin as the whole table looked on in horror. Cassidy and Aaron were panicked, and the preteen boys looked like they were about to flee the table. But Devin stood unwavering, arms crossed in front of his sweatshirt and his mouth pressed in a thin line.

He wasn't having it.

"What're you gonna do, emo boy?" Anthony taunted. Devin still didn't budge, his facial expression hard as a mask. "Go blab to the owner?"

"I *am* the owner," Devin growled. "Now get out of my shop."

Chapter 5

Thankfully, Anthony relented and stormed toward the front door. But as he did, he caught a glimpse of me standing in the back room, wide-eyed and pale as a ghost.

"Bitch," he hissed before throwing the door open, disappearing into the parking lot.

As soon as he left, my composure melted into a puddle and I fell to my knees. My heart was galloping madly in my chest, I was covered in cold sweat despite the shop being seventy degrees, and no amount of tensing my limbs would stop the uncontrollable shaking.

Is this... a panic attack?

"Avery." Devin rushed toward me, closing the storage room door so no one would see my reaction. I staggered to my feet, doing my best to hide my frenzied nerves. I would not break down in the middle of Critical Games.

I *especially* would not break down in front of Devin.

My breath hitched in my chest as I forced myself not to cry. Devin led me to the break area, plopping my shaky self down in a plastic chair. His hand lingered on my shoulder for a moment, and the feeling calmed me enough for my limbs to stop trembling.

"Stay here as long as you need."

Devin's voice was gentle, a tone I'd never heard from him. He was always a snarky, dry-humored, endlessly teasing pain in the ass. I'd never seen him like this before.

I nodded, worried that any amount of talking would cause me to immediately burst into tears.

"Here." Devin turned toward the mini-fridge. "Let me get you a water."

I heard light thumping noises as he rustled around the fridge, and he eventually pressed a cold miniature water bottle into my hands. The condensation on the outside cooled my sweaty palms—another small gesture that pulled me out of my panic attack and back to reality.

"Come join us when you're ready." Devin walked toward the door. "Or if you need to head home, no worries."

He left, leaving me alone in the breakroom, surrounded by silence and my own deafening thoughts. I took a few sips of the water bottle, surprised at how thirsty I was. Outside, I could hear Devin's muffled voice and a few laughs as their game resumed.

I placed the water bottle between my thighs. As sickening as the event was, I couldn't let Anthony get to me. I would spend some time in the breakroom, letting myself calm down, but I wouldn't leave. I would walk back out there and finish our *Creatures & Crypts* session; creepy online dates be damned.

Besides, I thought as I tossed my empty water bottle in the trash. *This session has been pretty fun.*

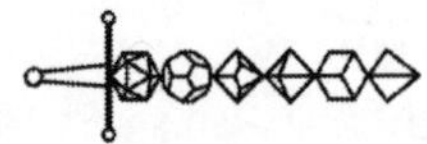

ONCE I REGAINED ENOUGH COMPOSURE TO GO back to my seat, my party had already accepted a quest to find a missing halfling, entered a creepy cave dungeon, and picked off a whole horde of goblins and kobolds.

I had made it back just in time for them to enter the boss's lair, where we all assumed the halfling was being imprisoned.

"But to make it through the door," Devin proclaimed in an exaggerated, malevolent voice, "you must solve the riddle that lines the sealed-off entrance."

"Okay," Cassidy remarked, studying her character sheet. "What language is it in?"

"Roll to investigate."

There was a hard plastic *thunk* as the die clattered onto the table. "Seventeen."

Chapter 5

"Well, the good news is, you passed," Devin grinned. "Bad news is, it isn't a language that you understand. But you're pretty sure it's written in Underling."

"Uh," Aaron frowned, looking down at his character sheet. "I can't read that language either."

"None of you can." Devon raised an eyebrow. "But using your collective knowledge of the Underworld and their alphabet, I bet you can all work together to decipher this."

Oh boy. I smiled and shook my head. *Here comes another of Devin's inane riddles.*

Devin pulled a sheet of paper from behind his Crypt Master screen and placed it in the middle of the table. On it was a short sentence written in a scratchy alphabet, similar to Nordic runes.

"For every successful arcane check you make, I'll tell you what one of the letters means," Devin announced, clapping his hands together. "Now, begin!"

While the other players huddled together, rolling a cacophony of dice while studying their character sheets, I stared intently at the riddle.

A twisted grin crept across my face. I recognized those symbols.

"It says, '*Observe the Observer's lair*'."

Everyone immediately stopped talking and swiveled their head in my direction. Devin's mouth hung open, his snakebite piercings jutting from his lower lip.

"H-how did you know that?!" he stammered.

"It's a popular fantasy font called *Dragonmark*."

"Once again," Devin repeated, his face even more bewildered, "*how did you know that*?"

"I've used it for work."

"*Work*?"

"Yeah. I work for a publishing company, dude. I'm the master of fonts."

Devin was speechless. He took a few moments to blink his way out of his disbelief, looking utterly defeated since his riddle was ruined.

"And an *Observer*, Devin?!" I continued. "We're level *eight*! Are you trying to get us all killed?"

He slumped behind his Crypt Master screen, his face buried in his fists. At first, regret burned through my stomach like acid. *I may have taken it too far...*

But as Devin began to shake, I realized he wasn't upset. He was laughing. He raised his head, cackling like a hyena as he slapped a palm on the table. Suddenly, everyone at the table, even the preteen boys, was full of giggles. It was a scene that bordered on near hysterics, everyone's faces red and eyes watering by the time we regained composure.

"Goddamnit, Avery," Devin wiped a tear from the corner of his eye. "Always the master at foiling my plans. And you know what?" His eyes narrowed. "I'm going to say that Sorcha spoke that aloud. Roll initiative."

I gulped.

"You're seriously having us face an Observer right now?"

Devin winked. "Better roll high."

My die fumbled onto the countertop, displaying a disappointing number five.

Well shit.

"Oh noooo," Devin teased in a drawn-out, mocking tone. "A *five*? Well, the Observer rolled a twenty-one, and you're standing right in the doorwayyyy..."

I scowled, but I knew I sort of deserved it for ruining Devin's riddle.

But when the giant eyeball-like creature's attack missed, I nearly leaped out of my seat with joy, once again thrilled to deflate Devin's ego. He huffed, rolling a die around in his fingers with a deep frown on his face.

"Alright, *fine*. He misses. Cass, you're up next."

Chapter 5

We went around the table, taking turns strategizing against the formidable creature. The Observer's central eye created an anti-magic area in whichever direction it was facing, so Liam and Cole used their fighter and barbarian characters to keep the Observer's attention. While they bashed it in the face with their weapons, the rest of us slung spells at the monstrosity from a safe distance.

The Observer's mythical actions were awful, with it having the ability to use the tentacles springing from its circular body to paralyze us, frighten us, or, if we were especially unlucky, instantly disintegrate us. After several rounds, we were all still standing, although Cassidy had taken a dangerous amount of necrotic damage from one of the tentacles.

While Aaron's character held back to heal Cassidy, it was my turn to attack. I was a feral magic sorcerer, meaning that my spells could have unpredictable results—good *or* bad. Devin knew this, and made me roll a d20 die to see if my spell went haywire. It did, and he howled with laughter, rubbing his hands together in a maniacal fashion.

"You know this could work in *my* favor, right?" I hissed as Devin flipped through his *Crypt Masters' Guide*.

He smirked. "Let's hope it doesn't."

"Alright, d100... I got a 28."

Devin switched to his *Player's Guide*, frantically flipping through the pages until he suddenly stopped. He was silent, and his smile was immediately wiped from his face.

I grinned. "So what effect do I get, dear Crypt Master?"

Devin gave a long, exasperated sigh, "On a 28, you can take another action immediately."

I raised my eyebrows. "You mean... I can cast *another* fire sphere?"

"Yup." I could see the disappointment in his glassy eyes. "Go for it."

To my surprise, right after I hurled yet another giant ball of fire at the Observer's backside, Devin announced that I had delivered the killing blow. Liam and Cole cheered, and I shook my head with a smile. Behind the dead Observer, the halfling we'd been searching for was imprisoned in a small cage.

And, conveniently, the ugly beast had the keyring wrapped around one of its head tentacles.

It was getting late, so we wrapped up the session by returning the kidnapped halfling to the tavern and obtaining our reward, a heaping chest of gold. The preteen boys were eager to spend their coin on more magical items, but Devin assured them they'd have plenty of time for shopping during their next session.

"Besides, boys, it looks like your mom is here," Devin gestured toward the front door, where a woman with the same sandy brown hair entered with a wave and a smile.

The boys excitedly babbled to their mom about their session, and Aaron and Cassidy were quickly swept up in their own conversation. Which left me and Devin sitting together at the gaming table.

"So I've gotta ask," I said as Devin packed up his books. "How did we manage to defeat that Observer? I have enough *C&C* knowledge to know we were way under-leveled for that."

Devin grinned, leaning towards me as if he had a secret. "Liam and Cole's favorite *C&C* monster is the Observer. They've been begging to fight one for weeks. So, I just nerfed the monster's hit points so it would die quicker."

I chuckled. "That's cheating."

Devin shrugged. "I mean, it was still a tough fight. But you throwing two fire spheres at its face in one turn took out a third of its health."

I laughed. Devin laughed too as he packed up the rest of his supplies.

"You know," he remarked as I walked towards the door. "You really should come to C&C more often. Today was fun."

I nodded. It really had been. "Sure. Now that work isn't so crazy, I'll come next week."

As I walked out the door, jogging to catch up with Cassidy and Aaron, I decided I liked Devin's campaign after all. I'd had so much fun that I'd forgotten about the harrowing incident from earlier.

I groaned as the memory of it trickled back over me. I knew that even safe in my townhouse, it would still haunt my sleep that night.

Chapter 6

My Sunday night was a restless one, spent tossing and turning in bed as I fretted about Anthony. I'd had plenty of lackluster dates that resulted in rejection, but this was the first time I'd had someone try to *stalk* me.

I still had no idea how he knew I was at Critical Games. I reassured myself by saying he just happened to show up at the right time, and he hadn't somehow managed to track my movements. And as I lay restless in bed, anxiety gripping my chest, the risks of online dating that I'd once been oblivious to now haunted me.

As a result, I started the next morning with exhaustion, a pounding headache, and blurry double vision. The words of the manuscript I'd been editing smeared together in a jumbled, inky mess, and not even two cups of coffee could shake my fatigue.

But I loved my job, constantly immersed in manuscripts, typesets, and cover designs, and I knew how to fight fatigue from years of god-awful periods. So I slogged through the day, reminding myself that I only had four left until the weekend returned and I could see Tristan again.

I grinned as I took a break and laid down on my bed. Working from home had its perks.

Over the following days, both my physical and mental state improved. I hadn't heard a word from Anthony since the game shop incident, which reassured me that Devin had scared him off for good. I had to admit that Devin was intimidating. He wasn't particularly muscular or tall, but his tattoos, facial piercings, and preference for all-black everything made many people balk at his appearance. I had too when I first met him, but over the years I realized that he was a kind, genuine person, if a bit obnoxious.

Friday came around as it did every week, although it seemed to take much longer than usual. I knew it was a side effect of anticipation—becoming painfully aware of every passing minute until an hour felt like an eternity. Friday was TCG Night, which was one of my favorite hobbies and something I looked forward to at the beginning of every weekend.

But this Friday was also my second date with Tristan. We had texted sporadically throughout the week and agreed to meet at a video game bar downtown. I initially assumed that I'd have to pass on TCG Night, but when we agreed on 8 p.m., I realized I would have enough time for a single round.

I exhaled sharply out of my mouth as I slid my laptop shut at 5 p.m., relieved that for the fourth weekend in a row, I didn't have to work overtime. It had kept me from regularly attending *Creatures & Crypts*, and it made it tough to schedule weekend activities with my friends.

Plus, it made dating difficult.

But we'd hired a new staff member, which meant we weren't overloaded with manuscripts for the foreseeable future. I had my weekends back, and at that moment, I was eager to spend some of it with Tristan.

I was buzzing with anticipation when I arrived at Critical Games an hour later. As usual, Devin greeted me and rang up my gaming fee, but I hardly paid him any attention. I was excited for TCG Night, but I was even more excited about what awaited me afterward.

"Hey Avery?"

I looked up, alarmed at the seriousness of Devin's tone. He had also referred to me by my full name, like he had done during my encounter with Anthony.

"Uh, yes?"

"I know this is awkward, but..." He shifted his weight from one foot to the other, scratching his shaggy black hair. "Please be careful, okay?"

"With what?"

"You know...all this online dating stuff. I grabbed some shots of that redhead from the security cameras, and I told my staff that he's banned from the shop. But I just...I don't want anything bad to happen."

I sighed. "Devin, you're not my dad."

Devin's expression sharpened. "No. But I am your friend. I care about you, and your safety. Just promise me you'll be careful."

As much as I hated it, Devin was right. I tended to wear my heart on my sleeve, diving headfirst into the dating pool without checking the depth first. I wasn't stupid; I knew there were weirdos and creeps out there. But I knew what I was getting into the first day I downloaded the app, and if online dating allowed me to find a partner who wouldn't judge my sexual shortcomings, it was worth the risk.

But that didn't stop Devin's words from knocking around my skull, making my heart thump in erratic, irrational ways.

I am your friend. I care about you.

And I hated every emotion it made me feel.

"Yeah yeah, you're right," I sighed. "I'll be careful."

"Thank you." There was a hint of relief in Devin's words as he handed me my receipt. "I hope you have fun tonight."

"Thanks. I appreciate it."

Cassidy and Aaron ushered me into a chair next to them as we waited for pairings to start. The three of us were placed in a pod with Chris, another regular who was good friends with Aaron. Cassidy was thrilled to play her new dinosaur-themed deck, and I had just added some new cards to my warrior deck.

But unfortunately, it wasn't enough for either of us to win. Chris and Cassidy took an early lead, but a card that wiped the board of creatures hurt Cassidy too much for her to recover. Chris took over, knocking me and Aaron out within two turns. His smug victory grin caused Aaron's face to twist into a scowl.

"You know, you didn't have to throw *two* infinite combos in that deck," he hissed at Chris.

"Of course I did. What's the fun of opening a $20 card out of a pack and not playing it?"

A hot trickle of anticipation seared through my veins. The game had lasted about an hour, meaning that I needed to head out and make my way to the video game bar.

"You're dropping again?" Devin looked confused as I gave him the news.

"Yup. Remove me from the pairings please."

Devin stopped typing on his computer keyboard, glancing me up and down with his blue-green eyes. A chill crept up my neck as I realized he was studying my outfit—a maroon dress with a black woven belt and velvety grey ankle-length boots. I had been showing up to the shop in dresses more often lately, since they were comfortable and didn't irritate my stomach during my bad periods. But today I looked especially dressed up.

He knew something was off.

"It's only been one round," he continued. "You sure?"

Irritation bubbled in my stomach again as my fingernails dug half-moons into my palms. Devin was my friend, and I appreciated his concern, but he was starting to get on my nerves.

"Yes, I'm sure." I had to force myself to not hiss my words. "I'll be here on Sunday for *C&C* though. I'll see you then!"

I spun around and sped out the front door before Devin had the chance to respond.

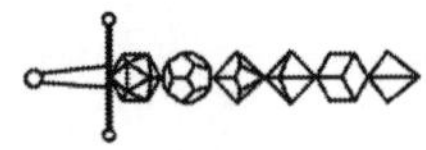

Just like before, Tristan was waiting for me when I arrived.

He swiveled around on his barstool, greeting me with an enthusiastic wave and a flash of his brilliantly white teeth. Once I reached the bar, he stood up to give me a hug, one far warmer and longer than the one during our first meetup.

He was even bold enough to place a quick peck on my cheek, which made me break out in a silly, infatuated grin.

As I took a seat, I peered around at my surroundings. *Joysticks* was a small, cozy establishment tucked into a strip mall near Universal Studios. It was a far drive for me, but I didn't mind since I was fond of the place. Cassidy and Aaron had dragged me there a few times, and while I typically didn't drink, I enjoyed playing lots of retro video games in the dark, quirky, neon-light-filled space.

"I'm so glad we came here tonight," Tristan grinned, rubbing his palms together. "My dad used to take me to old-school arcades when I was a kid. It reminded him of his childhood, and he was a master at *Galaga*. He used to get on the scoreboard at every arcade we visited."

I noticed Tristan was talking about his dad in the past tense, but I knew we weren't far along in our relationship, and I didn't want to pry. Instead, I studied the drink menu, searching for the beer with the lowest alcohol content.

We placed our orders and chatted while we waited for our drinks. Tristan asked me how my week went, and I used that question to tell him all about my job at the publishing company. He was fascinated, and I even confessed to him out of my far-flung dreams: to one day write my own book.

"What genre would you write?" he asked.

"I like romance," I shrugged. "Whether contemporary or fantasy. I just need an idea for a good story."

"I bet you'll find it," Tristan smiled. "Admittedly, I need to read more. I used to devour books like crazy as a kid, but ever since college I've completely given up on them."

"That happens to a lot of us," I reassured him. "I quit reading for a while, too. I think it's because of smartphones and social media. But since I read so much for work, I made it a habit to buy more books. And once I dove into fantasy romances, I couldn't put them down."

Our drinks arrived, and Tristan took a big, satisfied gulp of his beer while I took a hesitant sip of mine. It was sweet, with a hint of orange, and wasn't nearly as unpleasant as the cheap stuff kids used to sneak onto my college campus. I took another sip, knowing it wouldn't be long until the dizzying burn of intoxication seeped into my bloodstream.

I set my beer on the counter. I hated being a lightweight.

We spent the next few hours diving deeper into our personal lives, discussing our jobs, families, and friends over several rounds of *Super Smash Bros*. While our characters beat the crap out of each other, I told him more about

Critical Games and its regulars, Chris, Aaron, and of course, my best friend Cassidy.

But I decided to leave Devin off the list. The thought of adding him sent anxiety crawling up the back of my throat.

Eventually, Tristan decided he'd had enough of *Super Smash Bros.,* and he pulled me over to the vintage arcade cabinets to show off his *Galaga* skills. The buttons rattled beneath his fingers as he pressed them at lightning speed, his gaze locked on the old CRT monitor screen like a predator stalking its prey. He really was good at the game, picking off all the aliens while nimbly weaving through the maze of enemy fire. I'd been watching him for nearly thirty minutes when his ship blew up for a third and final time.

"Argh," he groaned, slapping a palm against the arcade console. But his white-toothed grin immediately lit up his face when he realized he'd made it onto the scoreboard.

"Hell yeah!" he laughed as he logged *TRK* into the computer.

I asked if those were his initials, and he nodded.

"Yup. Tristan Ryan Kleine. What're yours?"

I smiled. "*AAM*. Avery Annabelle Murphy."

Sharing my full name made my heart flutter. It was something new we were learning about each other, unlocking another piece of our puzzles.

Tristan seemed to share the same feeling as we stood motionless in front of the *Galaga* console, lost in each other's gazes. I seriously thought he was going to kiss me in the middle of the bar when he suddenly snapped back to reality and turned away, his face flushing red.

"I really like you."

His words struck me like a lightning bolt, sending warm, affectionate quivers down my spine. Between all the conversations and getting to know each other, this was the first time we'd acknowledged our budding relationship.

"Me too." I returned his starry gaze, flirtatiously pressing a finger to his nose.

But it was getting late. The neon-lit, windowless space distorted my sense of time, but I knew it had to be approaching midnight.

Once again, four hours had swept past in a heartbeat.

"You know," his smile disappeared, his face suddenly turning serious. "My apartment is only about twenty minutes from here."

Static rang in my ears, and I could feel the warmth draining from my face.

No. No, nonono...

I wasn't ready for this. I wasn't ready to tell him. I needed to let this illusion last a little longer, pretending that I was a normal, well-adjusted woman who definitely didn't have major sexual issues. I couldn't let him know the truth.

I couldn't let him know that I was broken.

Tristan's smile faded. I knew fear was written all over my face.

"We don't have to do anyth—ugh, sorry. I'm an idiot," he scratched his scalp, his face burning red as he tried to backtrack. "I just... really don't want this night to end. I didn't mean to push anything on you."

"It's o-okay," I stammered. "I'm just... not very experienced."

I could feel my insides cringing. *That's an understatement.*

He chuckled. "Neither am I. I'm just...excited, that's all. I started online dating a few months ago and I had yet to meet anyone I connected with. Especially someone as awesome as you. But I do tend to rush things, and I don't want to mess this up."

"Well, I'll tell you what," I smiled, my confidence beginning to return. "How about we play a few more games, then we'll close out our tabs and find a quieter venue to sit and talk. Somewhere more private."

Tristan nodded, deep in thought. "That's a great plan. And I know just the place. But first…" His eyes drifted over to the Nintendo Switch consoles. "Didn't you say you're good at *Mario Kart?*"

"Indeed." A smug grin crept into my face as I hopped onto a barstool and grabbed a controller. "C'mon, race me. Loser pays the tab."

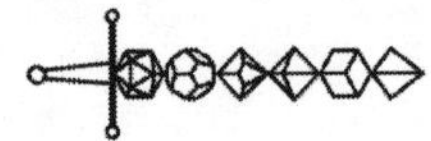

I SPENT MOST OF THE RACE IN THE LEAD, BUT IN the end, Tristan won by throwing a blue shell at me just seconds from the finish line.

I let out a frustrated scowl, plopping my controller on the glass countertop.

"I win," Tristan placed a hand on my shoulder and smirked. In response, I wrinkled my nose and laughed, swatting his hand off me.

"Yeah, yeah, you got lucky."

As serious as I was about winning Mario Kart, I couldn't be mad at him. Not with that beautiful, cheeky smile flashing back at me.

"Whelp, I'm true to my word." I leaned forward and scooped the tab off the countertop. "These drinks are on me."

"Not a chance." Tristan swiped the paper from my hands before I even had a chance to read the total. I didn't fight back, knowing the *fake-fighting-over-the-bill* game all too well, and gave a warm "thank you" as he plopped his credit card on the bar.

"Now, onward to your surprise venue?" I asked.

"Of course. I'll send you directions."

Chapter 6

At first, I was concerned about the prospect of ending up at an unknown destination in the middle of the night when a man I barely knew. But the knot in my stomach loosened when I noticed the address was for Sparrow's Roost Park. It was in a safe area, well-lit, and busy even deep into the night.

I wonder why he picked this place.

I drove in silence, not in the mood for music when my thoughts were already screaming in my mind. It felt so perfect, and yet it was all so fragile. The more I fell for Tristan, the more the truth about my sexual dysfunction ate away at me. It lurked in the back of my mind, reminding me that I was flawed, defective, *broken*.

No matter how much we enjoyed each other's company, no matter how perfect we were for each other, it wouldn't be enough. Because, in the end, who would want to be with a girl who couldn't have sex?

I was nearly shaking by the time I pulled into the parking lot. My hand spasmed as I pulled the keys out of the ignition, and I took a few deep, gulping breaths to calm myself.

Maybe I should've put some music on. I would've saved my anxiety from devouring me whole.

I stepped out of my car and into the damp night air. My anxiety about sex had dissipated, but it was now replaced by Devin's warning from earlier that day. I was suddenly aware of just how late it was, and I wondered if I was an idiot for trusting a man I'd only met twice.

I blinked a few times; my feet unsteady beneath me. Sparrow's Roost Park was right in the middle of downtown, with the rattle of the highway humming in the distance. Even at midnight, it was well-lit with a few pedestrians meandering around.

I smiled. It was a beautiful park, one of my favorites in Orlando. It was private without being too isolated, a perfect place to chat.

He means no harm, I assured myself as I strode towards the park. *Don't let Devin get under your skin.*

Tristan was waiting on a park bench, the streetlamp directly overhead bathing him in a stark white glow. As usual, his face lit up when he saw me. *Something that I could easily get used to,* I thought as I took a seat next to him.

"I love Sparrow's Roost," I remarked as we sat under the still night sky. "This was a good choice."

"Well..." Tristan shifted in his seat. "There's another reason why I picked this place."

"What's that?"

"Every time I feel stressed about life, even though I live way over in Oviedo, I come here. It's sentimental to me. See that apartment complex way over there?" Tristan pointed in the distance at a row of quaint buildings tucked beyond the trees. "That's where we lived after my dad passed away."

His dad is gone. I remembered the way Tristan talked about him at the bar, and a deep pang rattled through my heart.

"I'm sorry to hear that."

"Honestly, don't be," Tristan replied. "He was diagnosed with cancer when I was a toddler. He wasn't supposed to live past my third birthday, and yet he didn't pass away until I was in high school. He was a fighter, living on stolen time. When he died, I mourned his loss, but I was also grateful for the time I had with him. Time that, according to the doctors, we shouldn't have had."

My heart hung on every word, feeling his emotions as if they were my own as he shared the more personal parts of his life with me. It made me think of my parents, alive but distant, and I decided to bare my own soul.

Chapter 6

I told Tristan, a man I'd known for a week and seen in person twice, my life story. About how I was the daughter of two very religious parents who married at eighteen and had me at twenty. How my mother brought me to church every Sunday in beautiful dresses she sewed herself, instructing me to be on my very best behavior. How my mother worked tirelessly, day after day, to care for three children while my father remained physically and emotionally distant. How I'd never seen him wash a dish or fold a pair of pants in his life.

"I visit them once or twice a year," I told Tristan. I wore a stony, expressionless mask as I spoke, my fingers curled into fists in my lap. I knew if I let it crack, the tears would pour out like a faucet. "But I rarely speak with them otherwise, and I avoid their calls."

"It's hard, isn't it?" Tristan's words were soft and gentle. "Trying to be your own person. I still wonder if my dad would be happy with the way I turned out."

Tristan wrapped his arm around me, pulling me against his chest. A hint of fresh soap and evergreen lingered on his t-shirt, and I nuzzled into it, inhaling as much of the moment as I could.

The kisses came in an instant; deep, passionate, and utterly heart-melting. I didn't care if we'd just met. I didn't care that we were on a public park bench, at midnight, and someone could see us. At that moment, nothing else mattered. Every sense, every thought, every part of my being was wrapped up in him.

I finally broke the kiss, feeling the familiar dread of my sexual dysfunction crush me like a lead weight. This was dangerous. Not only was I falling for Tristan fast, maybe *too* fast, but every bit of affection was a risk. Every hug, every kiss, every touch of our bodies would always end in us wanting more.

And I was unable to provide it.

"I probably need to head home," I noted. It was disappointing, but it was the truth. It was nearly 1 a.m., and I could feel the late hour seeping into my bones. I needed sleep, and so did Tristan.

Besides, I thought. *This is a good stopping point for tonight.*

One step at a time, Avery.

Don't fall too fast.

Tristan walked me to my car, and we shared a final kiss, one that lingered on my lips and buzzed in my soul for the entire drive home. I was exhausted, but I knew the adrenalin from my newfound infatuation would make it hard to sleep.

You still have to tell him eventually.

Oh fuck off, I told the voice in my head, adjusting the rearview mirror as my nervous heart thumped in my chest.

But it was right.

It was only a matter of time before this all came crashing down.

And my heart would be crushed under it.

Chapter 7

I SAW TRISTAN TWO MORE TIMES THAT WEEK. Like before, he messaged me about a third date before I even made it home. Except this time, he was wondering if I'd like to have dinner with him after work on Tuesday.

My heart thumped with joy. He didn't want to wait until the weekend to see me.

Cassidy was her usual silly, fawning self as I prepared for my date, helping me pick an outfit and insisting on straightening my hair. The whole time, she preened on about how beautiful I looked and how she wished her hair was as thick as mine.

I used her glee over my dating life as an opportunity to ask about hers.

Specifically, about Aaron.

Cassidy froze like a statue, the flat iron steaming in her rigid grasp, and I realized I may have plucked a nerve. She and Aaron had known each other for years, but it was only within the past few months that he'd made his attraction obvious. As if some light bulb finally switched on in his brain.

"Oh, we're just friends," Cassidy replied in her usual cheery tone, although I could tell there was a bite to her words. A subtle warning not to push the topic further.

So I didn't. I dressed in a flowy pink sundress, my straightened hair now cascading down to my belly button. I studied myself in the mirror, wondering if I looked better this way or with my natural curls.

But when I greeted Tristan at the restaurant, he thought it looked fantastic. Our date was wonderful, full of flirty smiles, animated conversation, and plenty of good food. I was beginning to settle into our dates, learning his mannerisms and quirks, and he no longer felt like a stranger. In fact, it felt like I had known him for years.

This time, he didn't bring up going back to his house. The problem was that I really wanted to. I wanted to cook meals together and play video games curled up on the couch and all the other non-sexual things couples did at home. But that would always come with risks – a kiss lasting a bit too long, hands straying to places they shouldn't go... and all of it would end with me in a half-naked panic attack, unable to explain to Tristan why I was so terrified of sex.

But I didn't object when he pressed me against his car after our dinner date. I was in heaven, running my hands along his soft cotton t-shirt, feeling the firmness of his muscles hidden beneath his clothes. For a moment, I forgot all about my issues. I forgot all about my sexual dysfunction... until he slid his hand farther down my back. Too far.

It snapped be back to reality, reminding me what I couldn't give him. My anxiety sped into overdrive, and I scurried back to my own car with a quick goodbye before Tristan could comprehend what was happening.

Chapter 7

This "you're not experienced" crap isn't going to hold up much longer, I groaned as I butted my head against the steering wheel of my car.

Thirty minutes later, I pulled into the driveway of our townhouse with my nerves on fire, fingers trembling as I clutched the steering wheel. The whole way home, I wondered if I'd blown it... until a familiar notification lit up my screen.

> *Hey, want to meet me at Orange Blossom Coffee after work tomorrow? I figured we could talk about things.*

Oh no.

He wants to talk.

That's never a good sign.

Anxiety bubbled in the back of my throat the whole next day at work. I couldn't read a single line of the manuscript I was editing without my mind drifting off. Back toward the night before, leaned up against his car, when I turned what should've been an amorous moment into an awkward mess.

I leapt out of my seat the instant I clocked out for the day. I was supposed to meet Tristan at six, which gave me half an hour to pile five outfits on the bed and stare blankly at all of them before deciding on something else.

I peered at my reflection in my bathroom mirror, smoothing the fabric of my baby-blue, knee-length dress. If I was going to be a nervous wreck, I at least needed to look nice.

Just like a few weeks earlier, the traffic driving to Orange Blossom Coffee was ridiculous, made worse by the horde of terrible Florida drivers that got far too much use out of their brakes and horns. But I was too nervous to care. My mind was miles away, swimming in a sea of worry and anticipation. I dreaded what awaited me as I pulled into the parking lot.

I turned off my car ignition and stepped into the cool, damp evening air. I usually enjoyed going to coffee shops, but I wondered if tonight was a good night for my favorite drink. The anxiety pulsing through my veins made me feel like I'd already overdosed on caffeine.

Tristan was already inside when I arrived. He leaped up from his seat and pulled me into a hug, and my terror slowly began to dissipate.

Clearly, he still cares about me. It can't be that bad...can it?

"You okay?" Tristan rubbed my forearms. "You're shaking."

"Yeah." I forced out the word. "I'm just... nervous, that's all."

"Don't worry," he reassured me as we took a seat at a table. He already had a coffee in front of him, but it looked like he hadn't even taken a sip. "It's nothing bad. I did sound kind of cryptic, didn't I?"

I nodded sheepishly.

"I just wanted to have this conversation in person, not over text. Anyway... I really like you, Avery. I want a relationship with you. So that's why I need to ask..."

Uh oh.

Here it comes.

His voice lowered to a near-whisper. "Are you a virgin?"

I was so paralyzed with anticipation that I couldn't respond. He must've seen the ghostly-pale expression on my face, because his tone immediately softened. "It's okay if you are. It's not a big deal. I know it can be tough to talk about."

He sighed, his back slouching into his chair as he raked his fingers across his scalp. "I'm sorry. You look so scared."

"No, it's okay," I spoke up, extending a hand across the table. Tristan clasped it in his own, gently rubbing his thumb over my knuckles. "And you're right, I am. I should've just told you."

Chapter 7

It was true. I was a virgin. But it was only part of the truth, and that made it feel like lying. I feared that Tristan may not be receptive to the real reason why I'd been so flighty.

"You know, we can do this together," Tristan continued, his words warm and gentle. "My aunt has a condo out by the coast. I could see if it's available this weekend. I'll get candles, wine, condoms...anything you need to be comfortable."

He was so understanding, so willing to help, that it tore my terrified heart in half. To him, this would be a special, intimate night, one that ended with me successfully losing my virginity. A romantic getaway, in a cute little condo by the beach...it all sounded like a dream.

But that was all it was: a dream. I knew the reality would be Tristan struggling for hours while I alternated between crying and screaming in pain. Until he eventually got too frustrated and gave up on me. Walking away from his dysfunctional, broken partner, just like Tyler did.

I peered up at Tristan, then down to our interlocked hands. I studied the way his fingers trailed over mine, tracing the lines of my palm as if he needed to know every inch of me. It was a gentle, reassuring gesture, and I could feel his plea through his touch.

Please, do this with me. Let's spend the night together.

I knew I couldn't refuse. Not that Tristan was being pushy—he had been nothing but kind and understanding since I first met him. But he wanted a relationship, and with a relationship came the expectation of sex. If I wanted to be with him, I had to do this. I couldn't hold off intimacy forever.

My choices were to say no and never see him again, or take this chance and pray that my body wouldn't betray me. And amidst all the fear and pain, there was always a chance it would work. That I'd figure out a way to have sex.

And for Tristan, I would absolutely take that chance.

"Of course." I smiled, swallowing down my fear. "That sounds great."

"Awesome." I could see the stress melt away from Tristan's body as his shoulders loosened and he released a heavy breath. "Just remember, I care about you. You don't have to hide these things from me. Anyway," he said, as his usual warm, affectionate smile returned to his face. "now that that's out of the way, let's just sit and talk. About lighter stuff—gaming, work, friends...anything you want. I could talk to you all night."

"I agree," I smiled. Our conversation about sex was tucked away, at least for now. It felt like a massive weight off both our shoulders, but I knew it wouldn't stay off mine for long. It never did.

You don't have to hide these things from me.

My breath caught in my throat.

If only it were that easy, Tristan.

TRISTAN AND I TEXTED FREQUENTLY OVER THE next few days. He even called me on Thursday afternoon, both because "he wanted to hear my voice," and because he had news on his aunt's beach condo.

We were lucky. His aunt had a last-minute cancellation for Saturday night, and she said Tristan could use the condo if we paid the cleaning fee and left by 11 a.m. Sunday morning.

He sounded overjoyed, and I tried my best to sound the same. Even as the acidic burn of nausea seeped up my throat.

I stayed on the phone with him for another hour. It felt like a barrier had been broken between us, and we could freely laugh and talk and joke like a real couple. Because to him, nothing was wrong. I'd finally confessed my big secret, which to him was no big deal. He'd take me on a weekend getaway, take my virginity, and cement our newfound relationship. I knew it was a test; a sweet, romantic, exciting one, but still a test. And I was terrified of failing it.

Because an even bigger, uglier secret still hid below the surface, one that I knew he wouldn't be as accepting of.

Once our call ended, I spent the next twenty minutes flopped on my bed like a starfish, my eyes trailing the ceiling fan as it circled lazily overhead. I didn't know what to do with myself. The tension was fizzing inside me like a shaken soda can, and I needed to let it out.

I needed to talk to someone. I thought about knocking on Cassidy's door. I even made it as far as the hallway before I balked. It didn't make sense; she was my best friend, and we told each other everything. But I couldn't tell her. As painful as it was to have this secret lurking inside me, the thought of dredging it up in conversation made me want to vomit.

If I'm going to talk about this. I reasoned. *Maybe I should do it with a neutral third party. Someone I never have to see again if things go south.*

So, I turned to the internet, looking up therapists on various websites. I'd never done therapy before, and I knew it was going to be both expensive and time-consuming. But what I didn't expect was for there to be only two therapists within a reasonable drive that specialized in sexual dysfunction, and neither one took my insurance.

I huffed, about to slam my laptop shut when a question I should've asked myself years ago flooded my mind.

What exactly is sexual dysfunction?

I had no idea. I was terrified of seeing a gynecologist, and I didn't know what other medical professionals could help me. My sexual issues had always been something I shoved in a box and hid in the deepest recesses of my mind, pretending they didn't exist. But now I needed to face them, and I had no idea where to start.

I stared blankly at my web browser, and my throat tightened as I typed in *sexual dysfunction*.

I was immediately flooded with results, describing everything from lack of arousal to the inability to orgasm. *Okay, too broad. How do I describe what's wrong with me?*

Think...

This time, I typed in *painful penetration*.

This brought me to a medical website with a list of causes, which I scanned through with eager eyes. *Not enough lubrication.* I snorted, thinking of how Tyler had drowned my pelvic region in lube when we tried five years ago. Clearly that wasn't the problem. *Rough sex, trauma, negative feelings about a partner...*

I groaned in frustration. None of this was helping me. Despite my sexual dysfunction, I *did* have a sex drive, which made my inadequacies even more frustrating. I *wanted* to have sex with Tristan. More than anything. But no matter how attracted to him I was, no matter how aroused I became, my stubborn vagina had a mind of its own.

I exited the website, scrolling through more search results until I came across an intriguing term. *Vaginismus*. The website described it as involuntary muscle spasms that made the vagina too narrow for sexual activity.

That sounds about right. I thought back to five years ago, remembering how it felt like there was an impenetrable wall in my vagina.

I could feel the light bulb flashing in my head, the puzzle pieces finally clicking together. I scoured the website for more information, absorbing everything I could.

Ten minutes later, I finally understood my condition. And it made me want to hurl my phone across the room.

> *The condition requires there to be no anatomical issues and a desire for penetration.*

So this is all in my head? Nothing is actually wrong with me?

The thought terrified me. Physical problems were much easier to deal with. A few trips to the doctor, maybe a small surgical procedure, and I'd be all set. The human brain was a fickle instrument, and treating mental issues was a complicated, exhausting, and often lengthy process.

My nostrils flared as I kept reading:

> *Factors that cause vaginismus include chronic pain conditions, a negative emotional response to sexual activity, and strict conservative moral educati—*

Conservative moral education?!

Oh fucking hell.

This time I actually did hurl my phone across the room. It was undamaged, since it was in a thick case with a screen protector, but it still clattered loudly against my deck and flopped face down on the carpet like a dead bird.

I crossed my elbows in front of my body and plopped my head in the center, trying not to scream. When I decided to turn to the internet for a diagnosis, I expected some physical abnormality that could be treated. Even just being *scared* was an acceptable answer.

But this was my worst nightmare. My entire childhood had been entwined in religion, from home to church groups at my Catholic private school. I'd grown up thinking I needed to be a virgin, a good girl, a pure little flower for my future Christian husband. Sex before marriage was a sin; a dirty, repulsive, immoral act. Back then, even just thinking the word *sex* felt profane. I had fled that mindset five years ago, but maybe it still had a faint hold on me. Maybe my mind really was holding me back.

I remembered the night Tyler pressured me into having sex. Maybe that was why it hurt so much. Because my brain was screaming at me that sex before marriage was wrong, and no matter how much I wanted to believe otherwise, there was no fighting my upbringing. My subconscious wanted me to stay pure. But the sad, sick irony was that not having sex was what caused men to leave me. Being *pure* was ruining my life.

That night with Tyler changed everything, destroying the only world I knew.

And he got to walk away without consequences.

My hands were shaking, and tears brimmed in the corners of my eyes, threatening to spill like an overfilled water glass. I needed to punch something; take my anger out on the world around me so it didn't consume me whole.

No. Stop it.

I lowered my trembling fists. *Get ahold of yourself. Hitting your belongings isn't going to make you feel better.*

And Cassidy would hear it. She would know something was wrong.

Instead, I sat down on my bed, gripping the edges of my comforter until my knuckles turned white. I was broken. Truly, horrifically broken. I'd known this for years, but I'd always kept it at bay by avoiding relationships. But now that I wanted one, I had to face the truth. For the first time in my life, I'd been brave enough to research my condition.

So, stop the pity party, I told myself, *and do something about it.*

But what could I do? I had two days until my beach trip with Tristan; not nearly enough time to undo five years of sexual trauma.

I stood up and walked toward my desk, picking up my phone. I unlocked it, and the article about vaginismus flashed white on the screen, blinding my eyes and reminding me why I was so upset in the first place.

I scrolled to the bottom of the page, under treatment options. Much of it involved mental health treatment, something that wouldn't fix me before Saturday. But another solution caught my eye.

Pelvic physical therapy.

There was one in Orlando, about thirty minutes from my townhouse. I looked up their phone number and their hours. It was 5:45 p.m. —I had fifteen minutes until they closed.

With sweaty palms and a tensed throat, I made the call.

I was tired of being broken. And I was finally going to do something about it.

Chapter 8

I WALKED INTO THE WAITING ROOM THE FOLlowing evening with the same sweaty palms and locked-up throat.

I was lucky. They had a last-minute cancellation on Friday at 5 p.m. I was excited to finally receive treatment, but I also dreaded the poking and prodding I'd have to endure over the next hour. I could already feel my pelvic region tensing up, like a clamshell about to be pried open.

I slipped out of work a few minutes early and arrived just in time to complete a pile of paperwork. Once I got to the form outlining my sexual history, I gulped. Even five years after fleeing my religious household, discussing my sex life still made me squirm. And they wanted to know *everything*.

As I filled out the form, painfully outlining that I was an involuntary virgin in desperate need of help, I peered around the waiting room at my fellow patients. I noticed two of them were pregnant, and one carried a baby about six months old on her hip. That's when I realized the main reasons why people did pelvic physical therapy—for pregnancy and postpartum.

I shuddered, my vagina clamping down even further. I was far, *far* away from ever having to fathom that reality. I couldn't even get a tampon in there, much less push out an eight-pound baby.

They're cute, though. I smiled as the baby gazed at me with giant unblinking eyes. I waved, and he broke into a huge, toothless grin.

I finished the mound of paperwork, laying it face-down on the clipboard as I walked up to the front desk. I didn't want my sexual history to be on display for all to see, but I knew that the medical assistants would be rifling through it anyway. The receptionist was on the phone as I handed her the clipboard, and she took it without a word, barely glancing at its contents.

Alright. I settled back into my seat. *So far, so good. You can do this.*

You know you still have to tell the therapist all about your sex life, right?

Ugh. Shut up.

My eyes darted around the room as I squirmed uncomfortably in my chair. I didn't know what was worse; that I had to describe my sexual history to a doctor, or the fact that I hardly had one to begin with.

A nurse opened the door and called out a name that wasn't mine. One of the pregnant women stood up and waddled into the treatment area.

I hugged my arms across my chest. I was surrounded by pregnant and postpartum women who clearly had no issues having sex, and eventually I would have to walk back there and admit to the therapist that I was an almost 27-year-old virgin who couldn't even insert a tampon.

This is mortifying.

"Avery?"

I jolted as the door swung open. The nurse locked eyes with me, and I slowly rose to my feet, my ears ringing as I was led into the treatment area.

Down the hallway, the nurse led me into what looked like a typical exam room, except the "bed" was completely flat, with adjustable pieces for what I assumed were different exercises. It looked incredibly uncomfortable, and not just because it had very little padding.

At least it's not stirrups. I gulped as I sat down on the bench-bed-thing. It made of think of the first and only time I'd ever been to a gynecologist. It was a year after leaving college, when I was twenty-three years old. I was trembling before I even made it into the exam room, and the cold, impatient doctor had no sympathy for my condition. She shoved her fingers inside me without warning, and my cries were met with a flat, "Stop screaming."

I never went back. Which meant I'd never had a pap smear, although I doubted I had any sort of cancer. But it also meant that I'd never had my equipment checked to see if my pain was caused by a medical problem.

But after what I'd read online, I doubted it was. My pain was mental; I had a brain full of anxiety and religious trauma.

The door cracked open, and a face half-covered by a surgical mask peeked its way in.

"Hello? Ah, Avery, nice to meet you." The therapist was a brunette woman, possibly in her late thirties, but the mask made it difficult to tell. Her demeanor was cheerful and nurturing, and as she shook my hand, I realized I liked her better than the gynecologist already.

"So..." She plopped down in a chair, flipping through a clipboard in her lap. "My name is Jane, and I will be your physical therapist. Give me some background on what's going on."

Chapter 8

Ugh, where am I supposed to start?

Just saying the word *sex* felt painful, as if it burned on my lips, and uttering the proper names of genitalia was impossible. The doctor listened intently, with the occasional nod, as I struggled to spit out my story. As uncomfortable as I was, she was an excellent listener, and her attentive blue eyes reminded me of my mother.

"Alright, so from what I understand, you're having difficulty with penetration," Jane remarked, making some notes on her clipboard. "Have you ever had an actual penis inside of you, or just fingers? Toys?"

My whole body cringed at her bluntness. With my upbringing, this was going to take a *long* time to get used to. If I ever got used to it at all.

Thankfully, Jane sensed this, and she chuckled, "It's okay. I know it's tough to talk about these things with a stranger. But I'm a medical professional, and I need to know these things so I can help you. Why don't we go back a little further? What sort of sex education did you have growing up?"

"None." I spat out the word like it pained me.

"Ah, I see. Was it for religious reasons, or...?"

"Yes."

I swear, this woman can read me like a book.

"Is this common?" I asked, finally mustering the courage to squeak out a question. "Women who grew up in religious households having issues with sex?"

Jane smiled and nodded. "But it's not just religious households, or ones where there's no sex education. A lot of young women have trouble with penetration. It sometimes stems from deeper mental conditions, like anxiety disorders. But first, I need to rule out any medical causes. Have you been to a gynecologist?"

My uncomfortable silence gave her the answer she needed.

"Now, I do want you to try and see one," she instructed. "While there are plenty of exercises we can do to strengthen your pelvic floor, it will only do so much if there's a medical issue."

"What medical issues can cause this?"

"Quite a few. Pelvic inflammatory disease, endometriosis, ovarian cysts... that's why it's so important that you're checked out down there. Now, today I'm just going to do an external exam, check you for any painful spots..."

"So you won't be...*inserting* anything in me today?"

"I will not."

Part of me was relieved, but the other part of me felt sick. As terrified as I was, I needed to get over this issue, and it sounded like it wasn't something that could be fixed in a single physical therapy visit. After five years of putting this off, I had a feeling it would take *months* of therapy for me to even insert a finger.

Jane had me lie down on the table, and she left the room while I stripped off my underwear and hiked up the skirt of my dress. My legs trembled as they lay exposed on the table, covered by a flimsy paper sheet. The therapist wasn't even in the room, and my thighs were already clenched like steel.

Yup. I groaned, laying my head back on the table. *This is definitely going to take months.*

Jane returned, sitting on a stool next to me and steadying my shaking legs with her gloved hands. Just as she'd promised, she didn't insert anything into my vagina. Instead, she felt around the outside of my vulva and inner thighs, working on desensitization therapy for my incredibly tense muscles. Over the years, fear and anxiety had compounded my condition to the point where I was afraid of not just penetration, but of *any* touching below the belt.

"You did good today," Jane remarked half an hour later, as she finished the last of her examinations. As she stood up,

I could finally breathe again, and my thigh muscles ached as if I'd just run a marathon.

"This really is going to take months, isn't it?" I sighed.

She nodded. "It's the same for any form of physical therapy, not just pelvic. But if you keep working at it, I promise you'll see results. Now, I'll leave the room and let you put your underwear back on. But remember," she said as she opened the door with a loud click, "I want you to see the gynecologist before our next session, okay?"

I smiled and nodded, pretending that nausea wasn't rising up the back of my throat.

I got dressed, paid my co-pay at the front desk, and left the physical therapy office with mixed emotions and very sore legs. As I sat in the driver's seat of my car, I could still feel the therapist's fingers pressing against the strained muscles of my pelvis.

The visit wasn't what I had expected. I knew I wouldn't be cured in one visit, but I'd hoped she'd be able to do more for me than just poke around the outside of my vagina. It certainly wasn't enough to prepare for my weekend with Tristan.

You'll be more relaxed when you're aroused, I reassured myself, although I doubted that statement. *Besides, those exercises were still helpful. At least now I can be touched down there without panicking.*

Even if there wasn't a miracle cure for my condition, I was still satisfied with my visit to the physical therapist. Just being able to come to terms with my condition and seek out help was a relief. It made my sexual issues feel less like a hidden, shameful secret.

But the bad news was that the appointment made me late for TCG Night. Everyone was already paired up and several turns into their games once I arrived.

"Sorry about that." Devin frowned sympathetically as he stood behind the counter, sorting *C&C* cards with one hand and typing into his keyboard with another. "Work run late?"

"Doctor's appointment," I explained. "It's no big deal. I'll just wait around for the next game."

Devin stopped typing and locked eyes with me. I had never noticed what a vibrant color they were—deep blue-green with flecks of brown near his irises. He wore black studs in his snake-bite piercings that night, their deep color matching the shaggy hair that fell above his eyelas—

Stop it. I hissed at myself. *Why are you gawking at him?*

"Here." He reached under the counter and pulled out a small rectangular case the size of a shoebox. "I'll play with you."

"N-No, it's okay," I stuttered, feeling awkward. "I know you're busy, and—"

"Oh no, you're pulling me away from my thrilling night of cataloging thousands of trading cards," Devin droned in a sarcastic tone. "*The horror.*"

I scowled. "Fine. We'll play a game."

Devin grinned, and I noticed his teeth were remarkably white, if a bit crooked. He tucked the case under his arm and hopped over to one of the empty tables, pulling out a chair for me.

I struggled not to roll my eyes as I took a seat.

Devin unzipped the case, revealing half a dozen individually boxed *C&C* decks. I noticed they were all labeled, and I raised an eyebrow as he plucked a deck labeled *Vampires* from the middle of the case.

"Let me guess." I propped my elbows on the table. "It's a blood counter deck?"

"Nope." Devin removed the cards from the box and flung one of them at me like a frisbee. I picked it up and studied the artwork.

"*Lifestealer*?"

"Yup."

"Bold move. Not many people play *lifestealer* vampire decks."

Devin shrugged. "Draining people's life total is fun."

"You *would* play vampires."

"What's that supposed to mean?" Devin shot me a smug grin as he shuffled his cards. The sleeve of his sweatshirt slid halfway up his forearm, and I could see part of his dragon tattoo. "Am I being too stereotypical for a goth kid?"

"Well, *no*, but—"

"I could play dragons instead," Devin teased, flinging another card in my direction. This time, the artwork on the card depicted a dragon with a red body and five angry, snarling heads.

I knew exactly who she was: the vicious multi-headed dragon goddess of the Underworld.

"Cremara? Hell no. I'll take vampires, please."

Devon made an elaborate show of plopping the card back into its deck box. "That's what I thought."

"Wait a minute," I reached out and grabbed Devin's arm. He jolted at my touch; his nerves tense as I rolled up his sleeve. "I never realized, that your tattoo is of Cremara."

"Uh, yeah."

Devin pulled his arm away, quickly covering the tattoo with his sweatshirt sleeve. A cold trickle of embarrassment crept down my neck. *Why did you just grab his arm like that, you weirdo? Why do you care about his tattoo?*

But a single question, one that didn't involve my awkwardness, lingered stronger than the rest.

Why even have tattoos if you're going to cover them all the time?

In all the years I'd known Devin, he always wore a sweatshirt while working at the shop. Even in the hundred-degree summer heat of Florida, I never saw his bare arms except for the few times he rolled his sleeves up. And even then, he always seemed cautious of how he positioned them. Cassidy and I even joked about it once, mentioning that it was probably why Critical Games' A/C was always cranked up so high.

We continued setting up our game in silence. It made me uncomfortable, because just a few seconds earlier Devin had been his usual sarcastic, teasing self. Now, as he sat silently shuffling his cards, I knew something lurked behind those multicolored eyes. My tattoo comment had set his nerves on edge.

For the next hour, as we played our game, it lingered in the back of my mind.

Even once round two began and I joined another group, I kept an eye on him. For the rest of the night, he stayed behind the counter at his computer, his face deeply focused and devoid of emotion.

And not once did he roll up his sleeves. His arms remained covered for the rest of the night.

Chapter 9

SATURDAY MORNING ARRIVED, AND AS SOON as Tristan's pickup truck pulled in front of my townhouse, my anxiety's grip on my throat turned into a chokehold.

I should've been excited. An overnight trip to one of Florida's most popular beaches with a sweet, sexy guy would be paradise for any other woman. But as I climbed into the passenger seat, with a beach tote in my lap and sunglasses perched on my forehead, I felt a deep sense of impending doom.

Relax, Avery. I told myself. *You can do this. Everything will be fine.*

It was a 45-minute drive, and during that time, I was able to make small talk with Tristan to keep my nerves at bay. After we made it out of Orlando, he took my hand in mine, and our fingers laced together over the center console of his truck. It felt like heaven and hell at the same time.

The worst part was that my anxiety was obvious. It was plastered all over my face and emitted through my sweaty palms. Tristan noticed this, and to alleviate my worries, he suggested we listen to music.

His truck was old, likely from the early 2000s, with a CD player and an auxiliary port instead of a modern screen. He used a long black cable to hook up his phone, which rested in a plastic mount attached to one of the air vents.

"Any suggestions?" he asked as he flipped through his phone.

"What do you like to listen to?"

"Lots of stuff, but I'd say rock is my favorite."

"Let me take a look."

He handed me his phone, and I scrolled through his playlists until I settled on one called *'90s Rock*. Foo Fighters' heavy guitar riffs blared to life, vibrating throughout the whole car, and the knot in the pit of my stomach loosened.

"Excellent choice," Tristan chuckled, a single forearm propped on the steering wheel. The drive to Daytona was quiet; we were on a narrow strip of Interstate 4 with nothing but trees surrounding us. Florida's foliage was unusual; a mixture of forest and jungle, with towering pines flanked by plump, shrubby palmetto bushes. As we got closer to the coast, the trees gave way to open swampland, a maze of murky water and grass that sprawled across the horizon.

"I love Florida," Tristan remarked, a hazy, nostalgic smile on his face as he drove. "It's so beautiful out here."

"Me too. Being this close to the ocean makes me miss the panhandle."

This prompted Tristan to ask me more about my childhood, which made my insides squirm. I loved the scenic beauty of my hometown but hated almost everything else about it. Everything went sour after I broke up with Tyler and was kicked out of college, and thoughts of home sent all those emotions boiling back up to the surface.

But Tristan didn't seem to notice. We were still very early in our relationship, where our shields were up and we treaded carefully on conversations. The more I got to know him, the less our dates felt like interviews, but there was still a lot I wasn't ready to tell him. I needed time before I could expose the less pristine parts of myself.

It made me wish that sex could wait. But I knew that in modern dating, it was practically a requirement to start a relationship. It was the final test before becoming official. People my age spoke of "sexual compatibility", which made me feel even more inadequate. My sexuality was broken. I wasn't compatible with anyone.

So as "Best of You" blared on the radio, I lifted my head, cleared my throat, and sang away my worries. Tristan joined in, and our impromptu karaoke session devolved into joyous laughter as we approached the main strip of Daytona Beach.

"You're a really good singer." He smiled.

"Thank you!"

I'd been told that before. My mother's whole life revolved around church choir in her twenties, and I'd inherited some of her natural abilities. I hadn't performed in a choir in years, but I could at least belt out a few notes without sounding off-key.

"We're only a few minutes away from the rental." Tristan studied the GPS on his phone. "It's one of the high-rises further down the strip."

And as I stared out the window, I realized Daytona was nothing *but* high-rises. Huge hotels and condominiums sprawled along the shoreline, stretching twenty stories into the cloudless blue sky. It was an incredibly stereotypical beach town, jam-packed and heavily commercialized, with pristine resorts flanked by run-down arcades, greasy pizza joints, and a plethora of tattoo shops. Much of it looked like it hadn't been updated since the 1990s, giving it a garish, tacky charm that reminded me of beach trips in my childhood.

Further down the strip, where the flashy hotels faded away to more modest condominiums, we pulled into the parking lot of a tall white building crammed full of balconies. Tristan mentioned it was an older building, which meant we had to climb up four flights of stairs to reach our accommodation.

I was wheezing by the time Tristan unlocked the door. He'd jogged up the stairs without breaking a sweat, and I made a mental note to start working on my cardio.

"Here we are!" Tristan swung the door open, gesturing me inside. It was a cozy two-bedroom apartment, about the same size as the townhouse that Cassidy and I shared. It had stark white walls, wicker furniture in shades of cream and pale blue, and a whole trove of shells, starfish, and other beach-themed knickknacks. The smell of fresh linen and sunscreen hit my nose as soon as I walked in, and I inhaled the scent like I had just surfaced from below the ocean.

It was a perfect, nostalgic, sunny-and-cozy beach condo. As Tristan showed me around, plopping our belongings on the carpet in the larger bedroom, I started to feel like I was truly on vacation. Like this was a relaxing getaway, and not one of the most stressful overnight trips I would ever experience.

But that sense of relaxation came crashing down as soon as Tristan flopped down on the bed. It was king-size, with a plush seashell-patterned comforter and a variety of stiff, decorative throw pillows. He flashed me a beaming, wicked smile, his gentle eyes playfully inviting me to join him.

I wanted to. Every bone in my body wanted to leap onto the squishy mattress and lose myself in his embrace. To feel his soft cotton t-shirt against my skin and finally discover what was lurking underneath it. To let loose, strip away our clothes, and give each other what we both so desperately wanted.

But I couldn't. I stood there, dumbfounded, until Tristan's inviting smile gave way to a frown.

"You okay?"

I nodded, the stupid uncontrollable heat of tears prickling in my eyes.

"Sorry." He chuckled as he sat upright, smoothing the comforter. "I know you're scared. We don't have to do anything right now. Besides—" He pointed out the massive floor-to-ceiling windows, where the ocean's inviting waves roared in the distance. "—we should spend time on the beach while it's still daylight."

I nodded eagerly, relieved that Tristan was so understanding of my anxiety. Even if he didn't know the full truth.

Tristan pulled a pair of flip-flops out of his bag and tossed them onto the carpet, slipping his toes through them. He then lifted his shirt over his shoulders, and as soon as I caught a glimpse of his flat, tanned stomach, I knew I was in trouble.

"You ready? There are umbrellas and towels in the hallway closet."

I fingered the strap of my bathing suit, hidden under my beach dress. It was a bikini, one with a ruffled top to hide how flat my chest was.

"Of course." I grinned. "Let's go."

AS WE STEPPED ONTO THE BEACH, WITH SOFT sand sinking under our toes like pillows and a warm sea breeze carrying hints of salty brine and fried food, my stomach continued to sink.

I studied the ocean waves, churning and swirling in tall peaks, and knew this was the calm before the storm. It was all so picturesque: the sandy shoreline stretched out wide and flat next to the tumultuous sea, and the sound of churning waves, screaming children, and squawking seagulls hung in the salty air as Tristan shoved an umbrella into the ground. I couldn't help but admire him as he fumbled with the pole, the muscles in his deeply tanned upper arms and back flexing under the blisteringly bright sun.

I wanted him. But I didn't know if I'd be able to have him.

"Alright, should be in there good and deep." Tristan wiggled the umbrella for emphasis. I grabbed the bottom of my beach dress, preparing to lift it over my torso as Tristan's eyebrows wiggled in anticipation.

"Stripping on the beach, I see?"

"Shut up." I rolled my eyes, flinging my balled-up sundress onto an empty chair. I was now dressed in nothing but my frilly bikini, exposing my stick-thin frame and leaving little to Tristan's imagination.

I had reservations about my body, mainly my shrimpy figure and lack of curves. But that didn't stop Tristan from gazing curiously at me. It was subtle, especially with his eyes hidden behind his dark sunglasses, but I could see them flick up and down from my breasts to my way-too-pale legs.

He pretended not to stare, so I pretended not to notice. But our attraction was as obvious as a see-through curtain.

Heat prickled up the back of my neck as anxiety churned in my stomach. All the coyness was reminding me of the inevitable. I needed something to take my mind off our upcoming night together.

And nothing calmed me quite like being in the ocean.

Chapter 9

I plodded off as Tristan rifled through his beach bag, not bothering to wait for him. The water lapped at my feet, seeping between my toes and cooling my sand-scorched soles. Whether it was the beach or a bathtub, water had always been a comfort. It was as if the cool, clear liquid could wash my anxiety away, purifying every toxic thought in my worried head.

The rising water felt heavy on my thighs as I waded through it, eventually submerging my entire body at the three-foot mark. Daytona's waters were shallow, and I had to venture a long way out just to get to that depth. I was now far enough away from the shoreline for the tourist squabble to dissipate, and now all I could see and hear were churning waves.

As usual, it felt like I'd reached the end of the world. It was just me and the endless ocean.

I drifted for a while, letting the bobbing waves lift me and set me back down in long, sloping motions. The current was mild today, and I felt weightless beneath the thick turquoise sea. My breaths were long and slow, save for some accidental gulps of briny water that burned my insides. And even as the salt stung my eyes and the waves whipped my hair into a ratty mess, I'd never felt more at home.

"Hey Avery!"

A faint shout carried through the salty air. I turned around and saw Tristan a few dozen feet away, his jogging pace creating a ruckus of splashes.

I grinned and waved as a sudden current sent me rolling forward. We collided with each other, my lips banging against his shoulder, and my stomach fluttered as he gathered me into his arms.

I laughed. Tristan laughed, and our joy filled the air in a cacophony of sweet bliss. Tristan raised his hand, placing it on my cheek, and pulled my wet, salty self in for a kiss. It was deep and passionate, one that nearly sent me tumbling back into the water, and I let myself get lost in it. Tristan's wet hands slid up my back, and I wrapped my arms around his hips as we drifted, alone and at peace, in our hazy embrace.

Maybe everything would be alright. Maybe he would understand. Maybe this wasn't the end I'd been dreading, and our night together wouldn't be one of frustration and pain.

Maybe this was just the beginning.

And as Tristan broke our kiss, his sun-soaked eyes shining with affection, I begged with every strand of my soul that it would be.

Chapter 10

WE SPENT THE REST OF THE AFTERNOON ON the beach, soaking up the sun and basking in the warmth of our budding relationship. In between dips in the ocean, we lounged in our beach chairs under the sparse shade of the umbrella. I took the opportunity to unwind from my normally busy schedule and take a nap. Tristan had a paperback book in one hand while the other one rested on my thigh. His touch sent warm pulses through my body as I dozed off.

Every hour or so, our heat-drenched bodies would beg for a dip in the cool ocean. Out in the open water, surrounded by waves with the beach activity just a faint blur behind us, we pushed the boundaries of our relationship even further. More salty kisses, more of our wet half-clothed bodies pressed against each other. Tristan's affection evolved into desire, and I had to hold back a moan as he slid the tip of his thumb underneath my bikini bottoms.

Once evening arrived and the salty air grew dimmer, we packed up and headed inside for the night. My mind raced and my stomach swirled as hot anticipation made my body flush.

I would not be afraid.

Fear would only make sex more painful.

Fear was the enemy.

We barely managed to haul the chairs and towels inside before Tristan had me pinned against the wall. This time, I didn't stifle the sounds that escaped me as his kisses cascaded down my body. Our teasing the entire afternoon paled in comparison to this; it was like a pressure valve had been released. I was still dripping saltwater as his hands trailed up to my breasts, and a bulge was already visible through his bathing suit.

Heat prickled up my temples and around the back of my ears until they rang like gongs. My nerves crackled with electricity, and my pulse whirred through my head and into my pelvis like a hurricane.

I was so lost in a sea of passionate kisses and roaming hands that by the time we made it to the bed, I hadn't realized Tristan had undone my bathing suit. The frilly fabric slid off the bed in a sea of loose straps, leaving my sandy breasts exposed.

I'd put on some weight since college and was now a respectable B-cup, but I still felt insecure as Tristan cupped them in his hands.

"They're lovely," he breathed as he covered them in more kisses.

We were fully unclothed in less than a minute, our bathing suits a wet, forgotten heap of fabric on the floor. We were both a mess, our skin still sandy and sticky with saltwater and our hair tangled and unkempt from the ocean wind. But somehow, it made the feeling of his body against mine even more pleasurable. Even more arousing.

Chapter 10

I loved how he was so forceful yet so gentle at the same time. He had an overwhelming desire for me, but he still knew I was a virgin and to take it slow. He started with a single finger pressed against the top of my vulva, rubbing in steady circles until my whole body was on fire.

It felt amazing. It was the most amazing thing I'd ever experienced in my entire life.

Tristan sat up, positioning himself between my legs. As he fumbled with a condom, I took a moment to admire him. He was bigger than Tyler, and a lot girthier. I knew girls normally preferred them larger, but it only made me more nervous.

If Tyler's couldn't fit, how could his?

"It's okay," Tristan whispered in a soothing tone, pressing my body against the soft comforter. "Deep breaths. I'll go slow."

He steadied his hands on my thighs, slowly pulling his hips closer to mine.

It was time.

I'm not afraid.

I refused to be afraid.

I refus—

I screamed. As soon as Tristan realized it wasn't one of pleasure, he scrambled backward as if I'd just kicked him in the genitals.

"What's wrong?" he asked, his face twisted in bewilderment.

I paused to catch my breath, forcing the tension out of my legs as my thigh muscles softened. "Sorry, sorry. I panicked. Can we try again?"

Tristan nodded. He crawled back into bed, reassuring me with a few hungry kisses placed on my collarbone and breasts. It felt so good. *He* felt so good.

I wanted this more than anything. Why did my body always act otherwise?

As Tristan entered me, he placed his hands on my vulva, attempting to spread my lips to make more room. This resulted in another scream, as pain burned through my vagina like it was on fire.

Tristan fumbled backward, now more concerned than confused. This was no longer just anxiety from being a virgin. He knew something was wrong.

"It's that painful?" he asked with a raised eyebrow.

I nodded, tears threatening to spill from my eyes as my breath caught in my throat. "I'm so sorry…I thought this time it wouldn't hurt as much, and…"

"Wait. This isn't your first time?"

My mouth snapped shut. I realized that by not telling Tristan the whole truth, I'd made him think I'd never been with a guy before.

"My ex, back in college. We tried a few times."

"And it was always this painful?"

I nodded. My limbs began to shake.

His brows narrowed. "And you didn't think to tell me this beforehand?"

It was as if a bomb had gone off in my stomach. I sat upright, my mouth hanging open but unable to utter a single word.

I was an idiot. It had never occurred to me that concealing my issues would make him upset. Maybe this wasn't just about sex. It was about honesty. Trust. Hiding the truth from someone I was forming a relationship with wasn't my best idea.

Even when it was the most painful truth of my life.

Tristan sighed. "Look, I'm sorry. I get it. I imagine that's tough to talk about. It's just…I sort of feel betrayed. If we're going to be in a relationship, I need you to trust me enough to tell me these things."

"But is it a dealbreaker?"

"What?"

"My sexual issues." I crawled off the bed and stood up. My impending tears had vanished, my fear replaced by hard, cold indignation. "Because the truth is, I've had this problem my whole life. Sex has always been too painful for me. I finally got help yesterday and went to a physical therapist, but I don't know how long it will take for me to fix this. It could be weeks. Months, even. Is that going to be a dealbreaker for you?"

Tristan didn't say a word. His face was hard as stone, and I could see the realization sinking into his features.

After nearly a minute, I couldn't handle the silence. Tears poured freely from my eyes, staining the carpet at my feet.

"That's what I thought," I hissed, barely able to hide the anger in my voice. "I like you, Tristan. A lot. If you're going to get upset with me for not telling the truth, don't you dare act like it's not an issue. So, please, tell me honestly...*is this a dealbreaker*?"

Tristan was still silent. He looked...upset. Maybe even angry. His head hung low at his shoulders, and he refused to make eye contact. Instead, he slunk off the bed, grabbing a pair of boxers as his deep sigh of frustration hung in the heavy air.

I didn't want to wait around for him to say something. I already knew what his answer was, and I couldn't handle another round of tears. I stormed away from the bed, threw my beach dress back over my head, and wheeled my suitcase out of the condo.

Tristan was still lingering near the bed when I slammed the door behind me. He didn't bother to pursue me, which gave me an even more definite answer.

I managed to hold in the tears until I was in the parking lot. My shaking fingers struggled to dial Cassidy's number.

"Hello?"

"Cass? It's me."

"Avery? What's wrong? Are you crying?"

She could hear it through the phone. My voice was muffled with sobs.

"Can you come pick me up from Daytona?"

"Of course. Can you text me the address?"

"Yes."

"I'll be there soon. Hold on, Avery. It'll be ok."

More sobs erupted as I hung up the phone. Avery didn't ask what was wrong, but she already knew. Me calling and asking for a ride meant something went wrong with Tristan.

I sniffled, wiping my nose. I knew this weekend might end badly, and sobbing into a phone in a beach condo parking lot was one of the worst possible outcomes.

And the worst part was that he had every right to reject me. I was broken. Truly, horribly broken.

I couldn't expect him to stick around and pick up the pieces.

I feared no guy ever would.

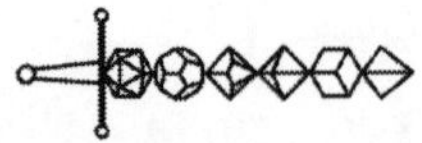

By the time Cassidy's car pulled onto the condominium parking lot, it was already dark. Which was good, because it hid how red and splotchy my face was after almost an hour of crying.

I didn't say much on the way home, and Cassidy didn't press me for answers. She drove in silence, the car stereo playing pop songs at a low volume. But she occasionally reached out to place a hand on my shoulder.

Chapter 10

I wasn't ready to talk. My throat was too choked up to speak, and my mind was still processing what had happened. All weekend long, this is what I had feared. It was what I had anticipated from the moment I agreed to this trip. But what had kept me together, what prevented me from breaking down entirely, was hope. Hope that despite my fears and past trauma, I would be able to finally lose my virginity. Hope that our night would end with me curled up on his chest in post-orgasmic bliss, and not with me sobbing in a parking lot.

But now that hope was gone. And there was nothing left to keep me from coming undone.

I kept my sobs to a minimum on the drive home, letting defiant tears fall silently down my cheeks. But as soon as we made it home and I was alone in the suffocating sanctity of my room, I let it all out. As I howled into my pillow, I remembered how frustrated I felt when I learned about vaginismus a few days earlier. How I was so angry that I wanted to punch something.

Now I wanted to tear the whole bedroom apart. I wanted to watch it crumble around me. It already felt like the rest of my world was.

But I couldn't. Because I still needed to wake up tomorrow, and the next day, and the day after that, and continue life as normal. I had to pretend that I wasn't a rejected, broken mess, with my heart hollowed out from the inside. I had to move on.

So I took my rage out on my pillow instead, gripping it in my fists until my knuckles lost blood flow. I remained that way for nearly an hour when a sudden buzz of my phone pulled me out of my distraught trance.

I scooped it up, and my stomach twisted when I saw Tristan's name.

Don't.

Don't open it.

But I had to. The anticipation would eat me alive if I didn't.

> *Hey Avery. I'm so sorry about that. I panicked, and you deserved a proper response and not me just sitting there like an idiot. You're an amazing person, you really are. But intimacy is important to me, and I don't think I can handle—*

I didn't bother to read the rest. I tossed my phone across the bed, and it skidded across the comforter before smacking against the opposite wall and plummeting to the ground.

He can't handle this.

Of course he can't.

Even I can't handle it.

It was over. That damning text was the final door closing on our relationship. I'd likely never see him again, and I needed to delete his messages and number before they consumed me whole.

Tristan decided my sexual dysfunction was too much for him. The problem was that I still had to live with it, and my ability to handle heartbreak was rapidly running out.

I grabbed my phone off the floor and tapped open my dating app.

There. Deleted.

No more online dating for me.

I was done. I couldn't handle it anymore.

My illness had won.

Chapter 11

IT ALL CAME BACK TO HAUNT ME THE NEXT morning.

As soon as my eyes fluttered open and I caught a glimpse of the ceiling fan swirling lazily over my head, the previous night's events hit me like a brick. For the past few weeks, dating Tristan had left me giddy and excited, waking up with my head in the clouds and my body lighter as I went about my day. Now, it felt like gravity had tripled, and my limbs struggled to drag my body out of bed.

I hated this. I hated myself. I hated the stupid defective vagina that I was stuck with.

My gaze drifted over to my phone, and I remembered deleting Tristan's messages and number the night before. Part of me wished I hadn't, as I was dying to know what the rest of his final text said. But the rest of me was relieved. We were already done, and whatever else was in that message would only further amplify the ache in my chest. I needed to cut ties and move on.

But then I remembered that I'd deleted my dating app, which also filled me with both pain and relief. This time, moving on wouldn't involve hopping back online to find some new match to be heartbroken by. I would move on by focusing on myself.

There was a knock on my door, and that was when I realized it was almost 11 a.m.

Jesus, I slept in way too late.

"What is it Cass?"

"You coming to *C&C* today?"

Yes. Absolutely. Relief poured over my body like running water. I needed to get out of the house today. Right now, my wounds were still raw, and a distraction would help numb the pain.

"Yup. We leave in an hour, right?"

"Yes. Do you have your character sheet ready?"

I frowned, confused. I stepped out of bed, making sure my hair wasn't too bedraggled, and opened the door.

Cassidy was already fully dressed and showered, which made me feel like even more of a slouch.

"What do you mean?" I asked.

A teasing grin crept across her lips. "You forgot, didn't you? Today is the PvP event."

Shit. My face fell. With so much drama in my personal life, I completely forgot that I had signed up. The PvP, or player-vs-player, event was different than our normal *Creatures & Crypts* game. It was something Devin ran at the shop a few times a year, where instead of an adventuring party battling against CM-controlled enemies, players fought directly against each other in arena-style combat. It was one of my favorite events at Critical Games, and there was always a prize for the winner.

This time, it was any *Creatures & Crypts* book on the shelf. And I'd been eyeing the special edition of *Cremara's Horde of Dragons* for weeks.

I desperately wanted to win.

And I hadn't even put together a character.

I slammed the door as I bounded across my bedroom. Cassidy laughed as she reminded me through the door that the event was for level five characters. I dug through my desk drawer, pulling out a spare character sheet and a pencil, flying through the pages of my *Player's Guide* so fast that they gave me paper cuts.

A small bubble of excitement formed in my stomach, banishing my previous self-deprecating thoughts.

At that moment, my dating woes didn't matter.

I had a competition to win.

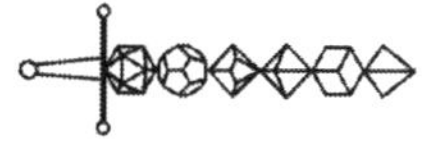

I WAS STILL SCRAMBLING TO PUT MY CHARACTER together an hour later, while Cassidy, Aaron, and I sat huddled around a table at Critical Games.

Cassidy and Aaron were sitting next to each other like always, having a heated discussion on the effectiveness of using the *hurry* spell in PvP combat. I picked up on bits and pieces of their conversation, and I was eager to chime in with my own opinion. But I still needed to finish writing down my freshly made character's spells.

"Tortoisefolk, huh?"

My shoulders hunched. I knew that voice.

I craned my neck over my shoulder, and sure enough, Devin was hovering over me, wearing a black sweatshirt with the *Creatures & Crypts* logo across the font and his hands shoved deep in the pockets of his dark grey jeans. His snakebite piercings held silver studs tonight, and the ones in his ears were tiny red d20 dice.

And, as usual, he had total disregard for my personal space.

"Yes." I slid my character sheet to the right so he had a better view, pointing at it with my pencil. "High armor class, and high wisdom for a cleric character."

"Battle cleric subclass?"

"Of course."

"It's just interesting," Devin noted, hunching forward to examine my character sheet. As he did, his sweatshirt sleeve brushed against my shoulder, sending a weird shiver down my spine. "I've never seen anyone play a tortoisefolk for a PvP event."

"Well, my giant tortoise-person is going to kick everyone's ass." I smirked.

Devin chuckled. "You do that. Good luck."

I hunched my shoulders as Devin walked away, burying my thoughts in my character build for the next ten minutes. Once I'd finally calculated the last stat and penciled in the last spell, I lifted my head and took a moment to surface. The shop was packed—at least thirty contestants hovered around the six large tables in the gaming area. The air was heavy with conversation, with many patrons flipping through their *Player's Guides* like I was. Character sheets were strewn everywhere, and the rolling of pencils and dice clattered across the tables.

Behind the counter, Devin was with one of his employees, a short blonde guy with a thick beard named Jordan. Jordan wore a bright baby-blue t-shirt and a pair of tan khakis, making him a stark contrast to Devin's usual all-black appearance. The pair hovered around the cash register, deep in conversation. The PvP matches were always crowded events, and Devin usually needed extra help to keep things running smoothly.

Chapter 11

I flicked my eyes to the far corner of the gaming room, where the huge *Wargavel* tables had been converted to *Creatures & Crypts* arenas for the event. I knew Devin had a knack for miniature painting and terrain building, but I hadn't realized the extent of his collection. There were four tables, each set up with intricate miniature forests full of trees, rocks, and scattered ruins to use for cover. Devin had a shelf full of painted miniatures for people to borrow, and curiosity pulled me toward them. I plucked a small Infernal character off the shelf, pinching it in my fingers as I inspected the paint job. It was incredible—not a single dab of color out of place, with full shading, a dark wash, and so much detail that even the character's rucksack had tiny silver buttons.

I was so immersed that I almost dropped the little figure when Devin whistled. The shrill noise pierced through everyone's conversations, causing them to fall silent.

"Alright, everyone." Devin clapped his hands together, stepping between the tables. I quickly placed the miniature back on the shelf and scurried over to my seat. "Here's how tonight's event is going to work: there are thirty-two of you, which makes my life easier, because that's exactly eight people per table. There are four tables, and the first round will be single elimination. Drop to zero hit points and you're out. The winners from each table will then face off in a final round. The top four players will get a dice set of their choice, and of course, the grand prize is any *Creatures & Crypts* book on the shelf."

Excited murmurs rumbled through the crowd, and Devin had to whistle to regain everyone's attention.

"If you haven't had your character's stats checked by Jordan yet, please do so. Otherwise, we start exactly at 1 p.m. Good luck!"

I grabbed my character sheet off the table and walked toward the counter, where a small line had formed for Jordan to approve everyone's characters. I knew that small mistakes were inevitable, but Devin's priority was to make sure no one was blatantly cheating.

"A tortoisefolk, huh?" Jordan remarked as I handed him my character sheet.

"That's what I said," Devin grinned as he slid behind Jordan to grab a dice set off the shelf. He placed it on the counter, typing into his computer for the awaiting customer. "Avie said her giant Bowser is going to kick everyone's asses."

I scoffed at him calling me Avie again.

"Bowser? Well, my character *does* need a name. But it's too bad I don't have spikes on my shell."

"Call him Koopa instead," Devin suggested, his eyes lit up by his fluorescent computer screen. "They don't have the shell spikes."

I shook my head, penciling *Koopa* into the *Character Name* line. I knew Devin would continue to tease me about the name later.

I stared at my character sheet as I strolled over to one of the tables. Cassidy and Aaron's group was already full, which meant I'd be on my own for the first round. Not that they would be much help. I was actually relieved that we wouldn't be pitted against each other.

Although, murdering Aaron's stupid barbarian would be pretty fun...

Everyone was picking miniatures off the shelf. To my surprise, there was a tortoisefolk character available, with a sword in one hand and a turtle-shell shield in the other.

"That's one of my favorites," Devin remarked. I cringed as he once again snuck up behind me and leaned in way too close. "I just painted him last week. Anyway..." He raised his voice. "Everyone ready?"

"Yeah!" A collective shout rang across the room.

Chapter 11

"I'm putting sixty minutes on the clock. Ready, set… begin round one!"

We rolled initiative - eight dice bumpily lurched across the table. My character didn't have high dexterity, so I ended up right in the middle of the turn order. I spent the first twenty minutes of the match utilizing my preferred strategy: setting up a variety of defenses while letting the more aggressive players pick each other off. It worked for a while; a wizard ended up backed into the corner and defeated by a pair of bloodthirsty fighters, while a barbarian got cocky and took on two opponents at once, eventually getting knocked down by a critical hit lightning bolt.

At the thirty-minute mark, six of us remained. My strategy was quickly running thin. As the number of contenders lessened, so did my ability to *not* draw attention. One of the fighters eventually realized I hadn't taken any damage and decided to charge my tortoise head-on.

I was prepared for this. Two turns ago, I'd cast *guardian fighters*, which allowed me to summon spirits to attack any players that came within 15 feet of me. The fighter, who was controlled by Chris, realized this too late, and I took a mere 9 damage while he took 18.

"Shit," he grumbled under his breath. I bit my lip to hide my smirk.

The spell also halved his speed, which allowed me to pummel him with attacks for the next two turns. Everyone else's health was already halved, which meant they didn't want to risk charging into my forcefield of doom.

But even if I did take damage, I had a huge advantage over the other players. Still in the fight were two fighters, a paladin, a wizard, and a druid. Out of all of us, I had the most healing abilities. With enough time and distance from the others, I could regenerate my lost hit points.

We reached the forty-five-minute mark. The paladin managed to break my tortoisefolk's concentration, causing my spell to dissipate and leaving me vulnerable to attack. But my character's naturally high armor caused a few hits to miss, leaving me with the most hit points of the four people left at the table.

"How's it going over here?" Devin whirled around the table, surveying the miniatures on the detailed terrain map. For once, I was glad he was hovering over me. I wanted him to see that I was winning.

"We've gotta take out the damn turtle," one of my opponents grumbled in response. I gulped, realizing that I was in trouble. Like in any multiplayer game, being in the lead also meant being a bigger target.

Devin nodded, wishing us all good luck before venturing off to the other tables. But as he left, I saw him tilt his chin back and wink at me. It sent a warm, burning flutter through my chest, but I was too deeply focused on our game to give the feeling much notice.

Three turns later, I was struggling. The wizard had been knocked out, meaning it was only me, the paladin, and the druid. I had now fallen below half of my original hit points, but I was still in the lead. The paladin was nearly dead, relying on his high armor class to deflect hits, while the druid desperately nature-shaped one last time to utilize her animal form's hit points.

I decided to take a risk and use a turn to heal myself instead of attacking. I got lucky; the druid's bear form missed with its claw attack, doing a mere 6 damage with its bite attack. On the next turn, I hit the druid hard enough to knock her out of her bear form and back into a wood elf. I could see the terror on Tracey's face as this happened. She was out of nature-shapes and had very few close-range attacks. She was trapped, and I had her knocked out within the next two turns.

Chapter 11

It was just me and the paladin. There were five minutes left, and we were one of only two tables left playing. This meant that we had a swarm of onlookers, including Cassidy and Aaron, who stood directly behind me and cheered me on. Across the table, Devin gazed at our battlefield with intense focus, his piercings glinting in the light as he chewed on his bottom lip.

Across the table, Andy glowered at me with fire in his eyes. He was a tall, heavyset guy, one with a patchy brown beard and large black gauges in his ears. I wasn't a big fan of him, and at the moment, the feeling was mutual.

His initiative roll had been low, which meant I went before him. My eyes flicked wildly across my character sheet. One more hit would kill him. I had to make it land.

My eyes lit up when I noticed *Guiding Hit* scrawled across my notes box in my scratchy handwriting.

> *When you attack, you can gain a +10 bonus to the roll.*

Piece of cake.

I rolled a d20. A nasty grin crept across Andy's face when he saw the 11, but it quickly turned to agony when I announced that the roll was actually a 21. He slapped his palms against his face, stumbling backward while a frustrated growl crept out of his mouth.

Cassidy and Aaron cheered. Devin's sly grin stretched all the way across his face.

I had won the first round.

Chapter 12

MY HEART WAS STILL HAMMERING IN MY chest as the rest of the tables finished up and Devin recorded the wins on his computer. Me, Cassidy, and Aaron watched as one last table went into overtime. At the sixty-minute mark, Devin had lightning start striking the field in random spaces, forcing the last two cowardly players out of their hiding spots. But one of them was a druid, and he was able to cast *Thorn Growth* to slow down his opponent, a dwarf fighter.

Now surrounded by dangerous thorns that slowed down his movement, the fighter was at the mercy of the lightning strikes. He struggled through the thorny field, painfully eating the damage with every step, until a well-placed lightning bolt dealt the finishing blow.

Another wave of cheers roared through the shop. Across the table, I saw Devin eye me as he clapped. He still had that mischievous grin on his face, and it set my reluctant heart aflutter.

Chapter 12

I gulped, hoping to slow my racing heartbeat, telling myself it was just from the adrenaline rush of winning and not because of how Devin's smile made my stomach flip. But as the applause slowed and the eliminated players slowly trickled out the door, I noticed that Cassidy hadn't been clapping. Instead, her eyes were locked on her phone, and her lips were pressed in a thin line.

"Something wrong?" I asked.

Cassidy let out a heaving sigh of frustration. "It's the newbie that's working tonight. One of the boarding dogs got out, and she can't find him. Joel is on vacation, so it looks like I'm gonna have to head down there and help."

I frowned. Cassidy was the lead veterinary technician at her animal hospital. It paid well and she enjoyed her work, but it also meant that difficult situations usually fell on her shoulders. This wasn't the first time she'd been texted late at night by an employee begging for help.

"I hope the dog is okay," I remarked as she packed up her belongings.

Cassidy shrugged. "I doubt he went far. The hospital doesn't border a main road, but it's gonna suck looking for him in the dark. And there's another problem."

"What?"

"We drove here together. I uh, may need to borrow your car."

My face fell. "Crap. You're right. Depending on how long the final round lasts, I may end up being here pretty late."

"That's okay, I can drive back over and pick you u—"

"It's okay," Aaron stepped in, having overheard our conversation. "I can drive you, Cass."

Cassidy's eyebrows shot up. "You sure? The hospital is thirty minutes away."

"It's no big deal." Aaron shrugged, his hands shoved deep in his pockets. "I was going to head home soon anyway. I'll drop you back off at the townhouse once we're done."

My heart lifted as I tried to hide the knowing smirk on my face. *Nice move, Aaron.* He could play hero by helping Cassidy find the missing dog and have some time alone with her to chat on the drive down there.

As they packed up their things and left, I silently wished them the best of luck. I knew Aaron had bottled up his feelings for a long time, and it was clear Cassidy liked him too.

I just didn't understand why she was so hesitant to admit it.

"Cass and Aaron leave?" Devin appeared behind me, a clipboard in his hands and a pencil tucked behind his ear.

"Yeah. Cass had a work emergency."

"And Aaron is driving her?" He raised a dark eyebrow. "Interesting move."

"Oh shut up," I sneered, though I was grinning too. "They'll figure it out."

"They'd better." Devin smirked as he strode over to the *Wargavel* tables. He clapped his hands together, preparing to make an announcement.

"Alright everyone, we have our winners from round one! Josh, Robbie, Cameron, and Avery, please come set up at the top right table."

Devin pointed, and the four of us settled around the table, laying out our character sheets and deciding our miniatures' starting positions. My strategy from before wouldn't work this time. There were only four of us, meaning that I couldn't hide away and wait for my opponents to pick each other off. Cameron even scoffed at me choosing to start in the abandoned ruins, where there was plenty of cover.

"Coward."

"Focus on your own character, you imp."

Chapter 12

Cameron huffed as he plopped his Infernal miniature into the center of the map. Everyone wore tense expressions on their faces, their eyes glued to the map as they wracked their brains for a strategy. My nostrils flared. Strategy only mattered so much. Ultimately, it was simple: kill or be killed.

"Alright, once again, you have one hour," Devin announced. He tapped a button on his computer, and a timer appeared on the television behind us. "You may begin!"

My heart soared as my die clattered across the table, displaying a triumphant number 18. But unfortunately, Cameron rolled a 21, which meant I was second in the turn order.

And he decided his first target was me. But he started with a low-level spell, dealing a mere 8 damage with a *Poison Splash*. I huffed. Like the rest of us, he was saving his big spells for the end, but being the first one to take damage made my stomach clench.

But on my turn, I knew better than to play into the taunt. I cast *Holy Weapon*, plopping a spectral sword right next to Cameron while he was still thirty feet away from me. I grinned. He was now locked in combat with the floating weapon, which meant he was unlikely to come after me. In addition, I could make an immediate attack with it, and I slashed the Infernal for 9 damage. Across the table, I saw Cameron's teeth clench.

We continued around the board. On Cameron's next turn, he managed to deal 10 damage to me with a ranged spell, but on my turn, he took another 7 damage from the sword. I also used my turn to re-cast *Guardian Fighters*. It caused my spectral weapon to dissipate as I broke concentration, but it would set up my defenses against the other two players on the board.

Josh was a fighter and Robbie was a druid, making them formidable opponents with high health and damage capacity. But Josh didn't have many ranged attacks and couldn't breach my defenses, and Robbie chose to go for the low-hanging fruit and attack Cameron. Now cornered by Robbie's dire wolf, Cameron's hit points were draining fast.

But during that time, Cameron also hit me with a *Fire Sphere*. I succeeded on my saving throw, but still took a whopping 14 damage. I panicked, spending the next turn shrouded in the ruins, healing myself while everyone else engaged in a bloody brawl.

Josh was knocked out at the thirty-minute mark. Cameron used his last third-level spell slot to hurl another *Fire Sphere*, and Josh wasn't so lucky with his saving throw. I gulped. Cameron was still blocked by Robbie's druid, although Robbie was now out of nature-shapes and forced to fight in his elf form.

My eyes flicked frantically between the board and my character sheet. I had to incentivize Cameron to knock Robbie out first. Robbie was more vulnerable, but he also had more hit points, while Cameron was struggling to stay alive. He'd taken a lot of damage, and since he'd already downed the one health potion we were allotted per game, I knew he was only one or two hits away from being knocked out.

It was my turn. Cameron and Robbie's characters were about thirty feet away, still locked in combat and unable to disengage without using up an action. I had one third-level spell slot left, and I had to use it wisely.

My fingers traced over my *Player's Guide*, pausing just below a spell that read *Striking Bolt.*

I knew how I was going to win.

"Alright," I announced after a few moments of silence. Cameron and Robbie had their gazes locked on me, anticipation dancing in their eyes like fire. "I'm going to cast *Striking Bolt* as a third-level spell, targeting Robbie."

They both gave a nervous nod, unsure where I was going with this.

"I make a ranged spell attack..." My die clattered out of my palm and onto the table.

17. Perfect.

Druids didn't wear metal armor, so it was an easy hit. Robbie didn't seem too concerned, until I revealed that he would be taking a whopping 22 damage. He reeled backward, a palm over his forehead, as if I'd just stuck him in the chest with a real spell and not an imaginary one.

A wicked grin crept across my face at his reaction.

"I'm dead." Robbie huffed in defeat.

A raucous mixture of applause and jeers echoed through the crowd. Many of the players knocked out in the first round had left, but we still had a handful of onlookers eager to watch the final round. My eyes flicked up to Devin, who was on the opposite side of the table. He was silent, his arms folded across the front of his black sweatshirt, but his pierced lips held the same smug smile that mine did.

"Uh, alright." Cameron looked visibly uncomfortable. "Well for my turn, I—"

"I'm not done."

Everyone's heads swiveled in my direction. I raised my eyebrows at Cameron.

Let's end this.

"The thing is, I can cast *Holy Weapon* as a bonus action," I remarked, my fingers trailing my character sheet. "So I will choose to re-cast it, and when I do, I can make an immediate attack with it."

All emotion drained from Cameron's face.

I rolled a d20, and an explosion of jeers echoed from the crowd as I rolled a measly 8. Cameron sneered, a nasty grin across his face.

"Hey, wait up!" I announced.

I waited for the crowd to fall silent, and I continued.

"I have *Guiding Hit,* dummies," I scoffed. "And I haven't used it yet this round. Which meant that 8 is actually an 18, so..."

Laughter, now aimed in Cameron's direction, roared through the crowd. I swore I could see angry steam wisping out of his pierced nostrils.

"And for damage," I continued. "I roll..."

"Don't bother," Cameron grumbled. "I only have two hit points. I'm dead."

More laughter, followed by cheers, flowed through my eardrums and left my brain buzzing as if I'd just downed a huge dose of caffeine. My heart thumped madly in my chest, and my limbs began to shake.

I had been so determined to win. But to have it actually *happen* was incredible.

"Congratulations, Avery!" Jordan announced as he and the few remaining spectators clapped. "Thank you to everyone for attending! Our final four players can collect their prizes at the front desk. Everyone else, have a good evening!"

The spectators shuffled out the door until only the top four players remained, all lined up at the cash register to obtain their prizes. Cameron flashed me a wicked glare as he stood behind me, his bulky frame towering over my petite one. But behind those fiery eyes, I saw a small, congratulatory smile.

Everyone at the shop was competitive. And as one of only three girls in the entire competition, it sent a small bubble of pride through my chest to have beaten the boys.

Chapter 12

"Congratulations, Avie."

That same familiar voice crept up behind me, just as it always did. But this time, I was overjoyed to hear it.

I turned around to see Devin's black-clothed frame hovering over me, his arms still crossed over his chest. But on his face was a smile. Not his usual smug, teasing smirk, but a genuine smile of praise. His green eyes swirled with a warmth that I rarely saw from him, and it made me beam from ear to ear like a giddy idiot.

"Thanks, Dev."

"What dice do you want? I can grab them for you."

My eyes flicked over to a stand atop the counter, where all the basic resin dice sets were stored. "I want the ones with little cows in them."

Devin snorted. "Why cows?"

I shrugged. "They're fun. When you already have like six full dice sets, you start picking up the more...*whimsical* ones."

"I see," Devin smiled, a hint of his usual smirk returning to his face. "Cows are cute. You'll have to play a minotaur character sometime and use them."

Cameron finished up ahead of me, and Jordan announced that he needed to head out to pick his toddler up from daycare.

"No problem," Devin waved Jordan away as he stepped behind the counter. "I can take care of things from here. Have a good evening. And thanks for all your help."

"Of course, man! Bye!"

Jordan strode out the front door, with Cameron right behind him. An uneasy silence settled over me as I realized Devin and I were the only ones left in the store.

"So, Koopa did win after all," Devin smirked. "Defeating Mario will be a piece of cake after dealing with everyone tonight."

I rolled my eyes. "You're such a dweeb."

"Am I?" Devin pressed a palm to his chest in mock offense. "Well, it's a good thing I run a game shop then."

I smiled. We truly were all dweebs here. But we were in good company, and Critical Games had been a lifesaver when I first moved to Orlando. *I wouldn't be who I am today without it.*

"So, one cow dice set," Devin plopped the plastic case on the counter in a dramatic fashion, resting his palm over it. "And if I remember correctly, you wanted *Cremara's Horde of Dragons*, didn't you?"

I scoffed. "Good memory. But specifically the special edition one, which...*crap*."

My eyes flicked to the shelf behind the counter, where the special edition books were stored. *Cremara's Horde of Dragons* was gone. *I swear there were two on the shelf earlier. Someone must've bought them while we were playing.*

"No worries." Devin strode out from behind the counter. "I'm pretty sure I have more copies in the back room. Follow me."

The storage room was far more cluttered than last time, with heaps of boxes, some opened with goods spilling out, stacked on top of each other. Devin rifled through them, cursing under his breath as he scoured through box after box, some of them toppling over at his feet.

"I know, I know," he grumbled as I took a seat in the break area. "It's a mess in here. I just got a huge shipment two days ago. I'm a one-man show most days, so keeping up with inventory can be tough."

I peered over at the minifridge, my mind flashing back to when Devin comforted me here after the situation with Anthony. I remembered how calmly and deftly he handled the situation, and how gentle his demeanor was. I could still feel the cold water bottle being pressed into my hands.

Chapter 12

Devin was right. I did need to be more careful when it came to online dating.

But at least I won't be doing it anymore. I'm done.

"So, how's it going with your new guy?"

I knew Devin was just trying to make small talk, but his words still sent fire burning through my veins. The wound that had been closing all night was just ripped wide open.

"We broke up," I replied flatly, in a tone that indicated I was not willing to explain further.

"Ah, that's too bad. Online dating can be tough." Devin didn't seem too fazed by my answer. "God, I swear it was in with the other *C&C* books..."

He was still scouring through boxes, stepping over a lopsided pile to reach the larger ones. It was hotter in the storage room than in the main storefront, and he had rolled his sweatshirt sleeves up to his elbows. I could see the muscles in his forearms straining as he lifted boxes, and my gaze was locked on his Cremara tattoo.

I could still feel it: the vibrant red dragon heads beneath my fingertips, the softness of his skin as I traced the design with my fingers.

The way he pulled away from me, as if my touch pained him.

"Hey Devin?"

He froze, still hunched over in front of a large box. "Yes?"

"I'm sorry about last week. I, uh, shouldn't have grabbed your arm like that when I was looking at your tattoo."

I had no idea why I was apologizing. I had no idea why I was even bringing it up. But there was this nagging urge, deep in my core, that was biting for answers.

"Oh, uh, it's okay," Devin stuttered his reply. He didn't seem upset, or even confused. He seemed...sad.

I gulped.

Stop prodding.

But I couldn't help myself.

"Can I ask you something else?"

"Sure."

I was silent for a moment, the heaviness of my question hanging in the air before I'd even asked it. I was suddenly fully aware that it was just the two of us, alone in a store-room in the back of a game shop that was about to close, and it made my heart pound wildly in my chest.

"If you have so many tattoos, why do you always cover them? We live in Florida, and you're always wearing heavy sweatshirts, even in the summer."

My words were like a knife slicing through the eerily still air. Devin had a bit of shock on his face, like someone zapped by static electricity. That's when I noticed that he'd found a copy of *Cremara's Horde of Dragons*, and it was in his left hand tucked behind his back.

You've really done it now. Just take your book and leave. Stop making a fool of yourse—

"Promise you won't tell anyone else about this?"

His sudden response made me jolt. My heart ached as I realized he was about to tell me something deeply personal about himself. Something he didn't want others to know.

"Of course."

He stepped toward me, placing the book on the break area table. My throat locked up. I had no idea what he was about to do next. I stood up, and our bodies were less than a foot away from each other. Normally his standing so close annoyed me, but now it felt like an invisible magnet was pulling me toward him.

He grabbed the bottom of his sweatshirt and began pulling it over his head. As he did so, his undershirt slid several inches up his torso, revealing his stomach all the way up to his belly button. I could see his full stomach tattoo now—it was a snake coiled around a fancy silver dagger, stretched horizontally just above the hem of his dark jeans. It was cut in half by a thin trail of hair, one that disappeared below his jeans and—

Stop it. Heat prickled my neck. *Why does he make me feel this way? Why am I not opposed to it?*

He tossed the sweatshirt over the back of the chair next to me. Underneath, he wore a black t-shirt with a menacing-looking Infernal character on the front. Its wicked, toothy grin stretched all the way across his chest.

But with the sweatshirt off, it allowed me to see the tattoos on his arms. That was when I realized that Cremara wasn't a single tattoo – it was part of a *Creatures & Crypts*-themed sleeve that covered his entire arm and disappeared into the sleeve of his shirt. He held it out for me to examine, and my eyes trailed over the intricate mural of monsters fighting an adventuring party. In addition to Cremara, there was an Observer and a Shifting Beast, each in elaborate fighting poses with tons of detail.

"Wow," I remarked, once again tempted to trace my fingers over the tattoos. "But I still don't understand why you cover them up."

I looked up, and my eyes met his. They didn't hold their usual emerald brightness. Instead, they look glazed over with pain.

"Look closer."

I leaned forward. And that was when, between the lines and colors, I saw them. On the surface of his skin, obscured by the artwork, were long red scars. They ran in jagged lines down his forearm, though they all seemed to be clustered around his veins.

It hit me like cold water being splashed on my face.

"Drugs," I whispered, more of a question than a remark.

Devin nodded. "Not just drugs. Self-harm scars too." He traced a few ragged marks below Cremara's wing. "I'm nine years clean, and I was hoping they would've healed more by now. But I think I'm stuck with them for life."

"What kind of drugs?"

"Mostly heroin. I really went off the deep end after my divorce."

Divorce!? I gave Devin a quizzical look. Marriage was a foreign concept to me, let alone the ending of one. I didn't know exactly how old Devin was, but he looked mid-to-late thirties. Meaning that he'd already completed nearly two decades of being an adult. At twenty-six, I still felt like I was just starting out.

Devin must have noticed my confusion, because he let out a big sigh. "Yeah, I guess you don't really know my story, do you? Before all this—" He gestured towards his tattoos and black clothing. "—I was a completely different person. Pastor's kid, raised on religion, always trying to please everyone. I married my high school girlfriend at nineteen."

My face dropped in disbelief. *Raised on religion.* Devin's upbringing was just like mine.

"You're kidding. I grew up in a super religious household too. I fled my hometown after getting kicked out of my bible-thumper college and ended up here."

Devin chuckled. "What got you kicked out?"

"Uh…I…got caught sleeping with my boyfriend."

Technically not a lie. I did sleep in bed with him. We just weren't successful with the sex part.

Devin laughed, the usual mischievous glint returning to his eyes. "Damn. You rebel."

"Oh shut up," I huffed. "Now it's your turn."

Devin bit his lip. "You want to know the rest of my story, don't you?"

I shrugged. "We've got time."

"Alright." Devin plopped in the chair next to me. My gaze was locked on his tattoo sleeve as he talked. "Well, let's start with my marriage. We lasted four years. It was fun at first, we were two kids fresh out of high school playing house and learning how to be adults. But as time passed, Jessica grew more and more restless. Our parents were pressuring us to have kids, and she wasn't ready. She was a dancer, and her dream was to go to an exclusive school in New York City. So when we were twenty-three, she applied behind my back."

"You didn't want her to go?"

"Quite the opposite. She panicked after she got accepted and confessed the whole thing to me. She swore she'd never actually leave, but our marriage was in ruin by that point. We were more roommates than husband and wife. I cared deeply about her, but we were no longer in love, and I didn't want to be the reason she gave up her dreams. I still remember driving her to the airport. I practically pushed her on the plane."

"Wow, that must've been hard. For both of you."

"It was. Both sets of parents threw a fit, and I was the one left behind in Georgia to deal with their fury. I fled the state as soon as the divorce was finalized, and I moved down here to be with my cousin. But I was an emotional wreck, and I started partying to numb the pain. And with parties came drinking, then drugs...and I lost control."

I felt Devin's pain, deep in my chest and through every nerve in my body. It reminded me of my parents' raging disappointment when they discovered I'd been kicked out of college—and why.

"I completely understand," I replied, my voice soft with empathy. "After college, I spent so many nights crying myself to sleep in my childhood bedroom until I finally snapped. One evening, after a particularly bad argument with my parents, I packed up all my essentials, shoved them in my beat-up Camry, and drove through the night until I ended up in Orlando."

"I remember," Devin said with a faint smirk. "You showed up here one afternoon, peeping through the door like a terrified kitten."

I scowled. "Oh come on. I was not that bad."

Devin laughed. "You most definitely were. I was standing behind the counter, and when I said hello, you gawked at me like I was the spawn of Satan."

"I did not!"

My nostrils flared; my cheeks scorching red with embarrassment. But Devin continued laughing.

My posture softened. I knew Devin was right, because I still remembered it myself. Growing up in such a sheltered community, I'd never been around anyone other than clean-cut church types. Walking into Critical Games on a whim was the first time I'd ever seen a goth guy with piercings and tattoos. It terrified me.

And now it filled me with regret.

I judged him without even knowing him.

It was hard to believe that, five years later, we were sitting alone in the back room of that same game shop, pouring out our life stories. Showing each other who we were beyond the gaming hijinks and snarky comments. It hit me that in all the years I'd known Devin, I'd never truly *known* him.

I'd never known how much our stories overlapped. How similar we were.

"I love it here," Devin continued, his voice hazy with contemplation. "I met Scott, the old owner, at one of my AA meetings. He hired me, a scrawny recovering addict with very little job history, to work at the shop. And I was so grateful for it. I started playing *Creatures & Crypts*, and it honestly saved my life. Tabletop gaming became my passion. I poured my heart and soul into this place, and after Scott's health issues got too severe, I took over the shop. It was having financial issues that took years to recover from, but Scott knew how much I cared about Critical Games. He still pops in here from time to time. He's more of a father to me than my own dad."

The warmth in his voice suddenly chilled over. "But I still get scared. There are nights when it all comes back to haunt me, when I remember who I used to be. And these—" He pointed at his scars. "—won't let me forget."

"But you have all of us." I gestured toward the front of his shop. "Everyone here loves you. You've built an incredible community here. They'd never judge you for your past."

"Maybe not my immediate friends," Devin sighed. "But others would. I'm a Crypt Master for kids for hell's sake, imagine if their parents saw my scars and knew I used to be an addict..."

His voice broke, and I saw the anguish consume his face as he fought back tears. My heart plummeted. In the five years I'd known Devin, I'd always labeled him as a cocky, smug, yet slightly endearing pain in the ass. But now my emotions lay raw in front of me, and I couldn't deny it anymore. I cared about him, and I couldn't stand to see him in so much pain.

"Listen to me." I placed a hand over his forearm, rubbing his scars with my fingers. "I know I call you a pain, and a dweeb, and a lot of other things. But the truth is that you, Devin Lancaster, are one of the most incredible people I've ever met. I walked in here five years ago as a terrified kid with no home, no friends, and a ton of emotional trauma. I was afraid of you, and yet you sat me down and taught me how to play *C&C* like we'd known each other for years. I left the shop that day with hope that maybe life in Orlando wouldn't be that bad. Then I met Cassidy, and Aaron, and all my other friends. I built a new life here. And it's all because of you. So don't *ever* let anyone judge you because of your past. Because I sure as hell won't let them judge me for mine."

Devin was silent. I looked up, my fingers still rubbing his scars, and locked eyes with him. I was close enough to see all the little details, every fleck of color in his blue-green irises. But most importantly, I saw him. Not the snarky older brother figure who liked to tease me. Not the cocky game shop owner who invaded my space and made snide comments about my dating life. Instead, I saw the first friend I made when I arrived in Orlando. The geeky, tattooed goth guy who had just as much baggage as I did. I saw the kindest soul I knew, the one that for years I'd been too stubborn to admit my feelings for.

And at that moment, I wanted him more than anything else in the world.

He leaned toward me, hesitant, his subtle movements asking a question. Testing the waters to see if his feelings were reciprocated. I threw every fear, every worry, every bit of sanity out the window and pressed my lips to his.

It was gentle at first. He was soft and warm, and I felt the spark within me roar into a searing flame the moment he deepened our kiss. He embraced me, wrapping his arms around my hips and pulling me towards him. I responded by running my fingers through his soft black hair, my heart melting like a burning candle.

This wasn't like my first kiss with Tristan. Or even with Tyler. This was five long years of repressed feelings and pent-up attraction. It was glorious and soul-consuming, and it wasn't long before our affections got out of control.

Devin leaned forward, pushing me back and forcing me to use the break room table as a seat. But he didn't stop there. His hands trailed their way up my back, gripping me with a ferocity that nearly brought me to tears. Our kisses grew deeper and more fervent as we allowed our attraction to consume us.

"Avie..." he breathed in my ear.

I had never loved that nickname so much in my life.

A slight gasp of pleasure escaped me, and that drove him wild. He pressed his lips against my neck in a sea of kisses while his hands slid to the side of my breasts. I bit my lip until I tasted blood, determined not to let out a moan in the back room of the shop. Critical Games was closed, and we were out of sight of the windows, but I still didn't want to risk it. This felt so wrong, and yet so horribly, wonderfully right.

I couldn't break away. I was still propped on the table, engulfed in his embrace, and I could feel the bulge in his jeans pressed against me. I wrapped my legs around his hips and pulled him closer to me. I wanted to feel him. I wanted all of him.

He gasped in my ear, and it set my entire body on fire. But amidst our heated embrace, it also allowed me a moment of clarity.

Wait.

What the fuck am I doing?

This wouldn't work. It would never work. Because in my stupid infatuated haze, I'd forgotten why I'd been dumped so many times in the first place.

I had no reason to believe that Devin and I would end any other way.

I practically shoved him away from me, stumbling off the table and trying to ignore the fact that all the blood flow in my body had pooled in my pelvis. My breath came in shallow, rapid gulps as my mind attempted to process what had just happened.

You idiot.

You absolute idiot.

"Avie, are you okay?" Devin asked, taking a moment to catch his breath. He looked confused.

"I... I—"

I was speechless. I couldn't tell him the truth. Tristan's rejection was bad enough. Devin's rejection would break me.

That left me with only one option.

I had to reject *him* instead.

"I...I have to go."

Devin's arms fell to his sides as his whole body drained of color. I could see the shattered expression on his face, the way it made his eyes glisten with fear.

"W-what do you mean?"

"I can't do this."

Devin took a step forward, and I took a step back.

"Avie, wait, please." His voice was strained with panic. "I'm sorry. I know this is going really fast, and you just broke up with the online dating guy. We can slow down. We can take all the time you need. Just please..." He extended a hand toward me. My eyes trailed up his arm, studying his tattoos and scars, the ones I'd been caressing just moments earlier.

"I can't. I'm sorry."

"But why not?" Devin stepped closer. His movements were slow and hesitant, as if he were trying to coax a spooked cat. As if he were afraid I'd bolt any second. "Avie, the truth is, I've had feelings for you for a long time. Talking to you tonight...I told you things I never tell anyone, and you said things to me that I've needed to hear for years. Like how I was one of the most incredible people you've ever met. What did you mean by that?"

"I... I..."

There was no stopping it. Silent tears fell like rain down my cheeks.

"Do you have feelings for me too?"

I couldn't lie to him. "Yes."

"Then what's wrong? Please, just tell me. I promise we'll work through it together."

I desperately wanted to believe him. I wanted to run back into his arms, tell him how sorry I was, and continue losing myself in his embrace. I wanted to tell him that every word I said was true, and that he was an incredible human being who I couldn't be without. He'd confessed so many secrets, so much pain, and here I was making it all worse.

I wasn't just broken. I was a monster.

"I can't. I'm sorry. I have to go."

"Avie, no, wait—"

"Don't call me Avie," I snapped. Saying those words felt like ripping my own heart in half, and it made Devin recoil away from me. I had never seen him—or anyone else—look so defeated. So heartbroken.

Dev, I'm so sorry.

I wish things were different.

I spun around and paced towards the door. I had to leave. The longer I stayed here, my gaze lingering on his, the more tempted I would be to tell him the truth. And the truth would only lead to him rejecting *me* instead.

What man would want a woman that couldn't have sex?

But I dared to look back one last time, once my hand was on the front door.

Devin was leaning against the counter, his sad eyes still full of longing. Confusion. And a heavy dose of pain.

"Please don't go."

It was one final plea. But as I pushed my way through the front door and let it slam behind me, I saw the last bit of hope fade from his eyes.

I ran to my car under the hazy setting sun, waiting until I was safely tucked away in the driver's seat to unleash my sobs. It took nearly fifteen minutes for me to calm down enough to turn my key in the ignition and back out of my parking spot.

Tyler, Tristan, online dating...none of it mattered anymore. Tonight had changed everything. Because now, my heart belonged to Devin, and I'd just ripped it out of my own chest.

I didn't know how I would ever recover from this.

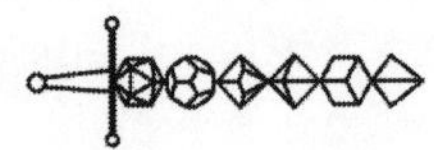

I MADE IT HOME TWENTY MINUTES LATER, MY face crusty and damp and my stomach still caught in my throat. I'd managed to keep it together for most of the car ride, as tear-stained vision was less than ideal for nighttime driving on busy streets. But now that I was home, I could turn off the car, crawl into my bedroom, and curl up in bed and let it all out.

It was going to be a long, *long* night.

And I still had to work the next day.

But as I entered the dark, eerily still house, I realized I wasn't the only one who had a rough night.

Faint, muffled cries emanated from behind Cassidy's bedroom door. I was surprised she was already home. Escaped pet situations usually kept her out all night. I was in no condition to console her with my own heartbreak still heavy on my mind, but Cassidy was my best friend. I couldn't just let her cry in her room alone.

I tapped my knuckles on the door, and the crying stopped.

"Go away," a sob-soaked voice shouted through the door.

"Cass? It's just me." I leaned against the doorframe. "Do you want to talk?"

"No."

I sighed. *She's just as stubborn as I am.*

Chapter 12

"Did something happen?"

There was silence on the other end of the door, until Cassidy spat out a reluctant "yes" followed by more sobs.

I took a deep breath, knowing I was about to ask a loaded question.

"Did it involve Aaron?"

She continued sobbing, but I could hear whisps of anger lacing her cries.

"I don't understand," I continued. "I thought you liked him. What went so wrong?"

"I *do not* like him."

"C'mon, Cass. We all know that's not true."

To my surprise, the door whizzed open, nearly toppling me over since I was leaning against the doorframe. Cassidy's face was just as blotchy and tear-stained as my own, but her eyes were full of fire and rage.

"You're one to talk," she hissed.

"What?"

"Don't pretend like you don't know. We've all seen you two flirting at the shop every weekend for *years*. And *I'm* the cowardly one?"

My stomach dropped. *No. Please don't bring him up.*

"I'm not interested in him," I replied flatly.

"Bullshit."

"What do you mean bullshit? We're always bickering!"

"Yeah, like an old married couple. I've seen the way you two stare at each other when you think no one is looking. He spent almost the entire PvP event at your table, watching *you*. He's completely in love with you."

"He is *not*!" I scream, hot tears threatening to burn my cheeks once again. "Besides, even if he was interested in me, I'm not interested in him. He's a smug, cocky asshole and way too old for me."

Cassidy glowered at me, clearly not believing a word out of my mouth. I could feel the blood pounding in my temples as my hands balled up into fists. I couldn't do this right now. Not after the night I'd had.

"Forget it," I scowled, marching toward my front door. "We're not discussing my love life if you refuse to discuss yours."

"Fine."

"Fine."

I slammed my door so loud the hinges rattled and flopped face-first onto my bed. Once I was certain Cassidy couldn't hear me, I wrapped my arms around a pillow and buried my face in it to keep from sobbing.

Thirty minutes ago, Devin and I were nearly tearing each other's clothes off in the storage room. And now I'd just called him an asshole, pretending that none of it ever happened.

I truly was a monster, and Devin deserved better. He'd poured his heart out to me, and I stomped all over it without so much as an explanation. I needed to figure out my sexual issues before I could ever be with someone, and that meant unpacking decades of trauma. It could take *years* for me to figure all this out and be ready for a relationship.

No more online dating.

No more dating, period.

I was done.

Chapter 13

THE REST OF THE WEEK WAS AN ABSOLUTE SLOG. Back when I was still fretting about Tristan, I'd been distracted, barely able to focus on my manuscripts without him drifting into my mind. But now, I threw myself into my work, immersing my brain in covers and typesets, completing projects in record time.

It kept me distracted. Because as soon as I clocked out every evening at 5 p.m., I had to face the fact that I was alone in a silent bedroom, with only the lazy whorls of the ceiling fan for company. And that's when it all came back to haunt me.

The worst of it was when I went to bed. Lying wide-eyed in the darkness, I still felt Devin's hands pressed against my back. I remembered his lips on my neck, his hips pressed against mine, and the way he breathed my name in my ear. It was so intoxicating, so euphoric, but those thoughts always left me a sobbing mess. I needed him, desperately, but our tryst was doomed to never happen again.

I wondered if he was still upset. If he hated me. If he also spent his nights lying alone in bed, paralyzed by his thoughts. Or maybe he was over it, and he'd forgotten about that night completely. Maybe he'd already tossed me out of his mind, while mine was still consumed with thoughts of him.

Five years. Five long, oblivious years, where I'd never thought of Devin as anything more than a snarky, annoying older brother figure.

How did my mind flip so quickly?

But I knew it hadn't. My feelings had been lurking beneath the surface for years, veiled with banter and snarky comments that now meant so much to me.

No matter who I met on my dating app, no matter how hard I fell for them, they would never compare.

It was always Devin.

And I could never have him.

I sighed, closing my eyes and praying that sleep wouldn't keep eluding me. I noted that I still needed to schedule a gynecologist appointment. I was going to confront my worst fear so that I could keep seeing the pelvic physical therapist. I didn't care how much pain and suffering it involved. I didn't care if it took weeks, months, or even years. I would overcome this.

But by then, Devin would likely have moved on.

I squeezed my eyelids tighter as a tear slid down the side of my face.

That meant I needed to move on too.

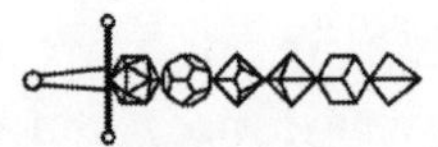

FRIDAY CAME QUICKER THAN I HAD ANTICIPATED. And it also filled me with dread. Because as the workday waned and the evening grew closer, it reminded me of

Critical Games. It was Friday, which was the night I usually played the *Creatures & Crypts TCG* at the shop. But it wasn't just any Friday. It was the pre-release event for the newest set.

Normally, Cassidy and I would've been itching to go. We loved pre-releases, and this set was one I'd been anticipating for a long time. But the thought of walking through those glass double doors and seeing Devin behind the counter made me want to vomit. Maybe we could get past this. Maybe we could still be friends. But it was still far too early to make amends, and I couldn't fathom seeing him just yet.

Cassidy had other plans. Fifteen minutes before my workday ended, she knocked on my bedroom door.

"Hello?" I swung it open, my greeting barely concealing my surprise. Cassidy and I hadn't talked all week. Just like me, she'd been holed away in her room, likely wrestling with memories and emotions that she wasn't ready to tell others about.

She'd just arrived home from work, still in her vet tech scrubs. Her face was no longer blotchy and tear-stained, but the same sorrowful cloud still hung over her. I could see it in her eyes.

"Look," she sighed. "I'm still not ready to talk about last weekend. I know neither of us want to go to the shop and confront the boys right now, but we'll have to face them eventually. And I really don't want to miss this pre-release. So, can we go tonight? Please?"

My heart softened at the pleading look in her eyes. She was right. We should go and enjoy prerelease; relationship problems be damned. Besides, the alternative was sitting around my bedroom on a Friday night, which would only dredge up more painful memories of Devin.

"Of course." I stepped toward her and extended my hands, offering a hug. She took it, wrapping her thin arms around me as we squeezed out our pain and frustration.

We both broke the hug before the tears returned, and shared a knowing glance of two women with broken hearts. We didn't have the full details of each other's relationship woes, but we still acknowledged each other's pain. I was eager to know what happened to my best friend, but I understood her silence. I wasn't ready to talk about Devin yet either.

"I'll drive," Cassidy offered. "Want to stop at Raceway and get frozen yogurt?"

I giggled. That was Cassidy's go-to when in a bad mood. "Of course. Let's go."

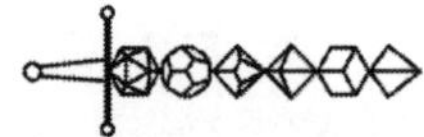

NOT EVEN A HEAPING CUP FULL OF FROZEN yogurt, topped with every form of sugary candy imaginable, could stop me from feeling sick the moment I stepped into Critical Games.

Cassidy had already finished hers and tossed the empty cup in the trash can next to the entrance, but mine was still half-full. And as soon as I caught a glimpse of him, standing behind the counter happily engaged in conversation with a few patrons, I suddenly couldn't handle another bite.

The bell above the doorframe chimed as we walked in. Devin glimpsed at the door like he did any time a customer entered the shop. But as soon as he saw me, his head snapped away like he was staring straight at the sun. Like I was painful to look at.

I stood there, dumbfounded, my spoon still frozen in my mouth as Cassidy stepped past me.

Chapter 13

"Damn, something really did happen between the two of you," she remarked as she approached the front counter. Devin was still chatting with customers, and I could tell he was pretending I wasn't there.

"I don't want to talk about it," I muttered in reply as I stepped in line behind her. I took another bite of my frozen yogurt, the sweet dessert suddenly tasting sour in my mouth. I debated tossing it before offering the rest to Cassidy.

She happily obliged, gulping the remaining third down in a few bites.

"Avery," she noted as she tossed the empty cup. "Calm down. You look like a deer caught in headlights."

I huffed, my nostrils flaring. Devin's current customer finished paying and stepped away, and the line moved forward. I was now one person closer to having to confront him. Relationship woes aside, he was still the shop owner, and I needed to interact with him to register for the event. And it filled me with nauseating dread.

Devin was oblivious to my presence, but I couldn't take my eyes off him. I studied his every feature like I was seeing him for the first time. He had little silver skulls in his earlobes, and his snakebites held studs that were long and pointed like arrows. As usual, he wore a black sweatshirt, although this one had artwork of a large red dragon curled around a d20 die. And just below his collar, against his bare chest, I saw both a thick silver chain necklace and the very top of his Critical Games tattoo. The one he'd shown me just a few weeks earlier.

As I studied him, it all came flooding back, just like it had all week. *His hands against my back, his lips against my neck, his hips against—*

"Uh, Avery?"

I spun around. Chris stood behind me, tapping me on the shoulder.

"You're up."

I turned back around and noticed Devin was staring at me from behind the counter.

Shit.

The few steps up to the front counter felt torturous. I hated the look on his face; how blank it was. The usual mischievous glint in his eye, the smug grin tugging at the corner of his lips…it was all gone. There was no smile, no recognition, no "hey there, Avie." He looked at me as if I were a stranger, just another customer in the shop.

"Uh…I'd like to register for prerelease, please."

His expression was still muted as he typed into his computer, pausing to grab a pen and write my name down on a clipboard. *Avery Murphy*, written in his scratchy handwriting, at the bottom of the list. It was the only indicator that he knew who I was, that I wasn't a stranger to him.

That last week wasn't just a horrible figment of my imagination.

"That'll be $32.50," he replied, still not looking away from his computer screen.

I dared to glance up at him as I swiped my credit card. This time, he was no longer looking at his computer. His gaze was now locked on me, but his eyes were still dull. Nothing. No hint of emotion.

As I walked away, I didn't know what I had expected. Less than a week ago, I had rejected him in the cruelest, most heartless way possible. I had said no to our relationship, and Devin was respecting that answer. He was giving me space.

The problem was that it was the opposite of what I wanted.

I slunk away, feeling dejected as I sat next to Cassidy. My chair made a loud squealing noise as I pulled it closer to the table, but Cassidy barely noticed. Her eyes were locked on Aaron, who sat at a table in the opposite corner of the room. Like Devin, Aaron was engaged in conversation, happily chatting with other patrons while he shuffled a deck of *C&C* cards. He'd decided he was no longer a fan of having green hair and had dyed it back to his usual sandy brown. My gaze flicked back to Cassidy, and I noticed she had the same hazy, longing look in her eyes that I did with Devin.

"Alright, everyone!"

My head twisted over my shoulder. Jordan stood at the back of the shop near the inventory walls with a large cardboard box at his feet. Jordan usually managed the shop on Mondays and Tuesdays when Devin was off, but like with the PvP event, pre-release was packed full of players. Which meant that Devin needed Jordan's help to manage everything.

As Jordan strolled down the aisles, plopping a pre-release kit in front of every seated player, my eyes flicked back to the front counter.

Devin's gaze was locked on his computer, with his sweatshirt sleeves rolled up to reveal his tattooed forearms. Every few seconds, he'd stop typing and scrawl notes on a sheet of paper in front of him.

He paid no notice to me, or Cassidy, or anyone else.

I shook my head, peeling my gaze away before he noticed me gawking like an idiot.

"Alright, you have forty-five minutes to open your packs and build a 40-card deck," Jordan shouted above the chattering crowd. "You may begin!"

The shop went quiet, the sounds of peeling cardboard and crinkling plastic filling the air instead. As usual, I flipped through my packs quickly, eager to reveal the high-value cards hidden at the back of the pack.

I had little luck. Six packs later, I hadn't pulled a single legendary rare.

"Avery, look!" Cassidy exclaimed next to me, revealing a foil dragon that she'd just pulled out of a pack. I smiled and congratulated her, hiding my envy. I hadn't drawn any high-power cards, which meant my deck would be at a disadvantage against the players who had.

Just my luck, I grumbled, biting my lip. Maybe it was karma after what I did to Devin.

But as I fumbled through my cards, sorting them into stacks by color like I always did, I realized I had a new problem. My head swirled with nausea, and a deep aching sensation pulsed in my pelvis and trickled its way up my torso.

Oh no.

I swear to God.

I couldn't deal with this right now. It took every bit of emotional stability I had left to march into the shop with Cassidy and play prerelease. To pretend that I wasn't pathetically pining for the guy behind the counter who acted like I didn't exist.

I am not going to let my period stop me tonight.

But ten minutes into deckbuilding, my vision was beginning to blur. The ache in my pelvis was growing stronger, sharper, sending even more nausea and fatigue rolling through my body. My body wavered in place as I struggled to sit upright. I desperately needed to go home and lie down in bed.

Fine. I practically threw my cards down on the table, shoving them into my pre-release box with little regard for the fact that they were made of delicate cardboard. *My period wins. Fuck prerelease, fuck my feelings for Devin, and most of all, fuck my stupid broken reproductive system.*

"Uh, Avery, you okay?"

I turned my head, which caused more nausea to bubble in my stomach. Cassidy had stopped deckbuilding and was staring at me with concern.

"Yeah," I groaned as I stood up, even though I wasn't. "Look, I'm gonna need to drop. Can I take the car and pick you up later?"

"Of course," Cassidy replied. "Is it..."

"Yeah."

Cassidy was aware of my period problems, although she never asked too many questions about them. Us women had an unspoken sympathy for each other's period pain, but I always felt queasy bringing it up around men.

Which made marching up to the counter and telling Devin I was dropping from the event even more awkward.

"Why?" He frowned, a dark eyebrow raised. "We haven't even started."

"I, uh, don't feel well."

I had prayed that he would let me go without asking too many questions. That he would keep that same icy mask of pretending not to know me. But Devin was a kind-hearted person, always concerned about the well-being of others. Which means no matter how much I fucked up our friendship, he wasn't going to let me just stumble out of there.

"You did this a few weeks ago," he noted, stepping out from behind the counter. "Are you sick? Do you need help?"

"No!" I hissed, recoiling away from him. "I'm fine. Just let me go home."

I stumbled away, my heart aching from snapping at him. But after a few paces, I stopped. The pain had amplified when I got up from the table, and it now nearly brought me to my knees.

"Avery, I can't just let you drive home when you're this sick." Out of the corner of my eye, I saw Devin stepping toward me. "Do you need me to call someone? What if you—shit!"

I collapsed.

Chapter 14

SOMETHING ISN'T RIGHT.

My mind stirred, drifting back into reality. My eyes were closed. I was clearly asleep a moment ago. But I wasn't at home. I couldn't feel my usual comforter wrapped around me like a cocoon, and there was no toasty Florida sun streaming through my window. Instead, I was engulfed in the smell of air freshener, cardboard, and a familiar light, earthy cologne.

A deep ache strained my pelvis, and I remembered everything.

I was just about to leave Critical Games. I told Devin I was dropping because I didn't feel well. He tried to stop me, and...

"C'mon Avery, wake up."

I was suddenly aware of the thick sweatshirt fabric cradling my back and legs.

I had fainted.

And Devin was carrying me into the storage room.

Chapter 14

He knelt down, and I felt cold, hard plastic beneath my body as he settled me into a chair. His hands gripped my shoulders as he gently rustled me awake.

I finally had the strength to open my eyes. My vision was blurry at first, but I knew that pale face and mop of choppy black hair.

"What happened?" I mumbled in a bleary tone.

"You passed out," Devin replied. Once he was convinced that I wouldn't topple out of my chair, he released his grip on my shoulders and pulled out his phone. As he furiously typed with one hand, I continued to regain consciousness, my vision sharpening and my mind becoming more aware of my surroundings.

It's even more of a mess in here than it was last week.

I winced as another deep, throbbing ache stabbed at my pelvis.

"What are you doing?" I asked Devin through clenched teeth as I fought through the pain.

He stopped typing and looked up. "I'm calling an ambulance."

"What? No! I'm oka—"

"Avery, you fainted! You're clearly not okay!"

Devin's sudden, sharp words made me snap my mouth shut. I wasn't used to him yelling, but I could see the flickers of concern in his eyes.

He sighed, scratching the back of his neck. "Sorry. Pardon my tone. But healthy people don't just pass out like that. Has this happened to you before?"

I hesitated before squeaking out a "yes." My period had caused me to faint a few times over the years. It always ended the same way – those around me freaking out and calling 911 while I frantically reassured them that I was fine. I was even once forced by paramedics to sign a denial of care waiver so they would pack up and leave.

I was *not* going to a hospital over a goddamn period.

Devin stood up straighter, crossing his arms over his chest. "Do you know keeps causing you to faint?"

Yes.

But there was no way I could tell him. Even though I'd escaped the clutches of my religious family five years earlier, discussing menstruation with others still made my insides churn.

Especially men.

"It's nothing," I huffed. I attempted to stand up, but Devin pressed his hands into my shoulders and forced me back down. "Just let me go home."

Devin snorted and raised an eyebrow. "Have I ever told you that you're the most stubborn person I know?"

I shrugged, in too much pain to fire back at Devin's snarky tone.

"Alright." Devin slid his phone into the back pocket of his jeans. "Here's how this is going to go. You either tell me what's going on, or I'm calling an ambulance."

My eyebrows furrowed as anger bubbled in my stomach. I'd just been pathetically pining for this man twenty minutes ago, and now he was giving me ultimatums like I was a child.

I opened my mouth, ready to tell Devin who *I* thought was stubborn, when a pang of sadness washed over my aching body. Devin wasn't acting like this to be an ass. He was acting like this because he was worried. Because even though I'd callously rejected him a week earlier, he still viewed me as his friend. He still cared about me, and I'd just fainted right in front of him and refused to tell him what was wrong.

I needed to suck it up and tell him the truth.

Goddamn you, Dev.

Why must you be so nice?

Chapter 14

"It's..." The words struggled to roll off my tongue. "It's just my period."

Devin's narrowed eyebrows suddenly raised with confusion and concern. "It's that bad?"

I nodded.

He gave a deep, heaving sigh as he pulled his phone back out. "Alright. No ambulance. But I still think you can see a doctor."

"For a *period*?"

"Look, Avery..." Devin plopped down in the chair next to me. "I have three older sisters and an ex-wife. I know I'm a guy, but I'm pretty sure it isn't supposed to hurt this much. And it's certainly not supposed to make you pass out. Besides, can't bad periods be a symptom of other health issues?"

Devin's words sent a lightbulb snapping on in my mind. Maybe he was right. I'd never been able to sit through a full gynecology exam, so I had no idea if there was anything wrong with my reproductive system.

And the thought of there being a cure for these god-awful periods was enticing.

"Alright," I sighed. "I'll go see a doctor."

Devin looked relieved. "There's an emergency room up the street. They take walk-ins."

"I'm not going to th—"

"You should, Avery. They can run tests and figure out what's wrong with you. Tonight. Don't you want to feel better?"

I clenched my teeth as another wave of pain shook my body. "Yes."

"Good." Devin stood up. A loud rubbery whir echoed across the cheap tile as he pushed his chair in. "Now let's go."

I froze. "*We?*"

"Yes."

"Devin." I frowned. "I can drive myself."

"Not when you're hunched over in pain every five minutes," he replied in a flat, sharp tone. One that indicated there was no talking him out of this. "Besides, didn't you ride here with Cass?"

Shit.

My eyes flicked to the doorway. In the main storefront, the low drone of chattering voices carried into the breakroom. I didn't want to pull Cassidy away from prerelease. Like me, she'd had a rough week, and she deserved to have fun tonight.

"Don't you have a shop to run?"

"Jordan will be fine without me." Devin stepped toward the doorway, gripping my bicep with his hand as I struggled to walk. In any other situation, Devin's touch would've sent warm pulses buzzing through my skull like caffeine. But right now, I was in too much pain to care.

"Fine," I grumbled. "Let's go."

"Great."

More pain, this time so severe it nearly made me fall over.

"Here, hold onto me," he wrapped an arm across my shoulder. "Otherwise, I'm gonna have to carry you again."

I scoffed. His tone almost sounded flirtatious.

We approached the front door, barely noticed by the busy prerelease players in the opposite room. And I realized that in a sick, twisted way, I'd gotten my wish. Devin was talking to me again. We'd still have to discuss that night eventually, but at least he was no longer pretending that I didn't exist.

Maybe he didn't hate me.

Maybe we could still be friends.

As we strode across the parking lot, I collapsed in the middle of the road. My muscles tensed as his hands gripped my legs and back, once again lifting me up.

"It's a good thing you're tiny," Devin chuckled as he walked across the parking lot, carrying me in his arms. Once again, the softness of his sweatshirt fabric contrasted with the firmness of his grip, and I had to resist the urge to press my head against his chest.

My heart plummeted.

I was never going to get over him.

I HAD NEVER BEEN INSIDE DEVIN'S CAR BEFORE, and being lowered into the passenger seat sent a weird tingle down my spine. It made me suddenly aware of how little I knew about him outside the realm of the game shop.

It felt so foreign, but it was also exactly what I had expected. The car was a dark grey Ford Escape, not brand-new but no more than a few years old. The backseat was piled with cardboard boxes full of bulk *C&C* cards, but the interior looked freshly vacuumed without any crumbs or dust on the floorboards. A set of fuzzy dice hung from the rearview mirror, bright red and shaped like d20s.

I slumped in my seat as Devin hopped in and turned his key in the ignition. The car roared to life as incredibly loud punk rock music blared from the speakers.

"Sorry," Devin muttered, turning the stereo down and flipping the transmission into reverse. I slouched down further, my body curling in on itself as another wave of pain pummeled my abdomen. I gritted my teeth and squeezed my eyes shut, determined to ride out the worst of it without making a sound. I didn't want Devin to think I was being dramatic.

Once the pain dulled to a low ache, I sat up and tilted my head to the left. Devin was silent, his glassy gaze focused on the road. He looked deep in thought, and I studied his shadowy form in the hazy evening light. He had one arm hanging over the steering wheel, driving with the bottom of his tattooed wrist, while the other hand was plopped on his lap. He wore different jewelry every time I saw him, and tonight that hand was adorned with a black wristband and two silver rings. His fingernails tapped nonchalantly against his jeans as he drove, and an overwhelming ache to slip my hand in his washed over my aching body.

I huffed, quashing the feeling like a candle being snuffed out.

We came to a rolling stop at an intersection, and when it became clear it would be a while until the light turned green, Devin sighed and grabbed the bottom of his sweatshirt. He pulled it over his head, tossing it in the backseat atop the cardboard boxes. His tattooed arms were once again on full display, and it sent a pang of longing down my pain-riddled abdomen.

But it also made my heart ache. Even with the sun almost gone, it was still eighty-five degrees outside, and the car's air conditioning did little to fight off the swampy humidity. I knew Devin took the sweatshirt off because he was warm.

But he also took it off because he had nothing to hide anymore. I'd already seen his scars. I already knew his secrets. And it made me realize that a part of him still trusted me. It made me hope that no matter how badly I'd fucked things up, no matter how callously I'd broken his heart, that we could move past this and be friends.

I gulped. The problem was that I didn't *want* to be friends.

I want to be so much more than frie—

"Gah!" I yelped as my weary body prepared for another round of cramping. My temples throbbed as my fingernails dug into my lower stomach, and I cursed myself for vocalizing my pain. *It's just period cramps. Stop being so dramatic...*

"Here."

Devin's voice was soft, but the car had been so silent that it rattled my eardrums. I managed to stop shaking enough to turn my head, and I noticed his open palm was resting on top of the center console.

"What?"

"You can squeeze my hand if you need to."

A hot bolt of electricity shot through my body, one nearly as painful as my period cramps. My head was swirling with emotions—embarrassment, guilt, fear...but mostly more longing. I'd just fantasized about holding his hand a minute ago, and now here he was offering my heartless self comfort when I didn't deserve it.

"I'm fine, thanks."

To my surprise, Devin didn't pull his hand away. It remained an open invitation just a few inches away from me, and it sent burning pangs of regret through my chest.

It was now nearly dark, but I could hear a long, slow exhale radiating from the driver's seat.

"I wish you'd just tell me why you left last Sunday."

That simple sentence was the most pain I'd felt all night. I peered back over at Devin, and I could see the tension on his face. It strained his cheeks and throat and made his eyes look dull. All this time, I'd assumed he was angry. That he hated me. But he wasn't. He was just...sad.

I opened my mouth, wanting to say a thousand things and yet unable to utter a sound. For Devin, he had nothing left to hide. I already knew his secrets. I couldn't imagine how hard it was to discuss his past, and there I was, too afraid to confess to the man I claimed to want, too afraid to rip open my wounds and be vulnerable.

Devin was the strongest person I knew.

And I was a coward.

Even if I wasn't paralyzed by my own guilt, I was out of time to give him an answer. Devin's car slowed as we pulled into a parking lot, and the blindingly white Emergency Room sign sent a new kind of fear galloping through my veins.

I hated hospitals.

"Here." Devin pulled his key out of the ignition, and the car fell silent. "I'll walk you in."

As I stepped out of the car, he offered me his hand again, but I muttered that I was fine and stumbled past him. It was only a few hundred feet from the car to the entrance, but it felt like miles as I struggled to put one foot in front of the other.

Another wave of pain made my knees buckle, and I felt a firm hand tug me upright.

"C'mon, Avie. You can do it."

He wrapped an arm around my back, and I tried not to focus on how his embrace made my nerves tingle as he dragged me through the giant, automatic glass doors.

It was bright, white, and sterile, and it immediately made me want to vomit. Devin noticed this, and he gripped me tighter as we approached the reception desk.

After chugging through the formalities and paperwork with pain in my abdomen that nearly rivaled childbirth, I plopped down on a hard, teal-colored cushion next to Devin. Now all that was left was to sit in the fluorescent nightmare of a waiting room while my fear of hospitals ate me alive.

"Have you ever noticed how hospital chairs are always the same color?"

"What?" I shook my head, the spontaneity of his odd question jolting my already frayed nerves.

Chapter 14

He slid his phone into his pocket. "Every time I've ever visited a hospital, the chairs are always the same color. It's like a...dull teal-green. I call it hospital green."

My eyes flicked down at the cushion beneath my legs. He did have a point.

"Vomit green would be a better name for it."

Devin chuckled. "Speaking of which, are you alright? You look sick, and not just from your period cramps."

"I hate hospitals," I muttered. Ever since I was a child, I'd never been a fan of visiting the doctor. And the fact that I was about to have my genitals poked and prodded was amplifying that dislike into cold, raw fear.

"Me too," Devin sighed. "Have you ever been in an ER before?"

"No."

"Well, let me give you the rundown. The first thing they always do is give you an IV."

My face immediately paled, and Devin patted me on the back.

"Don't like needles?"

"No. I hate them."

"Funny enough, despite all this—" Devin gestured toward his tattoos and scars. "—I do too. But the IV means they won't have to stick you again if they need to give you meds."

"Alright." My posture softened. I could handle one needle if it meant not dealing with multiple. "What's next?"

"They'll probably run some tests. CT scan, ultrasound, stuff like that. Until they figure out what's wrong with you. And after that...well, it depends on what they find."

I nodded, clasping my hands together to keep them from trembling. My legs were restless, and I bounced up and down on the tips of my toes as we waited. Devin, on the other hand, was completely still, lazily scrolling through his phone as if he were waiting at the DMV. It occurred to me that Devin knew much more about emergency rooms than I would expect from the average person. Then my eyes drifted back to his bare forearms, and a pang of sadness crept into my heart.

"You know, you don't have to stay." My shoulders slumped. "Cass can pick me up later."

Devin looked up from his phone, giving me a suspicious glare. "You're trembling like a chihuahua, and you want me to leave you here alone?"

I huffed, clenching the muscles in my arms. *Crap. He's right. I am shaking.*

"I am not."

To my surprise, he reached out and rubbed my shoulder. It made me want to both flinch away and sink into his touch, just like it had all night.

"You remember how I told you earlier that you're the most stubborn person I know?"

"Uh... yes?"

I didn't know where he was going with this.

"Well..." He cocked his head, a motion that I found adorable despite my situation. "You're also a bad liar."

I frowned. "I—"

"Avery Murphy?"

I snapped my mouth shut at the sound of my name.

Dread settled in my stomach like a rock as I stood up, fear thumping in my chest with every step I took toward the nurse. My nerves quelled slightly when I felt Devin's presence at my backside. He walked just a few inches behind me, ready to assist if another wave of pain made me fall over.

The nurse led me into a small, tiled room that smelled sickeningly of disinfectant and latex gloves. Another nurse, one wearing a surgical mask, awaited me at one of those extra-wide benches with large armrests. It was the same vomit green as the seats outside, and I knew exactly what it was for.

"Alright," she settled me into the oversized chair as she fiddled with her syringes. I was painfully aware of every heartbeat as they pounded like a gong in my chest.

Devin knelt next to me, once again offering his hand. This time I took it, squeezing tight as the nurse wrapped a tourniquet around my other arm. I winced. The tight rubber was almost as painful as the injection itself.

"Ready?"

I took a deep breath. I felt like I was on a rollercoaster at Disney World, about to take the big plunge.

My whole body jolted as the needle breached my skin. I hated the burning sensation it created, like acid being injected into my veins. I could feel my other hand, the one currently locked with Devin's, grow damp and clammy with nervous sweat. I was embarassed, but Devin only squeezed my hand tighter. The pressure was reassuring, like a weighted blanket.

I knew I needed to think of something soothing to get through this. So I let my mind flip back to that night, feeling Devin's lips pressed against mine and his arms gripping my back. I imagined myself embracing him, engulfed by him, like nothing else in the world mattered... and the nerves in my stomach settled.

"There," the nurse announced as she taped a cotton ball to my arm. "All done. Now, grab your things and I'll escort you to a room."

I locked eyes with Devin as I stood up, my arm still sore and stiff from the blood draw.

"You really don't have to stay," I insisted.

Devin chewed his bottom lip, his soft, gentle eyes locked on mine. "I know you're scared, and I don't want to leave you in a hospital all alone. The shop is fine, really. It's only two miles up the street, and Jordan can text me if he needs anything."

I swallowed hard as tears pooled in my eyes. Devin was no longer just a concerned friend. His insistence on staying, his desire to comfort me when I was scared, was his affection welling to the surface.

"Okay." I took his hand and pulled him upright. He placed a hand on my shoulder as we walked into the main ward of the hospital. It was then I realized how much comfort his presence truly brought me. I was a stubborn person, and I would brave the hospital alone if I had to. But there was no denying that I would be terrified.

I felt guilty for keeping him from the game shop.

But I also felt incredibly grateful.

"Hey Devin?" I asked as we walked down the eerily bright hallway.

"Yes?"

I smiled. A true, genuine, warm smile. "Thank you. For everything."

He smiled back. His eyes burned with affection, the same way they had last week.

"For you, always."

Chapter 15

AFTER A FEW HOURS OF SITTING IN A STIFF BED in a curtained off-room, I was itching to leave. The hospital was starting to feel like a prison.

I was exhausted yet restless at the same time - the thin, scratchy blankets offering little warmth or comfort. But I was still more comfortable than Devin, who was hunched over in a plastic chair next to my hospital bed. He spent most of the time scrolling his phone, as there wasn't much else to do between tests, but he always kept one hand locked with mine. I laced my fingers through his, feeling the cold metal of his rings pressing against my skin.

I ached to tell him the truth. In one night, he'd carried my unconscious self into the break room, driven me to the hospital despite my protests, and stayed with me in said hospital for hours. On the surface, it was because he was a kind-hearted person, and I was a friend in need of aid. But I knew it went so much deeper than that. Because he wouldn't be gripping my hand in his, rubbing his thumb along my knuckles, if I was merely a friend to him.

He noticed me staring at him and looked up from his phone. He smiled. It was the same warm, reassuring smile he'd given me all night, and it made me both overjoyed and sick with guilt.

I'd already had multiple tests done. The CT scan was easy, but when it came time for the ultrasound and I realized exactly where that long, thin wand was supposed to go, I panicked. I hated explaining to doctors that vaginal exams were too painful for me to undergo. Thankfully this doctor wasn't pushy, and he offered an abdominal ultrasound instead.

But that came with limits, he had explained. Without a full internal ultrasound or pelvic exam, they couldn't guarantee a good look at my reproductive organs. They could miss something that would normally lead to a diagnosis.

Which was why when the doctor finally made it into the room and told me all findings were normal, I nearly cried out in frustration. Even though I'd protested going to the hospital, once we were there, I was desperate for a diagnosis. I wanted there to be something wrong so that they could fix it.

No findings meant that I was stuck without answers.

Maybe my period pain really is just me being dramatic.

"Should I leave the room?" Devin asked, turning towards me.

I nodded. If I needed to disclose further information about my reproductive history, it was best that he did not hear it.

Devin released my hand and stood up, brushing the curtains out of the way as he left. The space between my fingers suddenly felt very empty without him.

"No findings means that we've ruled out most causes, such as ovarian cysts," The doctor continued. "But that also leaves us with another possible diagnosis."

Chapter 15

My ears perked up, and I sat upright, hanging on her words.

"I think you have endometriosis."

Endo—what?

Wait...

I had heard of that condition before. It was mentioned on the medical websites when I did my initial internet searches, and the pelvic physical therapist mentioned it during my session.

"What is that?"

"It's a condition where endometrial tissue, the kind that lines your uterus, grows in other parts of your body," the doctor explained. "It can stick to other organs in your abdomen and bind them together, causing a variety of health issues."

"What kinds of health issues?"

"It varies between cases, but common symptoms are severely painful or abnormal periods, digestion issues, bladder issues, sexual dysfunction, and..."

Upon hearing the last symptom, my torso shot up out of bed.

WHAT!?

"Sexual dysfunction?" I repeated, unsure if I'd heard her correctly.

"Yes. A lot of women with endometriosis suffer from painful sex or have difficulty with penetration."

I sat upright, frozen and stiff as a board, as my mind pieced together the reality of my diagnosis. *My sexual issues aren't all just in my head? There's actually something wrong with me?*

It felt nauseating and liberating at the same time. I wasn't imagining things. I was broken, but in a way that could be fixed.

A single hospital trip had just lifted years of emotional baggage off my shoulders. It was hard for me to process. The whole room seemed to swirl, like my head was stuck underwater.

"How do you treat endometriosis?" The question hurriedly shot out of my mouth.

"Well, the endometrial tissue won't show up in standard medical scans. The only way to get a confirmed diagnosis is through surgery. It's called a laparoscopy, and it's a minimally invasive procedure that only takes a few hours. It won't cure your endometriosis, but it will significantly improve your symptoms. There's a gynecological surgeon in Lakeland who specializes in endometriosis—I'll give you his contact information. Now, do you have any other questions?"

I had a million. But I was also eager to leap out of the hospital bed and return to Critical Games, so I decided to save my questions for the surgeon.

"Nope," I shook my head. "I'll contact the surgeon first thing tomorrow morning."

"Excellent." The nurse clasped her hands together. "I'll put together your discharge paperwork, and a nurse will be in shortly to administer some pain medication. It was a pleasure meeting you, Avery."

"Likewise."

As she walked away, she tilted her head over her shoulder. "Want me to let your boyfriend back in?"

"He's not..."

Oh fuck it. There was no point in correcting her.

"Um, yes, please, you can let him in."

She disappeared behind the rustling curtain, and Devin re-emerged a few seconds later. I couldn't help but notice the smug grin stretched across his face.

Chapter 15

"The doc said I could come back in," he said in a sing-song tone as he plopped back in his plastic chair. "To see my *girlfriend*."

I rolled my eyes as a hot, red flush tinted my cheeks.

"So what did she say?" he asked.

I sighed. "The doctor said I have a condition called endometriosis."

"What's that?"

"Long story short, it's a disease that causes a bunch of reproductive issues. She said I'm going to need surgery."

"Surgery?" Devin's eyebrows raised.

"She said it's minimally invasive. Shouldn't be a big deal." I tried to shrug it off, but on the inside my chest was quivering. I hated just stepping foot in hospitals, let alone being cut open in one.

Devin scoffed, as if he didn't believe me. But his gaze was warm and gentle as he rubbed my shoulder.

"I owe you another big thank you, by the way," I noted.

"What do you mean?"

"For insisting I come here. If it weren't for you, I never would've gotten a diagnosis."

"Well..." Devin shrugged. "You would've gone to the doctor sooner or later and found out."

I raised a disbelieving eyebrow. "Devin, I *really* hate hospitals. But you helped me face my fear tonight. So thank you. I owe you one."

"You're welcome." He smiled. "And you don't *owe* me anything, but I do have one question that I'd like you to answer."

"What is it?"

He took a long, deep breath, and my body tensed with anticipation.

"These medical issues you're having..." He paused, raking a hand through his hair. "They're not related to... you leaving me last week, are they?"

His words were like a punch to the stomach. He knew. There was no point in hiding it anymore.

Something burst within me, like a balloon filled with too much helium, and I exploded into sobs. I could barely breathe as I buried my face in my hands, both hysterical and mortified by my outburst.

"God, Avery..." Devin's eyes glistened with sympathy, and he wrapped his arms around my trembling body. He pulled me tight against his chest, squeezing me with more force than I'd ever felt from a hug in my life. It crushed my chest and made breathing even harder, but it also sent a wave of warm reassurance through my body. I reciprocated his embrace, pressing my fingers against his scalp and admiring the softness of his jet-black hair.

"Yes," I sputtered between sobs. "I...I have to...tell...you... something..."

God, I was a mess. My cheeks were crusty with tears, I didn't even want to know how terrible my puffy red face looked in a mirror. *Devin must think I'm a wreck.*

He pulled away, and his gaze showed nothing but compassion as he rubbed my thick, curly brown hair with his fingers. He looked at me as if I were the only woman in the world, and it made my brittle heart crack even more.

Because I was about to tell him the truth.

"I can't have sex." I blurted it out all at once, like ripping off a bandage. "At least...I've never been able to. It's too painful. The doctor thinks the endometriosis is what's causing it."

Devin nodded slowly, taking a few seconds to process the information.

"So you're a virgin?"

Chapter 15

"Yes."

"And... you thought I wouldn't want to be with you because of it?"

I burst into another round of sobs before I could reply. Hot, salty tears poured down my neck and stained the hospital blankets.

"Avie, I'm so sorry." He cupped my puffy, tear-stained cheeks in his palms. "It's okay. Really. It's not a big deal. We'll figure it out."

"I'm hoping the surgery helps...but even after that... I don't know how long it will be before I can have sex. Are you sure you're okay wi—"

"Yes," Devin replied, cutting me off with a firm, definitive answer. "Absolutely."

I blinked in disbelief. "Really?"

Devin chuckled, leaning back in his chair. He raised a dark eyebrow. "You know what I think?"

I gulped. "What?"

"I think you seriously underestimate how much I want to be with you."

His declaration shook me to the core. It made me stop crying, but it also left me paralyzed, unable to sputter out a response.

"It's been *years*, Avie. Five years of watching you turn from a timid college kid into the most incredible woman I've ever met. And these past few months, it really hit me hard. You were always on that dating app, meeting other people...I told myself I could handle being just friends. But I still ached for a chance with you. I thought about you all the time. I told myself I was going insane. I even confessed to my old friend Scott about my feelings. And you know what he told me? He said—and I quote— 'nut up and do something about it'. Well, now's my chance, and I'm not going to let it slip away. So no, the sex thing isn't a big deal. I'll wait however long you need."

"But what if—"

"No buts." Devin cut me off, placing a finger against my lips. "You're not getting rid of me that easily."

I grinned as more tears slid down my face. Then the giggles escaped me, and I sat there in my hospital bed, both laughing and crying while Devin gripped his hands in mine and smiled at me like nothing else mattered.

It was a horrible, messy, beautiful, perfect moment, one I would remember for the rest of my life.

Once the laughter died down, he pulled me towards him and placed his lips on mine. I kissed him back eagerly, and all my anxiety melted into thin air. This wasn't like our frenzied tryst in the storage room. There was no eager exploring of each other, no pushing the limits of our budding relationship. This was a simple, warm, comforting kiss. One that told me how much he cared. How everything was going to be okay.

It was his promise that he still wanted me, regardless of my sexual issues.

He broke our kiss first, glancing at me for a moment with those adoring eyes before pressing my head against his chest.

We remained there, locked in a peaceful embrace, until the nurse came back to send us both home.

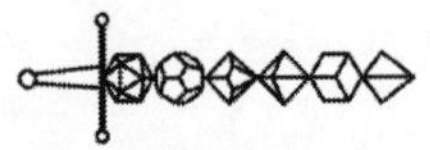

I HAD NO IDEA WHAT SORT OF PAIN MEDS THEY'D given me.

But I felt *fantastic*.

Chapter 15

My head floated in the clouds as I sat slumped in the passenger seat of Devin's car, humming along to his punk rock music while he drove down the dark city streets. We'd been at the hospital for hours, mainly because of how long we were waiting between tests, and pre-release was over by the time we made it back to Critical Games.

Jordan was still there, but Cassidy had just left.

Which meant Devin had to drive me home.

But as I sat in the car, my hand interlocked with his as I laid my head against the back of my seat, I wondered if I was even in proper shape to drive. The medication had eliminated my pain, and that alone was incredibly euphoric after enduring god-awful cramps for hours. But I also felt strangely...happy. Too happy.

Devin must've found it hilarious, because he kept snickering to himself as I belted out song lyrics in a very off-key tone.

"You're adorable," he remarked as we pulled into my neighborhood.

"No..." My body wavered in my seat. I extended a shaky hand across the center console and stroked his hair. "You're... adorable..."

"Avie, I'm driving." He smirked, pulling my hand away.

I normally knew better than to harass someone driving a car. But my head was still swimming in a fishbowl, and with my period pain quelled, it awoke a ravenous craving for my newly minted boyfriend. My hand reached across the seat again, this time landing on the soft denim fabric lining his inner thigh.

"Avie," he scolded as pulled my hand away. But despite how obnoxious I was being, Devin didn't seem frustrated. In fact, he looked like he was holding back laughter.

"Let's save that for when you're not drugged, silly," he remarked as we pulled into the driveway of my townhouse.

Thankfully, I had still been lucid enough to give him my address.

"Nice place." He turned his keys in the ignition and hopped out of the driver's seat, looping around to help my drug-addled self out of the car. "Looks a lot like my own."

"You live in a townhouse toooo?" My words slurred as Devin lifted an arm around my shoulders and hoisted me out of the car. I plodded forward, my body wobbling like a top with every step. "You should carry me agaaaaiinnn. Pleeease?"

Devin rolled his eyes, covering his mouth with his hand to hide his laughter. "C'mon loopy, it's only a few steps to the front door."

We managed to make it inside without me falling, but my unstable body practically spilled into the front hallway once Devin opened the door. Cassidy was sitting on the living room couch, waiting for me to arrive home.

"Avery!" she exclaimed, running towards us. She stopped and backed up a few steps once she realized how incoherent I was. "Uh...are you okay?"

"I'm fiiiiiiine." I mumbled as I wobbled in place.

Devin walked up behind me and wrapped his arm around my back, steadying my jelly-like spine and preventing me from collapsing.

"What did you do to her, dude?" Cassidy teased, crossing her arms over her chest.

"Oh hush, Cass," Devin retorted, his bicep straining as he held me upright. "The docs gave her heavy-duty pain meds, so she's high as a kite. I'm sure it'll wear off by morning."

Devin began walking my weary self towards my room, and Cassidy raised an eyebrow.

"You escorting her to bed?" she asked in a suspicious tone.

Devin scoffed, a wry smile on his face. "What else do you suggest, letting her fall asleep on the floor?"

Chapter 15

"I'm fiiiiiine," I lied, pressing a palm against Devin's chest. My lurking hand crept further up his shirt and slipped under his collar. I grinned seductively as my fingers traced his bare skin.

Cassidy burst out laughing. "Damn. What was in those drugs? She's all over you."

Devin shook his head, pulling my hand out of his shirt as he dragged me into my bedroom. I heard Cassidy shout something behind us as Devin closed the door, but I was too spaced out to comprehend it.

It was almost midnight, and in addition to being high on pain meds, I was also exhausted.

But that didn't stop me from pulling Devin into my lap once he helped me crawl into bed.

"You little tease," Devin growled in my ear. He tried to pull away, but I grabbed his wrists and pulled him back toward me.

"Deeeeev," I whined in a comically seductive tone. "Come hereeeeee."

He relented, and his body fell on top of mine again. I pressed kisses against his neck while he struggled to fight off my advances. I was in no shape for intimacy, but I knew Devin wanted me just as much as my drug-addled self wanted him. And that made it hard for him to say no.

One of my hands worked its way up his back, rubbing the muscles behind his shoulders, while the other one reached for his belt buckle. I was nearly there, loosening the strap with my shaky fingers, when he suddenly grasped my hand in his.

"Avie," he laughed. "That's enough. We're not doing this while you're drugged."

"Plllleeeeease?" I plopped another kiss on his cheek. A reluctant sigh of pleasure slipped out of him, breezing past my ear. At that moment, the pain meds weren't the only thing I was high on.

"Wear a condom!" Cassidy's shout carried from her bedroom.

Devin cringed and spun around, an exasperated frown on his face.

"Shut up Cass!" he shouted back across the townhouse.

I exploded into giggles, and Devin shook his head. An embarrassed smile caused his pale cheeks to tint pink.

He turned back to me, tucking a lock of curls behind my ear. "Sleep well, Avie. I'll text you in the morning."

"But..."

"No buts." He laughed as he stepped toward my door, cupping a hand around the brass-colored handle.

"Goodnight, my little drugged sweetheart."

He flicked off the light and disappeared through my door, leaving my loopy self alone in the silence of my dark bedroom. But as much as my heart ached for him not to leave, it was also buzzing at the fact that he'd called me *sweetheart*.

That word floated through my head, a soft and honeyed nickname that looped like a lullaby, until I descended into sleep.

Chapter 16

I DIDN'T KNOW IF IT WAS A SIDE EFFECT OF THE drugs or exhaustion from one of the most overwhelming nights of my life, but I slept until almost noon the next morning.

When my eyelids first fluttered open, it took a moment for it to all come back to me. I repeated each event to myself, one by one, as I attempted to piece it all together.

I had fainted during prerelease night. Devin took me to the hospital. I found out that both my period pain and my sexual issues were the result of a medical condition, and they could be fixed.

Also... I sat up, running my fingers through my messy curls. *I think Devin and I are...together now?*

Sprinkled in between the facts of the night before, I relived all the emotions I'd felt. I remembered the way he looked at me in the hospital room. The way my heart exploded like fireworks when we kissed. How this time, there were no more secrets. No more running away. I'd finally confessed, and he still wanted me.

Lastly, I remembered my hormonal, drug-addled self attempting to seduce him in my bedroom.

And that part made my cheeks flush with embarrassment.

Concerns still lurked in the back of my brain. I feared that he might change his mind down the road, depending on how long my sexual issues lasted. Even after I recovered from the surgery, I didn't know if I'd be able to do the deed right away.

Surgery.

My stomach fell. I'd never had surgery before. Not even for my wisdom teeth, which were still buried well beneath my gums.

A faint tap on the door knocked me back to reality. There could be only one person standing outside my bedroom, and I knew that she was itching for details on the night before.

"Hi Cass," I greeted with a smile as I swung the door open.

She stood with her arms crossed in the hallway, her eyebrows narrowed and a knowing smile spread across her face.

"Alright. Tell me everything."

"*Everything?*" I trilled in a sarcastic tone as I raised an eyebrow. "Not sure if I can do that. I was pretty messed up last night."

"He didn't... did he?"

"What? No." I shook my head. "He tucked my delirious self in bed and left."

"Good."

"I may have protested, though."

Cassidy laughed. "Just to clarify—you're together now? You figured out whatever mess happened last week?"

I sighed. I'd already braved telling Devin the truth; I needed to tell my best friend my secret too.

Chapter 16

"Yeah...I have a lot of explaining to do. And so do you, missy! What happened with you and Aaron?"

Cassidy's smile disappeared, and her arms unwound from her chest and fell by her sides. "That also involves a lot of explaining. I'll tell you what, I haven't had a full weekend off in forever, so let's go do something fun."

"Like what?"

Cassidy pursed her lips, taking a moment to think. "Well, if I'm gonna tell Aaron the truth and he still wants to go on a date, I need some clothes. I just rummaged through my closet, and all I have are work scrubs and geeky t-shirts. I need some cute dresses."

I perked up at the thought of going shopping. It had been *ages* since we'd had a girls' day.

"Absolutely," I grinned. "Let me just shower and get dressed. Give me twenty minutes?"

"Of course. I need to get dressed too. Also..." Cassidy plopped a blue flower-clad phone in my hand. "You left this in the kitchen last night. I heard it buzz earlier."

Realization zapped through my brain as I flipped open my phone screen. Just as I'd expected, I had a text from Devin. One that was sent three hours ago.

Crap. It was almost noon and he hadn't heard from me.

"Have fun chatting with your new boyfriend!" Cassidy grinned as she sauntered down the hallway and returned to her bedroom.

Once I was back on my bed, lying on my stomach with my body propped up on my elbows like a seal, I flipped open my messages.

Good morning Avie. You still drugged?

I scoffed. What a romantic greeting.

Aw c'mon. I don't get a "good morning beautiful," or something like that?

I could feel anticipation humming in my veins as soon as I hit send. But it must've been quiet at Critical Games, because the typing bubble appeared just a few minutes later.

Ah, of course. Let me try again. Good morning, my beautiful little Avie. You still drugged?

No. I am not.

Aw, bummer. That was pretty funny.

Yeah, yeah. I may have been all over you last night, but you're still a pain.

I promise that will never change.

Anyway, how's the shop?

Fine. Slow. Saturdays are Wargavel days, but the nerds don't generally start filing in here until two. Leaves me plenty of time to punch hundreds of cardboard pieces out of the new board games I ordered for the shop. Fun stuff.

Do you play Wargavel?

I know the rules, and I've played a few games. But I already have boxes full of D&D minis in my spare bedroom. If I got into Wargavel, my whole house would be overrun. Anyway, what are you doing today?

Chapter 16

Going shopping with Cass.

Nice. You need a fun day after everything that happened last night. I'll be at the shop late tonight, but will you be at C&C tomorrow?

Of course.

Awesome. You get to watch me entertain a table full of preteens. But the shop closes at five on Sundays, and I was wondering if you were free afterward?

Warm tingles ran down my limbs and made my heart gallop in my chest. It had finally happened.

You asking me out?

Absolutely. A completely unrelated question: what's your favorite kind of food?

Hmmm…definitely Greek food. My mom is Greek, and I grew up on her cooking.

Interesting. I love Greek food. There's a gyro shop next to Critical Games that I sometimes grab lunch from. Did you have any Greek restaurants in mind, or should I start searching?

My smile stretched so far that my cheeks started to hurt. In all the dates I'd ever been on, no one had ever asked what my favorite food was. The guys I met on my app often picked a place for us. They usually chose a bar, which made it awkward since I didn't drink.

Yes. It's in Oviedo, though, which is a bit far from the shop.

I don't mind. What's it called?

It's called Olive Tree Café. Although the sign out front just says, "Greek Food". It's a tiny little hole in the wall, but I go there every few weeks because it reminds me so much of home.

Is that where you'd like to go tomorrow night?

I paused. Part of me felt like I should pick a more... *formal* restaurant for my first date with Devin. But the thought of bringing him to one of my favorite places made me feel warm and happy. I went there often enough that the owners knew me. It wasn't a place I'd take a guy from my dating app to. But Devin was different.

Yes.

Perfect. Do I need to make a reservation?

No. Trust me, it's a tiny little café. You ok with that?

Yes. I am perfectly happy going anywhere with you.

Goddamnit. My face flushed red.

Chapter 16

Alright, Olive Tree Café it is.

Sweet. Hang back after C&C. I just need to take care of a few things before the shop closes. And heads up, I won't be very responsive this afternoon. Wargavel day keeps me busy.

Of course. I understand. Anyway, I need to get ready for shopping with Cass.

You do that. Goodbye Avie.

He ended his final message to me with a bright red heart. One that made my own heart flutter in my chest.

I sat my phone down on my desk, my mind still processing what had just happened.

I had a date.

With Devin Lancaster.

The snarky game shop owner I had been annoyed by for five years.

But...was I really annoyed? Details of our years of banter flicked through my mind, and I pondered the tone in which our exchanges were said. The look on Devin's face every time I stepped foot in the game shop. It wasn't the look of someone who dreaded seeing me.

It occurred to me that, even though I couldn't see my own face, I probably had that look too.

I'd been falling in love with him at a snail's pace without even realizing it.

Another warm smile stretched across my face. It stayed there as I showered, got dressed, and departed the townhouse with Cassidy.

I saw it reflected back at me in the rearview mirror as I turned my car on.

Yup.

Definitely falling in love with him.

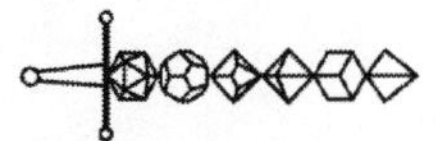

CASSIDY WAS EAGER FOR ME TO TELL HER THE full story as soon as we pulled out of our neighborhood. I watched out of the corner of my eye, pleading like an expectant puppy, and laughed.

"Alright, alright." I sighed. "God...where do I begin?"

"Let's start with what happened between the two of you after PvP night ended," Cassidy declared. "Did he confess his feelings? Did you?"

"Uh...it was sort of mutual."

"Let me guess...at some point, you two ended up alone in the shop together."

I cringed, my eyes twitching. *God, was it that obvious?*

"Yeah. We talked, and, well, turns out we're more alike than I thought."

"It took you *five years* to realize that?" Cassidy exclaimed. "I knew you two were meant for each other within a few months of meeting you."

"*What*!? You never told me about this!"

Cassidy shrugged. "He's like a decade older than you. And you didn't seem like you wanted a relationship at the time."

I nodded, my gaze locked on the road as I pulled up to a red light. *She's right. I wasn't ready back then. I don't even know if I'm ready now.*

"Anyway," Cassidy continued. "What happened that night? I'd assumed one of you rejected the other, but you both looked upset last night at prerelease."

My stomach clenched. That was where things got messy. But if I could handle telling the truth to Devin, the person I'd eventually end up being intimate with, then I could handle telling Cassidy. After all, she was my best friend.

"I can't have sex," I blurted out, in much the same way I'd done in the hospital with Devin. "It turns out I have a condition called endometriosis, which is also why my periods are so bad."

"Endometriosis? What's that?"

"The doctor at the ER explained it to me, but the details are still sort of fuzzy." I rubbed my head. "I meant to do more research on it later today. But long story short, I need surgery. Soon."

Cassidy's eyebrows shot up in alarm. *"Surgery*? God, Avery, I'm so sorry."

"It's alright," I lied, remembering how badly I'd been trembling at the hospital the night before. "The doctor said it's minimally invasive. It shouldn't be too bad."

"So all this time, with all that online dating...is that why you never found anyone? Is that why Tristan ended things?"

I didn't respond, but Cassidy could tell by the way my face hardened and my knuckles clenched the steering wheel what the answer was.

"God," she continued. "I didn't know any of this. We've... been really distant from each other lately, haven't we?"

I nodded, tightening the muscles in my throat to keep from crying.

"It's habit," I replied after a few moments of silence. "I bottle things up. I guess that's what happens when you flee a controlling family and try to make it on your own. It's hard."

"I feel that. My parents are poor as dirt and still chose to have six kids. I was almost completely on my own as soon as I turned eighteen."

A small crackle of realization seeped through my heart like electricity as I realized that my relationship with Cassidy was much like my relationship with Devin. We'd known each other for years, bonding over geeky hobbies and silly jokes, but we never prodded beneath our superficial exteriors. I didn't know much about Cassidy's life before I met her. I hadn't even known she had five siblings.

I decided that was something I needed to work on. My past caused me to avoid difficult conversations like the plague, which in turn made my emotions pressurize within me until they eventually burst. From then on, I vowed to be a more open, honest person. Not just with the people around me, but also with myself.

"But yeah, to wrap up my story," I continued. "when Devin dragged me to the hospital, I told him everything."

"And it didn't scare him away, did it?"

A warm, reminiscent smile lit up my face. "No. It didn't."

"God, that's so sweet." Cassidy sunk into her seat, her eyes hazy with longing. "I stayed up for a while after Devin put your drugged self to bed. I didn't know the full details at the time, but I knew that whatever had happened between you two, you managed to work past it. And it made me realize that I needed to do the same with Aaron."

"What do you mean?" I asked. "Did you reject him over personal issues too?"

Cassidy gave a dark chuckle, one laced with sadness. "Funny enough, yes. I also have a medical issue that I've never told you about. And now it's time."

"What is it?"

Cassidy's back stiffened as she took a deep breath. "I have herpes."

Chapter 16

I felt the blood drain from my limbs as I processed her words. "Wait, what?!"

"Yeah." Her gaze fell into her lap. "I never told you why things ended with my ex. Well...he cheated on me. That's how I ended up with an STD."

"God, Cass, I'm so sorry."

"It's okay. It's funny, because my story is so similar to yours. I was terrified that no one would want to be with me. That's why I haven't dated in the three years since Brian and I broke up. It's no secret that I want to be with Aaron, but people tend to run as soon as you mention an STD. So, when he confessed his feelings to me the night of the PvP event, I panicked and told him I didn't feel the same."

"And clearly, that's not true."

"Yeah." Her voice sank like a deflated balloon. "And I think he knows it, too. He even asked if we could talk last night at pre-release, and I brushed him off. But knowing that you and Devin are working past your sexual stuff...it made me realize maybe Aaron and I can too."

"He's crazy about you," I replied. "I think there's a good chance he'll be understanding if you explain things."

"Yup. That's what I plan to do. The truth is, if we use protection and don't have sex when I'm having an outbreak, the risk of transmission is extremely low. And even if it is a dealbreaker for him...well, it's better than awkwardly avoiding him for the rest of my life."

"I feel that. It's funny, when I was riding in the car with Devin to the ER, he really wanted to know why I rejected him. He looked so...sad. And when I finally told him, he swore he didn't care. He acted like it was no big deal."

"That's wonderful." Cassidy smiled, but it didn't quite wash away the anxiety in her eyes. "I hope the same happens for me too."

"I'm glad we had this talk." I flipped my turn signal on as we approached the entrance to the mall. "But for the rest of today, let's just focus on having fun. It's been a *long* week."

"Agreed. But before we try on clothes...can we stop at the bookstore?"

I grinned as the familiar large, concrete structure came into view. "Of course. In fact, I was about to suggest the same thing."

Chapter 17

Cassidy and I spent the rest of the day together. We browsed through the mall the entire afternoon, alternating between trying on clothes in the department stores and sitting in the bookstore café with iced coffees and piles of fantasy novels.

By the end of the day, we both had a small pile of shopping bags dumped on the floor next to our café table. But it wasn't just the thrill of bringing home new dresses and books that had me feeling relaxed and content. Shopping at a mall was nostalgic; it reminded me of my time as a teenager with my old high school friends, taking silly photos of ourselves in homecoming dresses until the sales clerk kicked us out. It was a time before online shopping and home deliveries, when malls were still the epicenter of activity on the weekends.

Now, the tiny mall near our condo was too decrepit to step foot into; full of empty storefronts, twitchy fluorescent lighting, and a dirty food court that even the popular fast-food chains had abandoned. Cassidy swore it was cursed. I joked that it was so creepy that they should run a haunted house there in October.

We had driven thirty minutes into the city center to shop at the bigger mall, one of the few left in Orlando worth visiting. After browsing the bookstore for another hour, we chucked our coffee cups and packed our acquired goods into my Camry. Cassidy teased me about popping into Critical Games and messing with Devin. After all, it was on our way home. I said hell no. I was not going to harass my new boyfriend while he was working.

"I don't think you'll be the one doing the harassing," Cassidy replied with a smirk.

"Oh shut up."

We stopped to go grocery shopping on the way home, and Cassidy insisted that we load up on ice cream. We spent the evening playing co-op games on her PlayStation, and once the sun set, we broke out the sugary desserts and watched YouTube videos until it was nearly midnight.

Once I'd finished my ice cream and tiredness began to seep into my bones, I turned off the television and rolled off the couch. Cassidy was asleep on the loveseat, her tall figure squished onto the tiny couch with a blanket draped over her legs. Her empty ice cream pint was on the floor, with wet drops of condensation dripping onto the linoleum. I chuckled as I scooped up her empty container and tossed it in the trash.

It had been months since we'd hung out like this. Spending a whole day together, laughing, talking, having conversations about our lives. We'd been living more like roommates and less like best friends ever since we moved in together.

I took a long, deep breath of contentment as I settled under the comforters in my dark bedroom.

It had been a good day.

And Sunday would be even better.

Chapter 17

I'd texted Devin sporadically throughout the evening when he wasn't busy with *Wargavel*, and now that I was alone in bed, I missed him. I both loved and despised the feeling. On one hand, I was thrilled that we were finally together. But I also felt weird about pining for a man I was yet to have a proper date with.

Either way, the thought of him sent warm, fuzzy pulses through my body as I succumbed to sleep. And I ended up dreaming about him that night.

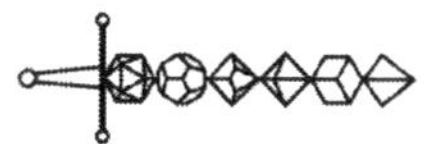

I WOKE UP EARLIER THAN USUAL THE NEXT MORNING. I spent extra time on my hair, making sure my curls were perfect ringlets instead of a frizzy mess. I laid three sundresses on my bed before deciding on a light purple one, and I slipped a quartz crystal necklace that Cassidy had given me over my head. It settled perfectly in the center of my chest, right above my cleavage. Which, conveniently, this dress showed off a tiny bit of.

It was perfect. Which meant Cassidy immediately commented on it once I walked out the door.

"Aw, dressing up for your boyfriend?"

I glanced down, smoothing out the bottom of my dress. "Well, I figured I wouldn't go to dinner with him in jeans and a t-shirt."

Cassidy's eyes widened to the size of dinner plates. "Oh, I forgot! Your date is right after the shop closes. Well, I hope you two have fun."

"We will."

"Let me know if you need any... privacy in the townhouse afterward."

"Cass! It's just dinner. I'm not ready for that yet."

A smug smile made her eyes narrow. "You certainly were when you were drugged."

"Oh my god," I scoffed as I grabbed my purse off its hanger. "You're as impossible as he is. Now let's go."

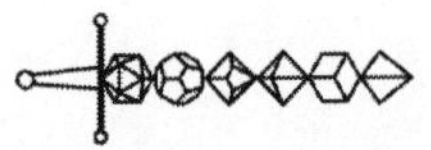

MY HEART WAS GIDDY WITH HAPPINESS BY THE TIME Cassidy and I made it through the doors of Critical Games.

The shop was packed for *Creatures & Crypts* day, with the six tables occupied by full parties and strewn with books, character sheets, dice, and miniatures. Several patrons hovered around the front counter, picking up last-minute supplies. And at the register, typing away at his computer as he rang up a teenager buying dice, was my current favorite person in the world.

He only looked at me for a moment, but it was enough time for me to see the adoring sparkle in his eyes. My gaze was focused on the black ring around his pointer finger as he fiddled with the credit card reader. He wore a long-sleeved black t-shirt with a heavy metal band logo, one whose font was too scratchy for me to read. I also noticed that both sleeves were rolled up, revealing his colorful tattoo-clad forearms.

I wondered if he'd been feeling less self-conscious about his scars lately. Or maybe it was because it was nearly a hundred degrees outside and air conditioning was expensive. Either way, it made me happy to see him feeling so confident. In all the years I'd known him, it had never occurred to me how handsome he was.

I sighed, eager for his attention but not wanting to look like a needy puppy. So I scurried away to Sam's table, where the heavyset, heavily bearded CM greeted me with an enthusiastic smile.

Chapter 17

"Good afternoon, Avery. Cassidy." He adjusted his CM screen. Sam was older, likely in his fifties, and had a deep voice and a warm, fatherly personality. He was a regular at Critical Games and beloved by everyone, much like Devin. I knew the two of them were close, with Devin occasionally attending board game nights at Sam's huge house out in the suburbs.

Cassidy and I settled down at the table, engaging in friendly conversation about the past week's events while we waited for everyone else to arrive. Ten minutes later, I noticed Devin make his way to his table, where six preteen boys squabbled in their seats.

"Alright, it looks like everyone's here!" he announced. "For the newbies: we run four-hour sessions here, so we'll be wrapping up around 4:30. Feel free to begin!"

A warm pulse flickered in my chest. I swore Devin's gaze had locked on me several times during his announcement.

I loved our current homebrew session, one set in the dinosaur-occupied land of Atali, but that afternoon I struggled to keep my focus. It was especially bad whenever we entered combat and I had to wait for my turn. That was when my eyes began to drift over to Devin's table.

Critical Games was a very family-friendly place, but it could be hard to find a Crypt Master willing to work with a group full of preteen boys. Most of the CMs wanted to hang out with their own friends, and when the kids acted up it could feel a lot like an unpaid babysitting job.

But Devin was a natural. His over-the-top playstyle managed to keep the squirrely kids engaged, and he had the patience to rapidly quell arguments or tell the freckly redhead in the far corner to put his phone away for the third time. It had been particularly bad a few months earlier, when Devin had to separate a physical fight between two of the boys who were known for not getting along.

But tonight, all was well. The kids erupted in giggles when Devin started up his ridiculous Scottish barkeep accent, and they were all squabbling to be the first one to pull a quest off the job board. While the rest of the CMs were comfortably perched in their chairs, Devin was standing up, moving his arms in wild motions when the kids entered a battle. I wondered if he preferred to be standing since he was on his feet all day managing the shop.

I watched as he pulled a large, bright green dragon miniature from behind his CM screen, plopping it dramatically in the middle of the gaming map. The kids erupted in shouts and laughter, and Devin cackled like the maniacal Crypt Master that he always was.

I was smiling so much my face hurt.

I couldn't believe it took me five years to realize how much I adored that man.

"Uh, Avery?"

My head snapped back toward my own table. Sam was staring expectantly at me.

"Your turn."

"Oh, I, uh..." *Shit.* I had no idea what had happened the past few combat turns, and didn't know which enemy would be best to hit.

"You make it so obvious," Cassidy whispered under her breath, a stupid taunting grin on her face.

My face hardened as I forced myself not to react to Cassidy's teasing.

"Hush," I muttered. "I need to focus."

"What are we making obvious?" Sam asked with a raised eyebrow. Cassidy was sitting right next to him, meaning that even at a whisper, he heard everything she said.

I cringed. *Goddamnit Cass.*

"Avery and Devin are dating," Cassidy blurted out.

"Cass!!"

Chapter 17

Suddenly we had the entire table's attention. Some of the players were shocked, while others shared knowing glances. My face burned red as I realized our thinly veiled flirting over the years may have been more obvious than I realized.

"Oh really? Can't say I'm surprised," Sam grinned. "You know, I may have prodded Devin about his thoughts on the ladies here a few months ago. With most of them, he shrugged. But when I mentioned you…well, he denied it like hell. That's how I knew he was into you."

The table erupted in laughter, and I covered my face with my palms to avoid exposing my tomato-red face.

Yup. Definitely more obvious than I realized.

The giggling eventually died down, though I knew the gossip wouldn't for a long time. I shot Devin another quick glance before sinking into my seat. *Pay attention,* I scolded myself. *Focus on Devin tonight at dinner. Not now.*

And I did just that for the rest of the afternoon. I engrossed myself in our campaign, studying our scenarios to determine the best use of my spells. I was even able to use a *Repair* spell to fix a busted wheel on our party's horse-drawn carriage. We still got ambushed by bandits, but at least we didn't have to walk on foot to the next town afterward.

The hours flew by, and it was nearly 4 p.m. when I realized I'd chugged my seltzer water too quickly and needed to use the restroom. As I stood up and walked away from the table, I got the first glimpse of Devin's group that I'd had in a while. He wasn't at the table, and the boys were currently bickering over who had the fanciest dice set.

The restrooms were right next to the storage room, and I was so lost in thought that I hardly noticed a figure emerge from there. What I did notice was that figure pausing next to me and grabbing my hip.

I jolted, even as my body warmed to his touch.

"*Devin,*" I hissed under my breath.

He pulled away and stepped backward, a cocky grin on his face, "What? It was an accident."

"It was not!" I frowned. "We can't be acting all couple-y in the middle of—!"

He leaned forward and planted a kiss on my cheek, which left me a stuttering, red-faced mess.

"That was also an accident." He smirked as he walked back towards the gaming tables. "Your cheek was in the way."

Once Devin was gone and I had recovered from the sudden rush of affection, I scanned the crowd to make sure no one had noticed his antics. All six tables were deeply focused on their game, and not a single pair of eyes were glancing in my direction.

Good, I huffed as I opened the restroom door. But as I finished up and returned to my seat, I couldn't ignore that feeling. The intoxicating burn of attraction, the all-consuming desire for more; the way his touch seeped into my skin like a healing balm.

I couldn't help but smile to myself as we wrapped up our session.

Devin was always going to drive me nuts.

And I would always be wanting more of it.

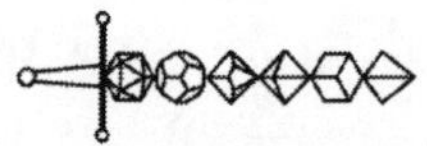

I LINGERED AROUND THE SHOP AFTER *CREATURES & Crypts* ended, saying goodbye to my friends while I kept tabs on Devin out of the corner of my eye. A few patrons hung around to make some last-minute purchases, which kept him busy at the register. I kept myself occupied by studying the vast wall of miniatures on the far-left wall, near the *Wargavel* tables. There were hundreds of them. I couldn't believe Devin had painted them all himself.

Chapter 17

The last few bits of chatter died down, and before I could realize we were the last two people in the shop, Devin swept in behind me and pulled me in for a kiss.

I practically melted against the game shop wall as the rest of the world blurred around me. I had needed this all day. I needed this every day.

He broke away, a huge, beaming grin on his face as he stroked my cheek.

"Let me guess," I taunted. "That was also an accident?"

"Of course not," Devin squeezed my waist as he walked away. "That was very much intentional. Now, this is the less exciting part of our date. I've gotta clean up, cash out, and grab my stuff. Should take about thirty minutes."

"I can help," I offered.

"Not a chance," he replied as he rolled a vacuum out of the storage room. "You sit and relax. I won't be long."

The vacuum whirred to life with a loud, hollow roar as I plopped down in a chair by the *Wargavel* tables.

"Boys, seriously?" I heard Devin mutter to himself over the sound of the vacuum. "So many crumbs..."

I chuckled. Like most game shops, Devin had a shelf stocked with snacks for clients to purchase, and he allowed outside food in Critical Games. His *C&C* group had treated themselves to tacos from the food truck across the street, and based on my own experiences with little brothers, they tended to be messy creatures.

I crouched down to look under the *Wargavel* tables and noticed a stack of player's guides hidden underneath. In addition to the books for sale, Devin had store copies of the basic roleplaying and tabletop books for patrons to use. *Though they're often not in great shape,* I noted as I flipped one of the books open, running my fingers down the worn spine.

I spent the next thirty minutes engrossing myself in *Wargavel* rules and lore as Devin scurried around the shop. He wiped down the tables, refilled the *C&C TCG* packs behind the counter, and balanced the register before turning the lights off.

My head shot up, surprised by the sudden darkness. It was only 5:30, so light was still streaming in from the front windows, but the whole shop was cast in greyscale.

"Alright, Avie." Devin twirled a set of keys around his pointer finger. They made metallic scraping noises as they clanged against his black ring. "You ready?"

I grinned, placing the *Wargavel* book back under the table. "Of course."

Devin slid his arm around my waist as we left the shop, and that same giddy grin made my face burn with happiness.

"You look fantastic in that dress, by the way," he complimented, opening the passenger door of his car for me to climb in. "You got directions?"

"Yup." I fiddled with my phone's GPS. "Should be about twenty minutes."

We spent most of the drive discussing our afternoon *C&C* campaigns, which devolved into Devin telling me funny stories of the boys acting up at his table.

"The day that still bewilders me," Devin explained as we turned off the highway and into Oviedo. "Was when two of the boys snuck silly string into their bags and used it on each other during an in-game fight."

I snorted as laughter erupted from me, "Seriously?"

"Yeah. *Silly string*. I didn't even think they still made that stuff." Devin shook his head. "So naturally, I told their mothers and made the two lunatics clean it all up. Fun times. I'm pretty sure Sam took video of it."

"My god. What a mess that must've made."

Devin rolled his eyes. "I was still picking bits of the stuff off the floor two weeks later. Anyway..." He pointed. "Is that it right there? I see a sign that says, 'Greek Food.'"

I smiled. Sure enough, the nondescript, bright red neon sign hung proudly above a quiet strip mall near the university.

"Yes, it is."

As we approached the little café and swung open the heavy glass door, the first thing that hit us was a blast of chilly air conditioning, one that carried the earthy, aromatic scent of oregano, dill, and bay leaves. The shop was empty except for a lone figure tucked away at a table near the restrooms, happily chowing down on a gyro.

It was small and cramped, as the six sets of tan tables with squeaky metal chairs had barely any room between them. In the kitchen behind the register, the savory sounds of popping and sizzling radiated through the restaurant. The storefront was likely a pizza parlor at one point, as it had the stereotypical black-and-white checkered tile and red, translucent plastic cups next to an old soda machine. But the walls were lined with huge, framed photos of various tourist locations in Greece, and old Greek folk songs hummed through the wall speakers.

To me, it felt cozy and nostalgic. The décor and music brought me back to my early childhood spent with my grandparents, who were Greek immigrants. But they died when I was in elementary school, so the food was more reminiscent of afternoons spent in the kitchen with my mother. Even as an adult, Greek food was still my favorite.

But I also wondered what Devin thought of the place. I peered over at him, wondering if my bringing him to a homey little café for our first date was the best idea. But he was smiling, his vibrant blue-green eyes surveying the artwork on the walls as a waitress hustled over to us.

"It smells fantastic," he noted as we took a seat at a tiny table next to the window. "I've barely eaten all day."

I scoured the laminated menu in front of me, deciding which of my favorite dishes to order. It didn't take me long, as I already knew the menu by heart, but when I looked up, Devin was still tracing his fingers over the words, occasionally stopping to look things up.

Even though I'd already kissed him multiple times, including our initial episode in the breakroom where we nearly stripped each other's clothes off, this still felt weird. Because sitting across from him at a restaurant table made it truly occur to me that I was on a *date*. With Devin. The game shop owner who I had bickered with for years.

A month ago, it would've seemed absurd.

Or would it...?

"So," Devin looked up from his menu, plopping his arms on the table. "What do you recommend?"

"Well, what do you like?"

"I usually go for a gyro, but I'm thinking I should be more... adventurous. Although I'm not gonna lie, I don't know what a lot of these menu items are."

I knew them all, since most of them were dishes that my mother made for us growing up. But upon hearing the word *adventurous*, I decided to test Devin's culinary limits.

After all, our budding relationship was built on messing with each other.

"Adventurous, you say?" I raised an eyebrow. "In that case, I'm ordering the taramosalata as an appetizer."

"What's that?"

I gave a coy shrug. "I'll tell you after you try it. And if you don't like it, I'll eat it."

"Alright then." Devin grinned, leaning back in his chair. "Challenge accepted."

Chapter 17

The waitress came by to get our drink and appetizer order, and once she left, a stillness fell over the table that jittered my nerves. Devin was looking right at me, smiling like he always did, and somehow it tied my stomach up in knots. I was always nervous on dates, but this time it was especially palpable. *What do I do next? What should I say?*

"You alright?" Devin asked.

Shit. I always had a terrible poker face when it came to anxiety.

"Yeah. I know this sounds crazy after everything...but I'm nervous."

Devin stifled a laugh. "Aw. No need to be nervous. I'll tell you what: you tell me something about yourself I don't already know. And I'll do the same."

I chuckled. Devin and I already knew about each other's hobbies and passions through years of seeing each other at Critical Games. He loved roleplaying and card games, just like I did.

What doesn't he know about me?

Naturally, that brought me back to my past, before I moved to Orlando. The thought of my teenage and college years made my stomach turn, because I was a very different person back then. None of my close friends, including Cassidy, knew about that version of myself.

"Well, back when I was in college," I began, "my big thing was choir. I loved to sing; I took after my mom. I even did a few solo pieces at our concerts, and I competed in the state choir competition every year."

"Wow," Devin replied. "I'd love to hear you sometime. It's funny, because I can't sing worth crap, but here's something not many people know about me - I can play piano."

"Oh really?"

"Yeah. Years of lessons plus playing in my dad's church every Sunday. Once I broke free of all that, I started learning songs that weren't just religious hymns. But I'm pretty out of practice. I really need to get a keyboard for my condo."

I nodded, digging through my mental archives and wondering if I knew any public places with a piano for customers to use. Orange Blossom Coffee came to mind; they had an old one tucked away in the corner of their shop.

"Well, I want to hear you play. There's a coffee shop downtown with a piano."

"Only if I get to hear you sing."

"Not in public." My cheeks flushed. "I just sing in the car. And shower."

Devin laughed. "I remember you singing in my car the night I drove you home."

"That doesn't count. I was way too drugged to sing properly."

He shrugged. "It was still cute."

The waitress arrived, placing two glasses of water and a heaping plate of pita bread on the table. In the middle of the place was a small dish with a tan-colored spread that had the consistency of hummus, but a slight pinkish tint.

Devin picked up a piece of pita bread, giving me a suspicious glare as he held it above the dip.

"Go on," I taunted. "It's not like I'm trying to poison you."

He laughed, dipping the bread in and taking a large bite. He chewed for a few moments, his face quizzical as he wondered what sort of strange food I was having him try.

"That's pretty good," he commented. "It's...sour. What is it?"

I giggled. Devin rolled his eyes.

"C'mon, what is it?"

"It's fish eggs."

Devin's eyebrows furrowed. "Wait, really?"

"Yup."

"It doesn't taste like it," he pulled out his phone, and I knew he was looking it up. "Damn, you're right. Huh."

"I took Cass here once. I told her what it was, and she wouldn't touch it."

Devin shrugged as he grabbed another piece of pita bread. "I'll eat anything. Especially seafood. That's another thing about me: in addition to his church activities, my dad loved fishing. In his free time, he was always fixing up boats. I was his helper from the time I could walk."

"Wow. So you grew up out on the water?"

"Yup." He took another bite of pita bread. "Every family vacation revolved around the boat. Even today, being out by the water brings me so much inner peace. I miss the beach. I haven't been out there in months. Which is funny, because I sunburn in like five minutes."

"I love the beach." The thought of soft, warm sand under my feet as the shoreline lapped at my toes caused a wave of pleasure to wash over me.

"We'll have to go sometime," Devin smiled as he finished off the last of our appetizer.

I loved that idea. Spending a sunny afternoon out by the water with someone who I cared so deeply about sounded heavenly. And this time, there would be no fear, no anxiety, no impending worry for what was to come that night. I had never been on a date with someone who made me feel so free. So much like myself.

Someone who took my worries and insecurities away with a single adoring smile.

Our food arrived, and we spent the next ten minutes alternating between eating and engaging in more conversation. I learned all the little details about Devin. He was the youngest of four siblings, and the only boy. He was left-handed, something I'd noticed while he held his fork. His natural hair color was a dark chocolate brown, and he griped about how annoying hair dye could be while I giggled. When he was younger, he used to wear eyeliner and paint his nails black, although he fell out of many of his goth tendencies as he got older.

Which made a question pop into my head. One that was awkward to ask, but was one that I needed to know.

"Uh, Dev?"

"Yes?"

"Exactly how...uh, how old are you?"

Devin stifled a laugh, which turned into a cough as he chewed his food. "Yeah, I knew that question was going to come up. You're what, twenty-seven?"

"Almost. My birthday is next month."

"Oh damn, what day?"

"The tenth."

Devin's eyes widened. "Shit, that's just a few weeks away. I need to start planning."

"You don't have to—"

"Oh hush," he laughed, placing his fork on the table. He leaned back in his chair. "Well, I am quite a bit older than you."

"How much older?"

"I'll be thirty-six in December."

I nodded, slowly absorbing the information as I swallowed a bite of salad. That age was about what I'd expected. In some ways, Devin looked very young, being clean-shaven with a full head of shaggy black hair. He had a youthful face, but his eyes had always had a melancholy aura around them. I wondered if having a difficult life in his twenties had aged him.

"That's not an issue, is it?" He suddenly looked concerned. "I mean...we're both adults."

I smiled. "No, it's not. I always knew you were older. As long as you don't mind that I'm younger."

Chapter 17

Devin scoffed. "Please, you're a hell of a lot more mature than I was at your age."

We finished up our meals, engaging in more small talk and silly comments until the waitress came by with our bill.

Devin snatched it before I even had a chance to glance at the total.

"Thank you," I said warmly, blushing as he pulled out a black wallet with silver studs.

"No worries."

He slid his arm across the table, offering an outstretched hand. I took it, lacing his fingers through mine, and my blushing cheeks turned a vibrant shade of crimson.

I still couldn't believe Devin and I were on a date.

But it had been a nice one. Maybe even the nicest one I'd ever been on.

It got even nicer once we made it back to Critical Games. Before I could even begin to say goodbye, he swept me into his arms. I kissed him eagerly as I leaned against the passenger side of his car, my whole body sinking into the door. I never wanted it to end. I even considered making a joke about slipping away to the storage room for some privacy.

As he pulled away, he cupped my face in both hands. We were both grinning like idiots as he pressed his forehead against mine.

"Goodnight Avie."

"Goodnight Dev."

"Text me when you get home, okay?"

"Of course."

He gave me one more quick kiss before climbing into the driver's seat and turning on the car. I watched from the dark parking lot as he drove away, blending into the sea of headlights on the main road.

We'd had a wonderful first date.

I drove home in silence, keeping my music off, and returned to my bedroom where I would sleep alone tonight. I knew that the more time I spent with him, the more I'd ache for intimacy. Frustration curdled my insides as I pondered what cruelty it was to have a sex drive yet be unable to perform the act.

I needed him. But I wasn't ready. I didn't know when I'd be ready.

And that was the part that scared me.

My phone buzzed shortly after I crawled into bed, and in my stupid lovesick haze, I'd forgotten to let him know I arrived home.

Make it home okay?

Yes, I did, sorry!

I had a wonderful time. Did you?

Of course. Thank you for everything.

I know we've only been on one date, but just to confirm…you are my girlfriend, right?

I laughed, my cheeks prickling with heat again. It made my heart leap to have him call me that.

Of course! I had already assumed so.

Fantastic. Goodnight sweetheart. I'll text you in the morning.

Goodnight Dev. Sleep well.

I spent the rest of the night lying in bed, lost in the sickly-sweet fog of infatuation. But despite my happiness, I couldn't fall asleep. Because my bed suddenly felt far too big and empty for just me alone.

One thing at a time, I reminded myself as I stared up at the textured ceiling. *You'll get there.*

Even if it took a while, Devin had sworn he would wait.

And I truly, deeply believed him.

Chapter 18

A SINGLE THOUGHT PERMEATED MY MIND AS I awoke the next morning.

I'd had one hell of a weekend.

I slunk out of bed and changed into shorts and a t-shirt while my coffee brewed in the kitchen. It was my usual morning routine before I hopped on my computer and clocked into work. It all seemed so ordinary, so mundane... it was hard to believe everything that had happened over the past few days was real.

It all flashed through my mind as I settled into work, digging through files and scanning through manuscripts with Devin heavy on my mind. I relived it all, from the harrowing experience at the hospital to the heart-fluttering kisses in the parking lot after our first date. It left me feeling giddy, weightless, and a bit distracted.

Twenty minutes later, my phone buzzed with a message, and in turn, it made my heart buzz with happiness.

Chapter 18

Good morning sweetheart. I hope you're having a good day at work.

As much as I wanted to spend my morning conversing with him, I had manuscripts to typeset, so I exchanged a few quick texts with Devin before putting my phone aside. He was off on Mondays, but that didn't stop him from working. In addition to errands and chores, he planned to do some bookkeeping later that afternoon.

I loved how passionate Devin was about the shop. But I was also starting to realize that he was a workaholic.

It's a shame we never have the same days off.

But with warm, happy thoughts of Devin pushed out of my mind for later, it allowed another new reality of my crazy weekend to sink in.

The hospital visit. My endometriosis.

I need to call that doctor.

I did so on my lunch break, and I discovered that the surgeon was incredibly busy. The next available consult was several weeks away. I swore I could feel my period cramps resurging as frustration boiled in my stomach.

But just as I was about to resign myself to another few weeks of suffering, the medical assistant I was on the phone with exclaimed that she'd found a cancellation. The problem was that it was that same day. At 3:30 pm. Which was during work hours.

I felt both relief at being able to see a doctor right away and dread at the thought of telling my uppity boss that I needed to use personal time on such short notice. But now that I knew what was wrong with me, there was no way I was going through another period cycle from hell. I wanted that surgery.

The other issue was that Lakeland was over an hour away, which meant I would need to clock out at 2 p.m. and prepare for a long drive ahead of me. I slipped away at 1:45 since I needed to fill up my tank, and snacked on a gas station coffee and pretzel on the way to the doctor's office.

The gynecological surgeon was a specialist who was very familiar with endometriosis cases. They were one of the few surgeons in the area that performed the procedure, hence the 50-mile drive away from Orlando.

Once I got to the tiny office, I also realized the doctor was male.

It left me with a feeling of unease as I shook his hand. I'd only ever had female gynecologists. Not only was my religiously raised self uncomfortable with a man poking around down there, but I'd always had a bias against male doctors specializing in female anatomy. How could he possibly understand my condition? Would he be rough and callous like my previous gynecologist?

It turns out, my prejudices were mistaken. Dr. Rojas, a tall, tan-skinned man with thick glasses and an even thicker accent, quickly became my new favorite doctor. He was both knowledgeable and attentive, taking the time to explain my condition in full detail and answering my numerous questions. It nearly brought me to tears; after a decade of my symptoms being either brushed off or misdiagnosed, I felt acknowledged. I felt heard. I felt like it wasn't all in my head.

When I brought up the laparoscopy, he immediately agreed to perform the procedure and send me in to meet with his surgery scheduler. He did make sure I was aware that he couldn't definitively confirm my condition without the surgery, and that there was a chance they could be incorrect about me having endometriosis. But I didn't care. Every symptom he'd described matched up with what I was experiencing. Even when it came to symptoms that I didn't know were related, such as my sensitive stomach and digestive issues.

Chapter 18

I wanted this surgery more than anything.

But it wouldn't be immediate. The surgery was scheduled for the first Monday in July, exactly two weeks away. The scheduler explained that it was because they needed time to process everything through my health insurance. At least having the procedure two weeks away meant that I wouldn't have to go through another period in severe pain.

I left the doctor's office with a giant weight lifted off my shoulders. But a new one immediately came crashing down on me once I realized who I needed to call.

My parents.

Who I generally spoke with as little as possible.

I stared blankly at their number in my phone as I sat in my car. There was no way I could go through this surgery alone. The hospital wouldn't even let me drive myself home coming off anesthesia, and I likely wouldn't be able to take care of my stitched-up self for a few days. I needed them to come stay with me.

Which, after a brief phone call, my mother enthusiastically agreed to. She was shocked with I told her my initial diagnosis, expressing sympathy for not having picked up on my symptoms before.

It made my stressed-out heart soften. I loved my mother. Preconceptions aside, she was a warm, loving person, and I knew she missed me.

My father was a different story. Which meant that I was very surprised when my mother told me he would be coming along. She explained that he was worried about me, which nearly made me scoff. My father had never been one to show much emotion toward anything, let alone his own children. My brothers, who were fifteen and eighteen, were old enough to be left alone for a few days. I chuckled, wondering what sort of disaster my parents could come home to with two teenage boys ruling the house unattended.

Shortly after the call from my parents, I got a text from Devin. He wanted to know how I was doing, his message punctuated by a cute little heart emoji. I decided to take the initiative this time and asked when he was free again for dinner. He said the shop closed at 7 p.m. on Thursdays, so he could meet up with me then. I decided to take it a step further and asked him to take me to his favorite place in Orlando. He offered to pick me up from my townhouse, and I agreed, adding an extra layer of excitement by telling him to make our destination a surprise.

He loved it, sending me plenty of smiley faces and hearts throughout his texts. It made me feel light-headed and giddy the entire way home.

I couldn't wait for Thursday.

Thankfully, the next few days of work flew by, and Devin's surprise destination turned out to be a board game bar not far from Critical Games. Neither of us drank, but they had pretty good fantasy-themed food and a monstrous wall of games to pick from.

As much as I loved roleplaying and card games, I'd never played many board games. It turned out Devin was a huge fan of them. It made sense, as Critical Games was always well-stocked, and there was a small library of public board games available for patrons to freely play.

"I hadn't played much either until I started running the shop," Devin explained as he set up a game with a massive map. The tokens were cute woodland creatures, and I picked them up and studied the details of each one. They reminded me of *Creatures & Crypts* miniatures. "I did a deep dive into learning board games, so I'd know what to stock Critical Games with. Which has resulted in me having an overflowing collection at home."

I smiled. As fearful as I was of broaching the topic of intimacy, I couldn't wait to someday go over to his place. I wanted to enjoy all the peaceful, mundane bits of relationships—cooking meals, playing video games, cuddling on the couch. But I was still too afraid. Devin said he'd wait for me to overcome my sexual issues, but I still didn't want to give in to temptation and end up in bed with him.

Having a sex drive while simultaneously being unable to have sex was awful. It was a cruelty I wouldn't even inflict on my worst enemy.

We spent the next several hours jumping between games, filling up on soda and bar food in the process. Devin had to explain the games to me, and I noticed that he was an excellent teacher. Maybe too good, because I ended up beating him at the last game we played.

I loved how Devin beamed with pride when I won. If I had done this with Tyler, he would've been pouty over losing to a woman.

But it was a Thursday. Not only did we both have work the next morning, but since it was a weeknight, the bar closed at 10 p.m. And as Devin drove me home in his car, our intertwined fingers resting on the center console, the topic of my endometriosis came up.

"I was able to meet with the surgeon and get my surgery scheduled," I explained. "He was great. I'm nervous about the procedure, but I'm also relieved that I'm getting it done. I can't believe after all these years, I've finally gotten a diagnosis."

"Yeah, no kidding," Devin replied. "I was doing some reading on endometriosis, and it said that on average it takes ten *years* for a woman to get properly diagnosed. That's insane."

I smiled. It made my heart happy to know that Devin cared enough to research my condition. It was strange to think that less than two weeks earlier, I'd been afraid to even mention my period around him.

I concluded that he the most wonderful man I'd ever met.

And I was lucky he was mine.

"Ten years sounds about right," I sighed. "I've been having these issues since I was a teenager."

"And you just...lived like that? In that much pain?"

I shrugged. "What else was I supposed to do? Every doctor I'd ever met told me that all women experience period pain and to 'suck it up.' Okay, maybe not that exact wording. But you get the idea. Plus, talking about period pain is...awkward. Women are taught to hide that stuff. Especially in my bible-thumper family."

Devin shook his head with a slight scoff of disgust. "Jesus. I have to say, Avie...you are the strongest person I have ever met. I'm just glad you'll finally be free of your pain."

You are the strongest person I have ever met.

Those words looped in my mind, swirling through my ears and seeping into my heart. I gripped Devin's hand tighter, rubbing my thumb over the black metal ring on his pointer finger. He responded by lifting my hand in his and pulling it up to his lips, placing a slow, gentle kiss just below my knuckles.

God, no guy had ever made me feel like this before.

We turned into my neighborhood, and the desire to invite him inside and fall into bed with him was stronger than ever.

"It's funny," I said as we pulled into my driveway. "A few weeks ago, when you took me to the hospital, I thought the same thing about you."

Devin smiled. His multicolored eyes glistened with warmth and adoration as he turned to me.

I threw myself across the center console of the car, wrapping my arms around his back and pulling him in for a kiss. I didn't care who saw us out the windows. At that moment, as he dug his fingers through my curly hair and slid his thumb along the skirt of my dress, nothing else mattered.

It was amazing how strong the fireworks were with him. The way a single kiss, let alone our current frenzy, made me lose control. The way he made the rest of the world slip away. Even my fears about my sexual inadequacies dimmed as my raging attraction to him threatened to consume me whole.

I wanted to bring him inside.

I wanted him.

But I wasn't ready yet.

I pulled away, gazing into his vibrant eyes as our chests rose and fell with heavy, panting breaths. At this point, I was nearly in his lap, my Converse sneakers pressed against the center console.

"You okay, sweetheart?" he asked.

My heart fell at those words. But I had to be honest with him.

"I..." The words struggled to escape my mouth. "I'm not ready for this yet."

Devin's concern was quickly replaced with laughter. "Avie, it's okay. We can take this completely at your pace. You're in control. When you're ready to take things further, you let me know. Besides, you haven't even had your surgery yet."

I nodded, relief flooding my veins like cool saline. "Thank you. That means a lot to me."

"Do we have to stop though? This is nice."

My eyes darted out the driver's side window. "Someone is gonna see us."

Devin's eyes narrowed, and a devious grin crept across his face. "You say that like it's a problem."

"Devin!" I admonished. "You little—!"

He grabbed my face and kissed me, silencing my lips before I could say another word.

"Alright, alright." He broke away. "I'll let you go."

I plopped one more kiss on his cheek. "Goodnight, Dev."

"Goodnight, sweetheart."

My empty bedroom felt darker and lonelier than usual. I knew the routine by now: I'd curl up into bed, surrounded by silence, and ache for his presence until I eventually fell asleep. The more time we spent together, the stronger those desires became.

Just get through your surgery, I reassured myself. I knew the procedure wasn't an instant cure, and I'd likely need more medical help before I could have sex. But once my troublesome endometrial tissue was removed and my body had healed, at least I could start trying. It was the first step in breaking the wall down, brick by painful brick.

I wanted to have sex with him. More than I ever had with anyone.

And I knew it was because of my feelings for him. How much I cared for him.

More than I'd ever cared for a partner before.

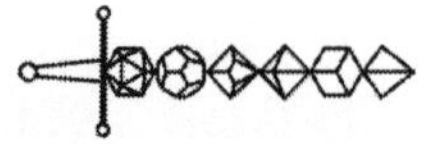

When Cassidy and I returned home from TCG Night the following evening, she couldn't hide it. A huge grin stretched across her face as she drove us home, her eyes sparkling with the telltale sign of being lost in a sea of dreamy thoughts.

"You told him, didn't you?" I asked, which caused Cassidy to jolt and come to a gut-lurching stop at a red light.

Cassidy smirked. "I'm just as obvious about it as you were, aren't I?"

"Yes. And now I'm realizing what a dopey, lovesick person I was. But it's wonderful. I'm happy for you two."

"He had concerns, obviously," Cassidy continued. "But he said he cared for me way too much to let something like this get in the way."

"That's exactly what Dev said to me."

"It made me think; to us, these conditions are terrifying," Cassidy pondered. "Growing up, I was taught that all boys wanted was sex. As if that was all women were good for."

I nodded in agreement, knowing that mindset all too well.

"Now that I'm older, I know that's not the case," she continued. "But it still lingers in the back of my mind. The idea that men *need* sex. But the way Aaron played it off like it wasn't a big deal...it made me realize how much more there is to relationships. And that sexuality can look and feel different for people who aren't 'normal.'"

Cassidy's last sentence clung to my mind. Since it would take time for me to heal and recover after the surgery, maybe Devin and I could find other ways to keep each other satisfied. But as a woman with little experience with intimacy, I had no idea what that would look like. Or where to start.

The thought lingered all weekend, even as Cassidy and I ran through our Saturday routine of chores and grocery shopping. I spent the evening alternating between playing video games and texting Devin. Although with a *Wargavel* tournament going on, it took him a long time for him to respond.

I fell asleep before he made it home, but I woke up the next morning to a beautiful message he'd sent well after midnight, just as he was crawling into his own bed.

> *Hey, I know you're probably already asleep, but I just wanted to say goodnight. And tell*

you that this bed feels very empty without you. I know you're not ready for intimacy, but I would still love to cuddle you all night.

I buried my face in my pillow as my cheeks burned. A month ago, I had no idea Devin could be so sappy. I didn't even know he was capable of it.

But it was already 9 a.m., which meant I only had to wait a few more hours to see him at *Creatures & Crypts*. I played video games until it was time to hop in the shower and get ready. And just like last time, I spent almost an hour fussing with my curls and debating which dress to wear.

I decided on a navy blue one, and I smoothed its soft cotton skirt over my knees as I drove myself and Cassidy to Critical Games. I usually dressed in jeans and some sort of geeky t-shirt when I went to events at the shop, but lately, I had been wearing more cute, flowy dresses.

And not just because I wanted to look nice for Devin. My stomach had been killing me lately. I'd always had digestive issues, which doctors always dismissed as IBS and told me to cut out inflammatory foods. But no matter what sort of diet I tried, my normally flat abdomen was spending more and more time swollen like a balloon. It made wearing tight jeans difficult, and I hated how form-fitting t-shirts made me look like I was well into my second trimester. I'd lost count of the times I had to reassure myself that I wasn't getting fat.

But now I knew why. Endometriosis affected more than just my reproductive system—the tissue wreaked havoc on whatever abdominal organ it decided to attach to. And in many cases, the doctor had told me, that organ would be the stomach or intestines. I wasn't gaining weight; my belly was just swollen from inflammation.

Which means the issue was never my digestive system in the first place, I grumbled, remembering how my stomach pains had nearly cost me the first job I had when I moved to Orlando.

Dwelling on my health issues made thoughts of my impending surgery creep into my mind. A small bubble of anxiety formed in my stomach, one that not even the sight of my sweet boyfriend behind the counter could dissolve. It stayed there for the next few hours as we played *Creatures & Crypts*. I went through the motions, making ability check rolls and engaging in combat, but my mind was too busy quivering with "what-ifs" for me to enjoy myself.

I knew that surgery shouldn't be a big deal, especially one that was minimally invasive. But I'd never had surgery before, and it was the fear of the unknown that kept me up at night. It was like when I first went to Universal Studios with Cassidy when I was twenty-three. I'd never been on a rollercoaster before, and the anxiety of waiting in the 45-minute line nearly turned my stomach inside out. But in the end, the ride was far less scary than I'd imagined. I even ended up loving rollercoasters and went on two others with Cassidy that day.

This feeling was similar, but instead of 45 minutes of impending dread, it was an entire week. And even if the surgery was easy, I doubted I'd be a fan of the whole procedure. In the end, rollercoasters were meant to be fun. Surgery was not.

Since I spent my days working from home and my evenings playing video games, I managed to keep my anxiety to myself. But by the time Thursday rolled around and Devin wanted to get dinner, I was starting to unravel. As much as I loved our date nights, my throat was too tight from anxiety for me to hold much conversation.

And Devin noticed right away.

"Alright, Avie, what's wrong?" he asked the moment we sat down at our table. We were at a Mexican restaurant, one that Devin had recommended. It was bright and colorful, full of music and activity. On any other night, I would've loved it. But at that moment, it was all too much. I just wanted to slip away to my quiet bedroom and pull my comforter over my head.

I opened my mouth to speak, but a sudden surge of emotion wrapped my neck in a chokehold. I couldn't utter a word for fear of bursting into tears.

God, I'm a mess.

"It is the surgery? That's on Monday, so…four days away?"

Relief allowed my windpipe to loosen. I didn't need to tell Devin what was wrong. We'd only been dating for two weeks, but after five years of knowing each other, he could read me as well as Cassidy could.

I nodded, still unable to choke out my words.

Devin reached across the table, cupping my hands in his. I studied his fingers; he wore different rings every time I saw him, but I'd grown used to their familiar metallic chill against my skin.

"We can get food to-go if you want," he offered. "Go to a park. Somewhere less hectic."

I sighed with relief. That was exactly what I needed.

"Yes. That sounds great."

We were near Baldwin Park, a ritzy neighborhood that had a walking path surrounding a large lake. The sun was just beginning to set, filling the air with a hazy, humid warmth that sunk into my skin and made my lungs loosen. The sky glowed a vibrant orange as we took a seat on a bench under the shade of a massive live oak tree. Since it was late in the day, we were mostly alone, except for the occasional jogger passing on the sidewalk.

Chapter 18

Devin reached into our to-go bag and handed me a Styrofoam container full of tacos. They were delicious, but my anxiety was making my stomach issues even worse than usual. I finished two of them before handing the rest of the container to Devin.

"You done?"

"I'm not that hungry."

"Avie..." He set his half-eaten container of tacos on the bench next to him, wrapping an arm around my back. "Do you want to talk?"

"I just..." My voice trailed off as my throat tightened again. "I don't know if there's much to talk about. I'm just nervous about my surgery. Am I overreacting?"

Devin shook his head. "No, that's normal."

"Have you ever had surgery?"

"Just wisdom teeth," he replied. "It wasn't that bad. I was really sore, but I got to skip my high school classes for a few days and lay in bed playing video games."

I chuckled. "That does sound nice. But what about the surgery part?"

"Well, I was afraid of being put under, but honestly it happens so fast that you don't have much time to think about it. It's not like dreaming, where you feel a passage of time. One second you're awake, then bam—you're opening your eyes and the surgery is over. It's wild."

"That is a bit reassuring," I replied, nestling my head into the crook of his neck. "Thank you, Dev."

"Of course."

He wrapped both arms around me and kissed my forehead. We remained that way, locked in a soothing embrace under the setting sun, for several minutes. I closed my eyes, trying my best to focus not on my surgery, but on how good it felt to have him hold me. The rhythmic rising and falling of his chest, combined with his thumping heartbeat, was a gentle remedy for my anxiety. I slowed my breaths until mine synced with his, and I became so relaxed that I nearly fell asleep.

"Here." Devin shifted his hip, pulling his phone out of his pocket. "I have something that might make you laugh."

"What's that?"

"You, uh, have to promise you'll never tell anyone about this."

I raised my eyebrow, now itching with curiosity. "Of course. Now what is it?"

Devin unlocked his phone, scrolling through years of photos at rapid speed. I caught brief glimpses at some of them: silly selfies with friends, his sisters, and what looked like family pets. Finally, once he was almost fifteen years back, I saw a flash of white, and it turned my stomach upside down. Those were wedding photos.

But they were gone in less than a second, and as Devin slowed his scrolling, he tapped on a video. One from eighteen years ago, likely passed down from cloud storage through multiple phones. I could tell it was old, because it was small and grainy, nothing like modern-day phone cameras.

But I knew exactly who the scrawny teenager lying wide-eyed in a dental chair was.

He was much smaller and thinner, with his arms bare of tattoos and his hair still chocolate brown. But I knew that face, even if it was almost two decades younger.

And in the video, that face was mumbling incoherently about attending church.

"Oh my god," I giggled. "Is that you?"

"Yup." Devin shook his head. "My parents took this after I woke up from my wisdom teeth surgery. I'm absolutely stoned. I'm rambling about my childhood youth group for fuck's sake."

Chapter 18

As the video went on, and seventeen-year-old Devin bounced from topic to topic with little cohesion to his ramblings, I continued giggling with my head pressed against current Devin's chest. He was right. This did make me feel better.

"The sad thing is, my dad stopped filming before the best part," Devin said as the video ended.

"What was that?"

"I told one of the nurses I thought she was hot."

I burst out laughing. "Well...was she?"

"She was like sixty."

My laughter erupted into hyena cackling as my face flushed red. Devin playfully scowled and ruffled my curly hair.

"I'm just glad you're less stressed now." He smiled. "Even if it comes at my expense."

"You're the best." I pressed my lips against his cheek.

Devin chuckled. "I try."

We sat there, wrapped in each other's arms, as we enjoyed the warmth and stillness of the evening sunset. From our spot on the bench, we had a perfect view of the lake, and I admired the way the melting orange sun cast a pastel glow on the inky water. In the distance, the faint rumbles of barking echoed from the nearby dog park, and a child's joyful scream cut across the field as he chased a plump, irritated duck.

I was getting used to being with Devin—at least, in a dating sense. The feeling of his lips on mine and the way our fingers interlaced when we held hands were growing more familiar. More comfortable. I was no longer nervous like I was on our first date at the Greek café.

Instead, I felt completely at peace with him. Which is exactly what I'd been searching for through my months of online dating. Warmth. Comfort.

Finally, for the first time in almost a week, my anxiety about my upcoming surgery faded away.

Because at that moment, it was just me and him. Nothing else mattered.

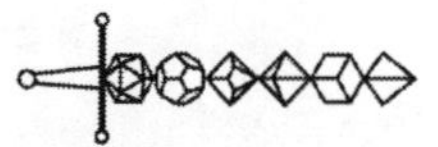

DEVIN DROVE ME HOME. I'D TOLD HIM SEVERAL times that I was perfectly capable of driving, though I noticed he always picked date spots that were close to my townhouse. But he'd explained that driving was something he enjoyed. He worked nearly sixty hours a week at Critical Games, and most of that time he was on his feet, bouncing from one task to another, surrounded by busy customers and plenty of noise. Being in the car was his one chance to sit down and relax. He could listen to music, focus on the road, and enjoy a brief period of solace.

"Plus." Devin grinned as we pulled into my driveway. "It gives me more time to talk to you."

I blushed, rubbing his shoulder. "I enjoy that too."

"So..." Devin shifted the car into park and leaned back in his seat. "Am I going to see you again before your surgery?"

"Other than the game shop, no," I sighed. "My parents are driving down from the panhandle on Sunday. They said they'd be here around three, and I'll probably be entertaining them for the evening. They've never been down here before."

"Really? You've lived in Orlando for five years and they've never come to visit?"

"Well, to be fair, I keep them at arm's length," I replied. "Although this time I don't have much of a choice."

Devin gave a long, deep exhale. "I hope it all goes well. I'll miss you. Text me once you're out of surgery."

"That may not be a good idea. My texts will be gibberish if I'm high as a kite on anesthesia."

"Exactly." Devin's usual devious grin returned to his face. "I eagerly await your drugged ramblings."

"Devin..."

"I promise I won't screenshot them."

"You brat," I scoffed, lightly shoving his shoulder. Devin took the opportunity to grab my arm and pull me in for a long, deep kiss.

When I broke the kiss a few seconds later, a sudden ache tugged at my chest. I desperately wanted him there with me when I had my surgery. In fact, I would've preferred him there over my parents. But there was a big, ugly elephant in the room, one that Devin and I both knew about but refused to acknowledge.

After only two weeks, I wasn't ready to introduce my new boyfriend to my parents. But the bigger problem was that I feared *ever* introducing him. It didn't matter how kind and sweet and wonderful Devin was, because my parents, with their uppity, staunch, traditional attitude, would take one look at his tattoos and piercings and write him off as a Satanic troublemaker.

They would never approve of him.

And it crushed my heart to think about it.

I lifted a hand to his face, brushing my fingers against his cheek. I slid a few strands of shaggy black hair out of his eyes and admired their sea-green beauty.

"I'll miss you too," I whispered, my voice both light and full of dreariness.

I turned my head away from him, studying both sides of the street. It was completely dark outside, and our driveway's floodlights were broken. The car was completely cloaked in shadows, and there were no signs of pedestrians on the sidewalk.

We were alone.

And tonight was my last night with Devin before my surgery.

Fuck it. I stepped over the center console and into Devin's lap, my legs straddling his hips. His eyes widened, both in alarm and intrigue, as a mischievous grin spread across his lips.

"Come here," he rumbled in a low, hungry tone, grabbing my back and pulling me forward. He started with my neck, pressing kisses deep against my throat until I could feel the hard metal of his piercings on my skin. I didn't hold back. I let out subtle gasps and cries as his hands explored me, feverishly and without restraint.

When they finally made their way up my legs and slipped under the skirt of my dress, I felt like I was about to explode with anticipation. The feeling of his hands rubbing my inner thighs made my cries louder and more heated.

This was dangerous.

But I couldn't stop if I tried.

"Avie..." Devin rasped between breaths, the rawness of his voice unlike anything I'd ever heard from him. "My sweet, beautiful, sexy girl..."

He continued in his heavy tone, whispering all the things he wanted to do to me while his fingers trailed further up my thigh. Once they made it up to my underwear and he pressed a finger against my vulva, hot electricity jolted through every nerve in my body.

Curse my stupid, broken vagina.

I would've taken him right there in the front seat of his car if I could.

His hands moved up to my breasts, and he'd nearly pulled the collar of my dress down to expose them when the sound of a door slamming shook us back to reality.

Chapter 18

I panicked, my arousal quickly replaced by adrenalin as I shot back into my own seat. It was a clumsy attempt; I ended up sideways with my legs still slayed over the center console. I pulled the skirt of my dress back down and the collar back up as I lay low and silent, fearing that someone would peep in the window at any moment.

"Avie," Dev whispered. He was still upright in his seat, though his heavy breaths hadn't returned to normal. "It's just Cass."

I lifted my head, peering out the passenger window. A tall, slim figure was bathed in the dull light of the front entryway. I squinted, and realized it was Cassidy grabbing a package off the front porch. She tucked the package under her arm and walked back inside without a single glance in our direction.

"Phew." I let out a sharp exhale. I craned my neck around, locking eyes with Devin, and we both burst out laughing.

But as the humor died down, and we were left sitting alone in the car after our interrupted lustfulness, a deep sadness washed over both of us like a dampening blanket.

"Will I be able to see you at all while you're recovering?" Devin asked, breaking the heavy tension in the air.

I sighed. "Probably not. My parents plan on being here all week."

Devin cupped his hand around my cheek and gave me a final kiss, one that was difficult to pull my lips away from. "Goodnight, sweetheart."

I felt hollow inside as I stepped out of the car and watched his Escape back out of the driveway. I could barely make out the black car's figure against the shadowy streets, only able to tell where it was by the ghostly white headlights. I stood in the entryway and watched until those lights disappeared, and the low hum of the engine faded away into silence.

Please don't go.

My heart sank at the sad yet beautiful irony of those words, and I was left with nothing else to do other than walk through the front door and call it a night.

Chapter 19

THE KNOT IN MY STOMACH HAD RETURNED BY Sunday morning.

Devin texted me shortly after I woke up, and we exchanged our usual sweet, honeyed good mornings as I showered, shaved, and blow-dried my curls with a diffuser.

And of course, I did all this naked while simultaneously texting Devin, which meant he had some amorous opinions on my current state of undress. I brushed him off, teasing him about how he'd have to wait until after my surgery. But his suggestive comments made me wonder what was beneath his own clothes and brought the same tingling curiosity to my own body.

I couldn't stop thinking about the past Thursday. About what I would give to go back to that moment; him exploring me both over and under my dress, ready to pull my bra away before Cassidy opened the door and interrupted us. I loved my best friend, but that part made me scowl.

You really had to have your package at that exact moment? It had been sitting on the front porch all day!

I shook my head. As much as I enjoyed the passionate memories, it was better for both of us if clothes finally came off in one of our beds and not in the front seat of a car.

Cassidy popped in to say hello around noon, shortly before she left for *Creatures & Crypts* day at Critical Games. My heart ached to go with her – I wanted to see Devin one last time before my surgery. I'd gone to TCG Night on Friday, but since the event was packed with players, he barely had time to say hello to us. He did slip me a quick kiss before I left that evening, and it had lingered on my lips all weekend.

But there was no point in going to *C&C*. I could only stay for an hour at most, and I hated the idea of having to leave in the middle of a session. Plus, Cassidy and I would have to take separate cars. So I stayed home and took my frustrations out on scrubbing the apartment from top the bottom.

I enjoyed cleaning; it kept my hands busy and my anxiety at bay. I coughed as I scrubbed the tile shower in my bathroom with bleach – the sour, burning chemical stinging my nostrils as I worked. If my parents were going to drive down from the panhandle and finally see where I'd been living all these years, I at least wanted it to be spotless.

But as I vacuumed, mopped, and wiped down countertops, memories of my childhood came trickling back into my mind. Part of me longed to see my mother, who despite her devout, old-fashioned beliefs, had always been a warm and comforting figure in my life. It was the man she was married to that made nausea swirl in my stomach.

I could count on two hands the number of times I'd seen my father smile, and it was usually when he had his church buddies over for a family dinner. I knew where he got it from: early memories of my grandfather revolved around him snapping his fingers at waitresses in restaurants and lounging in his recliner while my grandmother worked her fingers to the bone around the house.

Chapter 19

I knew my father had some kindness and charm in there somewhere; my mom married him for a reason. But most of the time he wore a stoic, hard mask, one that barked orders at us from across the house to keep it down so he could hear his football game on TV. This was all made worse by the fact that for the first eight years of my life, I was their only child – a girl.

I still remembered the two miscarriages my mother had between me and my younger brothers' births. The first time was a simple explanation: the baby was no longer in my mother's belly and had gone up to Heaven. But the second time, I'd caught my mom hunched over the toilet, howling the most horrific sobs my ten-year-old self had ever heard. My father was still at work, and my mother didn't bother to call him until after the whole ordeal was over.

As a child, I didn't understand—why would God do this to her? My mother, through her agonizing tears, patted me on the back and reassured me that He worked in mysterious ways. Looking back, it made me realize how incredibly strong she was. And it made my mind snap with the sudden realization that maybe I wasn't the only one with endometriosis.

I'd read online that one of the main side effects of the disease was infertility, and that miscarriages were common. I wondered if the disease was hereditary, and thinking about all the decades my mother had spent struggling through an undiagnosed illness made my chest hurt even more. I made a mental note to bring it up with her when she arrived. Alone, out of my father's earshot.

I finished wiping down the kitchen countertops and stowed my spray bottles and rags underneath the sink. The whole townhouse now had a sharp, lemony, sterile smell—a sure sign of a clean home.

I checked the time on my phone. It was almost 3 p.m., just enough time for me to get changed and make myself presentable before they arrived.

I slipped back into my room, stepped out of my gym shorts and faded Daytona Beach t-shirt, and tossed them in my laundry hamper. I decided on a cotton sunflower-print dress, one that came down just below my knees. My eyes flicked back to my hamper. Growing up, I was never allowed to wear shorts, and part of me wanted to put on the tightest ones I owned just to make a point. But I took a deep breath, reminding myself to get through this surgery and recover with as little drama as possible.

The sooner they go back up to the panhandle, the better.

I settled at my gaming PC, trying to stave off my nerves with some *Stardew Valley*. It helped, but I was barely through a single in-game day before the doorbell rang and made my whole body jolt.

My mother, Maria, squealed with joy the second I opened the door. She'd cut her long, curly black hair up to her collarbones, and her olive skin looked tanner than usual.

"Avery, sweetheart!" she exclaimed, pulling me into a hug even as the weight of her enormous purse weighed her arm down. A reluctant smile warmed my face as I embraced my mother. She smelled like rose and lavender, and it brought me back to my childhood.

But as soon as she broke the hug, I was left locking eyes with my father, James. He was a pale, square-jawed man with greying chestnut hair and a thick mustache that made it look like he was perpetually frowning. Which he usually was.

"Avery." His tone was blunt as he pulled me into a stiff one-armed hug. I peered into his eyes, which were the same chocolate-brown color as mine. I'd inherited those, his skin tone, and not much else. Otherwise, I was a carbon copy of my mother; one with freckles and hair that was dark brown instead of black.

I had no idea how my father always managed to look so dull. He had the emotional capacity of a robot, and he certainly hugged like one.

I led them both inside, silently observing as my mother oohed and aahed over the tiny townhouse, her enthusiasm almost making up for my father's sullen behavior. The only sign of activity from him was when he swiped a finger across the top of a shelving unit that I'd forgotten to wipe down.

My nostrils flared, but I refused to pay him much attention.

"And your bedroom is so cute!" My mother exclaimed as I opened the door. She admired my black Ikea shelving units and navy flower-print pillows, but I noticed her face scrunch up in confusion when she saw my geeky posters.

"Oh, what are these from, sweetie?"

"Video games," I replied flatly, not daring to look behind me to see my father's reaction.

"Ah. Well, they're very pretty." She admired one of Amaterasu, the wolf goddess from *Okami*, standing proudly in front of a blazing sunrise.

A figure stepped out from behind me and appeared at my right shoulder, and I realized it was my dad studying my gaming PC. He rubbed his chin with his thick hairy hands as he stood there with a dumbfounded expression on his face, like he'd never seen a computer before.

My gaze flicked up to an art piece of several *Creatures & Crypts* monsters that hung above him, and I silently prayed he wouldn't notice it. The scowl on his face was discouraging enough; I didn't need a full-on lecture on my "Satanic" hobbies.

"Well." My mother clapped her hands together, trying to dissipate the awkward tension in the room. "Are you hungry, sweetie? Your father and I haven't had anything to eat other than the road snacks we packed in the cooler."

"Yes." My reply shot out of my mouth. I was eager to leave my townhouse so my father could stop scrabbling around my gaming memorabilia. But going to a restaurant meant spending the next hour stuck at a table with my parents, where I'd be forced to engage in conversation about what I'd been doing in Orlando for the past five years.

"Well let's hop in the car and find a place," my mother replied, ushering us all out of my bedroom and toward the front door. "I'm sure you know where the best food in town is."

I did. But as we walked toward my parents' white pickup truck, I had a feeling the number of places my father would be willing to eat at would be limited.

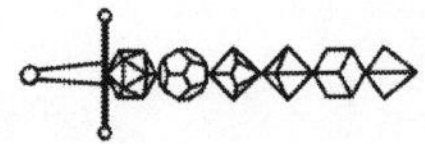

I WAS CORRECT, BECAUSE WE ENDED UP EATING at a small chain steakhouse not far from my townhouse. It was, in fact, the same chain steakhouse that was in my childhood hometown, being one of the few food options in the rural area besides fast-food chains and greasy breakfast joints.

Not that I minded. I wasn't a big fan of steak, but they had plenty of chicken and seafood options for me to pick from. Although this was a different location than the one in my tiny hometown, it had the same rustic décor and nearly the same layout. The walls were an earthy clay brown with generic framed photos of cows and farms, with the centerpiece being a giant taxidermy bull's head over the fake fireplace. At my age, it felt cheesy, but it also felt nostalgic, as big nights out to this chain steakhouse were a rare treat in my childhood.

"So Avery." My mother finally broke the silence after a few minutes of us burying our heads in our menus. "Tell me more about Orlando. How's your job? What do you like to do around here? Have you made lots of friends?"

Oh boy. I set my menu down, my stomach suddenly feeling less eager for food than before. Those were all loaded questions, and I knew I had to choose my answers carefully. Especially since my father was sitting right next to me in the booth. Our elbows were nearly touching.

"Well..." I paused, scrambling for words like I was about to give a carefully crafted speech. "Work is good. I mostly edit manuscripts and do cover design work in Photoshop. It's a lot of fun. We get all genres of books, but a lot of them are autobiographies. I've read a lot of interesting life stories."

"That sounds wonderful, sweetie. What fun."

The knot in my stomach loosened just a fraction. *So far, so good.*

"What about friends? You have a roommate, right?"

"Yes," I replied, glad that Cassidy wasn't home when my parents first arrived. She planned on staying with Aaron for the next week to give me some space to recover. *Not that she needs an excuse to stay with him,* I snickered.

Plus, our tiny townhouse would be crowded with four people. My parents had booked a hotel nearby, but I knew they'd be spending a lot of time at my place since I'd be incapacitated for at least the first few days.

"Her name is Cassidy," I continued. "She's my best friend. And I've made a lot of other good friends here too."

"Any coworker friends?"

"Nah. The company is mostly remote and based out of Miami."

"Ah. So how did you and Cassidy meet?"

Goddamnit. My fingers clenched around the napkin in my lap until my knuckles bulged.

"Uh, at a game shop."

"Oh, what's that?"

I wanted to be a smartass and say "*it's a shop where you play games*," but I knew there was no escaping this conversation. My mother wasn't a stone-faced, judgmental louse like my father, but she was still incredibly nosy. She'd keep digging and digging until she got to the truth.

"It's uh…where I play games with my friends."

"What kind of games?"

"Uh, tabletop stuff, like…"

"*Creatures & Crypts*?"

The sudden, unexpected interjection by my father caused both my mother and I to snap our mouths shut and swivel our heads in his direction.

I was nearly speechless, but I still managed to squeak out a "yes."

My father scoffed, shifting in his seat as his arms crossed over themselves. "I told you, Maria. She moves hours away to the big city, and now she's involved in demons and witchcraft."

My stomach clenched as I tried my hardest not to physically cringe at his words.

"It's not witchcraft," I replied weakly. "It's just a game."

"Is Satanism *just a game* to you?"

The dark undertone of his voice caused me to fall silent again.

Thankfully, that was when the waitress showed up with our appetizers, and I was able to stuff my face with fried onion strips instead of continuing with the conversation.

Once the appetizers had been reduced to crumbs, my mother steered the topic away from *Creatures & Crypts* and toward less polarizing subjects. They asked more about my job and the townhouse, conversations I was able to navigate through between bites of a massive fried chicken sandwich. My father was mostly silent, except for scolding me for not being "ladylike" in the way that I ate my food. My response was to glare daggers at him while I shoved an entire French fry in my mouth.

It made me wish I could be at *Creatures & Crypts* with Devin and not at this interrogation of a family dinner.

But the one topic I prayed they wouldn't touch never came up: my dating life. My parents had made offhand comments over the years, ranging from my mother's innocent prying to my father's straightforward attempts to pair me up with church boys in my hometown. But this time, they never asked.

Maybe it's because they're afraid of the answer, I scoffed as I finished the last of my fries.

Another topic that never came up was my surgery, but I knew why. That conversation would have to wait for a time when I was alone with my mother. Any mention of female anatomy, especially periods, made my father "uncomfortable."

As if I haven't been 'uncomfortable' for a fucking decade.

I was relieved when the bill finally showed up. My parents insisted on treating me, which was nice, but I would've been happy to pay the whole damn thing if it meant escaping the restaurant sooner. I couldn't handle any more uncomfortable conversations. My blood pressure was already spiking, like my veins were a soda can that had been shaken too hard and was about to explode.

"Well, sweetie." My mother resumed her sugary-sweet tone, trying to defuse the tension lingering around the table. "It's only four-thirty, and we're in no rush to check in to the hotel. Is there anything fun and exciting you'd like to do in Orlando?"

As much as I wanted to reply with a firm *no* and retreat to my townhouse without my parents, my father spoke up before I could open my mouth.

"I'd like to see that game shop."

I swallowed, a lump forming in my throat. On the surface, his request sounded innocent, but I could feel the disgust emanating from him like a noxious cloud. I'd gladly go anywhere in Orlando *other* than Critical Games. I did not want to expose Cassidy, Devin, or anyone else to my father's uptight scrutiny.

"Oh, uh…it's kind of far from here."

"Are you sure?" he asked. I peered at him out of the corner of my eye and had difficulty reading his facial expression underneath those hairy eyebrows and thick mustache. "I saw us pass a storefront that said 'Game Shop' a few miles back."

A cold chill crept through my veins as I wracked my brain for my mental map of the area. We *did* pass by Critical Games. I'd been too plagued with anxiety to notice.

"I, uh, I…they close at five. It's almost four-thirty."

"We've got time," my mother interjected, and more icy chills trickled through my limbs. "I'd love to see the place, honey. Since it's where you spend your free time."

My palms were hot and clammy, and I wiped them on the cloth napkin in my lap. I scrambled for an excuse, any excuse, but eventually the gears in my brain ground to a halt. I didn't see a way out of this.

And maybe I didn't need one. Visiting the shop would at least show them that *Creatures & Crypts* was just a role-playing game and not the evil demon-summoning ritual my father believed it to be. I knew my chances of winning him over were slim, but my mother's façade would be much easier to crack.

"Uh, alright," I stammered. "We'll need to leave soon though."

"No problem," my father replied. "I'm ready to head out."

As we walked towards the car, preparing for a less than ten-minute drive over to Critical Games, a sudden urgent thought blared through my mind like an alarm bell.

Devin.

I needed to warn him.

Devin, I know you're busy, but this is urgent.

My fingers fumbled with the tiny digital keyboard, and I was grateful that autocorrect was able to fix most of my sloppy texting. I was in the backseat of my parents' car, with my father driving and my mother examining her nails in the passenger seat. Outside the window, the familiar blur of gas stations and strip malls whizzed past, each one a warning that we were getting closer to the shop.

But I barely even glanced out the window. My attention was locked on my phone screen as I begged for the typing bubble to appear.

C'mon, Devin. Please.

The last thing I needed was for him to be ambushed by my judgmental parents without giving him a heads-up. *Creatures & Crypts* would be wrapping up right about now, which meant he'd be behind the counter ringing up final purchases and preparing to close the shop.

It took five minutes, which felt like an eternity, but Devin's response finally popped onto my phone screen.

Sorry. Just finished C&C. What's up?

Me and my parents are on our way to the shop.

Wait, what?

I'm so sorry. I couldn't talk them out of it. They insisted on seeing the place.

So let me guess… you need me to play the part of the unassuming shop owner who is definitely not your boyfriend?

I'm really sorry.

Don't be. I know you're not ready for me to meet your parents yet. Honestly, I'm not either. I'll keep quiet and stay out of the way.

Thank you. You're wonderful.

Of course, sweetheart.

I put my phone back in my pocket just as we pulled into the parking lot. Our last-minute texting conversation made me feel a little better, but that relief was quickly replaced with dread as we stepped out of the car and approached the glass double doors.

I took a deep breath as I grabbed the metal handle, feeling like I was about to jump off a cliff.

All was well at first. The A/C smacked us in the face with a soothing chill that helped wipe the muggy Florida heat from our skin. Since C&C was over, the shop only had a handful of patrons left, mainly stragglers looking to buy supplies and the few preteen boys that still needed to be picked up by their parents.

"Avery!" Cassidy shouted from across the shop. She was sitting at one of the *C&C* tables next to Aaron, their dice and miniatures packed in neat tote bags in front of them.

"Cass!" I jogged over and hugged my best friend. I introduced her to my parents, and my mother was quick to sweep her up in conversation with a flurry of excited questions. My father was quiet, but at least he didn't look as grumpy as usual.

I knew why. On the surface, Cassidy looked a lot like me, with her cheery round face, curly hair, and cute clothing. She wore a dress with high-top Converses, one of my favorite combinations, but nothing else about her screamed "roleplaying geek."

As Cassidy chatted with my mom, my gaze flicked over to Devin. He was at the register, chatting with Sam while he rang up a stack of boxed miniatures. My heart fluttered when Devin laughed at something Sam said, but it also drew my attention to his piercings. And his tattoos. And his black clothing.

All those things were a part of him, and I adored Devin exactly the way he was. But I hated that it would cause my parents to judge him before they even got to know him.

I gulped as I realized I'd let my gaze linger on Devin a bit too long. Because my father was now staring at him, and I could feel his hazy disgust polluting the air once again. He paced around the shop with his hands behind his back, inspecting the various miniatures, dice, and books like a cop at a crime scene. I swore I saw his frown deepen behind his curtain-like mustache.

My father finally made his way all around the shop, pausing at the glass display counters near the register. Devin had finished ringing up all the customers in line and was now busy at his computer. But I noticed him give my father a sideways glance.

"Can I help you find anything?" Devin asked in a sweetly oblivious tone, the same way he would with any customer.

My father looked up from the display cases, and the two men locked eyes for several seconds. Devin forced a polite smile, which my father didn't react to.

"I'm fine, thanks," he mumbled as he stepped away.

Once my father was gone, Devin peered at me from across the room. He held back an awkward chuckle as I mouthed the word "sorry."

I spun around, my attention drifting back to Cassidy's conversation with my mother. She and Aaron were all packed up, with their bags slung over their shoulders as I followed them to the front door.

"I'll be spending a few hours over at Aaron's place," Cassidy explained as she gave me a quick hug. "You gonna be okay tonight?"

"I'll be fine," I lied. I could already feel the nerves returning to my stomach, scrabbling around like a pit full of spiders. "Go have fun with your boyfriend."

Cassidy giggled as she and Aaron walked out the door. I could tell she wanted to say, "you too," but she could sense that I was trying to keep my relationship status a secret from my parents. Or she saw the way my father scowled at Devin earlier.

"We should get going too," I said in a hurried tone. My mother was already at the door with me, but my father was on the far side of the shop, glowering at a set of *Wargavel* miniatures on a wall-mounted shelf.

"C'mon, Dad." My voice was tense as I ushered him along.

He didn't respond at first.

"Dad, they're closing."

Chapter 19

My father finally pulled his gaze away from the miniatures, walking at a snail's pace toward the door. His eyes still flicked in every direction, as if he were trying to mentally photograph everything in the shop before we left. Meanwhile, Devin stood behind the counter, typing away at his computer.

He was the last thing my father's judgmental eyes fell upon, and Devin offered a sickeningly friendly smile and wave in response.

Good, I huffed. *Don't let him get to you.*

The car was silent for the first few moments as my father pulled out of the parking lot and onto the main road. My mother broke the tension, prattling on about how interesting the place was in a cheery but awkward tone.

"It's demonic is what it is, Maria," he muttered through gritted teeth. "I think we need to have a conversation with our daughter about her relationship with Christ."

"My relationship with Him is none of your business," I fired back. "I'm an adult. And like I said before, it's just a game. I'm not worshipping Satan."

"Maybe we should back off, dear," my mother replied in a hesitant tone. "After all, I'm glad she's found such good friends there. That girl—Cassidy, was it? She was lovely."

My father paused, rolling his tongue over his clenched front teeth. "What about the one behind the counter?"

I could feel the blood draining from my face. "What about him?"

"He had *piercings in his face*," my father's voice darkened. "And I saw those arms full of tattoos before he tried to hide them. Followers of the Lord do not mutilate their bodies for their own enjoyment."

A deep exhale rolled over me as I tried to steady my mounting anger. I knew that Devin covered himself in tattoos because he liked them, but I also couldn't forget the night he showed the scars that lurked beneath. The tattoos helped hide them. They helped him feel less ashamed.

They helped him recover and move on.

I didn't understand why God would bc against that.

But I knew there was no point in arguing with my father. I'd been doing that my entire adult life, and all I got in return was anger and resentment. Since he'd been rooted in his antiquated ways for almost fifty years of life, I had little hope of ever changing his mind.

And dwelling on it always made me feel like a disappointment. So this time, I didn't stoop to his level and stayed silent.

"Sweetie, can you come back to the hotel with us for a bit?" my mother asked. I knew why; she wanted the two of us to discuss my surgery in private. But I also knew she was desperate to steer the conversation away from Devin.

I wanted to say no. I wanted to tell my mother that I needed space, tell my father to fuck off, and hole myself up in my bedroom where I didn't have to listen to either one of them. But I needed to let my anxiety out, and my mother was still my mother. Even with our mismatched understanding of the world, the night before surgery was a time when I really needed her comfort.

Plus, my father wouldn't be around. We could kick him out and have him go for a nice, long walk.

Off a cliff, I scowled, before reminding myself not to stoop to his level.

"Okay," I replied. "But just for a little while."

"Excellent." My mother clapped her hands together, her lavender nails glinting in the fading sunlight. "The hotel's just a few miles up the street. It's very nice; I bet you'll love it!"

Chapter 20

DESPITE THE AWKWARDNESS OF DINNER and the game shop, I genuinely enjoyed the hotel. It was an upscale chain hotel on the outskirts of downtown Orlando, not far from my multiple failed dates at Orange Blossom Coffee. The lobby was sleek and elegant, with glossy cream-colored tiles and a rounded, cavernous ceiling that stretched up several stories. The hallways were decorated with soft yellow wall sconces, and the hotel room doors were impressively tall with huge, brassy handles.

"Your father had a bunch of hotel points saved up from his work trips," my mother explained as she unlocked the door with her key card. "It's up to you if you'd rather recover at home or here."

My father ended up going for a walk at a nearby park, so me and my mother had the hotel room to ourselves. In addition to the immaculate, puffy king-sized bed and sliding glass doors that overlooked downtown Orlando, my attention was locked on the sleek alcove bathtub lined with what looked like jacuzzi jets.

I placed a hand over my stomach, which was swollen and bloated from our earlier dinner. I didn't have a bathtub at home, and I longed to immerse my sore abdomen in the warm, bubbling water. My mother noticed me gawking at it, and she chuckled.

"Go ahead sweetie." She pulled a bathrobe out of the closet. "Make yourself comfortable. Once you're ready, we'll talk about your surgery."

I spent nearly half an hour soaking in the tub, enveloped in warmth and contentment. The water seemed to take the pressure off my swollen stomach, and by the time I stepped out of the bubble bath, it had shrunken down to a semi-normal size.

I released my hair from its updo and scrubbed myself dry, putting my clothes back on over my pruned skin. The bath made my whole body feel lighter.

We had another half-hour before my father returned from his walk, during which me and my mother sat on the bed and had our first heart-to-heart conversation in years. I still wasn't ready to tell her about Devin, but in-between discussions of my upcoming surgery, I revealed more about my life in Orlando. Like with the game shop, my mother seemed more open-minded than in the past, which lifted a huge weight off my shoulders. Back when I was in college, the thought of me being anything other than a pious church girl was unthinkable for her.

There were also further discussions about endometriosis and what it meant for my health post-surgery. I knew that the laparoscopy wasn't a cure, and that I would likely need medication for the rest of my life. There was also a chance I would be infertile, but I was nowhere near ready to contemplate that topic yet.

There were a few times where I was tempted to tell her about my sexual dysfunction. After all, it was a major symptom of my endometriosis, and what had caused me so much difficulty in adulthood. But talking through female medical issues with my mother was one thing. Discussing my sex life was uncharted territory that I wasn't ready to explore.

I was so grateful for the time alone with her that I was disappointed when a loud knock echoed from the hotel door. I gave my mother a quick goodbye hug, but there was one topic still lingering in the back of my mind: her own health issues. I wanted to mention my concerns that she might also have endometriosis, but I couldn't get the words out. Her miscarriages were a taboo, forbidden topic in my family, and I feared bringing them up would send my mother into another emotional spiral.

As we broke our hug, I gazed deeply into my mother's warm, smiling face. On the surface she looked happy, but I could see the way her eyes glistened under the bright hotel lights and how the wrinkles lining her eyes and mouth tugged at her features. I'd seen her so infrequently over the past five years, but she always looked spry and healthy for a woman in her late forties. I knew perimenopause likely staved off her pain for good, but I wondered if she suffered all the same symptoms I had in her younger years. If, like me, she felt the need to hide it for her own self-preservation.

But those questions remained in my head, unable to be spoken aloud, as I left the hotel and went home to await my surgery day.

It was well past 11 p.m.

And I couldn't sleep.

I felt like a coked-up zombie as I sat in front of my computer, the screen eyeball-scorchingly bright in comparison to my nearly pitch-black room. I was simultaneously exhausted and wired, and it made me feel like my brain was short-circuiting. In addition, my abdominal pain had returned, with my stomach twisting into more knots than a pretzel.

I had no idea I would be like this the night before my surgery. It reminded me of Christmas Eve in my childhood, when I'd lay restless in bed for hours while I thought about the presents that awaited me the next morning. Except this time, there were no presents, and the anxious bubble of excitement was instead one full of dread.

I'd texted Devin earlier, which helped alleviate some of my anxiety. But he'd said goodnight to me over an hour ago, and I assumed he was already asleep. I knew he didn't work on Mondays, but I also knew he did a lot of errands and bookkeeping on his days off, and I didn't want to bug him all night. Like with the period pains I'd dealt with for the past decade, I avoided asking for help when I was not feeling well. Even the night before a major surgery.

I tried lying down several times, but while my body was exhausted, my mind was in overdrive. All my attempts at sleep managed to do was give my brain more time to contemplate the thousands of ways my surgical procedure could go wrong.

I distracted myself with video games instead, even if it meant passing out from exhaustion at an ungodly early hour. What did it matter if I didn't get any sleep? The anesthesia would take care of that for me, and I'd be so drugged up on post-op pain meds that I'd be fast asleep for the rest of the day.

Thirty minutes passed. I was so restless that I could barely focus on video games, and milking cows and collecting eggs in my farming sims was starting to feel like actual chores. I couldn't turn on my television for fear of waking Cassidy in the next room, so I put some YouTube videos on my computer.

Halfway through a "Top 10" gaming list, I nearly threw my headphones off in frustration. None of this was helping with my anxiety, and I wanted to scream. It was now almost midnight, and with every passing minute on my phone screen, I was inching closer to my dreaded surgery. Within the next few hours, the sun would start peeking up above the horizon, and I'd be forced to endure this procedure full of both anxiety and exhaustion.

I opened my earlier texts from Devin, but my fingers were frozen above my keyboard.

Do I really want to do this?

Do I really want to bug him at midnight?

My phone buzzed with a notification, and it was so unexpected that my hands spazzed out and I nearly dropped the little device on the floor.

Hey, not sure if you're asleep yet.

It was Devin.

I was so relieved that I wanted to reach through the phone screen and hug him.

I'm not. I can't sleep.

I don't blame you. The night before surgery is rough. I'm having trouble sleeping too.

Why?

Honestly…I'm kind of worried about it too. I'm anxious that you're having surgery and I won't be there for you.

Aww. My anxious heart softened at his words.

I'll be okay, Devin. It's not a big deal.

It's okay to be scared, Avie. You don't have to brush those feelings off.

Okay, okay. I am scared. I just hate thinking about it.

Well…if you can't sleep and I can't sleep, maybe we should stay up together?

What do you mean?

Come over. You can spend the night here.

My heart screamed yes, but my brain had concerns. I knew it was unlikely that we could share a bed for a night without wanting to pull each other's clothes off, and I wasn't ready to practice having sex until after I'd recovered from surgery.

I just…I don't know if I'm ready for that.

Is it the sex part? I don't expect anything from you, Avie. It's okay.

It's not you, it's me, lol. I'm concerned that I'm going to be all over you if we share a bed.

You know, I've been thinking...if you did want to be intimate, you know we can do so without actual penetration, right?

Not really. What do you mean?

I felt stupid. Between my sexual dysfunction and my abstinence-focused upbringing, my knowledge of sexual activities was limited for someone my age.

Well, maybe you can't handle full-on sex, but we might be able to get a finger in there. There's also oral, or just external stuff. Lots of options.

A bubble of hope welled up in my chest. I craved the thought of spending all night with him, and I knew from my limited experience that sexual pleasure was a great way to stave off anxiety.

I looked up at my computer screen and then back down at my phone.

Fuck it.

What's your address?

Devin lived around the corner from Critical Games, less than twenty minutes from my townhouse. I recognized the name of the community he lived in; I often drove past it when running errands downtown.

Give me half an hour. Need to put some clothes on.

I mean...

Shut up.

As I scrambled out of my gaming chair and into the bathroom, desperate to make myself presentable at well past midnight, the reality of what I was doing sunk into my chest like a warm yet tingling blanket.

I was spending the night.

With Devin.

And I was both thrilled and terrified.

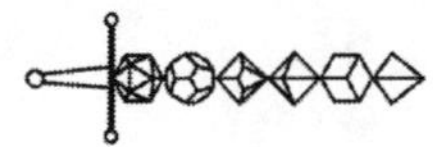

DEVIN LIVED IN A COMMUNITY CALLED WILLOW Grove, according to the worn wooden sign flanked with colorful flowers at the end of the main road. It was a small neighborhood, heavily shrouded by oak trees and centered around a large pond. While my townhouse building was in the middle of a traditional neighborhood, this community was entirely single-story townhomes, each with a garage, covered front porch, and muted blue paint. They were modern without being brand-new, built maybe twenty years ago based on the condition of the exteriors.

The long stretches of interconnected homes formed a maze, and I found myself going in circles, unable to understand the inane numbering system used to mark both the buildings and the individual residences. Finally, I came across building number 8, house number 342; an end unit next to a dense cluster of trees. I squeezed my Camry into a driveway that was barely big enough to accommodate it. There was no front yard, only a thin row of hedges that separated Devin's space from his neighbor's.

He had a patterned brick walkway leading to his porch, which I studied as I approached his front door in the darkness. An overhead wall lantern flicked on, bathing the front porch in yellow light and making me jolt.

Devin had a smart doorbell with a camera, so he likely already knew I was there. Instead of ringing it, I gave a faint knock, aware of how late it was and not wanting to disturb the neighbors.

I heard faint footsteps from further back in the house, but I startled when a much smaller, definitely-not-human figure appeared in the side window.

Devin has a cat?

The fluffy brown tabby, who had a white belly and four white paws, opened its mouth and let out a quick trill of meows. I couldn't tell if it was friendly, but I giggled as it raked its paws across the glass.

A metallic rattle shook the lock from inside the house, and the door swung open.

At first, my insides froze, fearing that I'd gone to the wrong residence and awoken a disgruntled neighbor. But even if I'd never seen him shirtless, with his impressive build and full tattoos on display, I knew that face smiling at me from the darkness.

I stepped forward, and Devin pulled me into a hug, closing the door behind me. We stood in silence for a few minutes, holding each other like we hadn't been together in weeks. I slid my arms around his back, tracing the muscles of his shoulders and biceps with my fingertips. His bare skin against mine felt so good. Too good. I feared I'd be tempted to jump into bed with him without so much as a hello.

"I'm so happy you're here." His words finally broke the sweet stillness. I could tell by the warmth in his voice that he was just as relieved to see me as I was to see him.

He pulled me back from our embrace, running his fingers along my jawline. In the dim light of the foyer, I could see his familiar face, including the holes below his lips and in his ears where he'd taken his piercings out. He was shirtless and barefoot, only wearing a pair of black gym shorts, and for the first time, I could see the full extent of his tattoos.

In addition to his *C&C* arm sleeve, which crested up his shoulder and ended just before his collarbone, he had a variety of random tattoos on his other arm, mostly of video game characters. He also had two on his chest, one on his stomach, and about half a dozen on his calves.

I pressed a hand to his chest, tracing my finger over the Critical Games logo just below his neck. I remembered the night he first showed it to me, almost two months earlier. I remembered how it made me wonder, shamefully at the time, what else was lurking underneath the black sweatshirts he always wore.

Now I had him. All of him.

"Want a quick tour?" Devin offered, sliding a hand around my waist.

I nodded. That was a good idea, as much as I would've rather focused on getting the rest of his clothes off.

The tabby slunk over from its spot by the window, letting out a funny-sounding meow and weaving between our legs as its chest rattled out a deep purr.

"You little bastard," Devin teased, scooping the cat up with one hand. The tabby yelped out its displeasure as Devin flipped it onto its back, holding it like a baby and exposing its fluffy white belly.

That was when I noticed that on Devin's wrist, nearly hidden by his tattoos, were old, scabbing claw marks.

"Who's this?" I asked.

"This is Gideon." Devin motioned for me to pet him. He had a wide head, with large, fluffy cheeks and vibrant yellow eyes. As unhappy as he was being held by Devin, he still purred when I scratched his ear.

Chapter 20

"See? He already likes you better than me," Devin laughed and plopped Gideon back on the ground. The cat shook himself off, sauntering away toward the kitchen with his long tail held high. "He's ten, and he pretty much rules the house. He belonged to my cousin back when he used to live here, but he moved in with his fiancé a year ago and she's allergic. So Giddy stayed with me. Mostly keeps to himself and just howls when he wants food."

I giggled. "I never imagined you as a cat person."

"I didn't either," Devin replied. "People sort of just dump pets on me."

He motioned for me to follow him into the kitchen. It was larger than mine but also more dated, with dull cream countertops and brassy cabinet handles. It was cluttered, with a variety of appliances lining the shelves, but it was also remarkably clean. Not a single dish was left hanging out in the sink.

As we continued throughout the townhouse, I noticed most of Devin's place was that way: incredibly cluttered, but also perfectly clean and organized. It was especially noticeable in the guest bedroom, which Devin referred to as the "storage room." Shelves lined two of the four walls, each overflowing with *Creatures & Crypts TCG* boxes, miniatures, and board games. A treadmill and weight set were shoved in the far corner, and the walls were full of framed posters from both rock bands and video games.

"There's so much stuff in here," I commented as I paced past the shelves, studying the contents of each one. I noticed that all the boxes, regardless of size, had detailed labels. "You certainly stay organized."

"Label maker," Devin commented as I ran my fingers over one of the labels. He pulled the device off a table next to the treadmill. "I needed one for the shop. I loved it so much I bought one for my place too."

I chuckled, coming to a stop at the end of the shelves. I was now less than a foot away from Devin, and I could feel the tension crackling off him. It jolted from my body to his like lightning between two conduits. Every moment of silence was a taunt, daring us to make the space between our bodies a lot smaller.

It tempted me, but just as I was about to lean into him, he asked if I wanted to see the master bedroom.

My stomach did a backflip as he took my hand and led me down the hall.

The first thing I noticed wasn't the low, metal-framed queen bed or black computer desk full of knickknacks. It wasn't even the plethora of *C&C* figurines on the wall-mounted shelf behind his Ikea dresser.

Instead, my gaze immediately shot to the giant PVC tank next to the bed. It rested on a heavy-duty shelving unit, the kind generally used for garages, and the décor inside indicated that it was home to some sort of pet reptile.

"This is what I mean by people dumping animals on me." Devin walked up to the tank, slid the glass door open with a loud squeak, and lifted a dark plastic hide. Inside, a chunky ball python was curled up in a tight cinnamon roll, and the sudden exposure caused him to flinch.

"This is Alistair." Devin lifted the sizable snake out of his hiding spot. Upon being picked up, the snake lifted its head and began flicking its dark pink tongue. "I was out fixing my car when I heard commotion from down the street. Someone moved out of one of the nearby units and just... left him. He was kind of skinny and he's got some old burn marks on his back, but he's an easy keeper. Sometimes I let him wander on my bed when I'm reading at night."

"Wow." I held out my hand, and Devin let Alistair crawl onto my outstretched arm. I was amazed at how soft and smooth his scales felt, not slimy like I'd been taught growing up. "He's beautiful. Poor little guy. Snakes are so misunderstood."

"Agreed. He's way less of a terror than Gideon, and tons of people have cats."

Devin placed the ball python back in his enclosure and slid the door shut. The snake lazily slithered back into his hide, his long body slowly disappearing into the darkness.

"That's not all I've collected over the years," Devin chuckled, taking a seat on the edge of the bed. "Travis had hamsters for a while, but he rehomed them after a near-fatal accident with Gideon. He also had a chinchilla, which lasted about a month. I swore he impulse-bought pets like candy. As for me, I used to have two ferrets, Cosmo and Nova. I loved those little munchkins, even if they did stink."

My ears perked up at the mention of ferrets. "Aw. What happened to them?"

"They passed. I only had them for a few years. Back when I was still recovering, I found them living in filth at a fellow AA member's house. Persuaded the guy to hand the little critters over for a hundred bucks. I knew nothing about ferrets, but I did tons of research and I like to think they lived out their senior years in peace. I miss them. I still have their cage tucked away in my closet."

I sat on the bed next to Devin, and the blooming warmth in my heart caused me to wrap my arms around him in a sappy hug.

"It's funny," I said softly with my lips just below his ear. "All these years, I never knew what a big heart you had under all that snarkiness."

Devin scoffed, leaning into my embrace. "I try. I like misfits. They've been through a lot, and so have I."

I smiled. *I think that's why I adore you so much.*

I pulled away and gazed into Devin's eyes. His face was inches away from mine, and he quickly closed the space with a long, deep kiss. He wrapped his hand around the back of my head, running his fingers through my scalp, and I wrapped my arms around his back.

My heart thrummed in my chest as anticipation made my nerves tingle. I knew what this was the beginning of.

And this time, there was no holding back. I pushed Devin backward, and he landed with a soft thud on the fluffy comforter while I sat just above his hips, straddling him with my dress splayed out and underwear pressed against his gym shorts.

I could feel that he was already aroused, and I pressed my hips tighter against his. He exhaled sharply, his breaths ragged with desire.

"Damn, you look fantastic up there," he sighed, rubbing his hands along the hourglass curve of my waist. His fingers curled around the fabric of my dress as he slid it over my head, slowly revealing my bare skin from my legs up to my chest.

There was a moment of silent musing from Devin, his gaze flicking up and down as he ran his hands across my torso. My breath hung in my chest, arousal mixing with anxiety as I wondered what he thought of my exposed self. A warm, dreamy smile stretched across his lips, and it made me break into a blushing grin.

"My god," he whispered. "You are perfect."

He hoisted himself up to a seated position, with my legs still wrapped around his hips. As eager as I was to slip his own clothes off, I wanted to give him a moment to further explore me.

Every brush of his fingers deepened the aches that consumed my entire body. He studied me like a map, determined to touch every inch of my bare skin. But the real quivers started when he reached my breasts. He gave them a few gentle squeezes before making his way inwards to my nipples.

As soon as he touched them, grabbing my breasts in his hands and running his thumbs over them like joysticks, I let out a gasp. Once the initial shock wore off, I realized how good it felt. I never knew those areas were so sensitive.

"Avie?" Devin paused, his gaze turning serious for a moment.

"Yes."

"I'm curious about something."

"Go on."

"It's just...I know you don't have much experience. But have you ever had an orgasm before?"

My stomach sank. With my staunch upbringing and painful sexual dysfunction, I barely even knew what that was.

"Uh... no. I haven't."

"Really?" he seemed shocked. "Damn. Well, we need to fix that."

"But..." My face burned with embarrassment. "How? I can't have sex."

Devin chuckled. "That's the joy of being a woman." He reached down to my pelvis, placing a finger at the top of my vaginal opening. "You have this thing called a clitoris. And from what I understand, it's even more sensitive than your vagina. And the best part? No penetration needed."

Clitoris? Another thing I knew nothing about.

I was wary of having his fingers down there, but as soon as he pressed down deeper, another yelp escaped me. And like with my nipples, it felt so foreign and so intoxicating at the same time.

Before, I was barely able to have anyone touch my vaginal area. But tonight was different. Here, there were no expectations. I could enjoy all the pleasure I wanted without the pressure of learning to have sex. I had no worries, no anxiety, and most importantly, no pain.

Devin's touch intensified as he used one hand to rub my clitoris and the other to rub my nipples. The smooth, deliberate, circular motions drove me wild, winding me up like a spring about to snap. I relished the pleasure, letting waves of it trail down my whole body, falling completely under his spell.

But what I hadn't expected was the tightening sensation within me. It was a strange yet euphoric buildup, like pressure inside a soda can. The heavier it became, the louder I cried, and the more intense the waves of pleasure felt. My breaths caught in my throat as I leaned into Devin's arms, the feeling of his bare skin against mine further heightening my ecstasy. I'd never felt like this before. And I never wanted it to end.

But it did, in the most glorious way. All that pressure exploded at once, escaping me with a loud cry, halfway between pleasure and pain. My shoulders trembled as my body gave out, falling against Devin's chest like I'd just run a marathon. I steadied my shaking fingers around his back as he embraced me, his warm laugh filling the amorous air.

"I—"

I tried to speak, but I could barely breathe, let alone utter a sound. Even sitting upright felt like too much effort.

"Here," Devin steadied my shoulders and laid me down on the bed, curling his own body around mine. Black dots and swirls clouded my eyes as the room wobbled in my blurry vision. I couldn't move, but it didn't matter. All I wanted to do was ride out this wave of euphoria in stillness and peace, embraced by the man who gave it to me.

"It's nice, isn't it?" Devin asked once my head stopped swirling like a lava lamp.

Chapter 20

"That was amazing," I replied breathlessly, still staring vacantly up at the ceiling.

He laughed, propping himself up on his shoulders so he hovered above me. He traced his fingers lazily up my thigh, which caused them to quiver with a sudden aftershock of pleasure.

But as the orgasm dissipated, it left room for my guilt to take over. Because the whole time I was in Devin's lap with him fingering me, all I wanted was more. He was still wearing his gym shorts, but I could feel him constantly pressing against me, and it made me ache to go further. I longed to have him fully inside me, us both giving and receiving at the same time. I wanted his cries to echo my own. I wanted to see him collapsed in post-orgasmic bliss like I was. But he wasn't, and it made me feel so selfish.

"You know..." Devin continued. "We don't have to stop. Women don't need breaks in between."

"We don't?"

"Yeah. Lucky," he scoffed with a smile on his face. "Besides, there's something I want to try."

He crept further down the bed, rubbing the sensitive skin of my upper thigh as he spread my legs apart.

"What about you?" I asked.

Devin shook his head. "We've got time. But first..." He tapped a finger against my vulva. "Have you ever had oral before?"

I shook my head.

"Well, it's not really penetration, so let's see if you can handle it. If it's too much, just tell me to stop."

"Okay." My voice wavered halfway between excitement and fear.

Like before, he started off gentle, positioning his head between my legs and pressing a small kiss against my opening. The pleasure caused me to gasp, starting the whole cycle over again. I was amazed that my body could recover from the orgasm so quickly.

Oral was even more intense than fingering. I clutched the pillow behind my head to keep the rapidly building tension from overflowing too early. Devin rubbed my hips and thighs as he explored me, and I had to be careful not to squeeze my legs too tightly around his head.

The second orgasm came quicker than the first, and this one left me even more exhausted and breathless. Devin crawled back up towards my head, taking great pleasure in watching me gasp and quiver next to him. I wish I'd known years ago that I could experience this amount of pleasure without penetration.

"Okay," I whispered once I could catch my breath. "That's enough. I'm done."

Devin laughed, wrapping his arms around me in a tight, full-body embrace. I grabbed the fabric of his gym shorts, pulling them down over his hips and tossing them over the bed.

Now we were both fully exposed, with nothing between us. I couldn't help but trace my fingers over his body, admiring his pale, lean frame covered in tattoos and muscle. Once I reached his chest, I studied the artwork that sprawled across it like a mural at an art museum.

He was beautiful.

"Now, it's your turn." I pressed a finger against the Critical Games tattoo below his collarbone. "What can I do for you?"

Devin raised an eyebrow. "Oh? Well, I have an idea. I need a shower, and we should probably get you cleaned up. Since I gave you oral, would you be interested in... reciprocating?"

I tilted my head quizzically. I'd never tried it before, but for Devin, I would try anything.

"Of course," I replied.

Devin cupped his hands around my breasts. "Excellent. Whenever you're ready. You may be shaky on your feet for a bit longer."

I curled up against him, nuzzling my head into his colorful chest. As eager as I was to return the favor, I didn't mind riding out the post-orgasmic bliss for a few more minutes.

But I also couldn't wait to hop in the shower with him. I knew his skin would feel even better against mine when we were both wet.

As midnight faded into early morning, Devin's deep, tender embrace kept all my fears and anxiety at bay. With my bare skin half-covered in bedsheets and our limbs entangled like puzzle pieces, I had never felt more at peace.

But I still didn't get a single second of sleep.

I was too busy riding out the high of emotions from our intimate night together. Traces of guilt still lingered in the back of my throat, but it was diluted by an overwhelming sense of joy and contentment. As I lay awake, I continued studying Devin's bare, sleeping figure, with our faces just inches from each other. He used one arm as a pillow, tucking it behind his head, and draped the other arm over my bare hip. My eyes trailed over the curves and definition of his biceps and the firmness of his chest. As his stomach rose and fell with every breath, I could see his abdominal muscles begin to peek through. Those features, topped with his colorful tattoos, tempted me to continue running my hands all over him. But Devin looked so peaceful in his sleep; I didn't want to risk waking him.

My gaze returned to his face. Strands of his shaggy black hair fell over his brows, obscuring his forehead and closed eyelids. I'd never noticed how thick and dark his eyelashes were, and I giggled when they twitched in his sleep. I wondered what he was dreaming about.

I wondered if he was dreaming about me.

His breath hitched, and my body tensed as he shifted the arm behind his head and tilted his body closer to mine. Just as I reached out to rub his shoulder, at the part where his tattoo sleeve faded away to bare skin, his blue-green eyes fluttered open.

He blinked a few times, rousing himself back to reality, and a warm smile slid across his lips as he caught a glimpse of me lying next to him.

"Good morning, sweetheart."

I replied by pulling him closer, so our chests were touching, then our foreheads, then our lips. I kissed him eagerly as heat flushed both our bodies, and I was tempted to give myself to him all over again.

"Did you sleep well?" Devin asked.

"Yes," I lied, snuggling closer to his bare chest. Despite my sleepless night, I was wide awake and buzzing with adrenaline.

We lay in silence for a few moments, with Devin rubbing my curly hair and me tracing the outlines of the tattoos on his chest. I let my thoughts drift back to our time in the shower, just like I had done repeatedly all morning. While the act itself was odd and took some acclimating, I took immense joy in how much pleasure it brought him. I ached to remember every detail: the way he braced himself against the shower wall with his fists gripping the side rails, the way he tilted his head back and cried out every time I went deeper. But most importantly, I could still feel the way he raked his fingers through my hair as I knelt before him, as he told me how wonderful and amazing and sexy I was between his ragged breaths.

Once we were finished, we held each other under the hissing stream of the waterfall shower, enjoying the warmth from both the hot water and our own burning attraction to each other. Water trailed down our faces and intermingled with our lips as we kissed, and I discovered that I thoroughly enjoyed the feeling of him pressing me against the shower wall.

And I was right. He felt even more amazing when we were both wet.

Now that we were both awake, I spent more time admiring him, tracing my hands over every unexplored inch of skin. I brushed strands of onyx-black hair away from his face, but my fingers paused above his dark eyebrow. A small, circular scar sat just above the hairline, and Devin gently pulled my fingers away and chuckled.

"Yeah...I used to have a lot more piercings," he explained, rubbing his eyebrow. "I had my right eyebrow done, but also my nose and the cartilage of my ear." He pointed to each scar and made a sideways gesture with his finger near the top of his ear. "I used to wear a bar through here."

"What made you take them all out?"

"Well...when I took over Critical Games, I decided I needed to look more like a proper business owner and not like a cashier at Hot Topic from 2008."

I giggled, and Devin crinkled his nose and rubbed my hair.

"Okay, well now I've gotta ask." A devious smile crept across my face as I peered below the sheets. "Did you ever get *it* pierced?"

Devin was silent for a moment before bursting into laughter and running a hand over his face. "No, I wasn't quite brave enough for that."

I peeked below the blankets, my gaze trailing down Devin's chest and bare hips. I wondered what it would feel like if he had been pierced. Part of me was intrigued, and part of me feared it would make the tension in my vagina even worse.

As much as I'd enjoyed the night before, another pang of guilt slammed into me like waves crashing against the shoreline. No matter how wonderful it was, it still wasn't sex. And I knew Devin wasn't a virgin, and that in the past other women had been able to give him what I could not.

What kind of partner did that make me?

"Hey," Devin rubbed my cheek with his thumb. "Something wrong? You look upset all of the sudden."

I shook my head.

"Did you enjoy last night?"

I nodded. "Yes. Of course I did. It's just…I'm sorry."

Devin scoffed, a wry smile on his face. "I spent the night with a beautiful, naked woman in my bed, one who gave me a fantastic blowjob in the shower. What could you possibly have to be sorry for?"

"Just…the fact that it wasn't sex. That's all."

"Avie…" Devin scolded in a gentle tone. "I think you're too hung up on this. We'll get there. Sex really isn't a big deal."

"But…" My voice trailed off. Telling him I was upset that I couldn't please him the way other women could was only going to make me sound petty and insecure.

"Let me tell you something," Devin continued, scooting himself closer to me. "Yes, I've had sex before. Many times. And you know what? Most of the time, I didn't really enjoy it. Because as I got older, I realized that sex wasn't actually what I wanted. I wanted intimacy, and it took me a long time to realize that those two things aren't always the same."

My gaze fell to the bedsheets, and Devin cupped a hand around my cheek.

Chapter 20

"This was, hands-down, the best night I've ever had with any woman. So stop worrying so much about sex. Please?"

"Okay," I replied in a reluctant tone. I wanted to believe him, but I knew my inadequacies and self-doubt would always lurk in the back of my mind.

Devin responded by wrapping his arm around me and pulling me toward his chest. As much as I loved his embrace, the tight, tense way he gripped me indicated that something heavy was on his mind.

"Listen, Avie..." His voice was soft with melancholy. "Just to give you some perspective on how insignificant this is. That night when you left..."

I cringed, embarrassment burning through my veins like acid. I hated thinking about that night.

"At first, I thought it was because of me. That my past drug addiction was too much for you."

"What? No, Dev, I would never—"

"I would've understood," he continued. His face was tense, like it was the night he first told me about his scars. "But it still killed me. So when I learned the real reason why you left, I wasn't upset at all. In fact, it felt like a huge weight had been lifted off my shoulders. I was relieved that the issue was something that, to me, is no big deal."

"I don't care about your past," I blurted out forcefully, adamant to calm the emotion I could see welling up behind those sea-green eyes. "That was nine years ago, Dev. You've been clean for a long time. Honestly, I'm amazed at how far you've come."

I pressed a hand against his cheek, and he took it in his and kissed the top of my knuckles.

"I meant it when I said you were incredible," I whispered.

Devin was silent for a moment, his expression stiff and contemplative as he ran his thumb over my fingers.

Something new was on his mind. And I wasn't sure if that was a good or bad thing.

"Can I say something?" he finally asked. I could hear the warble of uncertainty in his voice.

"Of course. Anything."

"It's going to sound insane. But I think you need to hear it. So you know how serious I am about you."

My chest fluttered with anticipation. "What is it?"

"I love you, Avie."

The world seemed to slow down after that, as those four words bounced around my skull like a pinball machine while I tried to process them. Shock was quickly replaced by joy, which then turned into the strongest feeling of adoration I'd ever had for anyone.

"I love you too, Dev."

There was no hesitation. I didn't need time to think it over. On the surface, it seemed insane to love someone after only two weeks of dating. But Dev and I went back way longer than that. I'd known him nearly my entire adult life. From our first kiss in the game shop, I knew he was the one. And even though I ran away, holding an unbearable secret that I feared would keep us apart, Devin still fought for me. His insistence on me going to the hospital was what got me my diagnosis. He comforted me when I was sick. He made me laugh when I got scared about my upcoming surgery.

But most importantly, he accepted me completely and wholly as I was. There was no act, no best-version-of-themselves façade that people often wore when they first started dating. After all, we'd made the decision to be together while I was lying in a hospital bed. He'd already seen me at my worst.

Our relationship could only get better from here.

I could feel Devin's hands shaking as he kissed me, wrapping his arms around my back and squeezing me like I was his whole world. I kissed him back, passionately, ferociously, and I would've gladly climbed back on top of him for round two if it weren't already almost 6 a.m.

"I have to go." The words hung ugly but true in the warm air as I pulled away from our embrace.

"Five more minutes," Devin pleaded like a sappy-eyed child, his arms still wrapped firmly around my back.

"Fine," I chuckled, settling back against his chest. He resumed stroking my curly hair, which I noticed was one of his favorite features of mine.

I wanted them to be the longest five minutes of my life. But I knew they'd pass in an instant.

There would be plenty of time for these moments later.

I just had to get through my surgery first.

Chapter 21

MY HEART THUMPED IN MY CHEST FOR THE entire hour-and-a-half drive to Lakeland. But once we approached the shiny, menacing hospital building, it was at a full-on gallop like a racehorse.

I had to admit, the inside was pretty. With its huge skylights, cavernous ceilings, and variety of artwork and potted plants, it almost felt like a hotel. At least, it did if I could ignore the weary-eyed patients slumped on benches with IV bandages strapped around their elbows.

Despite being almost twenty-seven years old, I hovered close to my mother for comfort. I realized that much like getting on a rollercoaster for the first time, it was the fact that I'd never had surgery before that made me so scared. Because the worst type of fear was the fear of the unknown.

Check-in was quick, and the holdup in the waiting room was brief. Only one person was allowed in the pre-operative area, so my mother came with me while my father stayed in the waiting room. The first thing the nurses had me do was change out of my comfy clothes and into a scratchy hospital gown that felt like it was made from paper towels. Once that was complete, they had me climb into a hospital bed, which felt much like climbing into a jail cell.

I knew what came next. Just like at the ER, they had to give me an IV.

But this time, having the tube inserted was no big deal. Maybe it was because I'd just had one two weeks earlier. Or maybe my fear of impending anesthesia overshadowed my fear of needles.

My anxiety was somewhat alleviated when my anesthesiologist popped in to say hello. He was a thin, balding, cheery middle-aged man. Almost too cheery for being in a hospital. In fact, I noticed most of the staff were that way - chatting and joking with each other while they worked. To them, it was just another day at the office.

The anesthesiologist explained the basics of how the anesthesia worked, but he also heavily emphasized that it would put me right to sleep and I wouldn't feel a thing. I wondered if he noticed the fear and anxiety written all over my face, because he gave the back of my hospital bed a reassuring pat and said he'd done thousands of procedures without any issues.

After he left, there was more waiting, which I hated. I'd brought my Kindle for situations like this, but as I attempted to engross myself in my latest fantasy novel, my anxiety made the words seem to melt off the page. It took a tremendous amount of willpower and eyestrain to keep my attention on the novel and not on my surgery. Even with a book to distract me, my hammering heartbeat never slowed.

"Alright, you ready?" The plastic scratching sound of curtains opening made my gaze shoot up from my Kindle.

My breaths sped up, nearly matching my racing heartbeat.

Oh no.

It's time.

The nurse had a warm, friendly voice, but the fact that she and the two other nurses behind her had their faces shielded by surgical masks made me even more antsy.

"I love you." My mom reached out and squeezed my hand. I could tell she was anxious too, even if she was desperately trying to hide it. "It'll all go by in a flash. They'll put you right to sleep."

There was a soft lurch in my hospital bed as one of the nurses stepped behind it, and then it began to move forward.

"We're going to give you some medication to help you relax before the anesthesia." The female nurse explained to me as she fiddled with my IV. The bed was now out of my curtained-off waiting area, and we were headed down a long hallway.

"I just need you to count to five." The nurse continued as she hooked a large syringe up to my IV. "Can you do that for me?"

I struggled to swallow. I couldn't tell if it was my anxiety or the medication, but the hallway was starting to spin.

"Okay." I forced my words out. "One... two... three..."

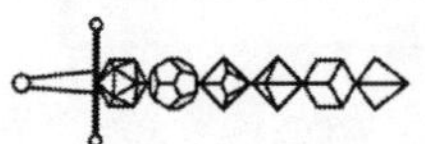

FOUR... FIVE...

Okay, I'm ready.

Wait...

Where am I?

Chapter 21

Devin was right about the anesthesia. One second, I was being wheeled down the hallway toward the surgery suite, and the next, I was lying bleary-eyed in the recovery room.

My head was spinning like a top, and I could barely open my eyes, but I felt no pain. I assumed it was because they'd heavily drugged me. As my clumsy hand brushed across my abdomen, I could feel the ragged bumps of the stitches.

It was over.

The surgery was done.

"Devin?" My voice was barely a whisper. There was no reply other than the various hums and beeps of hospital machinery.

"Devin?" I croaked, struggling to raise my voice loud enough to be heard. "Dev?"

Through my hazy vision, I noticed a light-skinned male hand next to my bed and instinctively grabbed it.

"Devin..." I whimpered. I missed him. I needed him.

I tried to rub my fingers over his knuckles like I always did, but the hand slipped away almost as soon as I grabbed it.

With my frustration growing and my rationality severely muddled by the anesthesia, I grabbed the hand again.

It pulled away, this time slower, and gave my own hand a gentle pat before returning to the keyboard it was typing on.

Keyboard?

I blinked a few times, and my vision began to stabilize. I was an idiot. Devin wasn't there. The hand belonged to a male nurse sitting next to my hospital bed. He was typing away at a computer with a stack of paperwork in his other hand. He chuckled when he noticed me gawking at him.

As embarrassed as I was, I assumed he was used to drugged-up patients being irrational. I'd seen videos of people coming out of surgery say and do worse things than hold a stranger's hand.

But being as drug-addled as I was, that didn't stop me from shouting Devin's name loudly across the recovery room. My cries were sharp and hoarse, and the nurse hid another chuckle behind his hand and told me my family would be allowed in soon.

A few minutes later, another nurse came in to check up on me. She had a cheery, motherly demeanor and was completely unfazed by my erratic speech and wobbling body. She said I needed to use the bathroom so she was sure that I could pee properly, and I clung to her shoulder as she helped me out of bed and led me down the hall.

Once I was alone in the restroom, I realized how much my vagina ached. The pain traveled further up my abdomen into what I assumed was my uterus. That was when I remembered that in addition to the laparoscopy, the surgeon had inserted a camera into my vagina to take a look around and collect a pap smear.

The pain wasn't unbearable, but I was incredibly sore. It felt like someone had taken a rough-edged spoon and scraped my entire uterus out.

It also burned when I peed. But the important part was that I *was* able to pee, and I assumed the discomfort would go away with time.

I took a moment to study myself in the mirror as I washed my hands. I was a pale, greasy-haired, puffy-eyed wreck. But the fear, the anticipation...it was all over. I'd made it through the worst part, and now I could spend the next week resting and recovering at home.

The more I thought about it, the more relief and joy it brought me, and I did a silly little dance in the hallway as the nurse escorted me back to my hospital bed.

Anesthesia was a hell of a drug.

My mother arrived not long after, fawning over me with hugs and kisses and congratulating me for being so brave. I hugged her back, her affection further amplifying my relief. Even as an adult, I would always appreciate my mother's comfort.

Maybe I should visit them more, I thought to myself. *I'll just steer clear of my grumpy father.*

"So the surgeon came out to the waiting room and told us about your procedure," My mother announced, which made my ears perk up.

"They were right. You did have endometriosis, and they were able to remove it all."

In my drug-addled state, I wasn't sure whether to cheer or cry. I ended up doing both, laughing joyously as tears streaked down my puffy face.

"You did it, sweetheart." My mother kissed my forehead.

Sweetheart...

Thoughts of lying in bed with Devin the night before, him rubbing my hair while calling me that same pet name, flooded my mind. I shot out of bed, which made my dizzy head swirl, and scrambled for my phone.

"Here it is, dear." My mother pulled the device out of her purse and handed it to me.

The screen seemed unnaturally bright, as if it were burning out my retinas. I could read my notifications—the text wasn't melting like it was on my Kindle earlier—but I had trouble keeping my hands steady and my eyes focused.

I had one message from Devin, from half an hour ago.

Hey sweetheart. You out of your surgery yet?

Hi Dev! I just got out! I did it!

That's great! You feeling okay?

I feel great! Well, drugged, but great! Not in much pain. And the doctor said I did have endometriosis! I was right!

Uh…Avie? You okay?

I froze, my eyebrows furrowing.

What do you mean? Of course I'm okay.

Avery…never mind. Just text me later when you're less drugged.

Confused by Devin's odd response but too high on anesthesia to let it bother me, I plopped my phone on the bed next to my hip and chatted with my mother while I waited to be discharged.

She explained that the doctor found endometriosis not only on the outside of my uterus and pelvic wall, but also around my stomach and intestines. That was a huge relief, because it explained why I had so many digestive issues. I hoped that going forward, my stomach wouldn't blow up like a balloon after every significant meal.

About fifteen minutes passed, and the nurse came in and announced that I could change back into my regular clothes. And as I did, alone in the restroom, I got my first look at my incisions. They were tiny, less than an inch across, and sealed with surgical glue and a row of tight black stitches. But despite their small size, they were incredibly sore, and my stomach was puffy and red from the procedure.

One, two, three...

The nurse said there were four incisions.

Where is...

Chapter 21

I tilted my head down at my stomach, and my insides twisted.

My belly button.

They'd cut open my belly button and stitched it back together.

A nauseating quiver ran down my limbs and up my throat as I scrambled to get dressed, trying to get visuals of how the surgery was performed out of my mind.

After that, I was itching to get out of the hospital as soon as possible. I was capable of walking, but the nurse insisted that I be brought to the car in a wheelchair. My father met us back in the waiting room, and to my surprise, he bent down to give me a hug, being careful not to touch my stomach. As he pulled away, I noticed the slightest hint of concern in his eyes.

He had been worried about me. Even if he barely showed it.

The nurse and my mother helped load me into the front seat of my father's truck. I insisted that I would be fine in the back, but my mother wanted me to be able to recline my seat and get some rest.

"I guarantee she'll be passed out the rest of the day," the nurse told my mom as she handed her a bundle of discharge paperwork. "Once she's awake, make sure she takes some pain meds. The injections we gave her will only last about 12 hours."

Injections. They gave me pain injections. No wonder my incisions don't hurt yet.

"Goodbye, Avery!" The nurse waved as she closed the door of the truck and my father pulled away from the hospital curb.

It was still surreal that the surgery was over. It had been less than an hour since I woke up, and I was already being discharged and sent home.

As my mother instructed, I leaned back in my seat and closed my eyes as a sudden wave of exhaustion rolled over me. We had a long drive home to Orlando, which was plenty of time for me to get some rest.

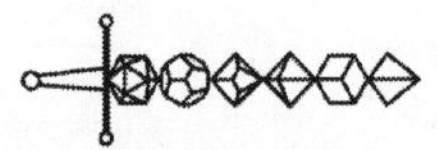

I MAY HAVE HAD A HAYWIRE BURST OF ENERGY immediately after my surgery, but by the time we made it home at nearly 3 pm, I felt like I hadn't slept in years. Just the short walk from the car to my bedroom was as exhausting as a marathon, and I needed both of my parents' assistance to not collapse along the way.

I fell asleep almost instantly; a series of bizarre, anesthesia-fueled dreams looping through my mind in erratic patterns as I slept. My weary body finally awoke in the early evening, when the amount of sunlight streaming through my window had significantly dimmed. Even with my eyes open and my mind alert, I still struggled to sit upright. My limbs felt like lead.

At this point, I assumed the anesthesia had worn off. The world no longer had a surreal, hazy tinge to it, like I was living in some sort of alternate reality. My eyes flicked over to my plain white end table, and I struggled to reach my phone without having to shift out of bed. I knew I likely had tons of messages awaiting me.

Cassidy, Aaron, and a few other members of the game shop had all texted me. Cassidy asked how I was feeling and told me to check my Steam account. She'd gifted me a video game, with a cute note telling me to enjoy it while I was recovering. Aaron said that Sam was asking about me and offered to host a board game night for all of us once I'd recovered.

I smiled, wading my way through the sea of "feel betters" and "get well soons" while a soothing warmth bloomed in my heart. I'd never realized how many true friends I had at Critical Games. How much of a community we'd become.

And of course, after I made my way through all my texts, I had saved the best for last.

I was just about to send him a sweet, loving message telling him that I was fine and that I missed him...until I caught a glimpse of my texts from earlier.

Dev! Jt I got out! I dd t!

I frowned. *What the hell?!*

Druged gat! Pan not. Docr endo petri has! Rite!

This message was followed up with several blood drop emojis, and I smacked a palm against my burning forehead.

I swear to God that's not what I typed...

No wonder Devin's texts didn't make sense. *My* texts didn't make sense. How could I feel so stable and be so incoherent at the same time?

Fucking anesthesia. I plopped my phone on my bed and took a few deep breaths. *Never again.*

Once I had a few moments to self-analyze and be certain that the anesthesia had made its way out of my system, I picked my phone back up and typed out a message to Devin.

Hey Dev. Just got a look at my texts from earlier. Sorry about that.

I checked the message three times before I sent it, making sure that my eyes weren't deceiving me.

Don't apologize. That was hilarious. And hello sweetheart. I'm assuming, based the fact that your message uses actual English, you're no longer drugged up?

I think so. The world isn't quite as weird anymore.

That's good to hear. You've recovered okay? Are you in pain?

Yeah, I'm fine. The stitches don't really hurt, I've just been sleeping a lot.

Well I need to ask since it's almost 5:30… have you received any deliveries today?

Deliveries?

I peered up at the top corner of my phone. It was 5:28 p.m.

I suppose I should go as Mom if anything arriv—

The doorbell rang - a sudden, sharp trill that echoed throughout the house and made my skin prickle. I could hear low chatter and shuffling feet from my parents in the kitchen. I wanted to answer the door, but it took a tremendous amount of willpower just to sit upright in bed.

Ow. I instinctively reached toward my aching stomach but pulled away since I knew touching the stitches would make it worse. The pain wasn't too severe, but I was very sore, and any movement of my abdomen further irritated my incisions.

The pain meds must be starting to wear off.

I heard the squeak of the door opening, and there was muffled but cheery chatter between my mother and whoever was at the door. I heard my mother's pitch grow louder and higher, as if she were surprised about something.

I peeled the covers off my legs, but they felt heavy and numb after hours stuck in bed. I attempted to slide my body off the edge, but a sudden, sharp tug at my stitches made me freeze and grit my teeth in pain.

Godamnit.

I was stuck. But it didn't take long to find out who was at the door, because my mother burst into my room right after they left.

Once I saw the glass vase in her hands, with a colorful assortment of flowers sprouting out in all directions, I felt my face turning red. The sensation of my heart fluttering and my stomach dropping at the same time made it feel like I was in freefall.

"Avie!" My mother exclaimed in her usual excited-squeaky voice as she entered the room. "Look what arrived for you!"

I was a stone statue in bed, able to hear my rapid heartbeat pounding in my ears, as she set the vase of flowers on my windowsill.

"That's not all," my mother continued, pointing out the door and into the hallway. "The lady also dropped off a large bag of takeout food. It smells delicious; the bag says it's from a place called Olive Tree Café?"

Dev...

I felt like I was going to melt into a lovesick, overwhelmed puddle.

He'd sent me flowers. No guy, in my entire life, had ever sent me flowers.

And food. From my favorite restaurant in Orlando.

My first instinct was to shoot out of bed, grab my phone, and text Devin that he was a wonderful, far too generous boyfriend and that I loved him very much. But of course, I couldn't do that without my mother becoming suspicious.

"Any idea who sent these, my dear?" she asked, inspecting the flowers by the window. "There's no card."

A faint chuckle escaped me. *Clever, Devin.*

"My friends," I blurted out, in a manner too abrupt and panicky for it to be true.

But whether my mother believed me or not, she didn't pry further. She offered to help me walk to the kitchen so I could eat dinner with my parents, but I excused myself to the restroom first, making sure my phone was tucked away in my pocket.

"Do you need help, dear?"

"No," I replied, my throat choking up as I tried to hide how much the stitches hurt. "I'll be fine. I'll meet you and Dad out there."

Once I was settled on the toilet seat and my stitches no longer felt tense and achy, I fired off a few quick messages to Devin.

Dev…you didn't have to do this.

So I take it the goods arrived?

Yes. You sent the flowers and food?

Yup! Avie, you had surgery and I'm not able to see you while you're recovering. Of course I'm going to send you flowers. And I figured you and your family would be tired after today and not up for cooking. So, enjoy the food.

You're an angel, Dev. I'm gonna go eat, but I'll talk to you later.

Lol. I am no angel, but thank you. I love you, sweetheart. I wish I could see you.

I know. I love you too.

I wish I could see you.

Those words ached more than my stitches ever could.

This was the sort of situation where people *needed* their partners around. I knew that the next few days would be relaxing, not having to worry about work and getting as much rest and video gaming time as I pleased. But it would be much easier to do it with Devin here. Just being able to curl up on the couch or bed with him would take so much of my pain away.

Would it be so terrible if I had him over? Would my parents really reject him?

Those questions swirled in my mind, pounding against my skull like a migraine, as I stumbled out of the bathroom and walked out to the kitchen to join my parents for dinner.

Chapter 22

"SO WHO GAVE YOU THE FLOWERS?"

I froze, my mouth mid-chew and my fork still stuck in my dinner. For the first few minutes of our meal, the three of us had been eating in silence, which I was perfectly content with.

My mother's sudden question had shattered any hope of a peaceful dinner.

"Uh...I told you, one of my friends." I quickly shoved another bite of food in my mouth, trying to keep my tone as level as possible and not reveal any deception.

"Which one? Was it one of the friends I met at the game shop?"

"Y-Yes."

I peered down at my Styrofoam takeout container, praying that my mother would get the hint and stop prying. But I knew that was wishful thinking. Since I rarely saw my parents, they were always eager for details on my personal life. At least my mother was.

Chapter 22

"That's so sweet of them," she continued, and my shoulders loosened. "They got you dolmades and spanakopita, your favorites. They must know you really well."

My shoulders tightened right back up. She wasn't going to let this go.

"Was it that curly-haired girl we were talking to? The one with the boyfriend?"

My mouth opened, then immediately snapped shut. It would be easy to just claim Cassidy had sent me the flowers. After all, she was still staying at Aaron's apartment and hadn't been by to say hello yet.

But it still wouldn't make sense. Why would Cassidy have flowers delivered instead of just driving over? Plus, if my mother ever saw Cassidy again, she'd thank her for sending the flowers, and Cassidy would have no idea what she was talking about.

God... I set my fork down on the table with a loud metallic clank. All the anxiety and plotting was giving me a headache.

I guess I could always just text Cass and warn her...

Wait... no.

You know what?

Fuck this.

I couldn't hide the truth forever, and concealing my relationship made me feel like a bad girlfriend. Whether I told my parents today or in six months, they would judge him all the same. Better to get it over with now.

"Was it not her?" my mother continued, and I could feel my jaw clenching. "Was it—?"

"I have a boyfriend."

It was like a bomb went off. The normal dinnertime sounds of food rustling, mouths chewing, and silverware scraping screeched to a grinding halt. My parents were frozen in an eerie, tense silence.

"Oh, sweetie." My mom fumbled for her words, shocked but not necessarily unhappy. "Congratulations! When did this happen?"

"A few weeks ago."

"Wow, so it just started? And he sent you flowers?"

"Well, we've known each other for a long time."

And he told me he loved me last night. But I kept that part to myself.

"Well." My mother sat up straighter, her excited-squeaky voice at an all-time high. "Who is he? What's his name?"

"Devin," I replied flatly, after doing a quick replay of our time at the Critical Games to confirm that I never mentioned his name.

"Does he go to your game shop too?"

Oh boy. We were inching closer to the truth. I felt like I was playing a racing game, about to turn the corner on the final lap and cross over a very dangerous finish line.

My eyes flicked up to my father. His face was set in stone, and I knew his mustache was concealing a heavy-set frown.

"He was the one behind the counter."

My mother's face twitched for a second, betraying her joyful exterior. I could see the muscles my father's neck tightening like a noose.

"The guy with the black hair?"

"Yes. He's the owner."

Absolute silence. I felt like my dinner was about to come crawling back up my throat.

"You see this?" My father's sudden exclamation made blood pound in my ears. "First she runs away from home, and then she spends the next five years avoiding us, not going to church, and now she ends up with—"

"What?" I suddenly found the courage to speak. "What were you about to call him?"

My father's bushy eyebrows narrowed.

Chapter 22

"You know nothing about him. You're just judging him based on his appearance, aren't you?"

"I know enough." A loud, grating squeak made me cringe as my father pushed his chair back and dumped his Styrofoam container in the garbage.

A low, pulsing ache stabbed at my abdomen, and I placed a hand over it. I needed to lie down and continue recovering from my surgery, one that I'd had just a few hours earlier. I did not need to be arguing with my father over this.

I stood up, ignoring the stinging tug of my stitches. *Be the bigger person.*

"Look, I'm finished eating, and I'm going to go lie down and get some rest. If you want to talk about this without acting like my boyfriend is a monster, feel free to knock on my door."

I dumped my own takeout container in the trash, determined to walk away from my dumbfounded parents and disappear into my bedroom while keeping a straight face.

But as soon as I was alone, all the air came bursting out of me. I sat down gingerly on the edge of my bed, taking a few deep beaths and trying to calm the adrenalin spike.

I peered over at my phone, which hovered on the edge of my end table.

Hey Dev?

Hey sweetheart. You done with dinner?

Yes, thank you so much. It was delicious. But I need to talk to you about something.

What is it?

Well…my parents prodded me for details about the flowers, and I let it slip that I have a boyfriend.

Ah, how'd they take that? And do they know it was the dude behind the counter at the game shop?

Not great, and yes. My mom wasn't too bad, but my dad's kind of…well, an ass. I'm sorry Dev. I hate this.

I know. It's okay. And trust me, I'm no stranger to it. I dealt with this with my own family.

There was a faint but firm knock on my door, and I sat there, phone in hand and stitches aching from sitting upright, as I debated whether to tell them to come in or go away.

They came in anyway. But thankfully, it was just my mother. I assumed my father was still angrily stewing in the kitchen.

"Hey, sweetheart." Her tone was soft but hesitant, like trying to coax a frightened animal. I remained frozen in bed, my lips pressed in a tight line and my phone clutched in my hands. I tried not to focus on how much I'd rather be texting Devin instead of talking with my mother.

"Hi." I replied bluntly.

"Listen, hun." She took a seat at the edge of the bed, so our shoulders were less than a foot apart. "I'm sorry about that."

"What? For Dad?"

"Well…"

"If he's sorry, then he should be the one to come in here and apologize."

Chapter 22

A long, deep sigh escaped my mother, and I knew she was frustrated with him too.

"You know how he is, Avery."

Always with the excuses. Being a pompous asshole shouldn't be treated like a personality quirk.

"But…" she continued. "I still think it's wonderful that he sent you flowers and food."

I turned my head towards my mother. "So, you're saying it *is* possible that my boyfriend is a good person and not whatever scum Dad believes him to be?"

She didn't reply to my biting, sarcastic tone, but I could tell by the way she chewed her bottom lip that she was deep in thought.

"I imagine you'd like to see him."

"A lot more than you two at the moment."

"Avery…" my mother scolded, but her frustration quickly softened. "You should invite him over. I'll make dinner."

"With Dad here? Sounds like a terrible idea."

"I'll handle your father," she assured me. Her gaze flicked down to my phone. "I'm assuming you've been texting him?"

I nodded.

"Well, it's up to you, but let me know if you do invite him over."

My mother got up and walked back into the kitchen, leaving me alone to ponder my decision. My gut screamed no; the last thing I needed was to subject my brand-new boyfriend to my judgmental tyrant of a father. There would be so much tension at dinner that I doubted I'd be able to stomach any food, even if it was my mother's amazing cooking.

But my heart ached to see Devin. I needed his comfort during one of the most uncomfortable and painful weeks of my life. Between the fatigue from the medication and the soreness from my stitches, all I wanted to do was be wrapped up in his arms. I doubted that would happen with my parents hovering around, but I knew I could at least sneak in a quick kiss.

Hey Dev. Sorry, my mom just came in.

What did she say?

Whelp…I have a proposition for you.

Go on.

The good news is we can see each other.

I very much like that news.

The bad news is it's because my parents want to meet you. Specifically, my mother.

I'm off tomorrow. I can stop by in the evening.

So…you're up for meeting them?

Well, I'm very much up for seeing you. As for your parents…well, they'll have to meet me sooner or later.

My mom isn't that bad. I think she'll be fine. My dad is the real issue.

Yup. I know the type. I'll be on my best behavior, but I can't guarantee I can change his dislike of me.

Chapter 22

I don't expect you to. I just really want to see you.

I know, sweetheart. In fact, I have an idea.

I could hear hushed but harsh conversation coming from the kitchen. I knew my parents were having a heated discussion about my newfound relationship. I couldn't make out their words, but I could tell by their tones that my mother was scolding my father, and my father was biting back with his usual gruff, demanding tone.

And based on the way her voice softened, I could tell my mom was running out of steam.

He always wins, I scowled.

What's that?

Well, I know you can't sit upright at your desk, but you have a Steam Deck, right?

Yup. I can play it in bed.

I'm pretty sure I added you on Steam a long time ago. I can look and see what games we share.

I looked up from my phone again. It was getting late, and I was less reliant on them than I thought I'd be after surgery. I could get through my nighttime routine and curl up in bed without assistance, so figured I could shoo them back to their hotel to have some gaming time with Devin.

That was partially what happened. My mother said there was no way in hell they were leaving me alone less than a day after surgery, even if I could get up and walk around without issue. They tried to persuade me to come with them to the hotel, but I wanted to recover in the comfort of my own house. Which was a problem, because my parents couldn't stay there as they would have nowhere to sleep.

Eventually, my father decided to head back to the hotel while my mother set up a makeshift bed on the couch. She was hesitant to even leave me alone in my room, but she relented when I told her I would be going to bed early anyway. I didn't need her help to sleep.

That was only a partial lie. Because as soon as my father left and my mother settled herself in the living room with the TV on, I curled up into bed with my Steam Deck. I felt guilty leaving her alone in the living room, but I'd had an eventful day, and after our tumultuous dinner I needed some time away from my parents.

Plus, I was exhausted. I wasn't even sure how long I'd be able to stay awake and game with Devin.

My phone buzzed with a message from him.

Damn, 300 hours in Stardew Valley?

Don't judge me.

Not judging. I love that game.

Really?

Yeah. With my hectic schedule, sometimes I just want to play something relaxing instead of shooting zombies or coordinating some complicated mission with my cousin.

I giggled. Another thing for me to love about him.

Chapter 22

So I take it you want to start a multi-player game?

Of course. Does this count as moving in together? Gosh, Avie, things might be going a bit too fast.

My nose crinkled. *You little brat.*

We're doing separate cabins, mister.

Fiiiine. I get to pick the cat though. I want the one that looks like Gideon.

I giggled as I booted up my Steam Deck, the handheld device's bright screen flashing like fireworks in my eyes.

We spent the rest of the night that way, alternating between texting and farming, until I eventually called it a night and went to sleep.

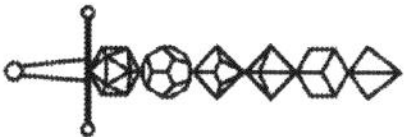

I WOKE UP THE NEXT MORNING AT 6 A.M. IN TERrible pain.

My stitches ached and burned with every movement. Even my own breaths making my stomach rise and fall felt like they were pulling my incisions apart.

I stumbled out of bed, my footsteps noticeably less steady than the night before, and staggered out of my bedroom and into the kitchen.

My pain meds were in an orange bottle on the counter. I fiddled with the lock on the container, slid two of them into my palm, and chugged them down with a mouthful of lukewarm water from the kitchen sink.

"Avie, sweetie..."

I looked up, the sink still running and water dripping from my lips. I'd awoken my mother, who sat upright twenty feet away on her makeshift couch-bed.

"It hurts," I croaked, my chest tightening.

"Come here sweetheart." My mother hurried across the kitchen and wrapped her arms around me. I swallowed hard, refusing to let the pain make me cry, and I realized that it had been years since I hugged my mother like this.

"The injected pain meds probably wore off," she explained, patting my curly hair. "Lie down and give it some time for the pills to kick in. You'll probably be like this for a few days."

She broke our embrace and took me by the hand, leading me back into my bedroom.

"I'll make you some breakfast," she promised in her warm, loving mom voice. "And you like tea, don't you?"

I nodded.

"Green or black?"

"Black. English breakfast—far right kitchen cabinet."

As my mother settled me in bed and turned around to leave, a sudden thought popped into my head.

"Hey Mom?"

She stopped by my bedroom door. "Yes sweetie?"

"How did you know how long the pain lasts? Have you ever had surgery?"

She nodded. "Yes."

"When?"

"I had a c-section when Allen was born."

My eyebrows shot up. Allen was my youngest brother, born when I was eleven years old.

"I don't remember you recovering from that."

My mother chuckled. "Admittedly I kept it hidden from you kids. And there's only so much recovering you can do with a newborn and two other children, plus a whole house to keep up with."

I opened my mouth, ready to reply with shock and confusion, when my mother turned away and closed the door.

With her gone, I slouched down in bed, the pain from my stitches further fueling the flames of my frustration.

Why is being a woman so difficult?

I SPENT THE REST OF THE MORNING ALTERnating between sleeping and gaming, and I was so exhausted and dizzy from the pain that my video games started showing up in my dreams. It made it difficult to tell where fantasy ended and reality began, and I didn't finally start to feel like myself until well into the afternoon.

By that time, my father had arrived from the hotel, and he and my mother were conversing in the kitchen when I woke up. I ran a hand over my stitches and realized that the pain was gone. I assumed that the medication was finally working without the loopy side effects. But just as I went to step out of bed, my mother crept in through the door carrying a ceramic plate.

"Oh, good, you're awake." she smiled, setting the plate on my end table. "I rolled some dolmades and made a whole tray of spanakopita while you were asleep. I just heated this piece up.

"Wow, Mom, thank you," I exclaimed in surprise. "Where did you even get the ingredients to make them?"

"There's an international grocery store about fifteen minutes away, although your local chain had everything except the grape leaves. Eat up, sweetheart. You need fuel to recover."

I smiled. The flaky spinach pie smelled delicious, and I could see the freshly microwaved steam wafting off the top.

"Mom. I'm not completely bed bound. I can eat in the kitchen."

"Okay, sweetie. Just be careful."

I stepped out into the kitchen and took a seat at the dining table, avoiding my father's gaze as I stabbed at my lunch with a fork.

"I also have all the ingredients to make some salad and moussaka when your boyfriend arrives," my mother announced, which made my shoulders twitch a fraction. "What time is he coming over, by the way?"

"Not until five," I replied.

"So, he *is* coming?" my father chimed in, although his tone was flat as always.

I nodded, although my gaze quickly returned to my spanakopita. I didn't like locking eyes with him any longer than necessary.

Out of the corner of my eye, I saw my mother shoot him a "be nice" look as she rifled through the fridge.

After I finished my lunch, I loaded my plate in the dishwasher and slunk back into my bedroom. I let out a long, deep yawn as I crawled into bed, one so big it made my jaw ache. My usual routine involved bouncing between work and the game shop, so I was always busy with something. Sleeping this much made me feel lazy and gross.

But I knew I needed rest, and I was asleep again within twenty minutes.

When I opened my eyes again, I was unaware of how much time had passed. But when I realized that the light in my room was growing dimmer, I shot out of bed and grabbed my phone off the end table.

Chapter 22

I sighed as I rubbed my aching abdomen. It was 4:20 pm., which meant I had a little over half an hour to make my sluggish, stitched-up self presentable for my boyfriend.

My eyes flicked toward the bathroom. *That needs to start with a shower.*

Thirty minutes later, I was clean and refreshed, with fluffy blow-dried hair and a loose, plain t-shirt dress that wouldn't irritate my abdominal stitches. I forced a smile across my face in my bathroom mirror. I looked considerably more presentable, but my face was still puffy and pale.

I was poking at the dark circles under my eyes when the doorbell rang.

"I'll get it!" I exclaimed, scurrying out of my bedroom and into the hallway. I didn't want Devin to be greeted by my overexcitable mother and judgmental father.

He smiled as soon as I opened the door. He looked different, but before I could take a good look at him, he craned his neck around me, peering through the front door.

I then realized he was making sure my parents couldn't see us, because he immediately grabbed my waist and pulled me in for a kiss.

It lasted far too short. I could still feel it lingering, buzzing on my lips, and I forced them into a polite, innocent smile as we pulled away.

"Hey there sweetheart," he said, just loud enough for me to hear.

Screw it. I stole another quick kiss.

Parents or no parents, I was thrilled that he was here.

Chapter 23

I COULD HEAR FOOTSTEPS SHUFFLING OUT OF the kitchen, which meant time for stolen affections with my boyfriend was coming to an end. As much as I wanted to pull him into bed with me and have my weak, recovering self fall asleep wrapped in his arms, I knew we both needed to be on our best behavior. My parents already had reservations about Devin; their first impressions of him shouldn't be a bunch of PDA.

"Hello there!" My mom's squeaky voice had returned, and like any Greek mother, she immediately swept him into a crushing hug. Devin smiled and laughed, but I could see him wince as she squeezed him a bit too tight.

With Devin now standing under the bright hallway lights, I managed to get a full glance at his appearance. The differences were subtle. He'd taken his piercings out, leaving just tiny holes in his earlobes and below his lips. He wore a long-sleeved, cream-colored shirt that fully covered his tattoos. It was the first time I'd ever seen him wear clothing that wasn't dark grey or black. Instead of his usual dark skinny jeans, he wore a pair of plain denim ones, and his black Converses were replaced with scuffed white sneakers.

My mother continued fussing over him, her high-pitched words a blur in my ears as Devin took off his shoes and followed her down the hallway. My father was still standing in the kitchen, having not budged an inch since Devin arrived. He didn't scowl as much as usual, but I noticed that he was eyeing Devin up and down like a steer at an auction. Seeking out any perceived flaws or imperfections. Trying to come up with reasons to not approve of him.

"It smells fantastic in here." Devin smiled as he took a seat at the dinette. My father's eyes remained locked on him, but Devin either didn't notice or pretended not to. He wore the same cheery, oblivious expression he'd had at the game shop.

"Why, thank you!" My mother beamed as she slipped her oven mitts on and pulled a tray out of the oven. "Did Avery tell you my parents are from Greece?"

"Yes, she did. She took me to a Greek restaurant on our first date."

"Oh, how lovely! Was it the one you sent the food from?"

"Yes. Avery told me it's her favorite."

"Thank you so much for that, by the way. It was very generous of you."

"Of course. I figured all of you would be exhausted and in need of an easy meal."

The whole time Devin and my mom were engaged in conversation, I noticed he was looking at me. He had that adoring sparkle in his eyes, the look he reserved only for me, and I think my mom noticed. My father, on the other hand, remained still as a statue, the steaming coffee mug pressed to his lips still hiding his facial expression.

Well, at least Devin is winning my mother over.

It was funny how with Devin's piercings gone, tattoos covered up, and lack of all-black clothing, he looked like someone my dad would normally approve of. It made me wonder what Devin was like in his early adulthood, back when he was still with his family and heavily involved in the church.

But the more I studied Devin's newly clean-cut appearance, the more I hated it. This wasn't him. I knew he wanted to make a good first impression, but he shouldn't have to hide who he was just to gain my uppity parents' approval.

"Well, the moussaka needs some time to cool, but we can start on the salad," my mother announced, placing a huge glass bowl in the center of the table. The salad was stuffed with peppers, feta cheese, and olives, and I could smell the vinegar and spices from the homemade dressing in the pitcher next to it.

I missed my mother's cooking.

"So, Devin," my mother continued as she placed four small bowls on the table. "tell us about yourself."

I let out a sharp exhale. I knew it was a typical question that parents asked their childrens' partners, but it was such an impossibly broad one. There were parts of Devin's life that he didn't like to talk about, and I knew that having to cobble together a pleasant enough answer was like sitting in a job interview.

"Well." Devin paused, taking a moment to scoop salad into his bowl. I could tell he was using the opportunity to think about how he wanted to answer. "As I'm sure you noticed on Sunday, I run the local game shop down the street."

"You own it?"

"Yes, ma'am. For the past seven years."

"Wow, that's certainly impressive! And that's where you have all your *Creatures & Coins* events?"

Across the table, I saw my father's face twitch.

Chapter 23

"*Creatures & Crypts*, but yes," Devin continued. "I have some relief staff during the week, but other than that I'm a one-man show. It's a lot of bookkeeping, which isn't too exciting, but my Sundays are my favorite since that's when I run the children's *C&C* group."

"Oh wow, you have kids that come and play your game?"

"Yes. Mostly preteen boys. They're a handful, but I enjoy them. Kids get so into it. They have such wild imaginations."

"I take it you enjoy working with children?"

"Yes." Devin paused to take a bite of his salad. "I love them. I love everyone who comes into the shop. It's grown into a real community."

"And how is this little endeavor financially feasible?"

My father's abrupt, impolite question was like a dampening blanket on Devin and my mother's cheery conversation. My mom shot him a dirty look, and I tried my best to relay an apology to Devin through my eyes.

God, my father is so rude.

But Devin wasn't even fazed. He smiled that same polite, unheeding smile as he wiped his mouth with a napkin.

"It's funny, I'm sure people wonder that a lot," Devin chuckled. "And the truth is, it's difficult. At least, for the first few years it was. I actually have a Bachelor's in IT management, so I took a day job at a call center and managed the shop at night and on the weekends. I finally managed to get us in the black two years ago, so I left the call center and now run the shop full time. It's a lot, though. I rarely work less than sixty hours a week."

"My goodness," my mother interjected. "Those are long hours."

"Oh, it's nothing. I was working closer to eighty before I left the call center."

"When did you sleep?"

Devin laughed. "I didn't."

Even I smiled. I'd never asked, but I had always wondered how Devin managed to run the game shop financially. I also hadn't realized he had a second job, but I remembered all the half-empty energy drinks he had behind the register for the first few years I lived in Orlando.

I peered back over at my father. Devin had answered his question perfectly, not falling victim to his sick little interrogations. But my dad still didn't look pleased, although it was hard to tell since his facial expressions never seemed to change.

"What are your plans for the future?"

Jesus Christ, Dad.

This isn't a fucking job interview.

Devin balked slightly at this question, taking a moment to swallow his food and cough. "My apologies, but what do you mean?"

"Well, do you intend to manage this little shop forever? Or do you have career plans?"

Little shop. I scowled. Critical Games was one of the largest game stores in Orlando.

"*Jim.*" My mother's scolding was soft, but her eyes flashed like lightning.

"What? I want to know."

Under the table, my hands balled into tight fists.

"Um, no, I plan to continue and expand the shop in the coming years," Devin replied, although I could hear the wavering unease in his voice. "My current project is doing more online sales, so I'm cataloging individual *Creatures & Crypts* cards in a database. But it's taking a long time. We have tens of thousands of cards. But once the project is done, I'm hoping it brings in enough extra revenue for me to hire more staff."

Chapter 23

My chest loosened. Devin was good at this. But it sent a pang of sadness through my heart as I wondered what sort of judgment he'd dealt with from his own family.

My father was silent. His eyes were still locked on Devin, his mind likely searching for more questions to stump him with. He'd already overstepped to the point of being cruel, and even though he was running out of steam, I feared he wasn't done.

"Roll your sleeves up."

Devin froze mid-bite, attempting to process what my father had just said.

"Dad!" I scolded, fury burning in my veins.

"Jim, that's enough." My mother's tone was sharper this time.

He completely ignored both of us, his eyes still locked on Devin. Inappropriate questions was bad enough; now he was trying to order my boyfriend around like he was some sort of animal.

Devin coughed, covering his mouth with the back of his hand. "I'm sorry, what was that?"

"You heard me. I want to see those tattoos on your arms."

"*Dad*," I hissed through gritted teeth. He ignored me.

Now Devin was beginning to crack. His expression was blank, his face drained of all color. The mask of sweet, charming obliviousness was gone. His eyes widened, his irises swirling with panic as he shifted his arms from the table to his lap.

This wasn't about the tattoos. Devin had no shame about them.

He didn't want my dad to see his scars.

"I told you," My father grumbled to my mother. "Tattoos are the mark of the devil, and he's covered in them. This is really the man you want courting our daughter?"

"DAD!!"

I yelled so loud I swore it shook the townhouse walls. My mom had her head buried in her hands, and Devin looked like he was about to be sick.

Dev...

I wanted to reach out. Hold his hand. Tell him how horribly sorry I was that I subjected him to this.

There was a loud screech against the tile floors as Devin pushed his seat back, muttered an "excuse me" that was barely audible, and retreated to my bedroom, closing the door behind him.

My attention snapped back to my dad, and I glowered at him with my brown eyes full of fire.

"Way to be an asshole, Dad."

"Avery!" he snapped, his eyes narrowing. "Language."

"*That's* what you're concerned about right now!?" I pushed my chair back and stood up, my fists coiling up in rage. I had never wanted to blip my father out of existence as much as I did at that moment.

"You'd better watch your attitude," he replied flatly, his face still taught as a rubber band pulled too tight.

I forced down a shaky swallow, and the tension in my fists loosened.

"You know what? I'm not doing this right now," I turned away and stormed off toward my bedroom.

"Avery!"

"Fuck off!"

I slammed the door behind me before my dad could respond.

Jesus Christ. I leaned my head against the textured wooden door, taking a few moments to catch my breath and let the adrenalin dissipate from my veins.

It was replaced with sorrow when I saw Devin sitting on the edge of my bed.

Chapter 23

His head hung low, which made his shaggy black hair fall forward and cover his face. His sleeves were rolled up, and I watched for a few moments as he ran his fingers along the scars that lined his forearms.

"God, Devin, I'm so sorry..." my voice croaked. I felt like this was all my fault. I was the one that invited him to dinner with my tyrannical father.

He lifted his head, and I could see those beautiful blue-green eyes shining through strands of dark hair. Eyes that were heavy with sadness.

"Come here," he pleaded, extending a hand in my direction. I threw my concerns for my parents walking in on us out the window and plopped down in his lap, wrapping my arms around his shoulders.

I kissed his cheek, but it didn't erase the melancholy look from his face. His gaze fell to his lap again, and he suddenly felt very distant.

"If they knew..." He ran his thumb over his scars again. "They wouldn't want me anywhere near you."

"Dev..."

"Or if they knew I was divorced."

"You know I don't care about any of those things." I kissed his cheek again. "And they don't make you a bad person."

"I tell myself that all the time. But sometimes..." He sniffled and ran a palm over his face. "I feel like my life has been this deep, dark pit. I keep crawling out, over and over again, but every time I see the surface and I feel like everything is going to be okay... someone pushes me back down again."

"Devin..."

"It's hard. I'm getting tired of it."

"I know." I ran my hand across his scalp, his soft black hair falling through my fingers. "But you know what? Fuck them. Push back. Because good people, the ones who love you and care about you and want you to succeed, won't judge you for your past. Everyone has skeletons in their closet, no matter how small."

I forced a smile, rubbing my thumb across his cheek. "Hell, sometimes I feel like I have a whole graveyard in there."

That elicited a small chuckle from Devin, which made my heavy heart lighten.

"Thank you, Avie."

He pulled me in for a long, deep kiss, and it nearly made a tear fall from my eye.

He always made me feel better. And I was glad I could do the same for him.

I pulled my lips away and spent a moment losing myself in those multicolored irises, until muffled shouts from the kitchen pulled me back to reality.

"They're fighting," I grumbled, and Devin gave an uncomfortable sigh.

"Here," I hopped up from his lap. "I'll be right back."

"What are you doing?" Devin asked as I approached my bedroom door.

I exhaled sharply, dread overtaking my body at what I was about to do.

"I'm going to go confront the *real* problem."

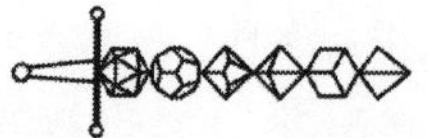

THE ARGUING CEASED AS SOON AS I OPENED THE DOOR.

I stepped hesitantly toward the kitchen table, with my parents' fiery gazes making me feel like a prey animal. My mom looked exasperated, and my dad looked pissed. Exactly the way I had left them.

Once I made my way back to the table, I glowered right back at them.

Especially my father.

Chapter 23

"I want you to leave," I hissed.

My father raised a bushy eyebrow. "Excuse me?"

"You heard me. It's my house. Get out."

"You do *not* talk to your father that way, young—"

"No, you do not talk to *me* that way," I retorted, cutting him off. "And do not call me 'young lady.' I am almost twenty-seven years old. I am an adult. Treat me like one."

"Absolutely not," he growled. "Your behavior over the past five years had been nothing but childish and defiant. You had your whole future set up for you, Avie—"

"Oh, don't you *dare* start that up again!" I threw my arms up in frustration.

"Tyler wanted to marry you. He was a fine young man from a good family, and you had to go and—"

"What, have sex with him?"

Both my parents balked, looked visibly uncomfortable.

My anger was boiling over, fizzing through my veins like lava in a volcano, and I was ready to erupt. Five years. Five long years, and they wouldn't let this go. They didn't care what I wanted. They didn't care if I was happy. I was supposed to fit into the pious little mold they'd crafted my entire life, and the moment I wanted to be something different, they acted as if I was no longer worthy of respect.

That I was *bad.*

Immoral.

Broken.

And you know what?

I don't care anymore.

I had no shame left. I'd fed them a lie for the past five years, and it was time to tell them the truth.

I didn't care how uncomfortable it made them.

"Well guess what?!" I leered toward my parents, my face burning an obscene shade of red. "Tyler didn't leave me because I had sex with him. He left me because I *didn't* have sex with him. You know why?! Because I. FUCKING. CAN'T!!"

I had never screamed so loudly at my parents in my life. I cringed, not because I had any concern over what they thought of me, but because I realized that Devin could likely hear this entire conversation from my bedroom.

My parents wore the most shattered expressions I had ever seen from them. It was a mixture of shock, horror, and disbelief, and it made me so uncomfortable that despite my rage, I took a timid step away from the table.

"Avery, sweetie." My mother's strained voice finally broke the silence. "What are you talking about?"

I took a deep, shaky, unsteady breath.

"I've never had sex. It's too painful. It's related to my endometriosis."

"God, sweetheart." My mother's eyes were glassy with remorse. "Why didn't you tell us?"

"*How* could I tell you!?" I exclaimed. "You act like even saying the word *sex* is a grave sin. And you expected me to talk to you about it? I was supposed to be *pure*. A perfect little virgin for my future husband. And instead, it became my curse."

"Avery..."

"I felt so ashamed. So broken. And because of the way you raised me, I felt like I had to keep it a secret from everyone. I know you're concerned that I'm almost twenty-seven and not married. Well, that's why. Because no man, including Tyler, wanted to be with a woman who couldn't have sex." I pointed to my bedroom door. "Until him."

"Sweetheart..."

"He doesn't care. In fact, he's the reason why I got my diagnosis. He insisted I go to the hospital. He stayed there with me all night. Because he loves me. He treats me better than anyone else. Far better than Tyler. But that's still not good enough for you, is it?"

My mother opened her mouth, but she couldn't say a word. Her jaw just hung there, gaping like a fish. I couldn't blame her. I'd just dropped a bombshell on them.

My father, on the other hand, was stoic as always. But his eyes betrayed his usual stony-faced appearance. I could see a glimmer of sadness within them.

"Well." I turned toward him. "Are you going to say something?"

This time, he was the one that couldn't make eye contact.

Nothing. Silence.

"That's what I thought," I hissed. I peered back over at my mother. "I'm going back to my room. I want you both gone by the time I come back out."

"Avery, but your surgery—"

"I'm fine," I grumbled as I walked toward my bedroom door. "I can take care of myself. All you two are doing is making it worse."

I slammed the door behind me before I could hear their response.

I steadied myself against the wall, my legs suddenly shaking now that all the adrenalin was wearing off. Out of the corner of my eye, I saw Devin rise from the edge of my bed and rush toward me.

"Avery..." He swept me into his arms. I knew from the look on his face that he'd heard everything.

I couldn't take it anymore.

The pipe burst, and I descended into frantic sobs. I could barely breathe as my legs gave out and Devin carried me over to my bed.

"It's okay. It's okay..." he laid me down gingerly before curling up next to me, rubbing my shoulder while his soothing words washed over me.

"You heard all that, didn't you?" I asked between hiccupping sobs.

"Well…yes."

"Am I an idiot?"

"No," Devin kissed the side of my forehead. "In fact, I think you're incredibly brave, finally telling your parents about your health issues after all these years."

"God…" I cringed. I hated the fact that I'd just brought up my sex life to my parents.

"Your illness is nothing to be ashamed of," Devin assured me. "And that includes your sexual issues. Sweetheart…I'm sorry you felt so alone in this for such a long time."

"I'm broken," I blubbered.

"You are not."

"I feel like I am."

Devin scooted closer to me, rolling up his sleeve and showing me his inner forearm.

"Do these make me broken?" he asked.

I pressed a finger against the largest scar, right before the crook of his elbow. "No."

"Then you're not either. Avie, we're human beings, not dolls. We don't *break*. We're so much more complex than that."

I turned over so I faced him, and a warm smile lit up his lips as he stroked my hair.

"Plus," he continued. "Part of being human means that we can heal." He pointed to my stitched-up abdomen. "That's exactly what your body is doing right now."

I smiled despite the tears. "Thank you, Devin."

"Of course. We'll get through this, sweetheart."

I nuzzled closer to his chest, breathing in his mint body wash as his heartbeat synched with my own.

"I love you, Avie."

Another wave of exhaustion rolled over me, and I closed my eyes.

"I love you too, Dev."

"AVIE. HEY, AVIE."

The soft voice intermingled with my dreams until they faded away and I was pulled back to reality. I opened my bleary eyes, blinking them a few times, until Devin's face in front of mine came into focus.

Realization made me lift my head. "Crap. How long was I asleep?"

"About a half hour," Devin chuckled. He was kneeling by my side, crouched on the carpet next to the bed. "You were out almost as soon as you laid down."

"Goddamnit."

"Avie, you *did* just have surgery."

"Yeah, yeah," I craned my neck to peer around Devin. "Are my parents still here?"

"Your mom is. I helped her clean up the kitchen, and we had a little talk."

"Talk?" My throat suddenly felt sour.

"Yeah. Nothing major, she mostly just wanted to learn more about me. Don't worry, there was no interrogation."

"And my dad?"

"He left and went back to the hotel. Both he and your mom thought it was best."

My chest relaxed at this news. I felt guilty for what I'd said earlier, about how them coming here only made things worse. But I knew my dad was terrible with ever admitting he was wrong, so letting him cool off at the hotel was a good thing.

I didn't mind that my mother was still there. She wasn't the one I was truly upset with.

"She does want to talk to you, though."

I nodded, struggling to sit upright. As I did so, a hot blast of pain burned through my stitches, causing me to wince and let out a yelp.

"Pain meds wearing off?" Devin asked.

"Yeah."

"I'll have your mom bring some more in for you." He stood up, giving my hand a final squeeze before walking toward the door. "Let me go get her."

Devin disappeared into the hallway, and a few minutes later, my mother emerged from it.

She had a look on her face that I'd never seen before. A heavy mixture of fatigue, sadness, and remorse. She forced a smile, and it seemed to exaggerate the wrinkles around her mouth more than usual.

"Hey, sweetheart." Her voice was soft and gentle. I didn't say anything as she stepped toward my bed and took a seat on the edge of it.

"Where do I start?" She gave a sad chuckle.

"I'm sorry, mom." A sudden ache tugged in my chest. I hated seeing her like this. "I sort of lost it earlier."

"No, it's alright. You don't need to apologize. Avery, sweetie, I wish I could go back in time and do things differently. After you left college, you needed support, and all we did was lecture you. I've realized how much we've driven you away over the past five years, and it fills me with so much regret. I miss you, sweetheart."

"You always acted like I was such a disappointment." Her honesty allowed my own regrets to seep through. "Just because I didn't turn out the way you wanted me to."

"I know. Avery, I love you so much. None of this was your fault. You are your own person, with your own thoughts and ideals, and as your parents, we need to learn to accept that. And Avery, you are not a disappointment. You are such a brave, smart, headstrong young woman. I'm so proud of the person you have become."

"You never acted like it. And it's hard for me to believe this…" I paused, swallowing hard. "Because you were always so strict with us growing up. The truth is, since I moved to Orlando, I haven't been to church once. I don't know what I believe anymore."

"I'm not upset with you over that."

"Dad is."

"Your father will have to come to terms with it," she replied. "Sweetheart, I've spent a lot of time praying lately. About your health and your recovery, but also about your relationship with the Lord. And I've concluded that your relationship with Him is your own, and that it's not my place to dictate it. I only ask that you continue to live in the light. To treat others the way you wish to be treated. Because that's what God truly wants from us."

"Thank you, Mom. That means a lot." My gaze drifted to my bedroom door. "You know, Devin is from a religious family too. His father is a pastor."

"Oh really?"

"Yeah. He's not the monster Dad thinks he is."

"Of course he's not." My mother scoffed, and it filled me with relief. "That's another thing I've come to believe: angels come to us in all forms. I can see what a kind, considerate, respectful young man he is. How much he loves you. I believe you two are blessed to have each other."

I lowered my head, my mind still processing the words my mother said to me. Realizing how much I'd needed to hear them.

It nearly brought me to tears, but I swallowed hard to keep them at bay.

"So, here's what we're going to do," my mother continued. "I'm going to go back to the hotel for the night. Devin said he wanted to spend some time with you, and I'm sure he can assist if you need help with anything."

I smiled and raised an eyebrow. "You're leaving me *alone* with a guy? That's new."

"You were right before, Avery. You're an adult, and I need to treat you like one. Now, dinner leftovers are in the fridge, and you're all stocked up with tea and seltzer. I'll be back in the morning."

My mother stood up, gave me a kiss on the forehead, and strode across my room to the door.

"Hey mom?"

She stopped with her hand on the door handle.

"Yes sweetie?"

"I love you."

My mother's face fell, and I realized that I hadn't said those words in a long time.

"I love you too, sweetheart. Thank you for talking with me. I hope you two have a lovely night. Sleep well."

Chapter 24

DESPITE MY ACHING STITCHES AND ACHING heart after the tumultuous evening with my parents, the rest of my night with Devin was absolute bliss.

I was still sore, so he heated up the dinner that we never got to eat in the oven and brought it into my bedroom. We set up a little picnic on my bed, where I gave Devin the details of my surgery and how it went. He especially enjoyed the fact that I'd been shouting his name in the recovery room when I woke up from anesthesia.

"I still wish I could've been there with you," Devin sighed.

"You're here now." I grinned, ruffling his hair as I shoved another bite of food in my mouth.

After dinner, we settled on the comfy L-shaped couch in the living room. It was a hand-me-down with sagging seats, but it was incredibly plush and comfortable. Perfect for cuddling with my boyfriend under a knit blanket while we watched *Creatures & Crypts* videos on YouTube.

A few hours later, after several heated debates about which cards from the latest set would be the strongest,

Devin and I got ready for bed. My twin mattress wasn't big enough for the two of us, but it did mean that Devin had to stay close to me all night.

"We'll have to do more sleepovers at your house," I noted as I turned off the light.

"Why?" Devin scooted closer until he was practically on top of me. "Am I too close?"

"Dev...my stitches."

"Oh, right. Sorry."

We both woke up at eight the next morning, and Devin was out the door by eight-thirty. Critical Games opened at ten, which meant he needed time to go home and get ready for work.

My mother showed up not long after, and she dug a box of pancake mix out of my kitchen cabinet and made us breakfast. I hadn't had pancakes in a long time. My father used to make them for us every Sunday morning after church, and those first few bites made me feel both nostalgic and sad.

The rest of the week continued that pattern: my mother kept me company during the day, and Devin showed up in the evenings after work. On Thursday night, he even brought over his Nintendo Switch, and we convinced my mom to join us for a game of Mario Party. She'd never played a video game before, and I had to teach her how to use the controller. But by the end of our hour-long playthrough, she was laughing and cheering just like me and Devin. She didn't get any stars, but since she'd used so many items during the game, she won enough bonus stars at the end to get second place.

Devin got first, which he bragged about while I tapped him on the head with a controller.

Friday night was tough. Devin wouldn't be over since it was TCG Night and the shop didn't close until 11 p.m., and

Chapter 24

after a week of sitting at home I was antsy and restless. I no longer needed pain medication, but I still couldn't sit upright for too long or my stitches would get sore.

"Are you sure you don't want me to drive you over there, sweetie?" my mother asked as she sat on the couch next to me, scrolling through her phone. "You can just stay for a little while. Say hi to your friends."

I shook my head. As much as I wanted to see them, I didn't think I could handle the twenty-minute car ride over there. Not only was sitting upright difficult, but the seatbelt would press against my stitches.

I fiddled with my Steam Deck, preparing for another night spent in my townhouse playing video games, when the doorbell rang.

My mother stood up and walked down the hall to answer it. I assumed it was just a package, until I heard a mix of chatter and laughter from several familiar voices.

"Avery!" My mom shouted down the hall. "Your friends are here!"

I burst off the couch, my stitches aching in the process. But the thrill of seeing my friends overrode the pain.

In the front doorway was Cassidy, Aaron, and Chris, carrying grocery bags of snack food and a Nintendo Switch case.

"Avery!" Cassidy exclaimed, giving me a big hug. I smiled and winced at the same time, reminding her to be careful with my abdomen.

"Oh, oops, sorry," she chuckled as she pulled away.

"What are you guys doing here?" I asked. "I thought you'd be at the shop."

Cassidy shrugged. "We decided to ditch and come hang out with you. Devin said you're almost recovered and have been really restless alone at home."

My heart fluttered. *Dev.* I knew he had a shop to manage, but part of me wished he could've been here with the rest of my friends.

"He says hi, by the way," Cassidy continued. "So, all my Switch games are in my bag, and I brought four controllers. Oh, and we got a little cake from the grocery store. A 'get well soon' cake."

"What kind?"

"Strawberry shortcake, of course," Cassidy grinned.

"I love you," I laughed. After being my roommate for almost four years, she knew all my favorites. "Anyway, come inside! Make yourselves at home!"

We spent the rest of the evening huddled on the couch, surrounded by open bags of potato chips and paper plates smeared with frosting as we played video games. My mother hung around for a little while before deciding to go to the hotel, and I told her she didn't have to return later. I was off the pain meds, and the stitches were healing well – the glue was even starting to peel off. She agreed, telling me to text her if I needed anything.

We ended up playing games until almost midnight. Cassidy fell asleep on the couch, and Aaron explained that she'd had a long day at the vet clinic as he and Chris fought each other in *Super Smash Bros.*

"How are you two doing, anyway?" I asked Aaron as he was thrown off the stage by Chris. He scowled, and Chris cackled.

"Really good!" Aaron exclaimed once he'd recovered. "I've loved having her over. It makes my apartment feel so much homier to have her there."

"That's awesome," I grinned, my cheeks flushing as I imagined what it would be like once I could spend more time over at Devin's.

Chapter 24

The boys played a few more rounds of Super Smash Bros. Aaron demanded rematches after being repeatedly defeated by Chris, until they both ran out of steam and called a truce.

"Cass." Aaron shook his sleeping girlfriend as she lay curled up next to him. "It's time to go home."

Cassidy's head rustled as her eyes fluttered open. "Jeez, how long was I out?"

"Only an hour." Aaron grinned and ruffled her curly hair. "Anyway, it's time for us to head out. I imagine Avery is tired."

I shrugged. "It's not that bad. I recovered a lot faster than I would've thought."

We cleaned up the living room, and I exchanged hugs with both the boys and Cassidy as I walked them to the front door.

"I was thinking of coming back over after *C&C* on Sunday," Cassidy told me as Aaron opened the door. "That sound good?"

"Yeah." I smiled. I knew she missed home, but I also knew that she enjoyed spending time at Aaron's apartment.

My friends shouted final goodbyes over their shoulders as I closed the door behind them. The silence of the now-empty townhouse rang like gongs in my ears.

But my heart felt lighter than it had all week.

I have good friends.

By the end of the following week, the surgical glue peeled off, taking my stitches with it, and I was left with nothing but faint pink scars.

At my follow-up appointment, the surgeon said I was healing perfectly, and since my wounds were healed, he cleared me to return to normal activities. I assumed that included sexual ones, but I didn't dare bring that up in front of my mother, who had insisted on coming to my follow-up.

She treated me to a celebratory lunch at Mexican restaurant near the doctor's office and began packing up her things as soon as we returned to my townhouse.

I was relieved that things were returning to normal. I was even glad that I could return to work the following Monday. But for the first time in a long time, I knew I was going to miss my mother.

I gave her a long, tight hug as we stood in the doorway, one that nearly brought me to tears.

"You've got this, sweetheart," she whispered in my ear. "I love you."

It was a vague encouragement, yet I knew exactly what it meant. It meant that she knew I could handle myself down in Orlando. It meant that she knew I'd continue recovering and overcome the lingering side effects of my illness.

And, most importantly, it meant that she was proud of the adult I'd become.

Watching her drive away felt like a door closing on that part of my life. That I was finally recovered and ready to continue my life post-surgery.

But the contemplative sadness was quickly replaced with a bubble of excitement. Because it was Friday evening, and even though my mother was gone, I had a party to attend in less than an hour.

I showered, blow-dried my hair, and put on my favorite lavender dress. As my stomach swelling continued to dissipate, I could go back to wearing pants again. But I decided that I loved the comfort and freedom of loose, flowy dresses. And after so many years of endometriosis pain, my closet was full of them.

The party was at Sam's house, and he'd asked us to bring either food or board games. I decided on both, packing up both my mother's leftover baklava from the night before and two of my favorite party games. I stacked them in a precarious pile in my arms as I shuffled out to my car in the driveway.

Sam lived on the eastern edge of Orlando, in a beautiful two-story home in a newer neighborhood. I hadn't been there in months, but it was easy to recognize, since it bordered a cul-de-sac and was painted a vibrant forest green. Sam's wife, Kathy, loved gardening, and the earthy, sweet scent of freshly planted flowers wafted past me as I rang the doorbell.

I was fifteen minutes late, which meant most of my very punctual friends were already there. Kathy answered the door, sweeping me up in her tight, motherly hug. Behind her, seated at Sam's enormous gaming table, half a dozen Critical Games patrons shouted my name and cheered.

I beamed as I approached the table, my smile spreading so widely across my face that it hurt. Plopped in the seats, snacking on potato chips and crackers, were Cassidy, Aaron, Chris, Devin, and Sam's two teenage sons, Jack and Danny.

But most of my attention was on Devin. For the first time in nearly a year, he'd taken a Friday night off and had Jordan manage the shop for the evening. I was glad he'd agreed to it—he desperately needed a break. And a casual gaming party with our closest friends was the best way for him to do so.

He was seated at the head of the table, closest to where I was standing. And as soon as he saw me, he stood up, pulled me into his arms, and kissed the top of my forehead.

"Feeling better?" he asked, even though I'd just seen him the day before.

"Yeah," I grinned. "Doc said I'm all clear. I've healed perfectly."

"So the rumors are true," Kathy remarked in a teasing tone, her short, plump frame leaning against the dining room archway. Like her husband Sam, she was an older woman, likely in her early fifties, with greying almond-brown hair pulled back in a messy ponytail.

Devin turned toward her with me still pulled against his chest. "Hey, I wasn't hiding anything. No rumors needed."

I grinned again, my face prickling with heat. I loved that Devin wasn't afraid to give me bits of affection in front of others. He took pride in the fact that I was his girlfriend. I looked up at his face, loving how genuine and bright his smile was. Tonight, he looked the happiest I'd seen him in a long time. Possibly ever.

Sam noted that we were waiting on one more person, but they'd likely be late, so we were free to start diving into the board games. We picked a simple card-drafting game, one that would accommodate so many people, and half an hour passed as we picked cards and totaled up our points.

Sam won, with Devin just two points behind him in second place. I'd never played this game before, so I was second to last. But it had been a lot of fun, and I made a mental note to pick this game up next time I was at the shop. I needed some easy, quick games for large numbers of players.

"I swear to god, you knew I needed that card." Devin scowled, pointing at the stacks of cards on the table in front of Sam. "It only scored you two points. I would've gotten nine."

"Sucks for you, young man," Sam teased, shrugging as he leaned back in his chair.

I giggled, finding it funny that Sam was old enough to be calling thirty-five-year-old Devin "young man," when the doorbell suddenly rang.

"I'll get it!" Devin bolted out of his chair.

I heard loud shouts and jeers from the foyer, so I crept down the hallway to see what was going on. Next to the large glass-inlaid front door, a man well into his sixties had Devin's neck in a light chokehold, rubbing the top of his head and sending his scruffy black hair everywhere.

"You pain in the ass." Devin shoved him away. At first I was concerned, but as Devin looked up, I saw the wide grin on his face.

"Good to see you too, bud." The man gave Devin a forceful pat on the back.

Unlike everyone else at the party, I didn't recognize him. In addition to being an older man, with receding snow-white hair and leathery, tanned skin, he was covered in almost as many tattoos as Devin was. Although his were much more faded, and instead of the studs that Devin normally wore in his ears, this man had bright gold hoops. He wore a worn blue tank top, khaki pants, and earth-toned sandals. He looked like he belonged on a boat or a motorcycle, not in Sam's house ready to play board games.

"Ah, is this her?" the man exclaimed, pointing toward me. I noticed he had a gruff voice, with a slight New England accent.

"Indeed it is," Devin replied, that same beaming grin on his face.

The man chuckled, which sounded more like a cackle, as he took my hand and gave me a vice grip of a handshake that left my fingers sore.

"Avery, this is Scott," Devin introduced, placing a hand on the man's bare shoulder. "The former owner of Critical Games, and an old friend of mine."

"And the one who taught this bastard everything he knows," Scott chortled. "Anyway, it's a pleasure to meet ya, Avery. Devin's told me all about ya. Never seen that boy so happy before."

Aw. More heat rose to my cheeks. Even Devin was blushing.

"Anyway, come on in." Devin gestured for Scott to follow us. "You're the last one here, like usual."

"Gotta make sure the party's goin' strong before I show up."

Scott exchanged greetings with Sam in the dining room, and I could tell they'd also known each other for a long time.

Everyone took a seat at the table, and Sam dumped a large pile of board games in the middle. There were ten of us, which was good because that was exactly how many people Sam's gaming table could hold. But it also meant that Sam only had a handful of games that could be played by that many people.

We spent most of the evening playing several rounds of a social deduction game that everyone enjoyed. Chris was the assassin in the first round, which everyone guessed because he had a terrible poker face. The next round, Devin kept insinuating that I was the assassin. I thought it was his usual flirtatious teasing, until it was time to reveal. The assassin got away, and it was Devin. He'd made everyone else think it was me.

I scrunched my face at him, and he responded by ruffling my curly hair and whispering "I love you" in my ear.

I blushed. Currently, those words were still a secret between the two of us.

But in the third round, *I* ended up being the assassin. And since I'd spent the entire last round being blamed, I managed to fly under the radar and survive the game without being caught.

"Alright, guys," Sam announced once the racket quieted down. The massive gaming table was beautiful, made of real wood with velvety inlays. But it was also a mess; chip bags and overturned cracker boxes were scattered across the table, with various crumbs making their way onto the floor. Between the snacks were random cards, game boxes, and d6 dice. I was glad Sam wasn't upset for us making such a mess.

"It's already past ten. Before we break out the *Jackbox* games, anyone want dessert?"

We all nodded eagerly.

"I brought some baklava that my mom made." I pointed to the tin-foil-coated tray on Sam's kitchen island.

Chapter 24

"That sounds delicious," Sam replied as he opened the fridge, rifling through the shelves. "But first...we all had something else in mind."

Sam pulled a large object wrapped in a shopping bag out of the fridge, and I noticed that Kathy was digging through one of her kitchen drawers. She pulled out a lighter and a few candles just as Sam revealed what was inside the bag: a beautiful chocolate cake with "Happy Birthday Avery" written in pink frosting.

"Guys!" I exclaimed. "You didn't have to do this!"

"It was Devin's idea," Cassidy laughed.

My twenty-seventh birthday was the following week, and Devin and I had plans to do a celebratory dinner date at a sushi restaurant. I hadn't expected a celebration during our game night, but as Kathy lit the candles and everyone began singing, I felt incredibly grateful.

For my friends. For my health.

For Devin.

He rubbed my shoulder as I stared at the lit candles, admiring the faint orange aura they gave off as they danced under the airy ceiling fans. Everyone insisted I make a wish, so I closed my eyes, dug deep into my mind, and wondered what I should ask for.

I could've done something silly, like wishing for a million dollars or to live to be a hundred. But then I reflected over the past few months. I'd finally gotten a diagnosis and treatment for my chronic health issues. I was on the path to mending my relationship with my parents.

And, of course, I now had a partner. Something I'd wanted for a long time.

I peered over at his face next to me, admiring the way his choppy black hair fell over his brows as the faint light of the candles danced in his pupils.

He smiled at me. I smiled back.

Then I knew my wish. I wished for this feeling of contentment, of having my life be complete, to last as long as possible. To remember this moment regardless of what the future held.

I blew out the candle, leaving only a faint plume of smoke trailing off a bent wick.

A small chorus of claps echoed from the table as my friends eagerly gathered around to grab a slice of cake. It looked delicious, with molten-black sponge cake and thick mocha frosting. And this time, I was able to happily consume an entire piece without my stomach feeling like it was about to explode. As we all collapsed on the couch in a sugar coma, I placed a hand over my abdomen. I could feel the texture of the pink scars below the fabric of my dress, but for once, I wasn't in pain.

Sam turned on the television, and we managed to get a few rounds of *Jackbox* games in before everyone got too tired. It wasn't even midnight, but most of us were either in our thirties or rapidly approaching it. My ability to stay awake into the early hours of the morning was waning as I got older.

Devin and I had taken separate cars, but he still insisted on walking me out to mine. I happily agreed, lacing my fingers through his as we trudged across Sam's dewy lawn in the darkness.

"Uh, Dev." I paused once we approached the sidewalk. "My car is that way."

"I know." He grinned, and I could tell he was up to something. "Hop in the car with me for a minute."

"Dev, we're not—"

"What?" He raised a dark eyebrow. "And I didn't mean *that*. But if you *do* want to stay the night..."

I crinkled my nose, a teasing smile on my face. "I suppose I could. I don't have work tomorrow."

Chapter 24

"And Critical Games doesn't open until noon on Sundays," Devin replied, slipping an arm around my hips and pulling me closer. I giggled as my chest pressed against his, the curves of our bodies palpable beneath the fabric of our clothing. "Follow me back to my place. I'll give you your gift there."

"Gift? My birthday isn't until next week."

"Yes, but I wanted to give it to you tonight so you could use it at *C&C* tomorrow," Devin gently pushed me toward my car. "C'mon, follow me back to my place."

Devin lived twenty minutes from Sam's house, and the whole time, my mind swirled with guesses as to what my gift could be. It would have to be something *C&C* related…I wondered if he got me a new book, or painted a miniature for me.

No matter what it was, I was excited about any gift from him.

It was only my second time at Devin's townhouse, but this time I remembered exactly how to get there. I smiled as I approached the front door, hoping that this place would become even more familiar with time.

"Alright." Devin paused once we made it to the kitchen. He pressed his hips against mine, and I propped myself up on his kitchen table. This made us both the same height, making it much easier for Devin to wrap his arms around me and kiss me until I melted in his arms.

Just as I was ready to slide my fingers down the waistband of his jeans, he pulled away and grabbed a small, wrapped object out of his pocket. It was about eight inches long and very thin, almost like a pencil case, and was topped with a tiny red bow.

"Happy birthday, Avie." He handed the gift to me.

I gave his lips another quick kiss. "*You* are my birthday present this year."

"Well, hey." He grinned, pressing himself tighter against me. "Now you get two presents. C'mon, open it."

I tore off the shiny red paper, revealing a black metal case. I flipped it over, and there was an image of a small red dragon wrapped around a d20 die on the front.

Wait a minute.

This is a dice case.

I pried the top off, now very curious about what was inside. I had at least half a dozen dice sets, but one of the rules of being a C&C player was that you could never have too many dice.

And as soon as I saw the rainbow sheen reflected off them, my heart leapt.

"Devin!!" I exclaimed, lifting the d20 out of its foam inlay. These weren't regular dice. They were made of prismatic glass, meaning they were clear dice that reflected light in an intense rainbow of colors.

I had always wanted prismatic glass dice. They were beautiful.

And also expensive, which made my cheeks flush.

"How did you know I wanted these?"

Devin shrugged, a coy smile on his face. "I cast *Mind Read* on you while you were sleeping in bed with me."

"Dev..."

"Just kidding. I asked Cass."

I laughed at my boyfriend's ridiculous sense of humor. "This is an incredible gift. You really didn't have to do this. I know these aren't cheap."

"Avie, I run a game shop," Devin chuckled, pressing his palms against my thighs as he stood between them. "I have ways of getting these things."

"Well thank you." I kissed him again. "This is honestly one of the best birthdays I've ever had."

"You know what would make it better?" Devin slid his hands further up my thighs.

I grabbed the bottom of his t-shirt, lifting it over his head. I ran my fingers over his chest as my stomach swirled with anticipation. "Oh, I already know."

"Excellent." Before I could react, Devin swept me off the table and into his arms, jogging as quickly as he could into his bedroom.

"Dev!" I shouted as we both collapsed on the bed, a heap of laughter and tangled limbs. I let out a deep sigh as he hovered on top of me, his legs pinning down my own.

"By the way," he asked. "When is your first post-op physical therapy appointment?"

"Tuesday," I replied. "I'll be going once a week."

"Good. That means we can start practicing after our date night on your birthday." He squeezed my breasts through the fabric of my dress. "But tonight, let's just focus on getting you more comfortable."

"What about you?"

"I mean…" He grinned and jabbed a thumb behind him. "The shower is that way."

I laughed, sweeping him up in my arms. His hands were already working their way up my dress, and I welcomed them with eager anticipation.

Because with Devin, I had nothing to fear.

Not tonight.

Not ever.

He was mine. I was his.

And my sexual issues would never change that.

Epilogue

As time passed, I tried to remember my wish. To remember the sense of contentment and peace I felt on at twenty-seventh birthday celebration, regardless of what the future held.

But it was difficult. Because while I knew that the surgery wasn't a cure for endometriosis, I wasn't prepared for how physically and mentally draining the next few months would be.

The first step post-surgery was to start proper medication to keep the endometrial tissue from growing back. And to my surprise, that medication was birth control. At first, I figured it would be no big deal. I'd heard that the side effects could suck, but lots of women took it, so how bad could it possibly be?

It ended up being one of the worst experiences I'd ever had. With the first brand the doctor put me on, I didn't even last one night. Nausea forced me awake at an ungodly early hour, and I barely made it to the bathroom in time to empty the meager contents of my stomach into the toilet.

The second pill was marginally better. For the first few days, life resumed as normal, giving me a false sense of security. But once the weekend rolled around, I began to feel fatigued and feverish, as if I had the flu. And on Sunday night, while I was hanging out over at Devin's house, I had the worst mental breakdown of my life.

I was inconsolable, howling furious tears into my sweaty palms as I confessed to Devin that I felt like my life had no meaning. It was a frightening episode of cognitive dissonance—I *knew* I wasn't suicidal, yet I couldn't shake the emotions that all those hormones had spawned in my mind. It was dark, terrifying, and eye-opening. I wondered if this was how depression felt.

Devin didn't leave my side all night, wrapping his body so tightly around mine that we were both soaked in sweat when we awoke the next morning. I called out of work, and thankfully Devin was off that day. We couldn't get ahold of my surgeon, so Devin insisted on scheduling an urgent appointment with a local gynecologist to get this sorted. He even came with me, which, despite my protests, ended up being a godsend. I was in no mental state to explain my health issues to the doctor, so he was able to do it for me.

This time, I was put on the "minipill," a progesterone-only pill that didn't contain any estrogen. Afterwards, we went home and spent the rest of the day together, in fragile but much-needed peace.

When Devin finally spoke of that night, many weeks later, he told me it was one of the most terrifying ones he'd ever had. How he was scared to let go of me while we slept, just in case the sickening combination of hormones caused me to do something drastic.

Even in the days after, Devin kept me close, lingering in the kitchen while I cooked and curling up next to me on the couch while I played video games. I spent most of my time at Devin's home now; what started as sleepover visits turned into me almost never leaving. I even worked from there several days a week to keep Gideon company.

Cassidy was doing the same with Aaron, meaning that our townhouse was empty most nights. The more time I spent at Devin's house, the less my own place felt like home. Sleeping by myself left me longing for his touch, and waking in my own bed felt foreign and uncomfortable.

By September, I was stable and comfortable on the minipill, and I was finally reaping the benefits of the surgery. My periods came and went as nothing more than a minor inconvenience, and I could wear whatever clothing I wanted without my stomach bulging like a hot air balloon. I wasn't cured, but I felt a lot better, and even the few bad days where my symptoms returned seemed like a luxury compared to all the nights I'd spent cramping in bed.

Spending so much time at Devin's house allowed us to develop a routine. We'd both wake early in the morning, and I would settle down with my work laptop while Devin made us breakfast. He preferred to hang around his house shirtless, even when cooking, which meant I was always stealing glances at his lean, tattooed figure as he bustled around the kitchen.

We'd sit at the dinette and eat breakfast together, which was one of my favorite parts of the day. I found it funny how often he made pancakes, and he told me it was nostalgic for him, as his dad would always make them on Sunday mornings after church.

It made me smile, as my dad did the same thing. But Devin explained it with a hint of sadness glazed over his eyes. Unlike me, he had no contact with his parents. He hadn't spoken to them in almost a decade. I broached the topic of reconnecting with them once, and Devin immediately shut the conversation down with a darkness in his eyes I rarely saw from him. I decided not to bring it up after that.

Critical Games usually opened in the late morning, no earlier than ten but no later than noon, which meant I had the townhouse to myself in the afternoons, with only Gideon for company. He was a haughty, standoffish cat, well into old age and very set in his ways, and the only scraps of affection I got from him was when he plopped his fluffy body behind my laptop fan. But according to Devin, he howled whenever I left the townhouse, so I guess he didn't dislike me as much as I thought.

My workday ended at 5 p.m. Devin's usually ended much later, so as soon as I shut my laptop for the day, I'd get started on dinner. Devin enjoyed cooking, but with his busy schedule, he rarely had time for it and usually resorted to takeout or frozen dinner. He was always so thrilled when he walked through the front door in the late evenings to a homemade meal packed away in the fridge for him.

On the days where he didn't get home super late, we'd eat together at the dinette, and Devin always insisted on cleaning up afterwards.

"You know something?" He crept up behind me one evening as I piled leftovers into the fridge.

"What?" I asked, flashing him a coy grin as he wrapped his arms around my hips.

"I don't tell you enough how much I appreciate you."

"Aw, Dev..."

"Seriously. This place finally feels like home now that you're here," He pointed into the fridge. "And I'm not just referring to your cooking. I'm just so happy to have you here. Waking up to you in the mornings, coming home to you after work, relaxing together on the couch after a long day..." His voice drifted off, and his eyes became warm and hazy. "My life feels so complete."

My heart bloomed with warmth as I leaned into Devin's embrace, but a pang of sadness lingered in my throat. As much as I appreciated his honeyed words, I knew our life together was still missing something.

Sex. Over the past two months, we'd made some progress. I'd been going to physical therapy once a week, and she'd recommended I buy vaginal dilators to practice with at home. My stomach had bundled up in knots as soon as they arrived through the mail. They were silicon bullet-shaped devices, very simple in design and function, but I still couldn't get over the fact that in my mind, these medical devices were thinly veiled sex toys.

It took a full month of daily practice for me to get the smallest dilator in. My therapist had suggested I try using them on myself first; she'd mentioned at one of my sessions that I seemed uncomfortable with that part of my body.

Gee, I wonder why. I scowled as I fiddled with the silicone device on Devin's bed. I may have made progress making amends with my parents, especially my mom, but my religious hang-ups about sexuality still lingered in my subconscious. The therapist told me to expect this. The burning sensation wasn't entirely from the endometriosis, as my body had to unlearn associating that area with both physical pain and emotional guilt.

But that didn't stop me from nearly screaming in celebration when I was finally able to get the first dilator in. Devin wasn't home, so I had to celebrate the achievement alone, but it was still an important first step. It made me feel like I really *could* do this. That sex wasn't an impossible dream.

But then I removed it, which was an uncomfortable, awkward sensation since I wasn't even aroused, and it occurred to me that the first dilator was even smaller than a tampon.

And I'd never been able to use those either.

I groaned as I lay naked in bed, flopping my head back on Devin's pillow.

I had a *long* way to go.

To shorten the amount of time it took to get the second dilator in, I enlisted Devin's help. We'd spend the evenings wrapped in each other's' amorous embraces, exploring each other with our hands and mouths as both he and I learned what turned me on. Even though I had such a primal fear of sex, I found that I loved straddling him, and we even experimented with him being at my entrance. It was an intoxicating feeling, one that drove me wild for *more*, but the one night where we decided to try ended with a burning vagina and molten tears streaming down my face.

"It's okay, Avie." Devin rubbed my shoulder, pressing a gentle kiss against my collarbone. "That was my fault. It's still too early to try."

Devin's soft words usually soothed me, but that night I ended up in a downward spiral about how broken I was and that I was doomed to be a virgin for the rest of my life. It took almost an hour, and numerous reassurances from my boyfriend, for me to calm down enough to get some sleep.

But over the next few weeks, it gave me a renewed sense of determination. I practiced with the dilators every single night. Sometimes even in the morning too. But I kept running into the same problem: putting them in was far more difficult when I wasn't aroused. And I couldn't always rely on Devin to get me worked up.

So, one Saturday afternoon, while Devin was working, I ended up alone in the apartment with a few hours of rare free time. Cassidy and I had brunch earlier that day – we were eager to see each other since we were barely roommates anymore. Afterwards, I picked up a few items for dinner, and it hit me that I hadn't been grocery shopping for my own townhouse in weeks.

I then picked up a refill of my birth control from the pharmacy, stopped at the pet store to pick up food for Gideon, and drove back to Devin's townhouse. But by then, it was only 2 p.m., and Devin wouldn't be home until much later that night.

I flopped on his bed, which was beginning to feel more like *our* bed, and ran my arms over the soft duvet like I was making a snow angel. It was October, which meant Critical Games was busier than ever. Devin was preparing for a big spooky *C&C* event the Sunday before Halloween, and he'd spent much of his free time hunched over his computer prepping horror-themed one-shot campaigns. He even planned on dressing up as Nikolai, a vampire character from one of his favorite campaigns.

And I still need to get a costume, I reminded myself, and a long, deep sigh escaped me.

I tilted my head, and my gaze drifted toward Devin's dresser. Specifically, the top drawer, where my dilators and lubricant were hiding underneath a mountain of socks and boxer briefs.

Twenty minutes later, I was naked, sore, and ready to scream in frustration. I'd managed to get the second dilator in a week ago, but the third one, which was about the same size as a guy on the smaller side, was proving to be my biggest hurdle yet. The instant I slid it in, my vagina burned as if the stupid not-a-dildo was coated in acid. No amount of lube helped. And the more frustrated I became, the more my anxiety heightened, and the more painful insertion became until I couldn't bear it at all.

I slammed the dilator base-first down on the nightstand, and it wobbled there like the pitiful excuse for a sex toy that it was. I needed help. But Devin wasn't here, and self-pleasure was still something I wasn't fully comfortable with.

I reached across the duvet and grabbed my phone, which was plopped face-down on the opposite corner of the bed.

How do I even know if I'm doing this right?

I didn't. Because I'd never had sex before.

My web searches started out innocent. I looked up techniques for inserting dilators on medical websites, but the cutaway diagrams that showed the device inserted into a vagina dug at a primal, forbidden part of my subconscious.

And a tempting, illicit question popped into my mind.

What does sex even look like?

I typed the three-letter word into my phone, and it responded with a sea of articles ranging from encyclopedia entries to mommy blogs with recommended sex positions. Some of it was what I'd expected, and other parts were mind-blowing.

I could feel the guilt and shame clawing at the back of my mind. But I ignored it. I needed to know more.

My searches intensified, my skittish self daring to type increasingly obscene search terms into my phone, until it finally happened.

I came across an actual video.

Of sex.

On a website that would've gotten me crucified if my parents ever knew.

The shame was strong. But my urges were stronger, consuming my entire mind in sweet flames that burned with arousal and desire.

So, I hit play.

Once the initial shock and slight disgust faded away, I was enchanted. *This* was sex? The thing I'd been desperately seeking my entire life? It was so strange, so utterly insane, but it was also glorious in a way that was hard to describe. It was like taking a bite of my favorite food when I was ravenously hungry. Feeling a cool blast of air conditioning after running around in the scorching Florida heat.

It was pleasure. Relief. Peace.

"Hey Avie?"

The house had been silent up until then, except for the faint shouts of pleasure coming from my phone speakers. My whole body startled upward, my limbs spazzing as if I had no control over them. My phone flew across the bed and clattered onto the floor, face-up and with its sights and sounds on full display.

I scrambled to cover myself with the bathrobe I'd stashed next to me on the bed, but it was too late. Devin was already standing in the doorway, and I was half-naked, surrounded by dilators, and caught red-handed watching something I shouldn't be.

He initially looked happy to see me, but his joy quickly turned to confusion when he saw the panicked look on my face. A sudden, loud gasp turned his attention to my phone, and panic tricked up my whole body like hot coals.

"Wait!" I let out a strangled cry just as Devin lifted my phone off the floor. His dark eyebrows knitted together for a moment as his mind processed what he was watching. But just as I was about to burst into tears, he burst out laughing.

"Damn, Avie." He tossed the phone back at me. "Didn't realize I was interrupting you."

"I... I—"

"What? Your face is red as a tomato, by the way."

I froze, taking a few deep breaths and letting the burning blood vessels in my face calm down.

"You're..." I stuttered. "You're not mad?"

He laughed again, as if my question was absurd. "No, Avie. Of course not. Is this the first time you've looked at porn?"

I remained silent, but nodded.

"Honestly, I think it's a good thing." He plopped down on the bed next to me. "I've noticed that you still have a lot of...*hang-ups* when it comes to sex."

I frowned. "I mean..."

"I did too when I was younger. But over the years, I learned to shed that shame. Just please remember, Avie, there is absolutely nothing evil or wrong about sex. It's completely natural, just like hunger or thirst. It's a part of being human. None of us would exist without it. So yes, I don't care if you look at porn. In fact, I *encourage* it, if it helps you overcome your pain."

"You're not jealous?" I asked.

Devin chuckled. "I mean, it's just a video." He shifted towards me, curling his fingers around my bare hips. "I'm the only one that *actually* gets to fuck you."

I giggled and kissed his cheek. "Thank you, Dev. That means a lot."

"Besides." He wiggled his dark eyebrows deviously. "If I had a problem with you watching it, I'd be a hypocrite."

My mouth fell open, ready to lovingly berate him for keeping such secrets, when he reached down and attempted to take my phone from me.

"What were you watching anyway?"

I yanked my hand away.

"Aw, c'mon," he teased. "I wanna know what you're into."

"Dev..." I scooted away from him, and he leered towards me with a devious grin on his face.

Just as he went to grab the phone again, I bolted off the bed and ran into the living room.

"Avieeeeeee, come back!" he shouted in a whiny tone as I leapt over couch cushions, screeching and laughing at the same time.

He dove onto the couch, and I scrambled into the armchair to get away from him, my bathrobe flying open in the process. Adrenaline pulsed through my veins like wildfire, but somehow it was more thrilling than terrifying. In fact, as he jumped onto the armchair and pinned my arms down, I found it very...arousing.

"You know what? It doesn't matter." His gaze trailed up to my phone, still clasped in my restrained hand, and he took it from me and tossed it on the end table. His fingers trailed my bare breasts and hips as they spilled out of my loose bathrobe, and I fought back a gasp. "I've found something I'm *far* more interested in."

Devin was on top of me, his body hunched over mine, with his remarkably strong arms pinning mine above my head. I never realized how much I loved being restrained by him. *God, this is wonderful.*

I was ready to submit, to welcome his kisses and fondling as he pulled away the rest of my bathrobe. He already had his lips pressed against my neck when the realization hit me, and it made it nearly impossible to say no.

"Dev," I fought to maintain my composure and not cry out in response to his touch. "You have to get back to work."

The neck kisses continued. "Jordan won't mind."

"*Dev.*"

A frustrated growl escaped him as he climbed off me. "*Fine*. You're right. I'll be a proper responsible adult and not seduce my girlfriend in the middle of a workday."

"Why are you here anyway?"

Devin stood up, digging into his back pocket and pulling out his wallet. "I forgot this. It was next to my desk since I was ordering stuff online last night."

"What made you come back for it now?"

"Well, I didn't pack a lunch, and I'd like to be able to eat today," he chuckled. "I'm starving. But I may just grab something here."

"There's leftover stir fry in the fridge."

Devin leaned down to give me a peck on the cheek. "Sounds good. I'll take that with me. Now, I'll be on my way, unless..." He suggestively raised a dark eyebrow.

"Devin Alexander Lancast—"

"Alright, alright. Don't have to go all full name on me. I'm leaving. Have a good afternoon, sweetheart. Love you."

"Love you too, you pain in the ass."

He flashed me one last cheeky grin as he disappeared down the hallway. I heard the front door open and close with a soft bang, followed by a firm click as he twisted the lock in place.

I shook my head at Devin's endearingly obnoxious behavior. I readjusted my bathrobe so I was no longer half-naked and picked up my phone. I unlocked it, and the video I'd been watching earlier was still active on my screen.

I was tempted to slip away to the bedroom again, but I thought better of it and closed the tab on my phone. I knew it would be better to practice with Devin later. But... the video *did* give me a feeling I'd never felt before. Practicing with Devin was one thing. *Seeing* what we were trying to accomplish was another.

It was decided. I'd explore this more with him when he returned from work.

A few hours later, we did exactly that.

And the best part?

It worked.

We got the third dilator in that night.

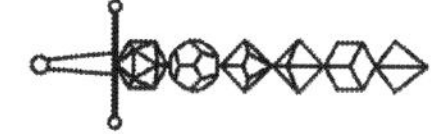

THE BIG DAY WAS FINALLY HERE.

Devin and I had just walked in the door to his townhouse, our feet sore and our limbs weary after walking around all day, and we were both ready to collapse.

We did so in his bedroom, enjoying the warmth, darkness, and solitude of being bundled up in the sheets together. I pressed my face into his soft sweatshirt as those familiar, colorful tattoo-adorned arms locked themselves around me. It was Christmas Eve, and we'd been together nearly six months. But his embrace would never cease to lull me into a calm, dreamy state.

For the first time in the five years since I'd left college, my parents decided to spend the holiday down in Orlando. And not just to visit me. Adam and Allen, my two teenage brothers, wanted to go to Universal Studios. And to my amazement, my parents agreed, and we all went together as a family as an early Christmas present.

In addition to me, my parents, and my brothers, Devin took the day off to join us. He usually closed Critical Games early on Christmas Eve, but decided this year to close it entirely for both Christmas Eve and Christmas Day. It made me happy and relieved: I knew how much the shop meant to him, but he also rarely took time off and never had both holidays to himself.

Plus, the idea of going to a theme park, something he hadn't done in years, enticed him.

We also had another member of my family join us: my cousin Evelyn and her two-year-old daughter Sadie. I hadn't seen Evelyn in years, but we'd spent a lot of time together at family events in our youth since we were less than a year apart in age. Her husband, who I'd never met, couldn't make it, but Evelyn had heard about my parents' Orlando trip and wanted to tag along. She'd never seen the parks before. I wondered if she'd ever even left the panhandle.

Sadie was precious; a plump, soft, smiley baby with wispy brown hair and shockingly blue eyes. She loved being on her feet, and could run impressively fast for a two-year-old, even if she did tend to bump into things. But Sadie stayed in her stroller for most of the day, and Devin happily volunteered to watch Sadie when Evelyn wanted to go on rides.

I thought it was a sweet gesture, but as I hung back with Devin while my family rode *VelociCoaster* for the second time, I noticed it wasn't just for Evelyn's benefit.

I knew that Devin loved children, but I'd never seen him around babies, and the way he interacted with them made my heart melt into a puddle. Sadie was getting fussy in her stroller, so Devin picked her up and propped her on his hip so she could watch the coaster from a distance. He cooed and baby-talked her with ease, his eyes lighting up just as much as hers did.

My parents had never been to a theme park before. While my mother wasn't too fond of the more intense rides, my father surprisingly loved them. It was a wonderful bonding moment for the four of us. On the two-seater rides, Adam and Allen would sit together, and I would sit with my dad. When we made the initial plunge on *VelociCoaster*, I was shocked that my normally reserved father threw his hands up in the air and cheered like the rest of the tourists. It made my own shouts mix with laughter and the adrenalin pump through my veins even faster.

I hadn't had an experience with my family like this in a long time. And I didn't want the day to end.

But my favorite moment wasn't the rides, or the scenery, or even the parks themselves. My favorite moment was when we went back to my family's hotel, a beautiful tropical resort on the outskirts of Universal Studios. We were all admiring the towering ceilings and glittering chandeliers when we entered the main lobby, but Devin's eyes were locked on something else.

Then I saw it. A sleek grand piano, tucked away in the corner of the lobby, with glistening white keys and an empty bench.

Devin quietly excused himself, and we all watched curiously as he walked over and settled himself in front of the piano.

He'd mentioned he used to play on our first date. But in the six months we'd been together, he'd never had an opportunity to showcase it.

I watched as he shifted in his seat, making himself comfortable, and propped his outstretched fingers on the keys. I watched, transfixed, as they danced slowly and deliberately across each note, the tune growing more familiar in my ears with every tap of the keys.

This is a Christmas song.

Wait... I know this.

I took a seat on the bench next to Devin. That was another thing we both had in common from our childhoods: church music. He had played piano, and I sang in the choir.

I pushed the words out, deep but gentle, and began the first few verses of "Have Yourself a Merry Little Christmas." I saw Devin's focused face break into a beaming grin as he played, and my whole family listened to our little concert in amazement. Even a few stray hotel guests stopped and watched us.

When the last word was sung and the last note played, a small chorus of applause emanated from our little audience.

Devin's grin grew wider as he wrapped an arm around me and nuzzled his lips against my cheek.

"I love you," he whispered.

"I love you too."

I looked up, with Devin's arm still wrapped around my shoulder, and noticed something that made my heart flutter with hope.

My dad, like everyone else, was clapping.

But he was also smiling. At Devin.

"That was impressive, son," he nodded at Devin as we stood up from the bench. "Where did you learn to play like that?"

"Years of lessons," Devin chuckled, scratching the back of his neck. "And years of playing in my dad's church."

"Your dad's church?"

"Yes," Devin nodded. "My father is a pastor."

My dad raised a curious eyebrow. I swore I could see the gears turning behind his usually steely eyes. As if he were slowly realizing that there was more to my boyfriend than he'd initially assumed.

And as we walked down the hotel hallways, eager to eat dinner at one of the restaurants after a long day at the park, I noticed Devin up ahead. He walked next to my father, shoulder to shoulder, with the two of them engaged in conversation.

Six months ago, my father had nearly insulted Devin to tears.

Now he was *talking* to him. Nodding. Smiling.

And it made me smile too. I knew change was less of a tidal wave and more of a subtle current, slowly pulling people along before they even realized what was happening. It would take a long time before my father truly accepted Devin as a member of the family.

But this? This was a start.

Now, several hours later, we were home, exhausted, full, and ready to settle into each other's arms. Our family had grown just a month earlier; as we laid down in bed, I could see two beady-eyed faces peeking out from behind Devin's old wire cage in the corner. Spending so much time at Devin's townhouse and hanging out with Gideon had made me realize how much I wanted a pet for myself. I spent weeks debating what to get, until a pair of two-year-old ferrets showed up in a social media marketplace ad. They were females, one dark brown and one cinnamon. I had named them Sylvie and Lyra, after two of my favorite *Creatures & Crypts* characters. I smiled at their adorable little faces and made a mental note to clean their litter box and let them out for exercise in the morning.

Devin's bedroom was dark, except for the boxy glow of Alistair's tank. But in just a few minutes, when the clock struck nine, the heat bulb would turn off for the night, leaving us shrouded in inky darkness.

My thoughts returned to the present. I focused on the feeling of Devin's fingers through my curly hair, his sweatshirt fabric against my cheek, and the softness of the plush duvet enveloping us both. It had been a long day, and my tired body longed to fall asleep in his arms.

But I couldn't.

Because tonight was a special night.

It was Christmas Eve, our first one together.

But it was also special for a different reason.

"Hey Dev?" I whispered as I lifted my head.

"Yes?"

"I have a surprise for you."

Devin shifted, a slight tired sigh emanating from him as he sat up. "Yeah? What is it?"

A beaming grin slipped across my lips. "Well, last night, while you were working...I got the fourth dilator in."

His previously sleepy eyes were now alight with surprise. "Wow, really?"

"Yup. And that's the largest one. I think it's about the same size as you."

Devin pursed his lips as he slid off the bed, digging through his top dresser drawer until he found the dilator. He studied it like a museum object, measuring its width with his fingers, before giving an approving nod.

"Yup. You're right. Does this mean...?"

"Yes," I lowered the collar of my sweater suggestively. "I'm ready."

Devin wasted no time. He practically leaped back into bed, pinning me down just like he'd done when he walked in on me just a few months earlier. My limbs initially tensed from the restraint, but they quickly softened as the sweet, heady burn of arousal tricked down my torso.

Finally. No more restraint. No more holding back.

He kissed my neck, and I let out a soft gasp, tilting my head to make it easier for him. Welcoming him in.

I loved the way his fingers trickled down my body, caressing each curve until he reached the bottom of my sweater. He lifted it over my head with ease and undid my bra with a single twist of his fingers. I relished the feeling of exposure, the sensitive skin of my bare breasts tightening under the chill of the ceiling fan.

I pulled his own sweatshirt over his head, sliding my hands up and down his body. The body that had become so familiar to me. The body that I knew almost as well as my own.

The growing pile of shed clothes slipped off the duvet and onto the floor. Finally, once we were both fully exposed, I wrapped my arms and legs around him, pulling his chest against my own. Our breaths were growing in speed and intensity, and there was a feral glint in Devin's aroused gaze. He knew this was it. No more restraining himself.

He ran his fingers over my breasts, squeezing them a few times before lowering his lips to my nipple. I burst into a chorus of gasps, with every pulse of pleasure in my own body making him tighten his grip. Driving him even more wild.

God, he is so good at this. I loved the way he worked me up, his fingers running along my body just as smoothly and skillfully as when he played piano. I remembered how afraid I was when we had our first night together, how I worried that his experienced past would make me seem inadequate. But now I relished his ability to make every part of my body burn under his touch.

He was perfect.

He was mine.

"You ready?" He paused, lifting his head. "I don't want to get you *too* worked up."

I nodded eagerly, my eyes sparkling with anticipation. He placed a quick kiss on my lips and stood up, walking over to the drawer to grab the condoms and lube I'd stashed there a few weeks ago.

I admired his bare figure as he fumbled through the drawer, my eyes trailing up and down his limbs as I examined his tattoos. I'd spent so many nights studying them while we lay in bed together, tracing my fingers over them as he slept. I knew every character, every detail, every line of ink across his body. They were a part of him, and I loved them.

"Here we go." Devin plopped a bottle of lubricant and a vibrator on the bed as he fiddled with the condom. I scooped up the vibrator, a plain pink device made of silicone, and pressed it against my vulva. It was much stronger than the tiny one I'd used back at my townhouse, and it made me quiver as soon as I turned it on.

Devin had insisted we get it. He knew it would help me relax, and he enjoyed the feeling of it too. We'd used it together many times while practicing with the dilators.

Devin crawled back on top of me, rubbing his hands down my thighs to relax them while I let the soft buzz of the vibrator build up my arousal. My pelvic muscles loosened as my core ached, this time with longing instead of pain.

I wanted this.

I wanted this more than anything.

"You ready?" Devin asked, a gentle smile on his face as he positioned himself between my legs.

I nodded. I was as ready as I would ever be.

I closed my eyes, directing my focus to the buzz of the vibrator. Keeping my legs relaxed. Not letting a single painful thought enter my blissful mind.

The first inch was always the most difficult. Despite all my preparation, actual sex was different than working with the dilators. After a few failed penetration attempts, my inner thighs began to clench.

Goddamnit. I forced my shaking legs to relax. I'd come this far. I wasn't going to let my sexual dysfunction win tonight.

Thankfully, Devin didn't seem fazed. There was no hint of frustration on his face, and he didn't look like he was ready to give up.

"Here." He crawled backwards, stepping off the bed so he was standing by the edge of it. He leaned forward, wrapped his arms around my waist, and pulled me towards him. "Let's try this."

I lay flat on my back with my legs dangling off the edge of the bed as Devin stood between them. My thigh muscles relaxed. He was right. This would be a better position; it offered an easier angle and more motion for him.

We hit the same roadblock again. Devin grabbed more lube, stroking my hair with his other hand as he did so. His loving smile reassured me. It told me not to give up.

I closed my eyes as he tried again, the vibrator's mechanical buzz still whirring in my ears. *Focus on the pleasure. Not the pain.*

There were a few stings, a few moments of burning, but they were blended with warmth and pleasure. Two opposing forces at war in my mind.

Relax.

I pressed the dilator deeper against my vagina.

Enjoy it.

I wouldn't let the pain win.

I gasped as a sudden smooth, sliding feeling shook my lower abdomen. Devin trembled, letting out a low groan.

He was in.

We did it.

"Yes!" I threw my hands up in the air and shouted with glee as exhilarating laughter filled my lungs. Finally. I couldn't believe it.

"Avie, Avie..." Devin let out a ragged chuckle, trying to regain my attention. "I know you're excited, but we've gotta focus."

I cringed, a blush tinting my cheeks. "Sorry."

"Okay, are you in pain right now?"

I craned my neck up so I could see my lower torso. Devin's hands were resting on my hips, and his pelvis was pressed directly against mine. He was in. There was no doubt about it.

"Nope, I'm fine."

"Okay. I'm going to move a little bit. Tell me if you need me to stop."

I nodded.

A full-body chill cascaded down me, spreading from my core all the way down my limbs and into the tips of my fingers and toes, as I felt him slide within me.

I grinned, and I looked up, I noticed Devin was having the same reaction.

"My god you're tight," he gasped with his teeth clenched.

"Are you okay?"

"Oh, yes," his chuckle was soft and breathy. "You feel fantastic."

"You can keep going," I insisted. "It doesn't hurt."

"Okay," Devin replied, adjusting his hold on my hips. "Remember, you can tell me to stop at any time."

"I know."

The movements started deep and slow, each one sending tremors through my abdomen as blood pounded in my core. I was sensitive. Really sensitive. Too sensitive.

I cried out, and Devin grinned my hips tighter. He seemed to take great satisfaction in watching my reactions, and after a few minutes, his gasps echoed my own.

Just as it was intensifying, becoming too much to bear, Devin leaned down and aggressively kissed my neck just below my jawline.

"I love you," he rasped in my ear.

"I love you too," I whispered back, in so much ecstasy that I could barely squeak out the words.

It felt so good, so mind-numbingly good, that I felt like I was losing my grip on reality. My whole body was under his spell, moving with him as if it had a will of its own. It was involuntary. Instinctual. Natural.

Now that I was twenty-seven and had experienced the world outside of my church bubble, I no longer believed that sex was a sin. That it was reserved for married couples and could only be done in certain ways and at certain times.

But there was no denying the feeling of otherworldliness that it evoked in me. Religion had taught me that it was a sacred binding of souls, and while I questioned the validity of such a statement, one thing was true: I had never felt closer to Devin than in that moment. This was a beautiful experience, and I was so grateful to be sharing it with someone that I loved so much.

It took twenty-seven years for this to happen.

But it was all worth it.

"Avie?" Devin gasped.

"Yes?"

"I..." He sighed as he slowed down. "I don't think I can last much longer."

I chuckled, flattered that he was enjoying this as much as I was. I reached up and pulled him towards me, so his slender torso hovered over mine. "Finish with me."

I could feel it too. The knot in my core getting tighter and tighter, threatening to snap at any moment. I wanted it to. I wanted it to be the most beautiful one I ever experienced. But it had to be at the same time as him.

I wrapped my arms around Devin, digging my fingers into his back until my nails made half-moons in his skin. I could feel his muscles tensing beneath my touch. He was now almost as loud as I was.

"Avie..."

"Dev..."

The knot snapped. I pressed the back of my head firmly into the mattress, my back arching as the electrifying pulses of my orgasm made my whole body tremble. My fingers dug further into Devin's back, and he gripped the soft curve of my hips until my skin went numb.

He pressed himself as far as he could into me, and I wrapped my legs around his lower back, locking my ankles in place.

I had orgasmed plenty of times since Devin and I got together six months ago, even a few times with the dilator inside me. But none of it compared to this, us locked in a crushing yet heartwarming embrace as we waited for the rolling waves of pleasure to give way to exhaustion.

Devin's breathing slowed, and he loosened his grip on my hips. He was still on top of me, my skin pressed against his, both of us flushed with heat and damp with sweat. Once he finally lifted his head from where it had been nestled below my chin, he gave me the most beautiful, adoring smile I'd ever seen.

"We did it," I sighed, my own massive grin mirroring his.

"*You* did it." He pointed a finger at my chest. "All those months working with the dilators, getting through the pain…I'm so proud of you."

I blushed. "Of course. I wanted this just as much as you did."

Devin rolled off me and curled up on my left side. We were both overwhelmed and exhausted; my limbs felt both light as air and heavy as lead. We needed to clean up and get ready for bed, but I knew it would be several minutes before either one of us would be steady enough to stand up.

"Sorry I couldn't last longer," Devin said sheepishly, breaking the dreamy stillness in the air.

I laughed, rolling onto my side and resting my arm on his chest. "I made you wait six months for sex, and *you're* the sorry one?"

Devin shrugged. "It's just been…a really long time."

"How long?"

I felt awkward asking, but I was also itching to know.

"A few years," he replied.

Years? Damn.

"Why so long?"

"Just didn't find anyone I liked enough to have sex with," he replied casually. "I sort of swore off dating until I met the right person. And I now know, without a doubt, that that person is you. You are the love of my life."

That sentence made my heart hammer in my chest. It felt like sex was the final hurdle for us to get past in our budding relationship. Now that we'd conquered that task... what was next?

I already knew. I'd known for a while now. With all the days and nights spent together in Devin's little townhouse, my old life felt so distant. I loved him so much, and I never wanted our time together to end.

"Hey Dev?" I asked, my tone hesitant.

"Yes?"

"I've been meaning to ask...we're coming up on six months now, and I just wanted to know..." I gulped. Spitting out the words was tougher than I thought. "What's our plan for the future?"

Devin shifted upright; his dreamy post-orgasmic state now replaced with serious contemplation. "By future...you mean marriage? Kids?"

"I didn't mean anytime soon," I backtracked, not wanting to freak him out. "It's just—"

"Avic," Devin chuckled, tucking a strand of curly hair behind my ear. "I will absolutely marry you. I agree, we're nowhere near ready, but that's always been my intention."

"Really?" My eyes lit up.

"Absolutely. Let me ask..." He suddenly looked nervous. "If I proposed next Christmas, would you say yes?"

My face was red with giddiness. "I think I'd be ready by then. But what about...after that? Do you want kids?"

That was a question I'd never been sure of myself. I liked children, but it had been hard to imagine myself as a mother. I felt like I was always so busy trying to manage my own life, let alone one of a tiny person that was completely dependent on me.

But with Devin, that was changing. Seeing what a smart, kind, mature person he was made me want to have a family with him. He was so good with kids; watching him interact with the childrens' group at Critical Games always brought a smile to my face. He would make an amazing father.

"Yes," Devin replied. "I do. Do you?"

"I think I do. Not a huge family though. Just one or two."

Devin laughed, a mixture of joy and relief in his eyes. I felt it too. It was reassuring to know that the man I loved wanted the same things out of life that I did.

"Imagine them running around the shop," I grinned, crinkling my nose.

Devin scoffed. "They'd either want to help me and play assistant manager or cause chaos by knocking every single miniature off the shelves."

"With you as their dad?" I teased. "Definitely."

"So…" A sly grin slipped onto Devin's face. "Now that we've had the whole 'future together' conversation…I have a proposal on our next steps."

"What's that?"

"When does your lease end?"

I paused to think. "End of May."

"Well, that's five months from now. We'll have been together almost a year. Do you think you'd…want to end your lease and move in with me?"

"Yes," I answered, without a single second of doubt. "Absolutely."

That would be perfect. I already spent so much time at Devin's place; my own townhouse was starting to feel foreign. It would make moving in together an easy transition. Then, we could truly spend all our downtime together—cooking, playing video games, and most importantly, curling up together every night.

Devin kissed my cheek. "Well as much as I've loved this conversation, we really do need to get some sleep. I'm exhausted."

"I know. Me too. Plus, tomorrow is our first Christmas together."

We spent the next fifteen minutes cleaning up, which involved us both stealing a few kisses in the shower, before settling into bed.

"Good night, sweetheart," Devin murmured in my ear as he wrapped his blanket-cloaked arm around me.

"Good night, Dev."

"I love you."

"I love you too."

That was it. We'd finally had sex. I was no longer an anxious, lonely virgin hiding her painful secret from the world. I'd set out on a journey to find the love of my life, and after many months of wading through dating apps, I'd found him in the most unexpected of places.

And now, we'd agreed to have each other for the rest of our lives.

I nuzzled into Devin's chest as we settled into slumber, grateful that he was loving and understanding enough to work through this with me.

And he was right.

I wasn't broken.

I never was.

But as I lay there in the darkness, engulfed in the arms of the man who was now my whole future, I couldn't help but feel complete.

A Note From the Author

Back in September of 2023, as I lay on the couch several days post-op from my laparoscopy surgery, a sudden thought formed in my still drug-addled mind.

What if I wrote a book about all of this?

Now almost exactly a year later, *Confessions of a Virgin on a Dating App* has been released to the world. I'm speaking candidly about my struggles for the first time, because while Avery and Devin's romance is entirely fictional, Avery's medical issues are less so. Her experience with endometriosis mirrors my life with the disease: from painful sex, to getting a diagnosis in an ER, to having laparoscopy surgery to help my symptoms. And just like Avery, it took me over a decade to get proper treatment.

If you've ever struggled with symptoms like Avery's, or know someone who is, don't brush them off for years like I did. Talk to a gynecologist. Find out what your options are. Endometriosis has no cure, but treatment can significantly improve your quality of life.

And remember, severe period pain isn't normal.

Painful sex isn't normal.

But you're not broken. You just need help.

And maybe, someday, we'll finally have a cure for one of the most common reproductive diseases affecting women.

- Sydney Wilder

Acknowledgments

THIS IS MY THIRD PUBLISHED BOOK, PREDATED by the first two books in my fantasy romance trilogy, *The Valley of Scales Saga*. And with every book I write, the list of people I owe gratitude to grows. Which is an incredible feeling as an author.

First, I have to thank those who helped make this book possible. Mary did an amazing job illustrating my cover. I'm so glad she reached out to me when I asked for illustrator recommendations online. You are so talented; as a designer, an illustrator, and a fellow romance author. I'm so glad I get to mention you in this book!

I also owe a huge thanks to Hailey, my editor, and Rae and Theresa, my beta readers. Those first few positive reviews are always such a relief to us authors, and you guys had wonderful praise and feedback for me!

I always must thank *Spellbound*, my local bookstore, in every book I write. They were the first bookstore to ever take one of my novels on consignment, and between my launch party and stocking my books on their shelves, they have been an amazing support system. And not just for me! Through their book clubs and writer's groups, they have formed such an incredible author and reader community here in Central Florida. I appreciate all of you!

And last, I have to thank Rob, the very best beta reader and cheerleader of a husband I could ask for. The one who both encourages me when I'm on a roll and tells me to take a break and play video games when I'm in over my head. I love you!

Other Books by Sydney Wilder

YA FANTASY ROMANCE

The Valley of Scales Saga
Daughter of Serpents
Heart of Venom
Strength of Scales (coming 2025)

ADULT CONTEMPORARY ROMANCE

Confessions of a Virgin on a Dating App

About the Author

Sydney Wilder is a writer, nerd, and reptile lover who has been living in Florida since she was a child. She loves writing and reading all things romance, although this is her first non-fantasy book. She was diagnosed with endometriosis at age 28 after nearly a decade of health issues and had surgery in September of 2023, which spawned the inspiration for *Confessions*. Her favorite authors are Julie Kagawa and Rebecca Ross, and her all-time favorite novel is *Divine Rivals*. When not writing, Sydney is an all-around nerd with a love of gaming, both video and tabletop. She is a longtime *Dungeons & Dragons* and *Magic: The Gathering* player and has been attending game shops for over a decade. She currently lives in Orlando with her loving husband and a menagerie of pets, including five adorable snakes.

Made in the USA
Columbia, SC
04 November 2024

45423947R00224